"*Elixir* is stylish, finely tuned and terrifying—the best thriller I've curled up with in a long while." —Michael Palmer

"Dorian Gray enters the world of the biotech thriller in a fast-paced and well-plotted debut novel. . . . The drug itself may produce a fatal addiction, but the story behind its development makes for an intoxicating read."
—*Publishers Weekly*

"Among the best of recent contributions to its genre because of its engaging plot and the issues it addresses, this is an outstanding addition to all fiction collections."
—*Library Journal*

"A fast-paced gem of a thriller."
—*The Capital Times,* Madison Wisconsin

"Gary Braver has produced a stimulating mixture of villainy, science and the philosophical and practical issues that underlie the new found ability to create 'immortality' or, at least, a major deferment of the aging process. Along the way, Mr. Braver introduces us to some of the scientific issues underlying the aging process, the role of telomerase and whether aging is in fact inevitable. . . . Enough science to make the narrative plausible, but not too much to paralyze the narrative development. . . . Once started, *Elixir* could not be easily put down. *Elixir* should be a deservedly popular read by scientists and non-scientists alike."
—*Pharmaceutical News, Vol. 7, No. 4*

"*Elixir* delivers all the suspense and excitement you could ask for, and asks a hard question, too: What would you do if you found that you could live forever? Read *Elixir* and find out."
—William Martin, *New York Times* bestselling author of *Cap Cod* and *Annapolis*

"Among the best of recent contributions to its genre because of its engaging plot and the issues it addresses, this is an outstanding addition to all fiction collections."
—*Library Journal*

"A terrifying novel . . . fast-paced, filled with action, twists and turns."
—*Midwest Book Review*

"This novel has some winning twists and even a nostalgic visit with Ronald Reagan. . . . *Elixir* is really bad science but awfully good fiction."

—*Tampa Tribune & Times*

"If you're tired of the Grisham legal drama and the Clancy spy novel, and if you're looking for an exciting, fun, read, pick up *Elixir*. It is wonderfully written. . . . The characters are beautifully realized. . . . Lots of drama; lots of suspense. This is a great thriller!"

—*Entertainment Tomorrow*

"A fantastic thriller and an intriguing ethical study. . . . A thrilling cascade of drama and paranoia."

—*The Northeastern News*

"A novel of commendable skill and literary craftsmanship."

—*The Armenian Mirror Spectator*

"Braver makes sure that every twist and turn makes sense. . . . He is a master craftsman when it comes to creating characters. There is not a single character major or minor, that feels as if they are two-dimensional, put on the pages as if to serve a purpose. . . . *Elixir* has all the makings of a great movie . . . I *expect* to see it on the silver screen."

—*Shelflife*

"I found myself thinking about this book every time I put it down. And it was very hard to put down. It races to a heart-stopping conclusion but lingers with you long after the last page. This is a *great* book for that long plane ride or a day at the beach."

—*Kate's Mystery Books Newsletter*

"[Braver] has tapped into an American obsession and come up with a relentless page-turner that manages to deal with technical, scientific, and medical material while still being entertaining, witty, and very unnerving."

—*Metrowest and Community Newspapers*

"Gary Braver's plot is informed by a real-world sensibility in which the heroes may be smart, but are given to blindness and ambition—and the bad guys, while evil, are far from stupid. A breathtaking series of moves and countermoves propels the story toward unforeseeable, tragic consequences, but at its heart the book remains a meditation on the nature of life and its need for family. This is one terrific thriller."

—*Wigglefish.com*

"A fasten-your-seatbelt thriller . . . with never an obvious or cliched moment. . . . *Elixir* not only gives us a complex story but also features characters who are complex and richly textured, and who act in ways that surprise but make perfect sense given what we come to know about their personalities. . . . While he has produced an unabashedly commercial page-turner, Braver has also probed, in a profound and often disturbing fashion, some fundamental questions about the ever-expanding role of biotechnology in modern life. . . . Perhaps *Elixir* is not only entertaining and provocative, but prophetic as well."

—*Northeastern University Magazine*

Elixir

GARY BRAVER

TOR®

A TOM DOHERTY ASSOCIATES BOOK
NEW YORK

This is a work of fiction. All the characters and events portrayed in this book are either products of the author's imagination or are used fictitiously.

ELIXIR

Copyright © 2000 by Gary Goshgarian

A Tor Book
Published by Tom Doherty Associates, LLC
175 Fifth Avenue
New York, NY 10010

ww.tor.com

Tor® is a registered trademark of Tom Doherty Associates, LLC.

ISBN: 0-812-57591-1
Library of Congress Catalog Card Number: 99-089057

First edition: April 2000
First mass market edition: August 2001

Printed in the United States of America

0 9 8 7 6 5 4 3 2

For Kathleen, Nathan, and David, as ever

And so, from hour to hour, we ripe and ripe,
And then, from hour to hour, we rot and rot,
And thereby hangs a tale.

—WILLIAM SHAKESPEARE, *AS YOU LIKE IT*

ACKNOWLEDGMENTS

A special thanks goes out to the following people for providing me with medical and other technical information.

From Northeastern University's College of Pharmacy and Allied Health Profession: Robert F. Raffauf, Barbara L. Waszczak, Carol Warner, Robert N. Hanson, Richard C. Deth, Wendy Smith, and Susan Sexton. Also, William J. DeAngelis, Department of Philosophy, and James R. Stellar, Department of Psychology.

Thanks also to Dr. John Neumeyer and Dr. William White of Research Biochemicals International; Mark Froimowitz, Pharm-Eco Laboratories, Inc.; David Lee-Parritz, New England Regional Primate Research Center; Dr. Changiz Geula of Beth Israel Hospital, Laboratory for Neurodegenerative and Aging Research; Ellen Kearns, Special Agent, Federal Bureau of Investigation, Boston; David Sturges, Professor of Economics, Colgate College; and Kenneth Van Cott, Director of the Pharmacy, Brattleboro Memorial Hospital.

I am greatly indebted to *How and Why We Age*, by Leonard Hayflick, Ph.D. (Ballantine Books, NY, 1994) whose own research with human cell tissues has been incorporated into this story.

A special thanks to William Martin, Charles O'Neill, Barbara Shapiro, Christopher Keane, Kathryn Goodfellow, and Alice Janjigian for their good suggestions. Also, to my terrific editor at Tor Books, Natalia Aponte.

A final word of appreciation to Susan Crawford who has always been more than an agent and who stood by me all the way.

PROLOGUE

There's no good way to die. But this was as bad as it gets.

Christopher Bacon raised the pistol at a spot in the bush, not certain if anybody was there or if it was all in his mind. What Iwati called "bush bugaboo"—when the tangle of green closed in, and shadows pulsed and shifted like some stalking beast. When mosquitoes buzzed to the core of your brain. And fatigue crossed with claustrophobia. And some damn juju flower filled the air with a cloying stench.

But Chris could sense movement—some rustling behind that black curtain of vines, whispers hovering at the threshold of awareness. He could see nothing in the dark—just shadows in the firelight. And the only sound was the electric buzz of insects and tree frogs—as if something was about to happen.

The rain had stopped, but the air was gluey. And he was wet—his shirt plastered to his chest, his pants chafing his legs, his toes gummy in his boots. Wet as he had been for two weeks even when it wasn't raining. So wet that his face felt like an aspic and the soles of his feet were covered with dead white skin that he could scrape off with his fingernails. The ground was a ripe-rot mud. And everything dripped. The rainforest always dripped.

A relentless green dripping. And it filled his head.

Maybe Iwati was right: Thirteen nights had unhinged him, reduced him to spikes of raw nerves, producing phantoms out of nothing.

Maybe.

But every instinct said he was not alone, that he was being watched—that just beyond those vines lurked a hungry presence that at any second would explode into the light and gut him.

For two days he had felt they were being stalked, ever since Iwati and five porters had led Chris into this remote region of the Sepik beyond the West Irian border—a *tabu* zone that even the Wanebabi tribe had warned them to avoid. But despite his porters' protests, Iwati had insisted on this side trip. So they hacked their way through jungle as dense as fur to this lake under the ancient cone of the Omafeki volcano—and all for that juju flower, the one that stank of apples and rotten flesh. And ever since, they had been on alert, certain that every errant sound was the Okamolu—the elusive highland tribe who stalked intruders with spears and arrows and a craving for "long pig."

But Iwati was unfazed, puffing his pipe and saying it was just tree kangaroos or bush rats. "Nothing to worry about, my friend. Nobody else here." Chris took refuge in the fact that his old schoolboy chum was shaman of the Tifalmin people and knew these parts. Tree kangaroos, Chris told himself—and an active imagination.

And where the hell was Iwati? While Chris had made a fire, Iwati led his men to a clearing to set up camp. But that was just down the trail. He had been gone for more than half an hour.

Chris crouched behind a fallen tree, the pistol gripped in both hands, ready to blast. Behind him the volcano brooded against the fiery sunset. It was nearly night.

"Iwati!"

No answer, but Chris's voice passed through the bush like a gunshot, exciting critters to a razor-edged chitter.

Invisible winged things were eating him alive. His eyes, ears, and lips were swollen, and some tiny boring beetles had gotten inside his boots and filled his feet with poison. During the day he had slathered himself with a repellent Iwati concocted of justica root and pigfat. But his face had been wiped clean, and the stuff was in Iwati's bag. Dozens of creatures in the Papuan bush were capable of killing a man—from black mambas to wild boars to eighteen-foot crocodiles. But it was the god-damn bugs that reduced you to lunacy. Unseen things that ate your blood and flesh. And that syrupy stench clogging his throat.

Suddenly a nasty thought rose up: What if Okamolus had killed Iwati? A sudden blitz of arrows, and Iwati and his men would be dead without commotion.

Or what if the porters had mutinied? They had been jumpy since leaving Wanebabi. What if they had put a knife in Iwati's back and fled for the river? Why not? The Okamolu's reputation for savagery was legendary. Chris remembered the war story of a Japanese patrol that had hacked its way out here to coerce locals into build-ing an airstrip and had found themselves surrounded by Okamolu warriors. After a standoff of spears and auto-matic rifles, the Japanese commander in a gesture of truce dropped his rifle. Following cue, the Okamolu leader stuck his spear into the ground. The crisis was over, so it seemed. That night all but one of the nine men had their throats cut in their sleep and ended up the next day headless and laid out like pigs on mumu fires with yams and tubers. The final memory of the sole sur-vivor was of children gnawing on a charred leg.

"Iwati!"

Still nothing.

Chris pressed himself against the tree, certain that if he survived the night he'd be feverish with malaria by dawn. *Bastards!* He wished they'd break the spell and get it over with. He had brought the gun for crocs, not a shootout with cannibals. Even if he could blast his way out, he'd never make it to the river on his own. Either he'd get lost or stumble into a pool of quick mud.

Then it happened. The tangle of vines slowly parted.

Chris's finger hummed on the trigger. Somebody was moving toward him. No trick of light. No insulin low. No hallucination. The vines were parting. The standoff was about to break. Showdown.

At the last moment, the image of Wendy rocking their baby son Ricky filled Chris Bacon's mind. And the thought: *This is my death.*

It had begun thirteen days ago. They had trekked out from the Tifalmin village gathering flora samples to take back to the States. Chris was a medicinal chemist working for Darby Pharmaceuticals, a Boston laboratory pioneering the synthesis of folk medicines. With the discovery that alkaloids from *Catharantus roseus* shrunk tumors from Hodgkin's disease, Darby had entered a race with other commercial labs, convinced that miracle drugs grew on trees. Specifically, Chris was testing for plant steroids capable of conversion to animal steroids for contraceptive purposes. Darby's goal was to produce the world's first male birth-control pill—a goal that, once realized, would rocket company stock to high heaven.

Chris Bacon was the Darby point man because he was their premier researcher and because he knew the Papuan bush. The son of the American ambassador to Australia in the late 1950s, Chris had attended Boys' Royal Academy in Port Moresby where at age fourteen he met Iwati, one of the few highland youths to attend the Academy. In 1943, Iwati's village had helped Australian-American forces build the airstrip near Tifalmin village, giving the Allies an interior foothold and access to the *chincona* tree whose bark was used to produce quinine, the most effective treatment for malaria. It was the Tifalmin's first contact with men with white skin and steel—a contact that resulted in Iwati growing up speaking English. And because he was bright, an Australian missionary group sponsored his education. Both diabetics, they met at the school's infirmary to have their blood sugar monitored and to receive insulin. Over the four years Chris and Iwati became friends—a relationship cemented forever during their last summer when Chris saved Iwati's life. Ironically, the boy was raised on the banks of the Sepik River but had never learned to swim—a fact Chris discovered when another boy pushed him into the deep end of a pool. Iwati went down like a rock and would have drowned had it not been for Chris.

Like his father before him, Iwati was the Tifalmin medicine man. In spite of the juju trinkets and mumbojumbo, he was thoroughly westernized, wearing Bermuda shorts, a Harvard T-shirt, and a new Bulova watch Chris had brought, while his men trudged through the bush naked but for penis gourds. Like his father, Iwati had a genius for telling which plants healed and which killed—a genius that brought Chris halfway around the globe. Iwati had a plant for every ailment—fevers, toothaches, ulcers, snakebites, lesions, malaria, and syphilis. And they pointed to the future of western world medicine.

For the third time in two years, Darby had sent Chris packing. But this time he managed to bring company money to build a school in the Tifalmin village. A longterm investment in shaman magic. And now it was to end in spears and arrows.

Chris cocked the gun and held his breath.

No trick of the light. No paranoid delusion. A figure took form out of the clotted shadows in the vines.

"Come out, you son-of-a-bitch!" Chris said.

The figure stopped, and for a moment the jungle turned to still life.

Suddenly the silence shattered in shrieks from all directions as the figure came rushing down on Chris. On reflex he shot and didn't stop until all six chambers of the Colt were empty and he was clicking at a naked body tied at the feet by vines and twisting in the air.

From the shoulder scarification marks, he recognized Maku, one of the porters. His chest had been shot open by the bullets, but he was already dead. His head was missing.

In horror Chris watched the body swing until it came to rest just feet away. He tore bullets off his belt to reload when a dozen Okamolu warriors materialized from the shadows, forming a circle around him, and jabbing the air with spears. Before Chris could reload, a little wrinkled man came up to him. He was naked like the rest but for a long white plume through his nose, a neckband crescent, and a headdress of feathers. His face was striped with white paint. The juju man.

In his hand was a spear with Maku's head still dripping blood. He approached Chris, jabbering in a tongue he didn't recognize. Chris tried to concentrate on slipping rounds into the chambers, but the juju man pushed Maku's head into his face. Black flies swarmed around it. He could smell the blood. Dark warm fluids dripped onto his shoes, making his gorge rise.

The juju man's eyes were wild and his mouth was bright red from chewing betel nuts. Every few seconds he would spit thick wads of red, as if he'd removed the head with his teeth. With his free hand he touched Chris's face and arms as if testing for paint. He yelled something, and his men mumbled back like a chorus. One of them shouted something angry, and the others agreed. It sounded like a death warrant. At once they began to chant and jab the air with their weapons again. As the old man backed away for clear shots, a ululating howl stunned the spears in place.

From the bush stepped a large man wearing a skirt of laplap grass and an elaborate bird-of-paradise headdress. What gave him a particularly fearsome appearance was the bright yellow face paint and red circled eyes. Instead of the shaman necklace of shells he wore a cord studded with crocodile teeth and weighted by a shrunken human head.

In perfect English he said, "They won't harm you."

Iwati.

He walked past Chris to the juju man and said something in a clear, even voice. Chris didn't understand a word, but the effect was immediate. The old man mumbled something, and the warriors lowered their weapons. Then, incredibly, they bobbed their heads in supplication.

Chris quickly loaded his gun. "You won't need that," Iwati said.

"Christ, man, look what they did." Maku's carcass dangled just feet away, blood still pouring from the neck hole.

Iwati nodded. "They won't harm you."

It wasn't just his appearance that held Chris. It was the Okamolu's reaction. They looked more like frightened schoolboys than notorious flesh-eaters.

"How come they're so scared? They've seen white men before."

Iwati did not answer.

"What do they want?"

"Just curious." Then Iwati said something in bush tongue.

The juju man muttered something to his men. He was dismissing them, and they looked grateful to leave. They turned around, then filed back into the black tangle the way they came. Before disappearing, each one looked back. And Chris could swear that what he saw in their faces was raw fear.

They buried the remains of Maku in a clearing and built a fire on the site to keep away scavengers. While the porters were back at camp, Iwati led Chris to the lake. The water looked like black glass. Silhouetted against the afterglow of the sun was the ancient Omafeki cone. A refreshing breeze had picked up, relieving the air of the nauseating sweetness. From under some mats of palms Iwati pushed out a small log canoe.

"Where're we going?"

Iwati pointed over the water. In the dim light, Chris could see a small island, maybe a quarter mile off shore. "What's out there?" he asked. Iwati didn't answer.

Chris squatted in front while Iwati paddled toward the island, guided by the moonlight. The closer they got, the more intense the sickening odor became. They pulled up at a small clearing surrounded by trees festooned with long vines. Chris made a move to get out when Iwati stopped him. From his sack he removed the carcass of a small tree kangaroo and hurled it high toward shore. In the moonlight Chris watched it arch to where the flowers hung. A split second before it splashed down, something huge exploded from the depths and caught it. Some violent thrashing and the rolling flash of underbelly; then it disappeared into the black. A massive crocodile.

"He waits for birds," Iwati said.

The animal surfaced in the distance, its tail etching a sinuous wake in the moonlight as it glided away like some ancient sentinel having collected his fee.

They pulled ashore, and sometime later they settled by a fire on a bluff above the water. Iwati put a bundle of banu sticks in the flames to keep mosquitoes away. To Chris's face he applied a poultice of piper leaves and the latex of mammea tree fruit which reduced the swelling and sting. Then he settled back and puffed his old briarwood pipe, acting strangely remote—probably from that weed he was smoking, Chris guessed.

The ride had calmed Chris, though he was still wondering why they were out here. Iwati had removed his headdress but not the shrunken head from his neck. The thing was repulsive, more so than a freshly severed one. This obscene parody was somebody's art. Iwati had sworn that his people had long ago given up cannibalism and headhunting—that only a few remote tribes like the Okamolu still maintained the practice in the belief that by consuming their enemy's flesh they absorbed his life forces.

Chris eyed the talisman, thinking how much he didn't know about Iwati. Yes, they'd been childhood pals, but twenty jungle years had separated them. Iwati could have been a physician practicing in Port Moresby or Sydney had he pursued his education, but he had chosen instead to return to the Stone Age—to the time-frozen ways of his ancestors, wearing grass skirts and shrunken heads instead of surgeon's white and stethoscope, and treating people with ground beetles and plant pastes instead of penicillin. No, much more than two decades had separated them: millennia. In his mind Chris saw Iwati hunched over the head, meticulously scooping out the eyes and picking brain matter from the sockets, crushing the skull and jawbones to be removed in pieces, stitching closed the eyelids and mouth with strips of wallaby gut, basting the skin sac with pigfat, and filling the sac with hot sand until it was cured and tanned and shrunk into that obscene little monkey face and shiny hair to be worn around his neck like a school ring.

"Iwati, what happened back there? Those men were spooked, and I think you know why."

Iwati puffed without response. Nor did he explain his shaman attire which, Chris understood, had been reserved for village rituals and intertribal sing-sings. But Iwati had brought it on the expedition.

"I asked you a question," Chris insisted. "You saved my life, but I'm not sure how."

Nothing.

"Then tell me why in God's name you dragged me all the way out here, man. I've got to leave the country in five days, and it's going to take us two just to reach the river, and two more to get to the coast." And then it was another four days of stop-and-go flights before he made it back to the clean well-lit world of Boston. "And while you're at it, why in hell are we out here and not back at camp? And by the way, what's that stink?"

From the fire Iwati relit his pipe. "Yes."

"Yes, *what*?"

"Yes, I'll explain to you. But you must promise not to tell anyone, my friend." Iwati kept his voice low even though his men were back at camp across the water, and none spoke English.

"Okay."

"Swear on your soul."

Chris began to smile at the silly old schoolboy ritual, but Iwati was dead serious. "I swear on my soul."

"Swear on your grandmother's soul."

"I swear on my grandmother's soul."

"Swear on the Queen's soul."

"I swear on the Queen's soul."

"Swear on the soul of Jesus."

"For godsakes, man, stop playing games."

"Swear it!" Iwati's eyes were intense.

"Okay, I swear on the soul of Jesus."

Iwati hadn't forgotten the order—the oath they had shared as kids sneaking cigarettes. But there was nothing in Iwati's face that said he was playing games.

When he was satisfied he uttered a single word: "Tabukari."

"Tabu what?"

"Tabukari."

Iwati walked over to a tree growing up from the water's edge. Hanging like pythons were thick vines clustered with small white flowers—the source of the sickeningly sweet air. He cut off a length of vine and gave it to Chris. "Tabukari. Special flower."

In the firelight the petals were thick and white, the interior funneling into a bloodspot. It was some kind of orchid, but unlike any other Chris had seen. The fleshy petals and bloodspot gave it a sensual, almost animal quality. But most unusual was the odor. From a distance it was a fruity perfume, but up close the sweetness yielded to a nauseating pungency—apples undercut by the stench of rotten flesh. What Eve passed on to Adam, Chris would later tell himself.

"The smell brings insects," Iwati said. "And the insects bring water birds."

"Which explains the croc."

"Yes. They come for the birds. This is the only place tabukari grows in the whole bush."

Chris was not a botanist, but he was certain its uniqueness had to do with the locale: the volcanic ash lacing the soil, the mineral-rich lake, the foggy elevation, and, of course, the rain forest. "What's so special about it?"

For the first time all evening Iwati smiled. "Everything." But he wouldn't elaborate.

"How do you use it?"

Iwati blew a cloud of smoke toward him. He'd been smoking the flower all along. "Sometimes I make tea. Sometimes put it in yam mash. But just for the medicine man. You want to try?"

"No."

A four-day side trip through a jungle full of mosquitoes, cannibals, and Godzilla crocs just to view Iwati's own private dope garden. Chris was tired and filthy and anxious to get back to camp and curl up in his cot. He couldn't wait to get back to Boston where the air was cool and dry, where he could eat a good steak and take a long hot bath without worrying about leeches and crocodiles. Where he could finally dry out. Where he could snuggle up against Wendy and Ricky and not fight off millipedes. Iwati had let him down.

"The name means 'forbidden flower of long day.' "

It struck Chris as a silly name, but he didn't say that. "And, I suppose, it makes you feel good."

"Yes."

"Well, so does scotch—and you don't have to cut through half the bloody bush."

"No, no, not like that." Then he added, "It's dangerous. Very addictive."

Probably a local species of coca, Chris guessed. "I see."

"No, you don't see. Addictive to the soul," he said and tapped his chest. "More dangerous than all your powders. Why it's called *tabu*." Iwati held up the vine and whispered, "Never grow old."

"Beg pardon?"

"Never grow old."

For a long moment the words hung in the air. Chris stared across the circle of embers at Iwati, whose eyes had deepened with shadows and looked like holes in his skull.

"I don't understand."

Iwati nodded. More silence.

But the ground seemed to shift slightly, as if a ripple of awareness had run through the earth and back. "You're saying this flower . . . prolongs life?"

"Yes."

"How long?"

"Long long."

"So, what has it done for you?"

He smiled. "I'm still here."

Through his grin shone teeth brown from years of smoking the stuff. But how many years? Twenty years ago in school Chris was sixteen, and he had assumed Iwati was about the same. The interim hadn't changed him much, though it was hard to tell with Papuans. Their skin was oily and they smeared themselves with vegetable pastes and mud for protection against the sun and insects. And being slender, Iwati could pass for a teenager.

"So, how old are you supposed to be?"

Iwati shook his head.

"You're not going to tell me that either?"

"I don't know how old."

Bush people lived by the movement of the sun; they

took note of the years. Besides, Iwati loved watches. "How can you not know how old you are, man?"

"I was born before the missionaries come."

That made sense. "The Red Cross missionaries were here during the war." Which meant he was born some-time in the early forties.

"Not Red Cross missionaries," Iwati said. "The Mar-ists."

A cold rash ran up Chris's back. "Marists? That was 1857."

"Yes."

"That's impossible! That would make you at least . . . a hundred and twenty-three." He started to laugh but the intensity in Iwati's eyes stopped him. "That's impossi-ble. You can't be more than forty."

Iwati smiled indulgently. "I am. Much much more."

"You *can't* be that old, Iwati. Our biology doesn't allow it."

"*Your* biology."

"Iwati, that's ridiculous." He wanted to say he was just trying to spook him, that for four years they had shared the same rational world of science—but suddenly that seemed so remote. So did Iwati.

"I was fifteen when I learned the tabukari power from my father."

"And when was he born?"

"Nobody knows. Sometime before the Contact."

"The Contact? Jesus, man, what kind of fool do you take me for? You're talking the seventeenth century."

Iwati nodded.

"And what happened to him?"

"The Portuguese killed him. The expedition led by Antonio d'Orbo."

Antonio d'Orbo was the first recorded white man to voyage up the Sepik in the middle of the last century, Chris recalled. Only a handful of his men made it back to tell.

"You don't believe me," Iwati said.

"Frankly, not a word."

Iwati stared at him for a moment, turning something over in his head. Then he removed the shrunken head from his neck and held it out to him. "Look. Look at it."

Repulsive as it was, Chris studied it in the firelight. The face was small and shriveled, its skin a darkened leather, the lips and eyelids stitched shut. He had seen several others in museums, but there was something distinctly different about this one. And for a moment he couldn't place it. Then it struck him: the hair. Unlike all the others, this was not black but a light brown, and not kinky but silky straight. Caucasian. The head had belonged to a westerner. Iwati lifted the plait, exposing one ear. It looked like a black apricot except for the lobe which was looped with metal and linked through a hole to a gold coin. The inscriptions were worn down some, but he could make out the Roman letters—the word *Anno Dei* and the Arabic numbers.

"It says 1866," Chris said. "What does that prove?"

"It's him."

"Who?"

"Antonio d'Orbo."

"Iwati, what the hell are you telling me?" But he did not answer. Just stared. "You're saying you did this— you killed Antonio d'Orbo and shrunk his head?"

"He killed my father."

Chris threw his hands into the air, shaking his head. "Sorry, my friend, but I don't believe you. None of it." He stood up and made a move to go. "Thanks for the bedtime story, but now I'd like to get some sleep."

Iwati rose. "Christopher, listen to me. I am telling you the truth. I swear it." Nothing in Iwati's manner betrayed his words. "I owe you for saving my life."

Chris stared into Iwati's eyes, but they held no guile. Suddenly the image of the Okamolu warriors flashed across Chris's mind. And the little juju man. They believed it.

They believed it!

Like his ears suddenly clearing, things began to make weird, terrifying sense. It wasn't Chris's skin that had reduced the Okamolu to frightened boys. They had seen white men before, probably had even eaten a few. Nor was it the gun. It was Iwati who had spooked them. Iwati! They weren't sure it was he in T-shirt, shorts, and sunglasses—not until he had changed into his ceremonial headdress and face paint and shrunken head. The declaration of his juju identity. Not just another tribal shaman, but Iwati of the secret tabukari magic. Maybe, too, it was the reason the porters regarded him as a god. The reason they had trudged for two weeks even into *tabu* land of flesh-eaters. The reason their own heads were still on their shoulders and not on Okamolu spears.

To their minds Iwati was deathless.

Iwati nodded as if reading Chris's mind. Then he shrugged and slipped the head back around his neck. "Maybe it's best, my friend," he said and tossed the flowered vine onto the fire.

The flames sputtered. But before they could claim the braid of small white blossoms, Chris's hand flew into the fire and snatched it away.

One

3,155,414,400 Seconds

52,590,240 Minutes

876,504 Hours

36,521 Days

5,218 Weeks

1,200 Months

400 Seasons

100 Years

1 Life

—LEONARD HAYFLICK

1

Quentin took a sip of his champagne. "My best offer is three million dollars, take it or leave it."

"Leave it," said Antoine Ducharme, not missing a beat.

You son-of-a-bitch! Quentin thought. "Then we have a problem."

"No, my friend, *you* have a problem. The fee is five million per ton."

Quentin Cross, Chief Financial Officer at thirty-seven and future CEO of Darby Pharmaceuticals, sat in uneasy silence on the rear deck of *Reef Madness*, a long sleek cruiser that Antoine's girlfriend, Lisa, maneuvered around the coral heads. Working the mooring line from the bow was Marcel, one of Antoine's security guards, who wore a snub-nosed revolver and pair of handcuffs on his belt.

They were inside the barrier reef on the northern coast of Apricot Cay, a palm-fringed island fifteen miles southeast of Jamaica and owned by Antoine Ducharme, an elegant and highly educated yachtsman, entrepreneur, and drug trafficker. Antoine, who looked to be in his mid-forties, was a tall, solidly built man with short salt-and-pepper hair, and an open face that appeared scholarly behind his rimless eyeglasses. It was a face that was used to making substantial decisions and one that could turn to stone in an instant.

Dressed in a green lounging suit, Antoine had arranged for his ten associates a sunset dinner of lobster tail, sautéed breadfruit, and French cheeses topped off with a dessert of fresh apricots, of course.

Quentin knew very little about the other men except that they were all part of an international group of very wealthy power brokers given to secret capital ventures and extravagances. But their association with Antoine Ducharme suggested that they had no ethical qualms about getting dirty. There were no introductions. The men ate separately, speaking French and German, then moved into the inner cabin to watch a soccer game beamed from a satellite dish. To Quentin they were simply "the Consortium."

Sitting with Quentin and Antoine was an American of about thirty-five named Vince Lucas, Antoine's "financial security officer." He was lean and attractive in a feral kind of way. He had smooth fleshy lips, a tanned, V-shaped face, and shiny black hair combed straight back to expose a deep widow's peak. His eyebrows were perfect black slashes, and his eyes were so dark that they appeared to be all pupil. On his forearm was a tattoo of a bird of prey with a death-head skull. He looked like no financial officer Quentin had ever met.

"If you ask me, five million is a bargain," Vince Lucas said.

"Five million dollars is out of the question," Quentin repeated. But he knew that they had him by the proverbial throat.

Lisa cleared the dishes. She was clad in a scant black bikini, a yellow headband, and a rose tattoo on her shoulder. She was a stunningly exotic woman in her early twenties with cocoa skin and deep, uninhibited eyes—eyes which when they fell on Quentin made him self-conscious of his large pink face, thinning hair, and pot belly swelling over his shorts. When she was finished, she gave Antoine, who was twice her age, a long passionate kiss and went below, Marcel tailing her to leave the men to their business.

"Listen to me, my friend," Antoine said, "We have over two thousand acres of mountain rainforest, another thousand acres of orchards with mountain streams for irrigation, protected harbors, your own airstrip, storage buildings—'the works,' as you Americans say. And most important: total privacy."

Quentin had heard all this before. He had toured the island including the rainforest. But biological diversity was not what interested him. Nor the acres of cannabis hidden in the orchards. Nor the camouflaged sheds where imported cocoa leaves were processed into cocaine for easy shipment northward—an operation which made Apricot Cay the Delmonte of dope in the Western Hemisphere.

What Quentin Cross wanted was apricots—and a particular species, *Prunus caribaeus*, unique to Apricot Cay. And he was willing to pay $3 million a ton for them.

No, Darby Pharms was not diversifying into the produce market. What made the species unique was the pits: They contained cyanogentic compounds highly toxic to cancer cells. In fact, the apricot toxogen had an astounding 80 percent success rate in the treatment of Mexican patients with malignant tumors. The FDA had not yet approved clinical testing in the U.S., but for Quentin the compound—with the potential trade name Veratox— promised to become the world's first cancer wonder drug.

Darby Pharms had kept the toxogen secret for two key reasons. First, they had not yet secured FDA approval; but that was no problem since Ross Darby was an old college buddy of Ronald Reagan. The second reason was Antoine Ducharme. Nobody at Darby but Quentin knew that he was an international drug baron, including Ross Darby, Quentin's father-in-law and current CEO—a man of impeccable scruples. If word got out, Darby Pharmaceuticals would not only lose its license to manufacture drugs, but it could end up in a criminal investigation that could put Quentin Cross and Ross Darby behind bars for years.

Antoine knew that and, thus, was asking for blood. What gnawed at Quentin's mind was the entrepreneur's unpredictability. Should Veratox turn out to be the world's hottest pharmaceutical, Antoine might double the price of subsequent shipments. Or he might set up an auction for bidders with limitless resources, such as Eli Lilly or Merck. The only solution was a commercially viable synthesis. But in spite of months of all-out efforts by Christopher Bacon, Darby's chief medical chemist, the toxogen was proving difficult to reproduce. The process required so many steps that the yield was infinitesimal. So far, *Prunus caribaeus* was an apricot that only nature could build.

"Let me remind you that it grows only on Apricot Cay. And do you know why?" Antoine flashed another toothy smile. "Because a particular fungus that blights only *Prunus caribaeus* mysteriously wiped out all the apricot crops on the other islands."

Quentin was about to ask where the blight came from, but something in Antoine's eyes said he could guess the answer. The son-of-a bitch was even more cunning than he had guessed.

"What prevents the blight from being introduced here?"

"The fact that nobody is allowed to disembark here without my permission."

That was true. He had ringed its beaches with elaborate electronic security systems—cameras, motion detectors, barbed-wire fences—not to mention armed guards on constant surveillance in towers and jeeps. He had even pushed old cars into the shallows of the bay for coral to build upon, making boat passage perilous. Apricot Cay was a tropical fortress.

"You're asking too much."

"Not according to the *Wall Street Journal*," Vince Lucas said. From his briefcase he pulled out a copy of the paper. "Darby Pharms' profitability increased 30 percent over the last year—some 50 million dollars. *Barron's* cites you as a growth company of choice. Besides, your Mr. Darby is an old friend of Ronald Reagan. Once you get FDA approval, Darby will be on the *Fortune* 500, *n'est-ce pas?*"

Quentin wished he had never mentioned the White House connection. In a moment of bravado he once boasted how Ross Darby and Reagan played football together at Eureka College and that Darby had contributed hundreds of thousands of dollars to Reagan's campaigns and raised millions more hosting Republican fund raisers. Ironically, Ross had even generously supported Nancy Reagan's "Just Say No" anti-drug initiative. That boast had probably doubled the cost of the apricots.

Quentin walked to the gunwale. The sun had set on the unbroken horizon, enameling the sea in burnt orange. Even with Reagan pressing the FDA Commissioner, it could take two years to win approval. Then another two before Veratox was on the market. Meanwhile, Darby would be another $25 million in debt to a Caribbean crook. Worse still, their ace microbiologist, Dexter Quinn, had retired two months ago, leaving only Chris Bacon and a couple of assistants on their premier project. They worked around the clock but had made no progress synthesizing the compound. But something bothered Quentin about Bacon. He seemed distracted all the time—as if he had another agenda just below the surface.

"Of course," said Antoine, joining him at the railing, "it's always possible that another firm would become interested in our fine harvest, no?" Antoine smiled broadly.

The bastard had him by the balls. On the table sat the leather-bound business plans containing all the lease conditions, the numbers, and paragraphs of legalese about the dummy corporation Quentin had established to export tropical fruit. It was all very sophisticated and legitimate, neatly spelled out in French and English and as negotiable as a firing squad.

Quentin felt himself cave in. Veratox was a billion-dollar molecule, and he was next in line to run the company. Once Chris Bacon's group could synthesize the extract, they would have no need of Antoine Ducharme and his island. "You drive a hard bargain."

"No such thing, my friend. Bargains are never hard."

Quentin shuffled back to the table and signed the contract. By November first, he would have to wire two and a half million dollars to a bank in Grand Bahamas as advance. A second payment of the same amount was due next June. And nobody would know because Quentin kept double books, siphoning funds from foreign sales of other products.

Antoine poured more champagne and they sat and watched the sky turn black while inside the others hooted over the game. After several minutes, Antoine stood up. "Trust, my friends. It is very important, no?"

The question threw Quentin. Vince Lucas just shrugged.

"More important than love." A strange intensity lit Antoine's eyes.

Quentin's first thought was that Antoine was drunk. But he moved purposefully to a wall unit by the boat's instruments and slid back a panel to reveal a small television screen. He hit a couple buttons and a color picture emerged. For a moment Quentin thought it was some kind of adult video. Two people were having sex. Antoine muttered something in French in a tone of harsh resignation, then turned a knob. The camera zoomed in on Lisa in the throes of an orgasm, Marcel, his red shirt still on, driving her from above.

Antoine's expression was a strange neutrality. He flicked off the set then picked up the phone and said something in French. Within a minute, Marcel climbed up from below. He was fully dressed, the holstered gun still belted around his waist.

Quentin could feel his heartbeat kick up.

"Everything okay below?" Antoine asked.

"Yes, of course," Marcel said, looking nervous.

"Good." Then he turned to Quentin. "Because my American associate here is joining us. He will be investing very heavily in our enterprise here, and we must assure him of flawless security, *n'est-ce-pas?*"

"But of course."

Antoine approached Marcel and raised a finger like a teacher making a key point. "Trust," he said, then reached around and unclipped the pistol from his holster. Marcel did not move. "See? Perfect trust." Marcel made an uncertain grin. Antoine raised a second finger. "Perfect security," he continued. "Essential ingredients for success, yes?"

Vince Lucas smiled and made a toasting gesture, encouraging Marcel to go along with the classroom charade.

Then Antoine motioned for Marcel to hold out his hands. The man looked perplexed, but Antoine was his boss making a point to impress his guest. So Marcel complied as Antoine removed the handcuffs from his belt and snapped one on his wrist. "Perfect trust, yes?"

Marcel nodded, then Antoine indicated for Marcel to turn around, which he did, half-proudly presenting his other hand behind him in perfect obedience. Antoine snapped on the second cuff, still keeping up his patter, while Quentin watched in anxious fascination. "Without trust, friendship fails, families dissolve, empires crumble."

He led Marcel to the portside edge. Across the water, Antoine's villa glowed like a jeweler's display. Above them spread an endless black vault fretted with a million stars and a crescent moon rocking just above the horizon. "And it is for all this," Antoine continued. "A paradise island in a paradise sea under a paradise sky—the stars, the moon, the air. All the moments we steal from the gods. We are as close to immortality as one can get."

"Yes, monsieur."

"Yes, monsieur," Antoine echoed. He directed Marcel to look straight down into the water. "But not the face of deceit."

Before Marcel could respond, Antoine nodded to Vince Lucas who in one smooth move heaved Marcel over the side.

Marcel bobbed to the surface, coughing and choking.

"You guarded the wrong body, my friend." Antoine said.

Marcel shouted pleas to Antoine to drop a rope or ladder, aware that they were half a mile out with an offshore wind pushing him toward where the surf pounded the jagged reef to foam.

Vince pulled a pistol from under his shirt and aimed it at Marcel's head to finish him off.

"No, let nature take its course," Antoine said, "and prolong the pleasure."

From below, Lisa climbed onto the deck. She had heard Marcel's cries. "What happened? What did you do to him?"

Antoine turned to her with fierce intensity. "He wanted to get his dick wet."

She looked at him in horror, then at the two other men standing with champagne glasses, the Consortium inside celebrating a goal. She started away when Antoine pushed her to the side. He was about to hurl her overboard when Quentin cried out. "No, please, Antoine. Don't do this. Please!"

Antoine's face snapped at him, furious at the intrusion. But he caught himself and released the woman. "You can go," he hissed. "But you won't make the same mistake twice, will you?"

She stood gasping in hideous disbelief as Marcel choked for his last few breaths of air.

"Will you?" Antoine repeated.

"No," she whined, then backed down the stairs to her cabin.

Frozen in horror, Quentin looked for help to Vince who just winked and pointed out a shooting star, while Antoine poured himself more champagne then returned to the gunwale to watch Marcel die.

For two wicked minutes he choked and begged for his life—his words gurgling through the night waves, his legs kicking with all he had to keep his head above night surf—until totally exhausted he sank into the black.

Quentin was too stricken with horror to say anything else. He hid in his glass, wondering at the cruel justice of Antoine Ducharme, at the casualness of Vince Lucas as if he'd witnessed murders all the time, at what miseries Antoine had in store for Lisa—but knowing with brilliant clarity that he was dealing with a species of people who lived in a dark and gaudy world—a world whose principles were alien to the rest of civilized society.

But what bothered Quentin Cross almost as much as watching the young man drown was knowing that he was now part of that world—an accomplice and partner who had signed his name in blood.

And that the only way out was Christopher Bacon.

Or his own death.

2

Karen Kimball couldn't put her finger on it, but the guy in the tan sportcoat looked vaguely familiar.

It was the eyes. The heavy lids, the dark blue flecked with stars. It's hard to forget eyes, no matter what happens to the rest of the face. These were eyes she knew from long ago. And the way they followed her. Not leering, not lewd, just a kind of warm speculation. But he was too young to be making eyes at her.

She mopped the table in the booth across from his and chided herself. Here she was an overweight fifty-nine year-old divorcée with three kids and a grandchild—not some teeniebopper flushing at each foxy guy who passed her way.

She dried her hands and pulled out her pad. "Would you like something to drink, sir?"

He eyed her waitress outfit. "Aren't you the owner?"

Everyone in town knew that. "One of my girls called in sick, so you're going to have to settle for me. What'll it be?"

"I think I'll have a black cow."

"A what?"

"Guess you stopped making them. Make it a Heineken instead."

For a moment Karen felt a blister of irritation rise. He

was putting her down for not having a bar that made fancy mixed drinks. But as she headed away, it occurred to her what he had asked for—a black cow: root beer and vanilla ice cream. She hadn't heard that name for years. Not since the days she had worked at the Lincoln Dairy, when she was a junior in high school.

Karen got the beer and returned, now feeling a low-grade uneasiness. She took his order, all the while studying his face. A good face: open and pleasant, with a thin, slightly crooked mouth, sharp cleft chin, thick brown hair, and those blue starburst eyes.

Jesus, I know this face, she told herself. And that look: Each time their eyes met she could feel something pass between them—something that went beyond customer and waitress.

She moved into the kitchen, and through the small window of the swing door she again studied the guy. She knew he knew her, though she could not place him in any context. And he seemed to enjoy his mystery. He looked to be in his thirties, so maybe he was the son of some friend, a guy she hadn't seen since he was a child. She called Freddie over. "You know that guy in booth seven?"

Freddie peered through the door. "Never saw him before. Why, he giving you trouble or something?"

"No, just looks familiar."

"Whyn't you ask him?"

She nodded, and for several moments let her mind rummage for a connection, watching him look around as if for familiar faces. The way he moved his head and ran his hand through his hair, and the slant of his chin. And those eyes. *Those eyes.*

Jesus! It was driving her to distraction. Maybe she'd seen him in the movies or on TV. But what would he be doing in the Casa Loma? It was a nice family place, but not the Ritz.

She stared through the glass concentrating as hard as she could, feeling it almost come to her—like a bird swooping in out of the dark, then just before landing turning sharply and flapping away.

This is ridiculous, she told herself. She delivered other orders, trying to look neutral but checking him out from the corner of her eye. By the time his meal was ready she had worked up the nerve to ask. "I don't mean to be impolite, but do I know you?"

The man smiled coyly. "You might."

"You from around here?"

"Not anymore." That same teasing smile. He sipped his beer.

"It's just that you look familiar."

"Well," he began, but decided to continue playing coy, letting her twist in the breeze.

"I guess not," she said and walked away, thinking, *The hell with this!* If he was somebody she was supposed to know, then, damn it, let him fess up. No way she was going to get into a mind game with some jerk looking for a little action before he blows back out of town.

Karen delivered his order without a word or a glance. She placed it on the place mat and turned on her heels just as cool and professional as she could be. But as she moved away, the man began to softly sing a refrain: *"Sometimes I wonder why I spend the lonely nights dreaming of a song. The melody haunts my reverie . . ."*

Karen pretended not to hear and headed across the floor and into the kitchen without looking back.

Freddie glanced up from the stove at her. "Hey, you okay? You look like you seen a ghost."

Karen was leaning against the wall staring out through the window. The eyes. That slightly crooked mouth. The little scar at the corner of his left eyebrow.

"Can't be," she said aloud.

"What 'can't be?' "

She shook her head to say it was nothing.

That song. "Stardust." Suddenly she was in the gym at Alfred E. Burr Junior High school dancing to Helen O'Connell and the Jimmy Dorsey Band. It was their favorite. She had said his eyes were like stardust.

Impossible! He's too young. Too young!

"That guy giving you some crap?"

"No, for chrissakes!" She didn't know why she flared up, but suddenly she felt upset and disoriented. She went out the back door and lit a cigarette trying to find her center again.

The parking lot was beginning to fill up. In the eastern sky, trees had lost their leaves and made scraggly patterns against the street lights. As she stared she was suddenly in a wooden backyard swing set on Brown Street in Canton's south end. He was beside her, smiling that silly crooked smile. And those stardust eyes. He was saying something about going to college and becoming a scientist someday, and how the next moment he was kissing her.

It came back to her in such a rush she felt faint.

She went back inside, crossed through the kitchen. Freddie asked her something, but she dismissed him with her hand and went into the staff toilet. Inside she fixed her hair and put fresh lipstick on. The face in the mirror looked at best five years this side of its age. And he looked like a kid.

It couldn't be him. So why was she shaking all of a sudden and fixing her face and gargling with mouthwash?

This was nuts!

She passed through the service door.

He had finished his meal, but was still sitting there and facing her. The same eyes. Same cleft in the chin. Same scar. She felt a strange fright, because it didn't make any sense. He looked half her age. While she tried to find the right words, she spotted something in his hand.

Then she realized that he wasn't smiling. And his eyes were huge and round. His mouth opened and a string of saliva poured out onto his shirt. And rising from his throat was a deep wet groan. Suddenly his chest began to heave.

Karen's first thought was he was choking, that he couldn't catch his breath, that she had to apply the Heimlich maneuver because his face was draining of color.

But then his body began to convulse as if experiencing electric shock. In a clean sweep of his hands, the dishes scattered to the floor, as his feet kicked in some awful reflex. But what made Karen scream was how his face tensed in agony and his head jerked back as if trying to free itself from his neck.

"Somebody get a doctor. Hurry."

My God! she thought, *he's having a heart attack.* She shouted to one of the waiters to call an ambulance.

Instantly the place was in a commotion, people shouting and jumping up to help, one man saying he was a physician.

While people swirled around her and the doctor tried to loosen the man's tie, Karen was frozen in place. Something was happening to the man's face.

As he weaved and bobbed his head, Karen could swear that the skin of his face was changing, shifting, beginning to darken with splotches. But more than that, it appeared to be moving, buckling, as if loosening from the inside—as if there were suddenly too much skin to cover his skull.

At first she couldn't believe what she was seeing, all too distracted by the convulsions and gurgling from his chest. Then she noticed his hands. The skin was changing—wrinkling and withering as if the flesh inside were dissolving, leaving a translucent parchment through which veins made long blue vees across the backs of his hands. Others noticed also, and their voices hushed as they stopped to take in the spectacle. Then people began to scream, calling for the doctor to do something.

But this was not a heart attack, nor a stroke, nor an aneurysm, nor anything else Karen could imagine. Nor anything any of the others who pressed against her could imagine, including the doctor. Futilely he had loosened the man's tie, knowing he was witnessing nothing he had seen before, nothing that his medical texts ever prepared him for—nothing that had anything to do with normal human pathology. What disease could reduce a human body to such a stage of debilitation and with such brutal virulence? No virus, bacteria, or plague he knew of. Whatever had struck the man had blitzed his cells at the DNA level.

While others gasped and shouted, Karen stood nailed to the floor, a scream bulbed in her throat as she watched the man age half-a-century before her eyes, simultaneously fleshing out and withering into a bloated mummy of his former self. Just minutes ago he had sat here a big handsome young guy. Now he was collapsed into the corner of the booth, his shoulders hunched forward, neck sunk into his frame, sightless rheumy eyes gaping at the onlookers, his mouth rimmed with cracked flesh frozen in a silent scream.

Then a long thin cry rose from Karen's lungs as she plied open the withered claw clutched around the black-and-white photograph he had brought her—one she knew so well, a bit faded and cracked but not enough to conceal the image of them in tuxedo and gown at their junior prom, "Stardust Night–1948"—a duplicate of which she had in her scrapbook at home with the inscription on the back: *With love forever, Dexter.*

3

Half-consciously Chris Bacon plucked a white hair from his eyebrow in the rearview mirror. "How old would you say you are if you didn't know how old you are?"

"Is this some kind of trick question?" his wife Wendy asked.

"No."

"Well, some days I feel about ninety," she chuckled.

"You know what I mean."

"I don't know, honey... Thirty-something, I suppose." Today was her forty-second birthday, although she looked at least ten years younger. She was slim and attractive, and her skin was smooth and fair. She had shiny chestnut-colored hair and large intelligent eyes of almost the same color. Her full expressive mouth, high cheekbones, and V-shaped chin gave her a regal quality that helped preserve her youthfulness. It also helped that Wendy took good care of herself and jogged regularly. "Why?"

"What if you could feel thirty-something the rest of your life?"

"I guess it depends on how long the rest of my life is."

"What if you could live, say, another hundred years and still feel thirty?"

Something in Wendy's expression said she was becoming uncomfortable with the subject. "But that's not going to happen."

"Let's say it could."

Wendy thought for a moment. Then she said, "Why would I want to live another hundred years?"

"Why? You mean you'd prefer three score and ten instead of twice that?"

"Well, only because everybody else I ever knew would be dead. I'd be a living anachronism. What kind of a life would that be?"

"How about if everybody had the same privilege?"

"Wouldn't that be worse? By the end of the century, there'd be ten billion people on the planet."

"What if it weren't accessible to everybody? I mean, just the people you love."

Wendy shifted restlessly in her seat. "Chris, can we please change the subject? None of what you're asking can happen."

"Honey, just pretend for the sake of argument: If you had the option to add another, say, fifty years onto your lifespan without aging, with me and your sister . . ."

"And how would you explain it to your neighbors when they grew old and you didn't?"

"We'd just move someplace else."

She started to laugh. "You mean every ten or fifteen years while everybody else is turning gray, we just pack up and go to another city?"

"Something like that."

"We'd be living like fugitives."

"Say we moved to your family place in the Adirondacks?"

"You mean live the last eighty years of our lives hiding in the woods? Frankly, I think I'd rather die young."

They were on their way to Logan airport to pick up Wendy's sister Jenny and her new baby who were visiting for the weekend. While they were in for Wendy's birthday, Chris was privately celebrating the birthday of a mouse.

Not Mickey. That was two years ago—and, Wendy swore, never again. No, this was a real mouse.

Although *mus musuclus sextonis* could be mistaken for any other laboratory rodent, it was a rare mutant with the dubious distinction of being the shortest-lived mouse—a mere eleven months compared to twenty-three for most others. Located at a breeder in Maine, Chris had ordered some five hundred of the animals over the years. Of the original batch, over 60 percent had defied their DNA clock by a factor of four. And one, a slender albino agouti male with pink eyes, had outlived them all as the sole survivor of years of secret experimentation—the one Chris had named Methuselah because he had exceeded his life expectancy by a factor of six, and today was celebrating his sixty-sixth month.

The best-laid plans of mice and men had *not* gone awry: Iwati's flower had worked!

Chris had been as good as his vow. For six years only one other person at Darby Pharms knew of his research. They had worked on the sly—nights and weekends—isolating, purifying, synthesizing, then testing the flower extract. And Chris got away with it because as senior researcher he had complete autonomy in the lab and could mask requisitions for material and animals. No one else from top management down had any inkling that during downtime on the apricot toxogen Chris was at work on the tabukari elixir. To the casual observer Dr. Christopher Bacon was the ideal employee—a man dedicated to his science, his company, and his fellow human beings.

Like the apricot toxogen, synthesis of tabukari was a complex process, but unlike Veratox the yield was very high. The active ingredient contained forty-six molecules, including a slight molecular variation of a steroid, fluoxymesterone, a hormonelike compound which Chris had never seen in a plant before—what he named *tabulone*.

In addition to testing tabulone on mice, Chris also applied it to cell cultures with astounding effects. From the medical literature he knew that normal, noncancerous animal cells reproduced a finite number of times between birth and death. For mice, it was an average of six replications; for chickens, twenty-five; for elephants, one hundred ten. For humans, about fifty. In a Petri dish four years ago, Chris had made a breakthrough discovery. He had taken two different batches of mouse brain tissue. One he treated with fluid nutrients and a nontoxic blue stain and incubated the mixture at body temperature. He did the same with the other but added tabulone. After five days, the first batch went through its full six replications, then died. Under the microscope, the walls of the cells had deteriorated to let the blue stain seep through. However, the cell batch treated with tabulone remained perfectly clear and healthy as on Day One. For all practical purposes, tabulone had stopped the biological clock. Today those same cells were still alive and thriving.

Somehow, tabulone had produced a protective shield around the test cells. Chris didn't understand what was happening on the molecular level, and he wished he could consult a geneticist. But six years and three hundred mice later he knew he had developed the closest thing to biological perpetuity. What started out as a quest for the perfect human birth control had, ironically, produced an eternal mouse. And Darby Pharms Inc. never knew. Nor would he tell them until he had worked out some nasty limitations of the compound.

Even then Chris was not sure. What staggered his mind was the magnitude of the implication: If tabulone could work the same for humans, he was at the threshold of the most astounding breakthrough in medical science—one that would redefine the very concept of life.

"You mean they don't die?" Wendy asked.

"No, they'll die eventually, but not from diseases associated with age—kidney failure, heart and liver diseases. Theoretically they could go on for a few more lifetimes."

"But a few mice outliving their life span doesn't mean you've discovered the fountain of youth for humans. You're a scientist, Chris. You know better than to make wild speculations."

"What about Iwati?"

"You want me to believe that some New Guinea bushman who claims to be a hundred and twenty three and doesn't look a day over thirty? Give me a break."

"What if he is?"

"Then I'd pity him because he'd be forced go on long after the people he loved grew old and died. He'd be a freak alone with his secret."

A freak alone with his secret.

The phrase stuck in Chris's mind like a thorn.

Maybe that was why Iwati had returned to the bush. It was the one place where time didn't move, where he could live to a hundred and fifty or more and never feel the press of change. In Port Moresby or Sydney or any other city, the future was happening by the moment. But in the Stone Age Papuan highlands, he had found indefinite life and exalted status. He was the Tifalmin's Constant Healer, dispensing balms for this ailment and that while keeping to himself the ultimate balm—the taboo to which only his offspring would be privy. And the ultimate bequest of a father to his firstborn son.

"Chris, death is what makes us human," Wendy said. "I want to live only long enough to become old."

They emerged from the Callahan tunnel to a line of

traffic and turned right, toward the entrance of Logan Airport.

"Wendy, most of the people in these cars won't be here in thirty years. They'd kill to double or triple their stay. You're an English teacher: Imagine what Shakespeare could have created had he lived another fifty years. Or Michelangelo or da Vinci or Einstein. The mind boggles. Just imagine how much more writing you could do, how much more life you could enjoy."

" 'Death is the mother of beauty,' " she quoted. Her voice was now flat, the earlier efforts to play along had vanished.

"Maybe, except that Wallace Stevens saw no alternative."

"Chris, we die for a reason. You're tampering with Nature—with processes refined over billions of years. And there's something dangerous in that. Besides, have you considered any of the social problems if the stuff actually worked on people—such as who could afford it? Or the population nightmare? Or if the stuff fell into the hands of criminals or a Hitler? The good thing about death is that it gets the bad guys too."

Chris made a dismissive gesture with his hand. "Precautions could be taken against all that. The point is, I like being alive. I like the moments of my life. And in thirty years I'll be dead forever. You know what *forever* means? It means never being conscious again. It means never waking up the next morning and seeing the world, of thinking, of being aware of colors and sounds. It means never seeing you again, and that sickens me."

"You've got at least another forty years ahead of you, maybe fifty given the way you take care of yourself."

It was true that he ate healthily and worked out regularly, jogging three miles each morning before going to work. And he had been doing that since his days at Yale where he competed on the wrestling team. At forty-two, and with a full head of sandy hair, he looked like a man ten years his junior—a young Nick Nolte, Wendy had once remarked. But his athletic good looks would pass sooner than later, and, at the moment, he refused to be placated.

As they continued into Logan, Chris asked, "What if Ricky could have been saved?"

Instantly Wendy's voice turned to gravel. "He wasn't!"

"No, but if he had been, you'd feel a lot different, right?"

"But he wasn't. And I don't want to talk about this anymore." Her voice began to crack.

They rode in prickly silence. Chris had opened that dreadful black box again. He hadn't wanted to, but he couldn't stop himself. He had to know. And as he drove into the airport with his wife trying to recompose herself, he thought of how he had multiplied the lifespan of a goddamn mouse but he couldn't save his own son by a day.

Mickey. The other mouse, and Ricky's favorite companion.

Mickey had been with him the day he died, along with Chris and Wendy who had sat on either side of his bed in Boston's Children's Hospital, each holding a hand. It was how he had left them. For two years they had tried everything including bone marrow transplants from Chris and a battery of experimental drugs. It was what kept Chris working on Veratox—hoping for a successful synthesis, hoping for a breakthrough that would win FDA approval and save his son before cancer cells claimed him.

It was what kept Chris going on tabulone. But time ran out. Ricky had died at the actuarial prime of life— the age when the fewest people in the nation die. The age when the statistical likelihood of living another day is higher than at any other time of human life: five years, eight months. Eaten by cannibals—minute and immortal.

When it was clear that no hope was left but life in a state of suspended decay, they asked that the respirator be removed so Ricky could pass away on his own. It took less than two hours. At his death, he had as much hair as he had at birth. But unlike his birth hair, this was wispy and dead looking, and his scalp was scaly, his face emaciated, his eyes sunken and slitted open and frozen in a blank stare. The cancer had ravished his little system, reducing him to a shriveled, bird-faced old man. They didn't know if at the end he was aware of their presence, but Wendy kept whispering in his ear that the angels would take care of him in heaven.

Three years later, the pain still throbbed, but they had grown hard around it. They both went through a period of anger—at the universe, at death for having claimed their baby. At God. Wendy, who had been brought up Roman Catholic, could not forgive Him on this one. After two miscarriages and Ricky's death, He had killed her will to ever have another child.

Chris pulled onto the United ramp thinking about Ricky and Wendy and Methuselah.

Thinking about the bedroom with the cowboy wallpaper and the PeeWee League trophy Ricky had won and the preschool class pictures on his bureau, Ricky's cherubic face beaming at the camera. How Wendy could not get herself to enter his room for weeks. How in a fit she tore the place apart, packed what she couldn't part with, gave clothes to Goodwill, and stripped the walls of every reminder of the son who would never grow up.

Thinking about his father in a Connecticut nursing home withered by arthritis and Alzheimer's disease. Thinking how that cruel predisposition might be etched in his own genes.

Thinking about Methuselah full of life—eating,

drinking, running his wheels and mazes like Mighty Mouse, a perpetual motion machine.

Thinking how he had the keys to the kingdom.

"When are you going to tell them?" Wendy asked. "I mean, it's been six years you've been skulking around the lab."

"I'm not sure I am."

"Why not?"

"It scares the hell out of me."

Six years of ingenious fraud was enough to get him fired, prosecuted, and blackballed in the industry. But what filled him with fear was not being caught, but the thought that once the genie was out of the lamp there was no getting him back in.

And behind that fear was Quentin Cross. Although Quentin would replace Ross Darby next year, Chris did not trust him. He took foolish risks and cut corners with FDA regulations. It was his idea to test Veratox on human subjects in Mexico, circumventing U.S. protocol. Quentin hadn't actually violated the law, just ethical practice. And that worried Chris. He couldn't predict what Quentin would do with tabulone.

The other problem was protocols for human testing. Even if it worked on higher species, the average rhesus monkey lived twenty-five years. Chris would be an old man by the time he had viable results for the next step. Not only did he lack the resources—financial and otherwise—he didn't have the time. *Nice irony*, he thought: *Not enough time to see if you could live forever!*

Worse still, he was now on his own. His sole assistant, a trusted and talented microbiologist, had retired from Darby Pharms a few months ago following a mild heart attack. He had said he wanted to make up for lost time while he still had some left.

They entered the United arrival area where Jenny was waiting for them with her luggage and baby daughter. Taxis and cars were moving helter-skelter. As Chris pulled up to the curb, he wondered what his only confidant at Darby was doing in his retirement. He had always been a nostalgic kind of guy, so he was probably back in Canton, Ohio, whooping it up with his old girlfriend.

Jesus, he missed Dexter Quinn!

4

O h, look, it's Auntie Wendy and Uncle Chris," Jenny chortled to the baby bundled in her arms.

It was their first time meeting Abigail, now four months old. As usual, Jenny was in high spirits despite air turbulence that had kept the baby fussing all the way from Kalamazoo. Jenny was just what Wendy needed to jump start her spirits. With Chris working around the clock, she had become bored and lonely. What she couldn't predict was how it would feel to have a baby in the house again.

Traffic was light, so they made it back to Carleton in half an hour. Chris and Wendy lived in an eight-room central-entrance colonial with a wide front lawn that was now covered with snow. The interior was decorated for Christmas, and while Jenny carried on about how festive the place looked, Chris brought her luggage up to the guest room. When Jenny was out of earshot he announced that he was going back to the lab.

"Back to the lab! They just arrived," Wendy said. "I thought we were going to have nice relaxing evening." A fire was going in the living room hearth beside the tree, and she had bought some good wine, cheeses, and pâtés.

"Honey, I'm sorry, but something critical's come up. I've got to get back."

Chris had two different colored eyes—one brown, the other green—that, someone once said, gave him the appearance of two different faces superimposed. At the moment, they appeared to be pulling apart by the distraction in them. It was a look Chris had gotten too often, and one that Wendy had come to resent.

"Can't it wait? You haven't seen her for a year. Besides, it's my birthday in case you forgot."

He had. "Oh, hell, I'm sorry. It completely slipped my mind, really."

But Wendy didn't care about that. Nor did she care how critical things were at the lab. At times she wished the place would blow up for how it had consumed him. And for what? Some foolish delusions about changing the course of human biology. She took his arm. "Chris, I don't want you to go." Her voice was beginning to tremble. She had envisioned a nice warm reunion around the fire. The three of them and the baby. "Please."

Chris slipped his gloves back on. "Honey, I can't. I'm sorry, but I have to. Quentin's been riding my ass to get a good yield."

"That's not why."

But Wendy stopped because Jenny had wandered into the living room with the baby in her arms. Instantly Jenny sensed the tension because she chortled something about how pretty the room was, then began straightening out sofa pillows and lining up the Christmas knick-knacks on a table. That was Jenny: She had an abnormal craving for neatness—emotional and otherwise. At all costs she would avoid conflicts, even if it meant forcing down hurt and anger with smiles and endless bubbles of chatter. There was a flip side to her obsession, however: You almost never knew when something troubled her.

Chris turned to Jenny. "Please don't be insulted, but I've really got to get back to the lab. We've got some time-sensitive tests, and my assistant is home in bed with the flu. It's lousy timing, I know."

If Jenny was offended, she didn't let on. In a good-natured voice, she said, "No-o-o problem. You go attend to your tests or whatever. We're here until Sunday. You'll get enough of us. Besides, you're going to save the world from cancer, right?"

"We're hoping."

Bull! Wendy thought. The apricot synthesis was a bust. It was that damned New Guinea flower that he was running back to.

"That's much more important than sitting around chewing the fat," Jenny continued. "Besides, your wife and I have a lot of boring sisterly stuff to catch up on."

"Jenny, listen, I'm sorry. Really. And Abby." He gave her a hug and kissed the baby on the head.

Then he turned and kissed Wendy on the forehead. "Happy birthday," he whispered. "Sorry."

Wendy looked into those impossible eyes and nodded, but she said nothing.

"Get going, get going. You're wasting precious time," Jenny sang out. "And she prefers Abigail."

Artfully, Jenny had let him off.

After a second glass of wine; Wendy felt better, although she was still disappointed and a little hurt that Chris had cut out on her birthday. No other project at the lab had consumed him so much. Nor had given him such profound satisfaction. And that's what bothered her even more than his absence. It was as if he were having an affair with some dark half-sister of Mother Nature.

When the baby was ready to go down, Wendy led them upstairs. She always felt a little self-conscious about her house when Jenny visited. It had that "lived-in" look, while Jenny kept her place obsessively neat—so much so that you felt as if you'd offend the furniture by using it. As they headed to the guest room, Jenny unconsciously straightened out pictures on the wall or rearranged table items. It was more than an aesthetic reflex. Jenny was positively harassed when things were out of place. Even as a child she had manifested an inordinate obsession for order. She would spend hours arranging things in her room—dolls, books, toys. One day when Jenny had nothing to do, Wendy found her at her desk lining the hundreds of seashells they'd collected over the years into a perfect spiral—the smallest ones in the center moving outward to the largest ones.

On the way Wendy showed Jenny the office she had made for herself out of the spare bedroom. Beside a new IBM PC and printer lay the nearly completed manuscript of a mystery novel she was writing. Her dream was to write herself out of Carleton High's English Department where she had been for eighteen years. By now she was burned out and tired of explaining things to kids.

"*If I Should Die*. Good title," Jenny said, riffling through the manuscript.

It was the first of a trilogy centered on a feisty forensic psychologist. Wendy hadn't thought out the plot of the sequels, but she had the titles: *Before I Wake* and *My Soul to Take*.

"You amaze me, Wendy. I can't tell a story at gunpoint."

Wendy chuckled. "I've had those days."

She watched as Jenny flipped through the manuscript. It had been over a year since they had last visited each other. Since her pregnancy, Jenny had put on weight. Yet unlike Wendy, who was still a size eight, Jenny had always been inclined toward plumpness. Because she avoided the aging effects of the sun, her skin was remarkably pale and creamy. She had their mother's deep brown eyes and dark hair which she wore in bangs and straightly cropped about her neck. With her bright round face and green-and-red plaid jumper, she looked like a Christmas pageant choirgirl.

Something on a page caught her eye. "Ceren Evadas! You put that in here."

"The old line about writing what you know."

When they were girls, Wendy would spin stories for Jenny at bedtime. It was how she forged her big-sister role while polishing her storytelling craft. One of the stories was about two girls who invented a secret hideaway where they could go to escape monsters. She named it "Ceren Evadas"—pronouncing it "serene evaders"—an anagram of Andrea's Cave near their summer lodge at Black Eagle Lake in the Adirondacks. Whenever they got the urge, they would whisper "Ceren Evadas," then take off to the cave. At the end of her novel, the heroine took refuge from the bad guys in such a childhood hideaway.

"What a pleasure it must be creating stories and characters and situations. You have complete control—like playing God."

And the good guys win, and bad guys don't, Wendy said to herself. *And children don't die of cancer*.

"Too bad real life's not like that." Jenny's face seemed to cloud over and she lay the page down.

"Are you okay?" Wendy asked.

"Me, of course, I'm wonderful. Oh, look at all the pictures." Something was bothering her, but Wendy didn't push.

Jenny moved to a small group of old family photos and picked up the one of Sam, Chris's father. He was posed beside Dwight Eisenhower. "How is he doing?"

Wendy shook her head sadly. "He's fading."

Samuel Adam Bacon—onetime American ambassador to Australia, professor of history at Trinity College, and great raconteur—was now living out the rest of his life in a nursing home in West Hartford, Connecticut. Two years ago he had been diagnosed with Alzheimer's disease. His mind, once strong and lucid—a mind that had helped draft important trade policies between the

United States and the Pacific nations—had begun to bump down the staircase to nothingness.

"Such a shame. How's Chris handling it?"

"As well as can be expected. Sam is only sixty-four." What she didn't mention was that behind Chris's grief lay fear of the same fate. Every time a name slipped his memory or he misplaced his keys he was certain his own mind was going.

They moved into the guest quarters—what used to be Ricky's room. Chris had dug up the old crib from its hiding place in the cellar, reassembled it, and moved it back in for Abigail. While Wendy watched, Jenny changed the baby and tucked her in. Her hair was like fine silk, and she had big, round, inquisitive blue eyes.

Wendy took one of Abigail's naked feet and chuckled lightly. "Her toes look like corn niblets," she said, and let her mind trip over the possibilities.

Jenny seemed to read her thoughts. "Why don't you have another one?"

"Because I don't think I'm ready for another baby. I'm not sure I even want another one."

"Wendy, it's been three years. It's time to move on. Time to start afresh. Chris would love to be a father again."

That was true. Since Jenny had gotten pregnant, he had suggested they do the same. "But I *am* forty-two, you recall."

"That's not old. A woman up the street from us had her first at forty-five. Look what you're missing. Abigail's the best thing that's happened to me."

Of course, Jenny hadn't always felt this way about children, because her first daughter, Kelly, now fifteen, had had problems since age five when her father died. By seven she required professional help. Today she was being treated for depression and drug abuse. Abigail was a second start for Jenny, who for years had declared that she would never have another child. "They just grow up and break your heart," she had said. Then, by accident, she got pregnant and would have sought an abortion had her second husband Ted not protested. For nine months she was nearly dysfunctional with anxiety. Then Abigail was born, and something magically snapped as Jenny embraced motherhood with pure joy.

The baby made a little sigh as she fell asleep. Then while they stood silently over the crib and watched, Jenny said in a voice barely audible, "Kelly tried to kill herself."

"What?"

"She tried to commit suicide."

"Oh, God, no."

"She took an overdose. But she's in a good hospital where they've got a special ward for young people. It's clean and the staff is very professional." Tears streamed down her face. "We talk freely. And I guess it's good. . . ." Her mood suddenly changed. "Wendy, she hates me. She says I made her crazy. She says she's going to grow up to be like me, living on pills and trying to stay sane." She let out a mirthless laugh. "She's a chip off the old block. She's got my crazy gene. Every family has one, I suppose, and I'm ours."

"Jenny, that's ridiculous! You're not crazy, for godsake."

"I sometimes feel crazy. I do."

"We all do at times. That's human. But you're not crazy, and you didn't make Kelly crazy."

"But something went wrong. I lost control. She's in a mental institution and I can't reach her. Something went wrong. I didn't watch her closely enough."

"Stop blaming yourself. Jim died and left you with a baby."

"Other single mothers manage. I lost control. I should have protected her better. I'm a nurse, for heaven's sake." She took a deep breath and adjusted the blanket around the baby. "But things will be different with her. She gives me strength to go on. She really does."

Wendy hugged Jennifer. "I know, and thank God you have her."

"Which is why I think you should have another."

"Nice how you circled back," Wendy laughed.

But Jenny did not respond as expected. As if talking to herself, she said, "Of course, we still have the 'terrible twos' around the corner, then the 'horrible threes' and 'furious fours.' Frankly, I think five's the best age. You're still the center of their universe, and they're not old enough to be influenced by others or reject you. Five. That's when they're most manageable. Don't you think?"

Jesus! Wendy thought. *Had she forgotten when Ricky had died*? But Wendy just said, "Yes."

Still in a semi-trance, Jenny gazed at her daughter. "I wish it could last forever." Then, as if at the snap of a magician's fingers, Jenny was back. "Oh, gosh, what's the matter with me?"

Wendy said nothing, suspecting that Jenny had had one of her spells.

When she was younger doctors had diagnosed her as mildly schizophrenic because she would occasionally recede into herself, unaware of her behavior. Medication had helped; so did the passage of time. By adulthood, her condition had stabilized, although she still had occasional blank-out spells.

Out of big-sister protectiveness, Wendy let it pass. "Even if I wanted to get pregnant," she continued as if nothing had happened, "Chris isn't around long enough to get down to business."

"Even big-time scientists have to go to bed on occasion." Jenny took Wendy's arm and headed for the door. "You have to be understanding. He's brilliant, and one day they'll give him a Nobel Prize for his cancer drug."

Because it was all so secret, Wendy could not tell her about his real research. Nor could she explain how obscene she found it. *Nobel Prize: If only his aspirations were so modest,* Wendy thought and turned off the lights.

Quentin's stomach leaked acid when he heard the voice.

Vince Lucas didn't have to explain why he had called. The $2.5 million for the apricot pits was supposed to have been wired to a Bahamian bank by November 1, and here it was the middle of December—two extensions later—and the next payment of equal amount was due in six months.

He had explained to Antoine his problems collecting debts from European jobbers. But the real reason was that Quentin was buying time for Chris Bacon to synthesize the toxogen. All else was in place—the chemical patent, fabulous clinical results, the marketing strategies. And with Ronald Reagan's help, FDA approval was just around the corner. All that was left was a commercially viable yield and he could pay what he owed and be out from under Antoine Ducharme, his Consortium, and his lousy apricots which were costing them nearly thirty dollars per pit—a rate which would make the toxogen astronomically expensive.

But that hadn't happened because Bacon said he needed more time—months more. The fucking golden boy with the youngest Ph.D. from M.I.T. in decades, and he couldn't come up with a decent yield!

What nearly stopped Quentin's heart was that Vince Lucas was in town. His message was brief: Meet him at nine that evening in the parking lot of Concord's Emerson Hospital which was a few miles from the lab. No mention of money or deadlines. But it would not be a social call. Nor was it like being indebted to legitimate creditors or the IRS. Quentin was beholden to men whose penalty for duplicity was execution.

But they couldn't do that to him, he assured himself. They needed him because he was the only link to the money. Ross knew nothing about Antoine. His sole concern was that his company not be ruled by the whims of Nature—invasion by some apricot-loving caterpillar or a tropical hurricane. If anything happened to Quentin, all deals were off.

Quentin's eyes drifted to the photo on the far wall—the 1932 Eureka football team with Ross standing behind Ronald Reagan who had signed it, "Win one for the Gipper." Two weeks ago, Quentin had pushed Ross to fly to Washington to get Reagan to expedite FDA testing. Ross first refused to exploit his friendship, but Quentin reminded him that Reagan prided himself on helping his friends. It was people like Ross who had put him in the White House—raising millions to support Nancy's White House decorations including all the fancy china.

Ross had conceded, but he lacked the Darwinian edge. He was not the opportunist Quentin was. Just as well he was retiring soon. He had become soft. He was an obstacle to progress.

A little before nine Quentin pulled his Mercedes into a slot under a lamp post. Only a handful of cars sat in the lot. A solitary ambulance was parked by the emergency room, its lights turned off. Christmas lights in a few upper windows gave the scene a comforting glow. To ease his nerves, he found a station playing Christmas carols. At about nine fifteen, midway through "Here Comes Santa Claus," Vince Lucas rolled up beside Quentin's Mercedes. He nodded for Quentin to get into his car. Quentin went over to the passenger door and opened it hesitantly.

"You're letting the heat out," Vince said.

His heart jogging, Quentin got in and closed the door. "Good to see you, Vince," he chirped and offered his hand like an old business colleague. Vince was wearing leather gloves but did not remove them, nor did he take Quentin's hand.

"Bullshit," Vince said. "It's not good to see me," and peeled onto the road.

Quentin's chest tightened. This was not going to be a good night. The car turned onto Route 2 then cut up a side street toward Concord center.

"Where're we going?" Quentin tried to affect an easy manner.

"For a ride."

"Uh-huh." After a long silence, Quentin said, "Look, Vince, I know why you're here. I explained to Antoine that I need until the turn of the year. There's money coming in from Switzerland. It's just taking more time than expected."

Vince still said nothing. From Concord they crossed into Lincoln not far from Quentin's neighborhood. Houses along the way were lit up with Christmas lights. Quentin tried again. "Vince, we're businessmen. We've got a contractual arrangement which I intend to fulfill, but these things happen around the end of the year, and Antoine knows all that. You'll get the money—"

Vince pulled the car over with a jerk. To Quentin's horror, they had stopped in front of his own house. The Christmas tree was visible through the family room window. The upper floor was dark except for the master bedroom where Margaret was in bed reading or watching television.

"Now, we talk," Vince said, turning in his seat to face Quentin. His face was half in shadows, making his teeth flash white as he spoke. "Antoine Ducharme is two thousand miles from here. The last time you talked, he gave you an extension until December first, twelve days ago. You missed it, which makes you *my* responsibility now. And I don't do extensions."

"Look, Vince, please . . . It's all the red tape with money transfers. I swear on my life."

"Your life doesn't have weight." He pointed to the dark upper corner of the house. "Just behind that 'TotFinder' sticker is a pretty pink bedroom with a pretty pink bed where your pretty pink daughter Robyn is asleep." Before Quentin could ask, Vince handed him three photographs, all of Robyn: at her bedroom window that morning, being dropped off at school, at recess.

"Listen, Vince—" he began.

Vince clamped his gloved hand on Quentin's jaw. "No, you listen." He pressed his face so close that Quentin could smell garlic on his breath from his dinner. In a feather-smooth voice he said, "You have until Friday. Understand? The day after tomorrow. If you renege again I look bad, and that I can't live with. Neither can your daughter." He squeezed so hard Quentin's jaw felt crushed. "Two days. Two-point-five million dollars. Plus another two hundred thousand visitation fee which you'll wire to another account. The number's on the back." And he stuffed one of his business cards into Quentin's pocket.

Quentin started to protest, but thought better. He grunted that he understood, and Vince snapped his face away. In dead silence they drove back to the Emerson, as Quentin massaged his jaw and wondered how to manipulate Darby funds, thinking how his daughter's life hung in the balance.

"This is me here," Quentin said as they rolled by his Mercedes. But they continued all the way to the emergency room. "But I'm back there."

When Vince stopped the car, he extended his gloved hand. Quentin took it, gratified that it would end with a gesture of civility. Except that Vince didn't let go. Instead, his other hand closed over Quentin's.

"This is closer."

"I don't follow."

Still holding Quentin's hand, Vince said, "You're going to need to see a doctor."

"What?"

Vince then clamped one hand onto his index finger and bent it all the way back until it broke at the joint with a sickening crack. Quentin jolted in place with a hectoring scream which Vince instantly caught in his glove. Pain jagged through Quentin like a bolt of lightning, searing nerve endings from his hand to his crown and through his genitals to the soles of his feet.

While Quentin yelled and squirmed in his seat, Vince kept his viselike grip on Quentin's mouth. For several minutes he held him until the cries subsided to whimpers.

Quentin's hand had swollen to twice its size, while his finger hung at a crazy angle like a dead root.

Vince then opened the passenger door, and in the same silky voice he said, "The next time it will be your daughter's neck."

And he shoved him out and drove off.

The morning after Jenny and Abigail returned home, Wendy stood naked before the full-length mirror and felt her heart slump. She looked all of forty-two. In her younger days she was a slender size six, and 120 pounds. Now she was two sizes and fifteen pounds heavier. Her waist and thighs were getting that thick puddingly look. Crows' feet were starting to spread around her eyes and mouth, and the smiles lines were becoming permanently etched.

Worse still, she could see herself as an old woman: a hunched and wrinkled thing with flabby skin, thinning hair, teeth chipped and gray, creasing eyes, a neck sunken into the widow's hunch of osteoporosis, her legs whitened sticks road-mapped with varicose veins, her hands patched and knobbed. It was the image of her mother staring back at her, a woman who had died of breast cancer at sixty-eight yet who looked fifteen years older because of a crippling stroke. The image was jolting.

While she had come to accept the grim inevitability, it was no less shocking to apprehend it in her own face. What Chris had dubbed the death gene—that nasty little

DNA switch that never failed to click on the long slide to the grave.

But, damn it! Wendy told herself, *Jenny was right: Forty-two is still young.* And she was still healthy. What benefit was there to wasting the good years left wringing her hands over mortality? No, she couldn't reverse gravity or cellular decay, but she could at least slow the progress.

"The wine is sweet whenever you drink it."

Chris's phrase hummed in her mind.

Feeling a surge, she put on her running suit and sneakers. A few minutes later she was pounding the pavement around Mystic Lake and debating with herself. *You're forty-two years old. Twenty years from now you'll be sixty-two. In thirty years, seventy-two.* It didn't make sense, not at her age.

But why not? And why not her?

She splashed through shafts of sunlight, thinking that the choices she made now would determine how she lived out the rest of her life: Her grief from Ricky's death would never leave her, but it was time to end the habit of mourning.

Half-consciously she rubbed her hand across her breast as she jogged along. As Jenny said, women over forty had babies all the time.

It was her visit that had done it—seeing Jenny's unequivocal joy. And hearing a baby in the house again— sounds that took her back to happier days. Jenny had given Wendy a pair of earrings, but the real birthday gift was leaving Wendy yearning for the same joy and feeling almost startled into the hope of it. Why not? She was still healthy.

"The wine is sweet whenever you drink it."

Yes! she told herself. *YES!* And she glided down the path thinking of baby names.

•   •   •

That night Chris peered through the eyepiece of his microscope and saw the landscape of eternity. And it took his breath away.

He was looking at the cells of his own body—cells that contained all the information that made him Christopher Bacon. Cells that should be turning bright blue, dying under his eye—but were thriving.

Eight weeks ago, he had scraped off some flesh from the inside of his cheek. He liquefied the sample and divided it into equal batches, one treated with nutrients—growth factors, hormones, vitamins, insulin, and a lot of other stuff—that sped up replication, collapsing the remaining life of his own forty-two-year-old cells into two weeks. The other he treated with the same nutrients plus tabulone. Within twenty-four hours the surface of each dish was covered with newly replicated cells. From those batches he made subcultures. He kept that up for four weeks until the untreated cells stopped subdividing and died. Meanwhile, the tabulone-treated cells continued to thrive. Two months later they were still replicating. If he had kept that up, he would have produced endless tons of his own cells.

The realization was staggering: The cells of his own flesh were reproducing indefinitely.

That could only mean that human death was not programmed in the genes but the result of a program of cell divisions—a finite process that climaxed in the eventual breakdown of cell walls. In other words, we lived as long as our cells kept replicating. But why did they stop at fifty?

He did not understand the genetics, but it confirmed his suspicion that aging had no clear evolutionary purpose. Traditional textbook reasoning about making room for the next generation made no sense since most animals never made it to old age. They were eaten by predators or died from disease. There was no reason for natural selection to genetically favor demise, Chris told himself. No purpose served.

His eye fell on the wall clock as the second hand made its circuit. Like all his clocks and watches, it was set ten minutes fast, a silly little habit to allow himself to pretend that it wasn't as late as it was—that he had a few more minutes free of charge.

While the radio played softly in the background, Chris watched the clock move inexorably around its course.

And he thought: During the next hour, ten thousand people would die—some by fire, some by floods, some by famine, some by accident, some by another's hand. But most deaths would be from "natural causes" brought on by aging—people over sixty-five. And nobody over 112. But who was to say that the upper limits couldn't be pushed? Or that people shouldn't die but by accident alone?

His eye slipped to the workbench where sat a solitary vial containing tabulone.

As he stared at it, a thought bulleted up from the recesses of his mind: *When are you going to try it, huh? When are you going to slip a couple ccs into your syringe and shoot up?*

Chris stiffened. *Dangerous thoughts*, he told himself. *Very dangerous*.

The kind of speculations he and Dexter Quinn would entertain after the third pint of Guiness. Mental idling that seemed okay when you were feeding a fine buzz—though he still recalled that weird gleam in Dexter's eyes, as if Dexter were giving the notion serious consideration. Chris could understand that: Dex was twenty years his senior and hated the thought of becoming old because he had never married and had no family to carry on. He also had an impaired heart.

"You want to know when you're old?" Dexter once said. "When you can't get it up and you don't care anymore that you can't get it up."

Chris had begun to chuckle when a look of sad resignation in Dexter's face stopped him.

It's when a tooth falls out and you don't go to the

dentist. When you stop coloring your hair. When you don't bother about that lump under your arm.

It's when you give up trying to do anything about it. What's called despair: *When all that's left is the count-down.*

Dexter was closer to the countdown than Chris, but Chris understood the mindset of defeat. He also understood the beer-soaked hankering for eternity. He had felt it himself. Every time he visited his father, it nipped at his heels: the groping for common words, the sudden confusion and bewilderment, the repetition of phrases and simple acts, the fading of memory. A man who once advised Eisenhower could not recall the current president. A man of trademark wit who now muttered in fragments. A man who last Memorial Day had to be reminded who Ricky was. What chilled Chris to the core was the thought that the same double-death was scored on his own genes.

It was too late for Sam, but not for him.

While he sat at his microscope, the realization hit him full force:

Admit it! The real reason you don't want anybody to know about tabulone is that you want it for yourself, good buddy. All that stuff about social problems, Frank-enstein nightmares, and getting yourself canned—just sweet-smelling bullshit you tell your wife and pillow. You're playing "Beat-the-Clock" against what stares back at you every time you look in the mirror—the little white hairs, the forehead wrinkles getting ever deeper, the turkey wattle beginning to form under the chin. The spells of forgetfulness.

The only thing between you and what's reducing Sam to a mindless sack of bones is that vial of colorless, odorless liquid on the shelf. Your private little fountain of youth.

Those were the thoughts swirling through Chris Bacon's head when Quentin Cross stormed into his lab.

•   •   •

His face looked chipped out of pink granite. He snapped off the radio in the middle of a news story about Reagan pledging an all-out war on drugs at home and abroad. "What's the latest yield with the new whatchamacalit enzymes?"

Quentin had a talent for irritating Chris. He was pompous, officious, and often wrong. And for Chief Financial Officer and the next CEO, he had the managerial polish of a warthog. "Not much better than ethyl acetate or any other solvent."

"Christ!" he shouted, and pounded the table with his good hand. His other was in a cast from a fall, he'd said. Quentin's eyes shrunk to twin ball bearings. "I'm telling you to increase the yield or this company and its employees are in deep shit."

"Why the red alert?"

"I asked what kind of yield."

Quentin was a soft portly man with a large fleshy face, which at the moment seemed to take up most of his space. Chris opened his notebook. "A kilo of starting material yielded only five milligrams of the toxogen."

"Five milligrams?" Quentin squealed. His left eye began to twitch the way it did when he got anxious. "Five milligrams?"

At that rate, they would need nearly half a ton to produce a single pound of the stuff—which, Chris had calculated, would cost a thousand dollars a milligram after all the impurities had been removed. It was hardly worth the effort.

"Try different chiral reagents, try different separation procedures, try different catalysts, different enzymes. Anything, I don't fucking care how expensive."

Quentin wasn't getting it. They had their best people working on it, following state-of-the-art procedures, and spending months and millions. "Quentin, I'm telling you we have tried them and they don't work." He had never seen Quentin so edged out. Something else was going on. Or he was suffering pathological denial. "Quentin, the molecule has multiple asymmetric centers—almost impossible to replicate. We can produce its molecular mirror image but not the isomer."

"Why the hell not?"

"Because nature is asymmetrical and organic chemistry isn't. It's like trying to put your right hand into a left-handed glove. It can't be done."

For a long moment Quentin stared at Chris, his big pink face struggling for an expression to settle on. He looked as if he were about to burst into tears. It didn't make sense. "Quentin, I'm sorry, but it's beyond our technology, maybe even our science."

"Then invent some new technology and science. You're the golden boy here. We're paying you sixty grand a year—fifteen thousand more than you'd get at Merck or Lilly. So, you better find a more efficient synthesis or we'll get somebody who can."

"Quentin, I'm not very sophisticated in the intricacies of international trade, but we're killing ourselves to manufacture a molecule that comes ready-made on trees. And we've got an endless supply of pits and exclusive rights. Please tell me what I'm missing here, because I don't get it."

"Just that we don't want to be dependent on raw materials from foreign sources."

Chris was about to respond when a small alarm went off in the rear lab.

"What's that?"

"It's nothing," Chris said vaguely, but the sound passed through his mind like a seismic crack. "Just one of the connectors." He wanted Quentin gone. The alarm was rigged to each of his control mice. An infusion tube had failed, which meant that an animal had been cut off from tabulone. He couldn't explain the potential consequences because Quentin Cross knew nothing of what Chris was doing back there. Nobody did. But he had to reconnect the animal immediately.

"What kind of connectors?"

"One of the animals." Chris made a dismissive gesture hoping Quentin would take the hint and leave. But he moved toward the back lab door.

Jesus! Of all times. Chris could be fired, even prosecuted for misuse of company equipment. And by the time Quentin got through, nobody in North America would hire him. "It's nothing." He tried to sound casual. But Quentin was at the door. Chris played it cool and pulled out his keys.

Inside were rows of glass cages with eighteen of his longest-lived animals. Each had a metal cannula permanently cemented to its skull with a feedback wire connected to an alarm should there be a rupture. After years of continuous supply, they were totally dependent on the serum, like diabetics or heroin addicts.

Quentin followed Chris inside to where a small red light pulsed.

Methuselah.

He had bitten through the tubing, and the stuff was draining into sawdust. Had it been one of the younger mice, there would be no problem. But Methuselah, the oldest, had been infused for nearly six years.

Chris shut off the alarm and auto-feed and gave the mouse an affectionate stroke with his finger. He still looked fine, but he needed to be reattached immediately. "I have to get him rehooked, so if you don't mind . . ."

But Quentin did mind. "What are you doing with all the mice?"

"Testing toxicity."

"Toxicity from what?"

"Veratox."

"That's preclinical. We're testing the stuff on people."

"I know that, but these animals have cancers."

"You mean you're trying to cure them?"

God! Why doesn't he leave?

"Look, I've really got to hook him up." But Quentin stayed as Chris reattached the tubing.

He was nearly finished when he saw something odd in Methuselah's movement. The animal sashayed across the cage as if drunk.

"What's his problem?"

Before Chris could answer, Methuselah stumbled into the corner, his eyes bulging like pink marbles.

Then for a long moment, Chris and Quentin stood paralyzed, trying to process what their eyes took in.

Methuselah flopped onto his back as his body began to wrack with spasms. His mouth shuddered open and a high-pitched squeal cut the air—an agonizing sound that seemed to arise from a much larger animal. Suddenly one of his eyes exploded from its socket, causing Quentin to gasp in horror. Methuselah's body appeared to ripple beneath the pelt, at the same time swelling, doubling in size with lumpy tumors, some splitting through his fur like shiny red mushrooms growing at an impossible rate.

"Jesus Christ!" Quentin screamed. "What the hell's happening to him?"

Chris was so stunned that he no longer registered Quentin's presence. Methuselah's body stopped erupting almost as fast as it began, only to shrivel up to a sack of knobbed and bloodied fur as if its insides were dehydrating at an wildfire rate. Its head withered to a furry cone half its original size, the contents draining from the mouth and eye socket. At the same time his feet curled up into tiny black fists. When the spasms eventually stopped, Methuselah lay a limbless, shapeless, dessicated pelt crusted with dark body fluids. A demise that would have taken weeks had been compressed into minutes.

"What happened to him?"

"I don't know." Chris had seen his mice die before, but never like this. Never.

"What do you mean, you don't know?" Quentin squealed. "What the hell were you pumping into him? What is that stuff?"

"The toxogen."

Quentin didn't believe him for a moment. "We animal-tested Veratox for a year and nothing like this ever happened."

Quentin's eyes raked Chris for an answer. "I guess the pathology somehow accelerated."

"Accelerated? There's nothing left of him. It's like he died on fast forward."

"I'll do a postmortem," Chris mumbled. "Maybe he had a prior condition, or maybe it's some unknown virus." He didn't know if Quentin would buy that or not, but he played it out and put on rubber gloves, put the remains of Methuselah into a plastic bag, and deposited it in the refrigerator for a necropsy when he was alone.

"I don't know what you're doing in here, but let me suggest you put your efforts into synthesizing Veratox— which is what the hell we're paying you for, and not saving a few goddamn mice."

Then he turned on his heal and stomped out, leaving Chris standing there frozen, the words echoing and ree-choing in his head: *It's like he died on fast forward.*

5

Chris arrived home around nine, still badly shaken. Methuselah's death was like nothing he had seen before. Other animals had experienced accelerated senescence before dying, but over a period of days or weeks—not minutes, and never so extreme. Held in submission for six years, cancer had apparently invaded healthy cells and replicated with explosive vengeance. To make things worse, Quentin was surely questioning Chris's dedication to Veratox.

As Chris stretched out on their big double bed, he knew his days at Darby Pharmaceuticals were numbered. Quentin had all but said he'd replace him, no doubt with some younger talent with hot new strategies on creating synthetic pathways. Now he'd been caught red-handed in his own private project, using company materials, time, and funds. How the hell at forty-two was he going to find a new job when the industry was hiring fresh grad students? How the hell were they going to live on an English teacher's salary?

Chris tried to compose his mind to rest. His eyes fell on the framed plaque on the opposite wall of their bedroom. It was an old Armenian wedding toast etched in beautiful calligraphy in the original language and English—a gift from a college friend on their marriage day.

"May both your heads grow old on one pillow."

For a long moment he stared at the words, then he closed his eyes.

Wendy was taking a shower, and the hush of the water filled his mind like whispered conversations. On the inside of his forehead he watched a closed-loop video of Methuselah erupting in cancerous growths, then shriveling up to a burnt-out pelt.

Who'd want to dip a needle into that?

Just ten wee minutes was all it took.

Like he died on fast forward.

It could take years to work out that limitation—first on mice, then rabbits and dogs, then primates. And that was assuming he could determine the genetic mechanism. Sadly, he had neither the expertise nor the equipment to do what was required. No way to do it alone and undercover.

No way.

No time . . .

Chris didn't know how long he had dozed—probably just a few minutes, but in that time his brain had dropped a few levels to dream mode. He was at the door of the nursing home, and Sam was sitting in his wheelchair, but everything had an *Alice in Wonderland* absurdity to it. The wheelchair was too big for Sam, who was the size of a child, sitting in diapers and grinning but still an old man in wispy hair and sad loose flesh. A little boy and old man at once. And he was waving. "Bye Bye, Sailor."

"Hey, sailor, wanna party?"

Chris's eyes snapped open.

Wendy was standing by the bed, naked but for a flimsy negligée.

The room was dimmed and from the tape deck Frank Sinatra filled the room with "Young at Heart."

"I said, you want to party?" She was grinning foolishly.

Suddenly Chris was fully awake. Wendy climbed onto the bed and straddled his thighs.

"My God!" he whispered. "It's the Whore of Babylon."

She laughed happily and kissed him.

"What's the occasion? Fancy meal, expensive French wine, now *Playboy After Dark*." He had bought the negligée as a Valentine's gift several years ago but had all but forgotten it.

The light from the bathroom gilded her features. "How about I'm in love with you."

"Even though I'm a madass Frankenstein trying to fool Mother Nature?"

"Love is blind."

"Thank God."

She smiled and brought his hands to her breast. He undid her negligée and dropped it on the floor. At least they could joke about it, he thought.

In a moment, he pushed away all the muck in his mind. And while Wendy fondled him, Chris lost himself in loving her. In the amber light, he studied the beautiful fine features of her face and large liquid eyes, her long arms and swanlike neck outlined in a fine phosphorescent arc.

Wendy guided his hands across her body from her breasts to her stomach and pubis. Gently he caressed her as she lowered her face to his, moving her hips in slow deliberate cadence to the music. She hadn't been this romantically aggressive in years.

The scent of her perfume filled his head. He kissed her and felt himself flood with sensations that rose up from a distant time. Suddenly he was back in their cramped little apartment in Cambridge where they had settled after marriage. She had just gotten her masters in English at Tufts, and he had finished his postdoc at Harvard. Greener days, when their passion seemed endless, and the sun sat idle in the sky.

"You're not wearing a diaphragm."

"That's right."

"Is it safe?"

"No."

"Isn't that taking a big chance?"

"Yes." She took his face in her hands. "Let's have a baby."

"What?"

"You heard me."

"Wendy, a-are you sure, I mean . . . ?"

She put a finger to his mouth. "Yes, I'm sure. Very."

"But we should maybe think about it, talk it over. I mean, we're forty-two. Aren't we a little long in the tooth?"

"But young at heart."

She was smiling and her eyes were radiant—as if a light had gone on inside of them, one long-extinguished. He wanted to ask what had brought on the change of heart, what magical snap of the fingers had ended the dark spell. Maybe it was four days of Abigail in the house.

"I want another baby. I do. Really."

His mind raced to catch hold of any objections but found none. For years he had wanted another child, but two miscarriages and Ricky's death had the effect of a long-acting poison. Wendy had refused to take another chance; he had complied, and had fallen into the mindset of remaining childless the rest of their lives.

She kissed him warmly and grinned. "What do you say?"

"Yeah, sure," he whispered.

"I love you."

He slipped himself into her and pulled her face to his. "I love you. Oh, do I ever!"

A moment later, they were in tight embrace and moving in rhythm to an all-but-forgotten love song.

●   ●   ●

"Christ!"

Quentin sat in his office hunched over the computer. Everybody else had gone for the day.

Three weeks ago he had wired Antoine $2.5 million for a single ton of apricot pits, and another two hundred thousand to Vince. He felt sick. He had juggled the books to disguise profits from a neuropeptide and other products sold to a Swiss firm. But his problems weren't over. In six months he'd have to pay another $2.5 million unless Chris Bacon's lab had some kind of breakthrough, which didn't seem likely. The only good news was that Ross's press on Reagan had paid off with the FDA giving top priority to expediting Veratox.

For nearly an hour Quentin had been studying financial records on the toxogen, nearly sick at how they had spent millions of research-and-development dollars for a compound too expensive to manufacture.

But as he scrolled the figures, something caught his eye that made no sense.

Over a six-year period, they had purchased some nine hundred mice from Jackson Labs in Maine—most for Chris Bacon's group. What bothered Quentin were the dates and prices. According to the catalogue he found in the office library, Jackson raised hundreds of different hybrid mice bred with any number of genetic mutations or biomedical conditions—diabetes, leukemia, hepatitis, etc.—including certain cancers.

There had to be some mistake. The average price for a mouse with malignant cancers was about four dollars— the price paid for some three hundred over the years. However, Darby's records showed that they had also ordered a breed listed as "special mutant" which at $170 each was the most expensive mouse in the catalogue by a factor of five. And over a six-year period they had purchased 582 of them, totaling nearly $99,000.

The signature on each was Christopher Bacon's.

But what held Quentin's attention was the catalogue notation: *"Shortest-lived breed—Gerontology studies."*

• • •

It was a quiet Friday morning a few weeks later when the envelope arrived. Chris had taken the day off because he was burned out. In seven months, sometimes working twelve hours a day, he had increased the yield of Veratox by a thousandth of a percent. The synthesis could not be done—not with the science he and his team knew. Wendy was seeing her doctor. She had missed her period, but she wanted to be sure because drugstore kits were not foolproof.

The envelope, whose postmark said Canton, Ohio, contained a small card and a newspaper clipping dated last month.

Canton, Ohio. Medical authorities are baffled by the unexplainable death of a former Ohio man, Dexter Quinn, who died while eating at the Casa Loma restaurant.

According to eyewitnesses, Quinn, 62, a recent retiree from a pharmaceutical company in Massachusetts, was just finishing dinner when he apparently experienced convulsions. Patrons and staff tried to aid the man, but Quinn appeared to rapidly age. "When it was over, he looked ninety years old, all wrinkled and scrunched up," reported Virginia Lawrence, who had sat in a nearby booth. "It was horrible. He just shriveled up like that."

Even more bizarre, several witnesses say that before the strange affliction, Quinn looked considerably younger than his age. "I thought he was about forty," said waiter Nick Hoffman. Karen Kimball, proprietor of the Casa Loma, who had served Mr. Quinn was too distraught to take questions.

According to George Megrich, the medical examiner who performed the autopsy, "no unusual chemicals signatures" were found in Quinn's system. But he did say that his internal organs resembled those of the elderly. "His prostate gland was greatly enlarged, and his liver and kidneys had the color and density associated with dysfunctions of older people."

Baffled, Megrich speculated that Quinn had died of some virulent form of Werner's syndrome, a rare genetic disorder that causes victims to age abnormally fast. "Fifty years of aging can be compressed into fifteen years," Megrich said, "but not fifteen minutes. Frankly, I have no idea what happened to this man. It's very very weird . . ."

"A medical card in his wallet had your name on the back." The card was signed: "Karen Kimball, an old friend of Dexter's."

Chris felt himself grow faint. He thought about flying out to consult with the doctor and medical examiner. But he knew what had happened.

No virus, no plague, no known diseases.

It was tabulone. Dexter Quinn had tried it on himself.

Veratox was the lead story on the eleven o'clock news.

With Wendy beside him, Chris tried to lose himself in the report, but his mind was elsewhere—stuck in a booth in a restaurant in Canton, Ohio. He had told her how he had just learned of Dexter's death, but did not show her the news clipping. He simply said it was a heart attack.

You want to know when you're old? When all that's left is the countdown.

Chris tried to convince himself that he just wanted to spare Wendy the horror. But deep down he knew the real reason. Wendy was dead set against the tabulone project. The truth would only confirm her revulsion.

What bothered him even more was how he had let his life split into a kind of dual existence—one open, the other hidden. Like Jekyll and Hyde.

The Channel 5 anchor announced that the FDA had approved a new and highly successful treatment for cancer called Veratox to be marketed by Lexington's own Darby Pharmaceuticals. It went on to describe the unprecedented results with malignant tumors. The report jumped from supermarket shots of apricots to cancer patients at the Massachusetts General Hospital to an interview with the head of oncology holding forth on what a miracle compound Veratox was.

But Chris could barely concentrate, and not just because all the TV hoopla was hollow—FDA approval nothwithstanding, they still couldn't synthesize the toxogen to make it marketable. What clutched his mind was that Dexter had died like Methuselah. He had probably absconded with undetectable amounts of tabulone and saved it to administer to himself after retiring. But something had gone horribly wrong. Maybe he had run out of supply. Maybe he missed a treatment. Maybe he had miscalculated the dosage. Maybe none of the above.

While physicians on the TV screen recommended hospitals everywhere give Veratox usage top priority, something scratched at Chris's mind.

"I thought he was about forty." How was a sixty-two-year-old man mistaken for one two-thirds his age, especially since Dexter was not a young-looking sextarian? He had a bad heart, so he couldn't exercise much. At best he could pass for the late fifties. *Not* forty. It was as if he had somehow rejuvenated.

Ross Darby beamed at the camera from his office desk. "I have every confidence that Veratox could prove to be a turning point in the battle against what is surely the greatest threat to human health and longevity. . . ."

Maybe Dexter's death is a dark little godsend, Chris told himself. *Maybe this is a warning to keep in mind the next time you think about jabbing a needle in yourself.*

"Congratulations." Wendy squeezed Chris's hand and snapped him back into the moment.

"You knew about this last week."

"I'm not talking about Veratox, silly." Wendy's eyes

were wide and intense, and she wore a huge grin, the kind that was just this side of erupting into giggles.

"What are you telling me?"

"Dada, mama, goo-goo."

Chris bolted upright. "What?"

"We are with child, my love—preggers, knocked up, all of the above." She was beaming happily.

"Yahooooooo!" And he pulled her to him.

"When's it due?"

"November third."

She wrapped her arms around him.

"I don't believe it," he said, and rocked her in his arms.

In a few moments the lights were out and they were naked under the covers, arms embraced. Chris let himself dissolve into the warm joy of the moment, as he made love to his wife and reveled in the thoughts of being a father again.

And through the window, a crescent moon smiled down on them through a bank of fast-moving clouds.

The same crescent moon smiled down on Antoine Ducharme, fifteen hundred miles to the south.

He woke with a start. Everything was still, including Lisa asleep in the big round bed beside him. The ceiling fan hummed, the only sound other than that of the Roman shades swaying gently in the breeze. If there had been an intruder, the security guards would have heard, and the dogs would be barking their brains out.

At forty-six years of age, Antoine had become a light sleeper; the slightest disturbance aroused him. But that was all right, since he would take a catch-up nap tomorrow. Besides, he loved the night from the balcony. It gave him a chance to reflect on his fortunes. And if he was still alert he would open a good book. Antoine was an avid reader of mystery novels, particularly women writers, both the classics—Agatha Christie and

Dorothy Sayers—and American contemporaries. He liked how women treated crime with such delicate sensibilities, driven by a greater urgency for order than male writers.

Antoine padded through the French doors onto the veranda off the master bedroom—a balustrade marble structure that overhung the northern peak of the island. His villa—named La Dolce Vita after the movie—was a palatial structure nestled high on a hilltop with a three-quarter view of the sea. The daytime vista was particularly splendid: voluptuous green slopes sweeping down to turquoise water edged by a white sand beach to the left and the small protected harbor to the right where night lights illuminated the flanks of *Reef Madness*. It was a view that could make the hardest man ache.

His watch said 3:12. On a chaise lounge he stretched out under an outrageously starry sky. As usual the midnight air was comfortably cool and laced with spices and apricot perfume. He poured himself some brandy and let the sweet miasma fill his head.

He knew the realities. Once Veratox was synthesized, Darby would have no need for his apricots. But he also knew that the synthesis was very difficult and could take years. Meanwhile, Antoine had Darby Pharms over the barrel, as the Americans liked to say. It had cost Quentin a finger, but he paid up. That was the nice part of being on top. You got others to do the enforcement. Not that Antoine had lost his stomach for it. He had killed eighteen people in his day, most when he was an upstart. He had even taken pleasure in killing. But he was in his middle years now and could afford others to do that, leaving him more time for more genteel pleasures. Life was good.

Out at sea a freighter blinked along the horizon. A few shooting stars streaked across the Pleides in the constellation of Taurus, which was unusual for this time of year. A portent, he thought. As he stared at the heavens, he thought about Lisa asleep inside, about waking her and making love. She had a goddesslike body which was a source of great physical pleasure for him—the key reason he had spared her life. After discovering her infidelity with Marcel, he had hired a homosexual guard who did not let her out of sight. She had begged Antoine to forgive and forget what had happened. He agreed to half her request. The day would come when she would get fat and he would tire of her—and retribution would need be redressed. But, now, things were in place. The center held.

At about 30 degrees northeast he could just make out Kingston airport. A few degrees further east the freighter's lights rippled in the air. Behind it, flashes of heat lightning. There would be rain tomorrow, but it would be short, then the sun would come out and dry things up—a pattern of nourishment and splendor, the natural rhythms of paradise. And he was part of them. In fact, he owned some of them.

He closed his eyes and thought about how rich life was. He thought how wonderful it would be to freeze his life at such moments to live them out forever. A pity man could not stop the clock. With all his millions, he was just as mortal as a pauper.

Antoine's eyes snapped open.

A strange sound. Beyond the crash of the waves against the shore. Beyond the chirping of tree frogs. Beyond the whispers of the Antilles trade winds through the bougainvillea. For a moment he thought it was the brandy playing tricks on him.

Engines. But not a security vehicle. Nor a boat. A persistent rumbling drone. From inside he returned with a powerful pair of binoculars. The sound grew louder.

No freighter. Too many lights and getting larger. Antoine felt his heart kick up. Airplanes were heading directly toward the island from the northeast. But no flights were scheduled tonight. And no planes ever approached from that direction. Nor so low. They couldn't be flying more than a hundred feet above the water. And so many.

There must have been half a dozen in tight formation bearing down on Apricot Cay. Small planes, and moving fast.

Somewhere the dogs began barking. Then guards were shouting. The security phone rang inside, but before he could get it, eight jet planes rocketed up from the water's surface about a mile off shore and fanned out over the island.

Suddenly there was a volley of explosions that shook the villa and lit up the heavens. The planes were bombing his island with napalm. In a matter of minutes the forests were ablaze with jellied fire and filling the sky with thick black smoke.

He could barely hear Lisa scream for the noise. Security alarms wailed and guards fired automatic weapons helplessly as bombs continued to rain across the island, filling the night with choking fumes from incendiaries and burning orchards of apricots and marijuana.

To the south two direct hits destroyed the marina and the processing plant as drums of ether sent flaming mushrooms into the sky. Another sweep took out the airstrip where three of his own planes were blown to shrapnel. When a bomb hit the road behind the villa, Antoine dashed inside. Lisa was on the floor crying hysterically, but no rockets had hit them. Antoine Ducharme's death was not the object of the raid. Just his operation—to destroy it now and forever.

It took less than thirty minutes for eight F-14 fighters to set ablaze half the island and every processing building and storage shed, including, Antoine would later learn, a small barge containing a load of apricot pits destined to leave tomorrow for Boston Harbor. And what the napalm didn't kill, a solitary B-52 bomber did in three passes over the southern slopes, spewing Agent Orange.

When it was all over one fighter jet peeled off from formation and sent two rockets into *Reef Madness*.

Crouched behind a window, Antoine Ducharme

watched the boat explode. As his rainforests raged with
fire, all Antoine Ducharme could think was that this was
not supposed to happen. That his man had a friend in
the White House. That his man's father-in-law was
"bosom buddies" with Ronald Reagan.

That weasely little bastard, Quentin Cross. He would
pay for this with all he had.

6

Ronald Reagan sat in his bathrobe in the private quarters of the west wing breakfasting on scrambled eggs and stewed apricots when his secretary called to say that Ross Darby was on the line with an urgent call. It was 6:55 A.M.

The President punched the lighted button. "I've got a seven-thirty meeting with Cap Weinberger, what's your excuse?"

"Sorry to call at this hour, Mr. President, but I have something of a problem."

Even though they had known each other for nearly half a century, Ross Darby just could not address his old pal by first name, because this was official business.

"I just got a call from an associate that U.S. naval jets bombed Apricot Cay in the Caribbean. I'm sure you're aware of that fact since you no doubt gave the orders."

There was a long pause as Darby waited for the president's response. Then Reagan cleared his throat and said, "Well, you put me in kind of a funny position, Ross. Frankly, these are matters of national security."

"National security?"

"Yes. What's the problem?"

"Mr. President, I don't know if you were aware that Apricot Cay was the sole habitat of the very species of apricot which our new cancer drug comes from. We just got FDA approval the other day, as you well know."

"The same island?"

"Yes, and from what I understand the entire crop and orchards have been incinerated. They were napalmed, every last tree, and it appears they finished off the place with some kind of defoliant."

More gaping silence as the president measured his words. "And you're calling to ask why."

"Ron, I invested millions in that island and staked the future of the company on that harvest, not to mention that we had a cure for many cancers in those trees."

"Hell, I'm sorry, Ross," Reagan's voice was low and scratchy. "But why in God's name did you pick the same island?"

"Same as what?"

"Ross, it's seven in the morning and I've got a long day ahead of me, so let's please stop playing games."

"I don't know what you are driving at."

"That Apricot Cay was trafficking ten to twenty billion dollars of cocaine and marijuana each year, and all of it heading for the American streets."

"What?"

"Ross, they had shipments moving in and out of there every day, by land and air, like it was New York Harbor. What I want to know is how you could have risked investing in such a place, especially given our anti-drug campaign. I don't know how to say it without saying it, but frankly I feel personally betrayed, as will Nancy."

"Ron, I didn't know."

"How in hell could you not know, for God's sake? You must have visited the place before you invested. You did, didn't you?"

"No."

"Well, whoever set up the deal for you must have known. They had to. Intelligence says the place was a fortress."

Darby listened in numbed silence as the president continued. Before he hung up, Reagan said, "Ross, I'm going to forget this call ever took place."

"Thank you, Mr. President," Ross said, and hung up.

For a long moment, Ross stared out the window into the gray light. He was shaking as if there were a brick of ice at the core of his body. Eighteen years ago he was Associate Professor of Pharmacology at Middlesex State University, and Darby Pharmaceuticals was a makeshift lab in his basement where he developed new compounds, selling the patents to companies such as Pfizer and Merck. Over the years he had turned Darby Pharms into a $70 million business because of his knack for developing pharmaceuticals with prestige, profit, and universal application, such as synthetic estrogenic hormones, cholesterol lowering drugs, and—Veratox. Yet he suddenly saw himself as a foolish old man everybody goes about humoring but never letting on with the truth that the sky is beginning to fall.

Quentin sat across from him studying the carpet, his eye twitching uncontrollably. Sometime around 4:30 that morning he had telephoned Ross with the news of the bombing. When pressed to explain the military's action, Quentin had no answer. That was when Ross dialed the White House.

"He said that the island was the major drug distribution center of the western hemisphere. Did you know that?"

Quentin could not raise his eyes to his. "You think I'd do business with a drug lord?"

"That's what the hell I'm asking you."

"I was there to buy apricots, period. I had no idea he was dealing in dope. None whatsoever."

Darby nodded, thinking what a miserable goddamn liar his son-in-law was. "We're ruined, I hope you know."

Quentin studied his cuticles without a word. Then he got up and walked to the window.

It was late November, and most of the trees had lost

their leaves. A fine rain fell and glazed his gray Mercedes coupe in the executive lot. Quentin could just make out the Nantucket sticker on the windshield. Last month workmen had finished constructing their summer home on an oceanside bluff in Siasconset—a big sprawling place, called NewDawn, that put him in enormous debt in anticipation of taking over the pharmaceutical company with a patent for the world's first cancer cure.

"I didn't know."

"Turn around!" Darby's voice was like a gunshot.

Quentin turned.

"Look me in the eyes and say that again."

"I—I . . . ," he trailed off, stuck on Darby's stare.

"Just what I thought," Ross said. He took a deep breath and hissed through his teeth. "According to your records we're half a million dollars in the hole to your drug buddy. Half a million for all the charcoal we could ever ask for." He slammed down his coffee cup. "He said the son-of-a-bitch was the Don Corleone of the Caribbean. He said he had a fortress down there with his own army, a fleet of planes, processing plants, and shipping docks. And you didn't know. The goddamn DEA's been watching him for a year from spy satellites three hundred miles up, and you couldn't tell from ground level. What the hell do you take me for?"

Quentin looked away. The real figure was $2.5 million, but Ross would never know. He would also not ask him to resign because there was nobody else in line. Besides, how would Ross explain that to Margaret and the kids?

"Not to mention another $2.8 million trying to synthesize the stuff for the last two years. That's another dead end. You've ruined us, Quentin, and you made me look like a blue-ribbon ass to the president of United States. It's probably out of pity I'm not facing federal prosecution.

"But I suppose there's a silver lining in everything: I can spend my retirement in financial ruin instead of financial ruin *and* federal prison." Darby flopped into his chair and closed his eyes and rubbed his temples.

A hush fell on the room, all but for the pattering of the rain against the windows.

"Maybe not," Quentin said.

Darby looked up. " 'Maybe not' *what?*"

While Ross glowered at him, Quentin picked up the phone and punched seven numbers.

Chris was in a deep sleep when the phone rang. He caught it, but not before Wendy woke up. It was Quentin Cross. His message was terse: Meet him and Ross in the office at eight-thirty.

"It's Saturday, for God's sake." She craned her neck to see the clock. It was a little after seven. "What did he say?"

"Just that it was urgent." He got up to get dressed. "Probably another hare-brained scheme to synthesize the toxogen."

"You don't believe that. They never call on Saturdays." His face had that fistlike tightness it got when something was bothering him. "Honey, what's going on?"

She could see that he didn't want to upset her, but it was time to fess up. "I think they're firing me."

"Firing you for what?"

"For not getting a better yield."

"That's ridiculous. They can't fire you if it can't be done."

"I didn't say it can't be done. It's just that *I* can't do it. So they'll find somebody who can."

"They can't do that," Wendy said. Tears sprung to her eyes. Chris was a decent man and brilliant scientist whose entire professional life had been dedicated to benefiting the human race. For two years he had labored tirelessly to synthesize the stuff. If they were terminating him, it was grossly unjust.

"It's their company. They can do what they want."

"Can't you fight them? Get a lawyer?"

"It's not against the law to get rid of somebody who's not doing his job."

"But you've been doing your job. It's not your fault you can't get the goddamn stuff to yield. Is there anybody you can call? Somebody who knows new techniques?"

"I've tried them all. If it can be done, it's beyond me." He got his clothes together.

"You're the best they've got."

"Maybe that's the problem." Chris wiped the tears from her face and kissed her. Then he took his insulin shot, got dressed, and left.

Darby Pharms was located in a small complex of buildings fashioned in a red brick Tudor motif. The original building was once a private residence that had since been expanded over the years as the company grew to sixty employees, creating a series of buildings handsomely landscaped to look like a small English village.

At 8:20 Chris pulled into his slot. In the Executive area sat two cars: Ross Darby's big black Mercedes sedan and Quentin's gray 450 SL Coupe. The colors of power and wannabe power.

Chris went inside. The interior was eerily quiet, as if holding its breath. He could sense the tension from the foyer. He cut through the maze of offices. Quentin was at the door of Ross's office suite holding a coffee mug. He was dressed in jeans and a sweatshirt and looked as if he'd been up all night.

"Have a seat," Darby said as Chris entered. He was also casually dressed—a blue shirt and black V-neck sweater. His face looked ashen and haggard. From their grim appearances, Chris was certain that this was his dismissal.

Quentin began. "Chris, we called you in because,

quite frankly, we have something of a problem with your work here. You have been with us for fifteen years, and in those fifteen years we counted on you—"

Chris cut him off. "Quentin, if you're firing me, please just say it and save us a lot of trouble."

Quentin's face filled with blood. "I don't like your attitude."

"And I don't like you calling me at seven o'clock on Saturday morning without explanation."

"It's about your mice," Quentin said.

"We've been through this already."

"I want Ross to hear."

Ross got up. It took him a moment to straighten up. He walked to the coffee machine, stretched a kink out of his lower lumbar, then poured himself another cup. In spite of chronic back problems, he looked good for a man over seventy. He was tall and still quite trim, and his face usually radiated with a rich, healthy luster—the product of regular games of tennis. It was easy to imagine the dashing young quarterback from Eureka. Today Ross Darby looked his age. They had probably been up for hours mulling over the terms of dismissal.

"Chris, I want to apologize for all the mystery, but I preferred to talk with you in person. Quentin told me what you said, but I'd like to hear it firsthand if you don't mind."

Chris liked Darby because he was classy at managing people. He always treated you with respect and patience, and never had to raise his voice. He made you feel that when you talked there was nothing else in the universe he wanted more to do than to listen. Unlike Quentin, he was never petty; if something bothered him, he never let on unless it was important. "As I explained, I tried to save us time by testing toxicity."

"We moved beyond animal testing over a year ago."

"I didn't want to see the animals die."

"So, for two years you played mouse doctor at our expense," Quentin said.

It was just like him to jawbone Chris about costs to impress Ross before announcing he was canned. When little men cast long shadows, you knew the sun was setting. "Yeah," Chris said.

"That's horseshit."

"Quentin, get on with it," Darby said.

Quentin removed a packet of papers and handed it to Chris. "Look familiar?"

"An inventory of some sort?" Chris said.

"That's right, and you know of what?"

Darby cut in again. "Quentin, this isn't *Perry Mason*."

"It's an inventory of requisitions from your lab," Quentin continued. "And maybe you can explain a few items."

"Like what?"

"Like how over a five-year period from 1980 you placed orders for 582 exotic mutant mice at $170 each—five times the next most expensive mouse, I should add—for a grand total of $98,940. I called Jackson Labs and they told me that *mus musculatus sextonis* stock number JR 004134 is an albino mutant Amazonian agouti—whatever the hell that is—with a lifespan of eleven months. What we'd like to know is what the hell you were doing with $100,000 worth of short-lived mutant mice."

"I was doing life-cycle studies."

"Really? For nearly one fiftieth the price you could have gotten mice with twice the life span. What the hell was the rush?"

"You're the one who insisted we couldn't depend on raw stock and needed to find a synthesis."

"Uh-huh. Then what about these chemical orders? You purchased organics that have nothing to do with apricots or any other interests of this lab. Like on September 23 five years ago, eighteen liters of acetonitrile."

"It's a solvent for extracting the toxogen out of the apricot pits."

"Is that right? Well, my chemistry's a little rusty, so

I checked. And everybody and his brother said that the solvent of choice is ethanol, not acetonitrile—which, as you well know, is used in organic procedures." He adjusted his glasses, feeling very clever. "Then in December '84, seventy-five grams of L–N5 iminoethyl ornithine, and three months later a total of twenty liters of hexamethylphosphamide. And before you try and fudge up another answer, I checked and, lo and behold, nobody has a fucking clue why you'd need such fancy organics. In fact, HMPA is a goddamn carcinogenic which, by the way, cost us two thousand dollars." He slapped down the inventory. "In fact, you've been ordering some rather strange materials ever since we sent you to Papua New Guinea back in 1980. You want to tell us just what the hell you've been doing in this lab for the last seven years while nobody was looking?"

They both stared at him for an explanation.

After a long moment, Chris said, "Nothing that matters." He got up to leave.

But Quentin continued. "Then what about that conference on neurology and gerontology at Yale last November? Two days you were supposedly taking as sick days?"

"You've been spying on me. I don't believe it."

"Believe it," Quentin said. "And believe it that misuse of company property and the misappropriation of funds is a criminal offense tantamount to stealing."

Chris moved to the door.

"Well, maybe this will tell me." Quentin was holding a black, bound ledger containing Chris's notes on the tabukari elixir and its effect on his animals all the way back to 1980. He had broken into locked files in Chris's office.

"And before you declare it's personal property, let me remind you of your contract which reads: 'All research material including equipment, animals, procedures, patents, inventions, discoveries, *and* notes are private property of Darby Pharmaceuticals.' Do I make myself clear?"

A photocopy of Chris's notes sat in front of Ross, who stared at Chris silently and without expression.

"And by the way," Quentin continued, his face all aglow, "that mouse that died horribly a few weeks ago? Well, I checked the files and found he was purchased over six years ago—I repeat, *six* years ago. Now, I don't know much about mice, but that struck me as unlikely, so I called Jackson and they confirmed that the original order of twenty such mice was placed in 1980. When I told them it was the same mouse, they said that was outright impossible because its life span was eleven months. There had to be some mistake because no mouse under the sun—no matter what breed or hybrid—lives six friggin' years."

They stared at him for an answer. "So what do you want?"

"What we want is for you to sit down and tell us all about your *tabukari* elixir."

7

Am I being fired or not?"
   They had read everything in his log. The entire
medical history of his mice was in those notes, including
Methuselah's—six years of secret employment at Darby.
If they wanted to, he could be out the door and facing
charges of grand larceny.

"Fired?" Ross Darby stood up and came around his
desk. "If you've developed something that's multiplied
the lifespan of mice, I want to know what it could do
for humans. And I want you to find out. In fact, I'd like
you to work on it full time."

Christ! The genie was out of the lamp, and they
wanted him to dance with it. "What about Veratox?"

"It's quite clear the synthesis won't work, and we've
spent more than enough money to find out. We appreciate your efforts, but these things happen."

"We still have another shipment of raw stock coming,
no?"

"I need not get into it, but we don't." Ross was being
evasive.

That explained the stoical attitude. Veratox was a bust,
and Chris's elixir had fallen into their laps to make up
the losses.

"So," Ross sang out, "what can it do for humans?"

Chris glanced at Quentin, who sat back waiting for him to spill. If he resisted or protested, they could still fire him, retaining his notes and the contents of his lab. Which would mean his genie would be dancing with someone else. "I don't know."

"Then how did you know about its longevity powers?"

"Rumors from New Guinea villagers."

"Such as?"

He measured his words. The exposure was too sudden. "That it can retard the aging process."

But Chris said nothing about Iwati. Neither did his name appear in the notes nor speculations about how the stuff might double or triple human lifespan or more. Only pharmacological and biological history of his mice—dosages, procedures, vital signs, blood and tissue chemistry, neurophysiology, and so forth.

"Well, I'm curious why all the secrecy," Darby said. "You worked on it since 1980 and never breathed a word."

"It didn't strike me as profitable research given the limitations."

"Not while you were here, that is," Quentin said.

"Pardon me?"

Quentin's face had a look of cagey cleverness he used to impress Darby. "I'm just wondering if you kept everything under wraps so you could perfect the stuff, then jump ship with the patent to start your own company."

"Quentin, I'm a biologist, not a crackerjack entrepreneur like yourself."

"I'm not interested in motives," Ross interjected. "You've developed a compound that's multiplied the lifespan of mice. That's one hell of a breakthrough. And that's what I'd like you to develop for us. Are you interested?"

To Chris, Ross Darby was the kind of businessman Ayn Rand would have swooned over. In less than twenty years he had taken his company out of his garage and into this multimillion-dollar complex. "Sure."

"You mentioned limitations."

"Accelerated senescence, rapid aging—what afflicted Methuselah."

"Then its elimination should be a prime objective," Ross said. "I have to admire you for pulling it off without notice. What bothers me is what that says about the quality of our bookkeeping." He glanced at Quentin. "I'd like to see these mice, if you don't mind."

Chris took them to the back lab and the cages of mice, each hooked up at the skull to supplies of tabulone.

"You've invested half a dozen years and increased the lifespan of mice by a factor of six, so you must see hope for the human race."

"Find the right chemicals," Chris said, "and there's no reason we can't extend our warranties without limit— like these guys."

Ross studied the mice as if he were glimpsing magical creatures. "An appealing prospect, especially when you're my age."

"We've got a huge baby boomer generation out there eating their oat bran and jogging their asses off," Quentin piped in. "We're talking about a billion-dollar molecule." His face glowed red at the prospect.

"What's the composition?" Ross asked.

Chris opened his log notes to a ring diagram he had drawn.

Ross studied it. "A steroidal structure, except the C and D rings are reversed. I've not seen anything like it before."

"I doubt anybody has," Chris said. What made the compound unique was the spiral ring system—two rings coming off a common carbon atom, something not found in steroidal structures.

"What's the plant?"

"A vine with small orchidlike flowers. I'm told it grows nowhere else in the world."

"That's what they said about the apricots," Ross muttered. He studied the diagram.

"Where did you get the elucidation and synthesis done?" Ross was concerned that outside labs could compromise Darby's exclusive patent on the compound, especially if the molecular profile got out. But Chris had anticipated all that. Without revealing its potentials, he had gotten analyses done at MIT, Northeastern University, and private labs without incurring interest. In his favor was the fact that nobody did steroid research anymore.

Darby stared at the clear liquid in the feeder tubes. "You've discovered a molecule that puts the cellular clock for mice on slow-mo. If you make it work for human beings, you'll have the fountain of youth."

"The operative word is *if*. Disconnect those tubes, and they'll age to death before your eyes."

Ross eyed a mouse in the nearest cage, its skull sporting electrodes like a tiny diver's helmet. "How old is this one?"

"Chronologically, sixty-two months. Biologically, I haven't got a clue. Like most animals, mice don't age in any noticeable way. They just get bigger. And smarter. Their cognitive powers have measurably heightened."

And in his mind Chris saw his father in two different shoes, tearing up as he struggled to find the right word . . . to recall his son's name. To block the fog that was slowly closing in.

"What do you think triggers this accelerated senescense?"

"I don't know, but my gut feeling is that it's in the molecule itself. It's huge, which means the problem might be in the binding sites. Maybe something in the compound attaches to neuroreceptors and blocks the natural process of aging, and once it's withdrawn the conditions causing senescence are heightened. Or maybe it works directly on the DNA sequence."

"Any rumors of people rapidly aging in New Guinea?"

"None I know of."

The intensity on Ross's face said he was becoming convinced of grand possibilities. "The first step will be to get a patent on it. That's essential."

Because secrecy was essential they would have to apply for a "composition of matter" patent rather than a "use" patent to avoid stipulating the compound's application as an anti-aging drug. Chris knew that the senescence effects would never pass FDA.

"What will it take to do the job?" Ross asked.

Chris was ready for him, and he ticked off the contents of his fantasy lab: High-speed computers with elaborate imaging software, nuclear magnetic resonance equipment, mass spectrometers, and so on. Ross snapped his fingers for Quentin to take it all down.

"Also, geneticists, pharmacists, physical chemists with pharmacology backgrounds. I can give you names. And test animals, especially rhesus monkeys—very old ones and virus-free."

When he finished, Quentin looked at the list he had taken down. "You're talking *major* capital investment."

"And it may not be successful," Chris added.

"But I think you're on to something extraordinary," Ross said. "So we'll do whatever it takes. I want you to put together the best team and lab that money can buy."

Chris nodded, amused how in less than two hours he

had passed from company crook to messiah. "I'll do my best."

"And the sooner the better," Darby said. "I'm just a couple years this side of my own warranty. You get it to work on old monkeys, and I'm next in line."

"If this works," Quentin said, "you'll be more famous than God and twice as rich."

Chris smiled. Fame and personal wealth were the least of his interests. He was by nature a private person and making enough of a salary to afford his and Wendy's needs. Yes, it would be nice to have a few extra thousand, what with a child on the way and Wendy's decision to take an extended maternity leave from teaching. But sudden wealth would only add an unnecessary edge of anxiety, like what put those Rocky Raccoon rings around Quentin's eyes. Maybe it was no longer fashionable, but he was a scientist motivated solely by intellectual challenges, not financial ones. Even if he could afford otherwise, he preferred L. L. Bean to Armani, a Jeep to a Mercedes, and vacations at Wendy's family lodge in the Adirondacks to *chateaux* on the Riviera.

Ross had one more question before they left. "Does anybody else know about this? Colleagues or friends?"

"Just my wife."

"Good," Darby said, "and let's keep it that way because if word leaks that we're putting our resources into an anti-aging drug, the media will be on us like vultures and competitors will be scrambling to learn what we've got. Think of this as our own Manhattan Project."

Later, while driving home, Darby's words buzzed in Chris's head. It wasn't the demand for secrecy that bothered him—he was used to that. It was recollection of the first words of Robert Oppenheimer moments after the original Manhattan Project made a ten-mile-high column of radioactive smoke over Almagordo: *"I have become Death."*

Two

"Old age is the most unexpected
of all the things that happen to a man."

—LEON TROTSKY

8

Chris didn't sleep much for the excitement. In a few months Wendy would give birth to their son or daughter. Meanwhile, Darby Pharms was going all out on tabulone. At times he could not distinguish which buoyed his spirits more.

Wendy's former apprehension about another baby had vanished like a low-grade fever. On the contrary, she happily anticipated the November birth and a year's leave of absence. To add to her delight, she had finished *If I Should Die*, and a literary agent had sold the manuscript on the second submission. It had garnered a modest advance, but her publisher loved the book and the series proposal. The publication date was February of next year. Wendy was ecstatic—a baby and a book, just months apart. It couldn't get much better than that.

Last week Jenny had flown down for another visit. The good news on that front was that her daughter Kelly was out of the hospital and planning to return to school in the fall. And Abigail was growing into a happy and healthy toddler.

Meanwhile, a SWAT team of workmen had over the months converted Chris's old lab into a state-of-the-art research site. Walls had been pushed out, and the floor space had doubled. Fancy equipment had arrived almost daily from all over the country. Also test animals. Mice they still procured from Jackson Labs. But finding the right monkeys presented problems. There were vendors all over the country, but only one had virus-free "retired breeders"—an isolated colony in the Florida Keys. Chris ordered two dozen ranging in age from twenty-one to twenty-nine—the oldest, named Jimbo, who was equivalent to a 105-year-old man. The younger animals cost four to six thousand dollars each. Because he might have been the oldest virus-free rhesus macaque in the world, Jimbo went for a cool ten thousand.

As director, Chris had also sought out the best talent he could find. But wooing them required special artfulness since he had to make the project alluring without revealing the objective. He explained that Darby had launched a project never before attempted in the pharmaceutical industry. As expected, his recruits were intrigued that a reputable company was investing millions of dollars in a steroid. Unique as its crystalline structure was, steroids was an area very few bothered with today. Intriguing also were the starting salaries—twice what they were earning. By the time Chris was through, he had hired six fulltime class-A researchers—two pharmacologists plus a medicinal chemist, a microbiologist, a protein chemist, and a geneticist. It was a pharmaceutical dream team.

The other good news was that Darby had received a patent on tabulone, which meant that no other institution could research the molecule for seventeen years.

By midwinter, the cancer toxogen had mysteriously dropped off the boards in spite of the initial media blitz. The official explanation was that a blight had killed off the apricot crops. The loss had cost the company dearly, and Chris guessed Quentin took some flak. Whatever the real story, Ross had managed to raise millions for the new lab from select venture capitalists. And he had done so with fantasies of developing a fountain-of-youth drug and turning investors into billionaires.

• • •

Toward that end, a special meeting was held in June with Chris, Quentin, Ross Darby, and a couple others to come up with a trade name for investors, research documents, and the FDA application. They met in the conference room where Chris wrote the suggestions on the black-board. "Tabulone" did not impress anyone, given the product's momentous promise. Quentin said it sounded like an Italian dessert.

"What we need is something striking," Ross said. "Something that suggests what it's for—*longevity*, but not so literal. You know, something exotic and catchy."

So for nearly two hours they kicked around names until the blackboard was full and Chris was covered with chalk.

> *Eternity*
> *Vitalong*
> *VitaYou*
> *VitaLife*
> *AgeNot*

For awhile they got stuck on puns, odd spellings, until the suggestions turned silly. They then moved on to var-ious associations with time, clocks, life, then Latin and Greek roots, mythological and biblical names. And be-cause the compound was a steroid not too unlike testos-terone, they bandied around the *-one* suffix which produced some goofy tongue-twisters like *Immorticone* and *Methuselone*.

Next they played with prefixes like *ever-* and *eva-*, which yielded *Evagreen, EvaYoung, EvaYou*, and so on. That gave way to combos with *vita-mega-*, and *omni-*. Breaking the frustration somebody suggested *Fuk4Eva* and they all cheered.

Finally, into their second hour, Chris moved to the blackboard and in large block letters he wrote:

ELIXIR

For a moment everybody fell silent as they let the word sink in. Then heads began to nod. Ross straightened up in his chair, his eyes wide as he tested the suggestion. "Yes, I like it. Exotic, but not arcane. Overtones of alchemy yet with a sexy scientific *X* dead center." He slapped the table and rose. "That's it. *Elixir*," he said as if mouthing a spell. "Elixir. It's perfect, and can't you just imagine the great TV ads and promotional material? Yes! That's what we'll call it. Elixir!"

And everybody agreed.

Elixir.

"Elixir?"

"What do you think?"

"It's catchy."

It was the first time Wendy had visited the lab in years. Chris had brought her in to see the new facilities. Boxes of materials were stacked on the floor, but the structural work had been completed and equipment was functioning.

Wendy feigned interest as Chris showed her all the fancy instruments. In one room was his pride and joy, a mass spectrometer for determining chemical compositions and molecular weights. In another room, looking like something from a science fiction movie, sat the high resolution nuclear magnetometer. "Very nice," she said. "What does it do?"

"Tells us the number of atoms in the molecule, as well as their structural relations. Tabulone is very sophisticated—lots of interesting branches and bondings."

"Why's that important?"

"To help figure out the senescence problem. It's possible the flatness of the molecule lets it wedge itself between the coils of the DNA promoting mutagenesis. If that's the case, we may be able to alter the problem structure. Otherwise, no Elixir."

"But you don't even know if it works on humans."

"Except for Iwati."

She had almost forgotten. New Guinea juju was alive and well and living in twentieth-century Boston. "If he suddenly went off the stuff, would he age?"

"I really don't know. The next step is to see what happens to primates, which means determining dosages. They're just a few genetic steps up from mice, but my guess is that the stuff will prolong their lives, too."

Wendy was happy that Chris was finally out of the shadows and that his sideshow study was now a major scientific inquiry. She could also enjoy his excitement because he seemed like a different person, a great big, handsome, lovable kid. However, while she kept it to herself, all she saw on her tour was scientists producing false hopes of finding a cure for death itself. There were no magic cures, she told herself. People got sick and died. Like Ricky. It was an inevitability that Chris would not accept. A grand illusion. She just prayed that when that discovery hit home, he would not be crushed.

Chris led her to a computer station nearby where he tapped some keys and, like magic, the Elixir molecule appeared on the monitor in different colored balls. Slowly the figure rotated like a bubble dancer, turning itself around in 3-D to show off its endless cheeks.

She put her hands on his shoulders and peered at the monitor. "Pretty. So what do you do with it?"

"If you know binding sites, you can see how atoms fit together, then manipulate the geometry." He clipped off a hydrogen/oxygen stem and added a carbon-hydrogen cluster. "Now we have a different molecule with different properties."

"You're designing new matter."

"More like redesigning old."

"Improving on nature," she said.

He looked up at her with a blank face. "Wendy,

you're not going to give me your Imperial Margarine lecture, are you?"

"Now that you mention it . . ." she joked.

The last stop was the monkeys. They were kept in rows of steel cages lined up along one long wall. Each contained a single rhesus. Wendy stopped at one cage tagged FRED and his birthdate, 3/13/65. He looked at her with quick anxious eyes. It was so unfair, she thought. In a few weeks his head would be in clamps, his body paralyzed, the skull cap removed, his brains exposed and sprouting electrodes to monitor his death. "Poor little guy."

"I know what you're thinking. But if it's any consolation, he may teach us how to prolong human life."

"I don't approve of that either."

"Not exactly a news flash," he chuckled. "But frankly, it appeals to me."

She knew what he was getting at. "Honey, you don't have Alzheimer's."

"You don't know that."

"Nor do you."

"Yeah, but sometimes I almost feel it coming. Yesterday I couldn't remember Stan's extension. There are days I'd call him half a dozen times. How could I forget?"

"That's natural. You're under a lot of stress."

"Then what about forgetting our anniversary last week? The first time in sixteen years that's happened. Or your birthday last year?"

"You're just preoccupied. Besides, Alzheimer's affects people in their sixties and seventies, not forties."

"That's not true, I checked. It could start in the late thirties even."

Wendy stared into Chris's two-tone eyes. As an old friend had once said, it was like two different faces superimposed. At the moment, he was at once the brilliant, cool-minded scientist and an irrational kid. "Chris, you're being ridiculous. You don't have Alzheimer's disease."

"Maybe not. But every instinct tells me it's in the cards. Whatever, the bottom line is that aging stinks. All that stuff about wisdom in the years is a lot of feel-good garbage."

Wendy watched Fred stir the wood chips with his fingers. She felt the tired old debate coming on but pushed it aside. "Just one question: Say it works, say you eliminate the senescence problem. How would people relate if some grew old while others didn't?"

"I haven't thought that far ahead."

"Maybe you should if the future's going to make sense."

Chris said nothing but handed Fred an orange wedge. It was his cue to change the subject.

"And what if it's so expensive only the rich can afford it?"

"That's what they said about penicillin and the polio vaccine, and they're available to everybody in the world today."

"And what about the population?"

"That can be worked out with proper regulations."

"Sure, maybe they can set up a Ministry of Birth."

"In spite of all the doomsday caveats, 1984 turned into 1985. And, by the way, I thought you said just one question."

Wendy was about to go on when movement inside made her suck in her breath.

"What the matter? What is it?" Chris asked.

Wendy smiled and took his hand and lay it on her belly to feel. "One future that's going to make sense."

It was another miserable night. Antoine had called from Puerto Rico to say that another $2.5 million was due July 1. Yes, the apricots had been destroyed in Reagan's fireblitz last year, but he wanted his money no matter what. And Quentin had no choice. But he would have to pay from his own pocket because financial restructuring over Elixir made it impossible to skim funds again. His net worth, some $2 million, was tied up in investments he couldn't touch without his wife finding out. And she was still fuming that he had nearly destroyed her father's name and business. His only option was secret bank loans.

What gave him night sweats was that this wouldn't be another wire transfer. The exchange would take place in person at the statue of George Washington in the Boston Garden at 2:30 on Friday the 1st—in unmarked hundred-dollar bills, twenty-five thousand of them.

"Chris, I think you better come in as soon as possible."

It was Vartan Dolat, the molecular biologist Chris had hired from MIT. He was at the lab, and as usual he was exercising telephone caution. His voice was devoid of inflection.

But Chris's heart started to hammer. It was nine in the morning on his day off. "Do we have a problem?"

But Vartan deflected the question. "See you at ten."

Chris arrived and was met by Vartan outside the lab. "It's Jimbo."

"Is he okay?"

Vartan didn't answer but hustled him to the lab while Chris said a silent prayer that he wouldn't find Jimbo withered and dying.

Waiting for them were Stan Chow, Derek Wyman, and Betsy Watkins, a geneticist from Northeastern specializing in human aging. Chris could hear monkeys chattering, but Jimbo's cage was empty. Betsy opened the rear door to the large enclosed pen outside where the animals could move about in fresh air. Chris could see the nontoxic red *J* painted on his chest. "Is that him?"

Jimbo was sitting on a high perch casually grooming Fred, a male ten years his junior.

"He's quiet now, but for the last two hours he's been jumping around like a kid," Vartan said.

Jimbo saw Chris and hooted a hello.

"I don't believe it."

When Jimbo had arrived four months ago, all he did was sit in a corner or sleep. What movements he made were crimped by arthritis. When put in the group pen, he'd either ignore the other animals or whack them if they approached. Twenty-nine years had reduced Jimbo to a lethargic, flabby, antisocial curmudgeon. Incredibly, he looked reborn.

"He even made a move on Molly," Betsy said.

"You're kidding."

"He went through some courtship gestures then he tried to mount her. We had to separate them because she's still fertile."

Chris beamed at the animal. "You old gunslinger, you."

Vartan handed Chris Jimbo's vital functions charts. "What's interesting is that he's eating less, yet he's gained nearly a pound, mostly in muscle mass."

Fred decided it was time to play and leapt to the ceiling bars. Instantly, Jimbo was behind him, chattering and swinging across the pen. His movements were slower but still fluid. It was like watching an elderly man on amphetamines.

"Even more remarkable, his blood sugars are down by 80 percent. And so are the protein substances that block arteries, stiffen joints, produce cataracts, and gum up brain tissue."

"All the signs of aging," Chris said.

"Yes. Tabulone seems to have reversed the process. I don't think he'll turn into a juvenile again, but the stuff's kicked him back a few years. My guess is that it will stabilize as with the mice."

Chris was stunned. They just hadn't noticed the effect in the mice.

Not only did Elixir prolong life, it had some initial rejuvenating effects.

Even more bizarre, several witnesses say that before the strange affliction, Quinn looked thirty years younger than his age.

My God! thought Chris, It's what took hold of Dexter.

He had a damaged heart which he knew would kill him soon. Maybe on an impulse he'd tried it on himself and experienced a backward thrust like Jimbo. It must have been like nothing else he had ever experienced. Nothing out of a medicine jar or syringe. The ultimate high: the fires of spring redux.

Betsy Watkins, who had a reputation for being a no-nonsense researcher rarely given to superlatives, was also amazed. "Tabulone appears to restore the DNA to effect a kind of cellular retrogression. I've seen nothing like it before. I don't think anyone has. It's nothing short of a miracle."

"Does Ross know?" Chris asked.

"Yes, he does." Around the corner came Quentin. He was beaming. "The real question is, What's the next step?"

Chris could smell alcohol on his breath and it wasn't even noon. What Quentin really wanted to know was when they could file application with the FDA. "I think we're talking a few years."

"Years? Why so long? I mean, you've got a monkey who's regressed a decade. We should be thinking about moving on to human subjects and all."

"We have protocol to follow. You know that," Betsy said incredulously. "Disconnect these animals, and they'll die."

"Don't disconnect them and they'll go on forever."

Betsy began to laugh, but caught herself because Quentin was perfectly serious. "Quentin, this is a compound that will make you die of old age on the spot if you overdose or underdose. It's hardly ready for human trial."

"Betsy, we supply most hospitals and clinics with Proctizam which is highly toxic."

"Proctizam is an experimental drug for cancer patients near death," Betsy shot back.

"So is Elixir! There are people who would pay dearly to have it the way it is, with all the risks."

Chris could feel the others stiffen. It wasn't just that they were dedicated university scientists not used to corporate bullying. They couldn't quite believe Quentin's suggestion. It bordered dangerously on blind desperation.

"Quentin," Betsy said, "speculation like that is not within the interests of any responsible pharmaceutical company."

Quentin's face flushed as if it had been slapped. He sucked in his breath and recomposed himself. "Well, let's just say I'm getting a tad frustrated. We've got too many important people invested in this project who don't want to wait a bunch of years to see this go to market. If you'll excuse me."

And he walked away, leaving the others wondering what that was all about.

9

I think your sister's a little paranoid." What Chris really meant was that she was getting wackier. "She carried on about the evils of the modern world for half an hour."

It was a few days later, and Jenny had flown in for a quick visit. After driving her to the airport he had returned home to work with Wendy on the nursery. Pressure from Quentin had him working long days so he almost forgot how good it was to share time with her. Presently he was hanging wallpaper while she was putting up curtains.

"She can get like that. I wonder what set her off?"

"A radio report about drugs at some junior high. She carried on like the Antichrist was dealing in every schoolyard in the country. No wonder Kelly's so screwed up."

"Chris, Jenny's a great mother. She gave up a nursing career for Kelly. Nobody could have predicted her problems."

"Well, she's trying to make up for them with Abigail. The kid's a year old, and she's already thinking about home schooling."

"Maybe it's second motherhood. She's determined to make this one work."

So are we, Chris thought. The old wound was healing. Wendy was loving the prospect of motherhood. And with it, they had moved closer over the months. It was like going back in time themselves, happy in love all over again.

Last month they had learned that their baby would be a boy. So Chris hung paper with sailboats on a field of blue, while Wendy made nautical curtains. They bought a new crib and set up a bookcase with a collection of kiddie stories, a Jack-in-the-box, and a few stuffed animals including a big goofy Garfield cat.

"It's costing her and Ted a fortune," he said.

While shopping yesterday, Jenny had spent hundreds of dollars on toys including an inlaid pearl music box that played "Frere Jacques." While he was fond of Jenny, he worried about her influence on Wendy. It wasn't just the mood swings or neatness obsession. It was her hangups. Some people got worked up over the Russians, others the environment. For Jenny it was how our culture killed childhood innocence. At the slightest provocation, she'd hold forth on the usual demons— drugs, rock and roll, alcohol, TV violence—and how kids didn't have a chance to be kids anymore. Wendy didn't need that kind of talk. It was hard enough to get her to decide to have another child without the hyped-up ravings.

Wendy returned from the other room. "Did you see Kelly's photo—the one at her fifth birthday? It was sitting with the others in the office." She wanted to group early family shots on a shelf in the nursery.

"No."

"That's odd, it's missing."

"Maybe Jenny took it."

"But she would have said something."

"Unless she had one of her spells." Jenny was known to have moments of confusion—vestiges of childhood schizophrenia that slipped through the medication.

"I'll ask her," Wendy said vaguely. She had hung up

a watercolor of children at a yellow beach against a sun-lit ocean. "What do you think?"

Chris came over and put his arm around her. "Looks good."

"Hey, why don't we go away someplace tropical—just the two of us, before I'm too big to fit on a plane."

"Like where?"

"Anywhere as long as it's romantic and far from mass spectrometers and rhesus macaques."

"No such place," he grinned.

"That's the problem. You spend more time with your monkeys than you do with me. I'm starting to feel like Jane in the Tarzan movies."

He laughed and gave her a squeeze. The suggestion was wonderful. The tough part was finding the time. He would check the lab schedule to see when he could take off a week. "Sure."

"Good. Maybe Jamaica or Barbados—someplace with beaches, palm trees, and a big double bed."

"You have no shame," he said.

"How would you know?"

He could see the glint in her eyes. He kissed her lips. Instantly his body flooded with warmth as she flicked her tongue in his mouth and ground her hips against him. "I'll never kiss Jimbo again."

She laughed and pulled him to the couch. In a moment he was naked and lying across the cushions, an erection poking in the air.

"You're obscene," she said, slipping out of her pants.

"I hope five minutes from now you still think so."

For a moment Wendy's face clouded over as something rippled through her. "Everything will be all right, won't it?"

There it was again, the old wound that just wouldn't heal. In a flash all defenses had dropped.

"Of course, it will. He'll be fine. We'll all be fine." He held out his hand to hers.

The moment passed, and she smiled again.

Her breasts were beginning to swell, and her belly looked as if she had swallowed a football. She climbed onto the couch and straddled him. "Ever do it with an old heifer?"

"Always a first time for everything."

"You're supposed to say you're not old or heiferey."

"You're not old."

"Moo you," she said, and they made love while Garfield looked on with a sly grin.

Chris had anticipated Betsy Watkins's presentation, but he was not prepared for what he heard.

They met, as scheduled, at ten on Friday morning in the lab conference room. Gathered were Derek Wyman, Stan Chow, company chemist, Vartan Dolat, and Quentin. For the last several months, Betsy had taken over the cell studies.

Betsy was a compact woman with a sharp and pleasant face and wide intelligent eyes. She had dark loose curly hair that only emphasized the hard cool substance of her mind. Armed with notes and board chalk, she reviewed recent breakthroughs in the science then launched into a description of how Elixir worked at the cell level.

"Capping mammal chromosomes is a DNA sequence called 'telomeres,' " she explained. "Like the plastic tips on shoelaces, they function to protect chromosomal molecules from proteins that trigger the cell deterioration associated with aging."

She illustrated her point with diagrams on the board. "Each time a cell divides, telomeres of offspring cells become shorter and shorter. In healthy young cells, there is an enzyme called 'telomerase' containing the genetic code for restoring telomeres, allowing cells to divide by keeping the telomeres long. But as the cell gets old, the telomerase activity decreases and the telomeres get shorter until after a half a dozen replications in mice—

fifty in humans—the sequence shortens until the cells die.

"But as we've discovered, cells treated with Elixir don't senesce. Instead, telomeres in treated animals held their length while cells continued to replicate. My guess is that tabulone activates the genes that produces telomerase, thereby maintaining a constant supply to keep the telomeres long and cells young."

"How does that jive with the literature?" Chris asked.

"Well, all aging studies hit the same brick wall: how to switch on telomerase production indefinitely." She held up an ampule of Elixir. "It's the magic bullet. It triggers an endless source of telomerase—the Fountain of Youth, if you will."

Betsy's reasoning was brilliant. But it also raised some fundamental questions. "Are you saying, then, that the cells of our bodies are genetically programmed to die?" Vartan asked.

Betsy hesitated to answer because of the enormity of the implications. "No, because that would mean that death is an evolutionary necessity. And, frankly, I don't believe that aging is the result of evolutionary forces," she answered. "And the reason is that Nature is a red-toothed demon that kills off most animals before they reach reproductive age, and those that make it almost never live long enough for aging to have become part of the natural selection process."

Chris felt a warm flow of satisfaction because it was the same conclusion he had reached years ago. More than that, he felt considerable admiration for Betsy and pride that a scientist with such fierce intelligence and authority was on his team.

Betsy continued, "There are so-called 'big-bang' exceptions like the Pacific salmon which seem genetically programmed to spawn and die within a few days. But on balance, death seems clearly to be the result of cell deterioration at the molecular level and not natural selection."

"Which means that aging could be stalled as long as the cells are protected," Chris added.

"Exactly, and tabulone appears to do just that. As long as the antioxidant binds to the DNA telomere sequence, cell death will not occur."

"What about the rejuvenating effect?" Chris asked.

Betsy nodded in anticipation of the query. "My guess is that it reverses the process. Say we started Jimbo on treatment on his twenty-seventh out of a max of thirty replications. As Elixir turns on the telomerase gene, instead of going twenty-eight, twenty-nine, thirty, death!, the replications went twenty-seven, twenty-six, twenty-five until he reached a steady state. Telomere lengths were restored with each division, and in the meantime he experiences moderate rejuvenation. That's still conjecture, but the important thing is that tabulone is a natural telomerase activator."

Chris was dumbfounded: What Betsy was describing was a breakthrough in cell biology. Under ordinary circumstances such findings would be winged to every major scientific journal. But they were sworn to secrecy.

The next step—Phase 2—was the rapid senescence problem. While the molecular work would be conducted by the others, Chris would concentrate on determining dosages—when exactly senescence began and how to reverse it.

"There's one more thing," Betsy said. Her expression had suddenly darkened. "While our successes don't guarantee prolongevity for humans, we're moving inexorably closer. I need not remind you how stupendous a discovery that is. But it's imperative we consider the higher implications before we blindly push onward."

There was a hushed moment.

"In fact, I suggest we stop right where we are."

"Stop? What are you saying?" It was Quentin from the rear of the room—the first words he had uttered in nearly two hours.

"I know how you feel, but there are some serious

moral and social ramifications to what we're doing."

Quentin bolted upright in his chair. "Betsy, let me remind you that this project is guided by FDA protocol and good manufacturing principles as with all our work at Darby."

"I know that, Quentin, but Elixir is not like any other pharmaceutical in history. We're not talking about adding ten years to a person's life but doubling or tripling it."

"I fail to see the problem."

"The problem is we're no longer playing scientist, but God. And, frankly, I don't have the credentials! I'm asking, do we really want to open that door?"

"What door, for godsakes?" Quentin was losing his composure by the second.

"To all the nightmare potentials. If suddenly we introduce a compound that keeps the next generation from dying, the population in a hundred years would be twenty-six billion. Meanwhile, resources run out, the environment is devastated, and wars erupt between the Elixirs and the Elixir-nots—"

Quentin cut her off. "Betsy, your nightmare may be the only hope for patients suffering multiple sclerosis, or Lou Gehrig's Disease . . . or Alzheimer's."

That was intended to ingratiate Chris. But from Quentin it was a smarmy jab. He didn't give a damn about ethics or humanity. His sole interest was his billion-dollar dream.

"The potential impact is unimaginable," Betsy continued, "and we had better think about it while we still have time."

The others nodded in agreement. Sensing a conspiracy, Quentin shot Chris a look for help. But Chris remained silent. "You mean you want to pull the plug because it might be too successful?"

"Yes—because we should be working on improving the quality of the life, not trying to prolong it."

"Prolonging it *is* improving the quality, damn it!"

"Then we should get Public Citizen or some other watchdog agency to monitor its development."

"Jesus Christ! We don't need to have Ralph Nader and his people hanging over us again."

Four years ago, the medical arm of Nader's consumer group got the FDA to withdraw one of Darby's high-profit arthritis drugs because it caused heart failure in some patients. The very mention of the organization made Quentin apoplectic.

"Please," said Vartan holding up his hands. "Betsy's making an important point. There are too many big unknowns to grapple with. It's only ethical we reassess matters."

Derek and Stan agreed. It was clear that they had discussed matters among themselves already. Only Quentin and Chris were hearing the dissent for the first time.

Chris felt the battle lines divide them. He did not like being on the same side as Quentin. He also felt the rising expectation to say something. It was his project, after all. Suddenly his people were talking about halting a seven-year investment of his mind and soul—and at the very threshold of the kingdom. And they were expecting him to resolve what smacked of being the ultimate conflict between science and ethics.

No longer able to stall, he said, "I think you're both right. Betsy, you raise some troublesome potentials, things we should consider. But unwanted possibilities are no reason to call a halt. Cocaine or heroin are dangerous when abused, but lots of people take them and nobody's twisting their arms. Should we stop manufacturing them because it's become a social problem? Of course not, because of all the legitimate uses in medicine. Even nuclear fission: It's not innately evil, just one of its potential applications."

"That's like saying climb the mountain because it's there: Knowledge for its own sake," Betsy said.

"Yes, but I see nothing wrong with that."

"Not all knowledge is good."

"True, but science shouldn't be prohibited from extending frontiers, especially in human biology. Like cloning, prolongevity was bound to be discovered, so why not do it right? And we're the best team there is."

"Hear, hear!" shouted Quentin and flashed Chris a thumbs-up. The man was a damn fool, and Chris resented the assumption of complicity.

"Then maybe you can tell us what exactly our objective is," Betsy said, "because I've lost sight."

Iwati's face rose up in Chris's mind. *Never grow old.*

"Our objective is to continue the headway we've made with an eye to moving to clinical. The fact is, the accelerated senescence may stop us before our conscience does."

Another flashcard image—Sam in the hospital, looking up at Chris, wondering who he was.

"If you're worried about it being too successful," Quentin said, "why not modify the compound so that it's good for, say, for ten or twenty years—chemically fine-tune it, kind of?"

Betsy took a deep breath of exasperation. It was a ludicrous suggestion. "Even if we discovered some built-in timers for molecules, activation would constitute mass murder."

"Oh hell, you can work out something," Quentin snapped back. "The point is that if Elixir can add a decade or two to human life, I'm all for it. So is Darby Pharms *and* so is the human race, damn it! We're not going to have a work stoppage. Period! Besides, we don't even know if it works on humans."

"Frankly, I hope it doesn't," Betsy said, and picked up her things and left.

The meeting was over, and Derek, Stan, and Vartan exited without a word.

When they were alone, Quentin turned to Chris. "What the hell's wrong with her? This might be the greatest discovery in all of science, and she's trying to

fucking sabotage it. Jesus! Where the hell did you find
that woman in the first place?"

Chris looked at the big pink musk-melon face. The
same face that for weeks would mooch into his lab to
check on progress, to reiterate how important Elixir was
to the company, to remind him how there would be no
Elixir project without Quentin. Chris did all he could to
keep from whacking that face. "Quentin, I'm sure you
have work to do."

Quentin gave him an offended look then left.

Chris's insides felt scooped out. Maybe they would
talk, but they were not going to shut the project down.
No way. He needed Betsy, but if she became a liability,
he would ask her to find another lab.

He was about to leave when he looked back at the
chalkboard notes and diagrams. *Do we really want to
open that door?*

And a small voice in his head whispered: *Yes, oh yes*.

Dexter had messed up—yielded to a crazy nostalgic
impulse. A last-ditch effort to bathe in the fires of spring.
But when the time came, Chris wouldn't be so foolish.
No way.

10

Quentin arrived at two-thirty and paced in circles around George Washington and his horse for half an hour. In a shoulder bag he carried unmarked hundred-dollar bills. But not twenty-five thousand of them. Over the week he had raised only $1.5 million—a million shy of what he owed.

It was a cool drizzly day, and only a few people were in the Garden. Quentin's stomach was a cauldron of acid. He chewed Tums, thinking that Antoine was being cagey, probably waiting to see if he had brought police or narcs. The thought had never crossed his mind. About three o'clock a kid in jeans and a slicker approached him. "He's waiting for you in the lounge across the street." He pointed to the Ritz-Carlton Hotel then took off in the opposite direction.

Quentin crossed Arlington Street, feeling relief they were meeting in a civilized place. The lounge was dim and only a couple of businessmen sat by the window. A waiter directed Quentin to a table in the far corner where a man sat, but it was not Antoine Ducharme.

"How's the finger?" asked Vince Lucas.

Instantly, Quentin's hand began to throb. The finger had a permanent crook which made Vince smile.

"Where's Antoine?"

"Let's just say it's inconvenient for Antoine to travel."

Quentin sat and the waiter took their orders—a Chivas on the rocks for Quentin, a second Perrier for Vince. Quentin clenched the bag of money between his feet. He could not stop trembling. All he could think of was his daughter, Robyn.

"You got a problem?" Vince asked. "You seem a bit jumpy."

"It's just I'm out of breath from running over," he stammered and mopped his face with the napkins.

The waiter brought the drinks. Lucas's eyes were deep black and totally unreadable. He wore a gray suit, blue shirt, and paisley tie, like a stockbroker. Quentin's heart pounded so hard that he wondered if Lucas could hear it. He called the waiter back to bring some nuts. When the waiter left, Lucas said, "Do you have the money, Mr. Cross?

"Oh, sure." He shoved a handful of nuts into his mouth.

Lucas reached over and pulled the bag over. Quentin started to protest, but choked it back. It took Lucas a few seconds to estimate the contents. "Where's the rest?"

"That's what I want to talk to Antoine about."

Lucas sighed. "Mr. Cross, I told you a long time ago that I speak for Antoine, understand? And he's not happy." His eyes had hardened into flat onyx marbles.

Suddenly a thought occurred to Quentin—an interesting one that sent a ripple through his bowels. He finished his drink and flagged the waiter for a refill. Meanwhile, Lucas watched him squirm and gobble down nuts—his face an uncompromising blank.

"We're both businessmen, correct?" Quentin began. "And you're successful I assume. I mean, you're well dressed and all . . ." He tapered off.

More gaping silence as Lucas tried to read Quentin.

"As you may recall, I'm the Chief Financial Officer of a very reputable pharmaceutical company—"

"Cut the blah-blah and get to the point."

"Okay, there's nearly a million and a half dollars in there. I know it's short, and I have every intention of paying the balance, but frankly, I simply can't raise that kind of money without serious consequences. But Darby Pharms is on the verge of something with cosmic potential."

The waiter came with more nuts and Quentin's drink.

"How old are you, Mr. Lucas?"

Lucas narrowed his eyes at Quentin without response then checked his watch.

"I'd guess thirty-five." Quentin removed a half-eaten roll of Tums from his pocket and placed it on the table. "What would you pay for a compound that could freeze you at thirty-five for another hundred years?"

Lucas glanced at the Tums then gave Quentin the same menacingly blank look. "You asking me real questions, or is this your idea of conversation? By the way, you've got three minutes."

Quentin felt a burst of panic. "For what?"

"To settle the rest of your debt."

Quentin's mind flooded with all sorts of horrors—being dragged to a waiting car outside, or maybe even shot dead right here with a silencer, fast when nobody was looking. He glanced desperately to the table of businessmen at the window.

"They're with me," Lucas said. "You were saying?"

Oh, God. Quentin thought. There was no compromising these people. No extensions. No second chances. It was all he had left. "Look, please. I'm serious. I'm . . . I'm talking about something historic. . . . Something we're developing while we speak, in fact. It's for real. What if those weren't antacids but pills that prevented you from aging?"

"What's the catch?"

"There is no catch."

"Sounds like bullshit."

"It's not. It works. The stuff exists. I'm telling you, it's for real."

"How many people have you tried it on?"

"Nobody yet, but it works on lab animals—mice and monkeys."

"Maybe you should think about moving to people, because I wouldn't give you a dime till I was certain."

"But suppose it worked? What do you think such a compound would be worth to the company manufacturing it?"

"Sky's the limit, I guess. Why, you people making this stuff?"

Quentin felt a rush of relief. He had captured Lucas's interest. "Yes." Quentin did not mention the accelerated senescence. "We've still got some testing left and FDA approval, then we're rolling."

Suddenly Betsy Watkins's pointy little self-righteous face rose up in his mind. He pushed it down when another face shot up. Ross Darby's. *"I need not remind you that this is supremely confidential."* But they didn't get it. None of them did. His back was against the wall with a professional killer glowering at him point-blank. He had no choice, so he told Vince Lucas about the mice and rhesus monkeys in detail. And Lucas listened intently.

"You're talking months if not years to get this marketed. Antoine wants his money today."

"Vince, you're a successful businessman—"

Vince reached across the table and grabbed Quentin's index finger. "Get to your point or I'm going to snap these off one by one."

"M-my point is I am offering you a percentage of Elixir. We can work out the details later, but I am offering you a piece of Darby stock in return for a capital investment that would cover our debt to Mr. Ducharme."

Vince Lucas stared at him incredulously. "You want me to lend you a million dollars to pay off Antoine?"

"No, not a loan. An investment in Elixir."

Lucas smiled. "That's a new one."

"We're talking about the ultimate miracle drug, a little pill that would prolong life indefinitely. And I'm offering you an opportunity to be part of it—part of untold fortunes. It's a chance of a lifetime, literally."

Quentin continued in his smoothest entrepreneurial manner. He produced the capital-raising literature Ross had presented to the small coterie of investors, a video of the lab animals, and legal financial documents should Lucas agree to come aboard. All the stuff he had intended to unload on Antoine Ducharme.

Lucas studied the material, fingering through the figures and graphs. "Looks interesting."

"Interesting! Mr. Lucas, these are road maps to the Garden of Eden!"

"No, Mr. Cross, these are pieces of paper. You could have made up all this stuff and had it printed."

"Then what can I do to convince you?"

"Show me your hundred-year-old monkeys."

"You mean you want to visit the labs?"

"Unless you brought them with you."

Quentin hadn't expected this. He said he could bring him in on Monday after hours. But Vince insisted on today.

"There're too many people around today."

"What time do they go home?"

Of course, he could bring him in after the place closed up. "Tonight at nine."

"You still haven't said anything about money."

"For forgiving my debt, I guarantee you that your million dollars will turn into two and a half million dollars in two years. An increase of 150 percent."

"What if your Elixir doesn't work on people?"

"Then I'll pay you out of my own pocket, even if it means selling my home. That's how much I believe in this." Lucas studied him in more opaque silence. "So, what do you think?

"I think you're going to need this Elixir yourself, the way you're packing in the nuts and booze."

Quentin made a nervous chuckle. "I'd like to add, that this deal must be held in the utmost confidence."

Lucas reached into an inner pocket of his jacket and pulled out a portable phone. He tapped some numbers. "It's me. Something's come up. Yeah, everything's fine. Stay low. Yeah. Catch you later." Then he clicked off. He handed the phone to Quentin. "Tell your wife you won't be coming home for supper."

"But she's not home."

"She's home, and so is your daughter."

Jesus! People were watching his family while they were here. "Did you think I'd bring the police?"

"It's your track record on payment." He pushed the phone into his hand. "Call your wife."

Shaking, Quentin called his wife to say he'd not be home until late. Then Vince slung the bag of money on his shoulder and led Quentin to the elevator in the lobby. They rode to the top floor alone. "Tell me this," Vince said halfway up. "Can your Elixir keep you from dying? Say, if somebody put a bullet through your head?"

Quentin flinched. "Well, n-no, not really."

"Then here's how this works. I want 300 percent, not 150."

"That's four million dollars!"

"Correct."

"That's an awful lot of money. . . ."

"How much is your daughter's life worth to you?"

"Okay, okay. Four million."

"And I want half next year at this time—two million next July first. Another two the following July. And if you don't deliver, you take a bullet in the head—end of story."

The elevator door opened onto an empty floor.

Vince nudged him out. "And you deliver it yourself in front of me." The door closed with a loud crack.

Vince Lucas led them down the hall to his suite. He unlocked the door and opened it. "So far, your Elixir seems to work."

Two days later Vince flew to Puerto Rico where in a villa on a bluff overlooking the ocean he delivered $2.5 million in cash to Antoine. He did not let on that a million was his own money. Nor did he mention Elixir or the video Quentin had given him or what he had seen in the Darby labs that night. This was his own private investment. If it didn't work out, he could always recoup. Quentin had equity—a fancy house, a summer place, and ownership in the company which he'd take over in January.

But if it worked out, it could be one monster bonanza.

August came and, once again, Chris postponed their Caribbean trip. Things were just too crazy at the lab to get away, he told Wendy. Understandably, she was disappointed.

Then on August 5 Jenny called to say that Kelly had been readmitted to the hospital. She didn't explain why. In fact, she purposely talked down the matter, saying simply that everybody thought it was best. But Jenny's evasiveness bothered Wendy so much that she decided to go out there herself. Jenny protested that everything was fine, but she finally gave in since she was having a first-birthday party for Abigail the following week and Wendy could join them.

"It was so strange," Wendy said the night she returned from Kalamazoo. "Kelly had had another nervous breakdown, yet Jenny pretended she was at a retreat."

"Did you get to see her?" Chris asked as they drove back from the airport.

"Only after I insisted. Not only did she not want to take me to the hospital, she didn't even want to go into the conference room with me. And when she did, she chattered away about the pictures on the walls and how superior the food was to the usual hospital fare."

"Talk about denial!" Chris said. "How was Kelly?"

Wendy shook her head woefully. "Like a zombie. Maybe it's all the medication, but I couldn't believe how she looked. You remember what a big and strong kid she used to be. Well, she was all skin and bones and stooped over. She looked elderly. It was frightening. When I asked how she felt, she looked at me with dead eyes and said, 'Crazy.'

"Jenny heard her and blurted out something about what lovely doctors she had, when Kelly cut her off. 'I was in a coma for three days,' she said. 'I took forty tabs of her Lithium, but they found me and pumped it out.'

"What struck me, Chris, was that she sounded disappointed they had gotten to her in time. All I could think was how she was sixteen years old with so much life ahead of her and she wanted to die. It's so sad, at only sixteen," she said, thinking that Ricky had never made it to six.

"That must have shaken Jenny," Chris said.

"It was hard to tell. She sat there with a twisted grin on her face looking as if she was about to start laughing or screaming. Instead, she got up and left the ward. I made a move to stop her, but Kelly said, 'Don't bother. It's how she deals with stuff she can't handle.'

"A few minutes later when we were alone, Kelly asked how I felt about having another baby. I told her I was happy. She asked if we planned to have any more. I said no. She nodded, then said, 'Our baby's an only child too.' She meant her!"

"God, the poor kid," Chris said.

Wendy nodded. "When I left I hugged her goodbye and said 'Take care of yourself,' and she looked at me as if to ask *why*."

"Sounds like she's going to be in there for a long time."

"I'm afraid so. I left the ward and found Jenny downstairs in the gift shop buying toys for Abigail and joking with the sales clerk. Then two days later, she had a big party for her. The place was full of parents and small kids, and they all put on hats and sang 'Happy Birthday' and ate a huge yellow Big Bird cake and ice cream. The way Jenny carried on you'd never know that her other daughter was in a psychiatric ward for trying to kill herself for the second time just days before. I felt like Alice in Wonderland."

After a few minutes of silence, Wendy said, "And remember that missing photo of Kelly? Well, it's sitting on Jenny's vanity table in her bedroom among some baby pictures of her. She had taken it."

"Where was Ted in all this?" Chris asked.

"He wasn't around much," Wendy said. "During the party he was at work, and at night he went out with friends. As for Kelly, he keeps his distance—she's Jenny's daughter."

"And you wonder why she tried to kill herself. He wants nothing to do with her and Jenny can't forgive her for growing up."

The month of August passed, and 7.2 million people had died.

Included among the dead were Jack Lescoulie, 75, former *Today* show host; Richard Egan, 65, actor; John Houston, 81, world-class movie director; Vincent Persichetti, 72, American composer and educator; Lee Marvin, 63, actor; Bayard Ruston, 85, political philosopher and civil rights activist; Pola Negri, silent film star; Jesse Unruh, 64, politically powerful California assemblyman; David Martin, 50, rock singer and bassist for Sam the

Sham and the Pharaohs; Joseph E. Levine, 81, movie mogul; Jim Bishop, 79, author of bestsellers *The Day Lincoln Was Shot* and *The Day Christ Died*; and Rudolf Hess, 93, the last survivor of Hitler's inner circle.

Except for Hess who hanged himself in Spandau Prison, all the other deaths had all been listed as "natural causes."

Natural causes: A handy medical phrase which to Chris's mind meant that attending physicians didn't have a clue. Almost nobody over 75 was autopsied anymore, because most cases had revealed no clear cause—no specific disease. To satisfy the law, death certificates simply listed "natural causes" which translated as the loss of physiological function attributed to aging.

What those death certificates didn't say was that the cells of the victims had ceased to replicate and, thus, had deteriorated to the point that the vital organs failed.

The process was universal. They had gone to their ends, the rich, the famous, the powerful, unprotected— unprotected, as every other human being who ever lived.

Except Iwati.

September came and went, and once again Chris put off their trip. Maybe they'd go after the baby was born.

On September 18, Sam Bacon was permanently confined to his nursing home bed because he could no longer remember how to sit up.

On the tenth of October, Vince Lucas called Quentin to check on Elixir's progress. Quentin had nothing new to report because these things took time. But the lab team was giving its all to perfecting the serum and winning federal approval by early next year. Lucas seemed satisfied, then asked for the names of the head scientist and his wife. Quentin gladly told him.

•   •   •

During the month of November, 10 million people were born in the world. One of them was Baby Boy Bacon. They named him Adam.

11

A dam Samuel Bacon was born on November 4, 1987 at 8:10 A.M. at Beth Israel Hospital in Boston. He weighed seven pounds, nine ounces.

Because his head was so large, the doctors performed an episiotomy. Throughout the delivery, Chris held Wendy's hand, whispering words of encouragement and how he loved her. While the doctors stitched her up, the nurses brought Adam to her. She and Chris cried and laughed at the same time.

For several minutes, Chris curled his finger around the tiny pink miniature of his son's, thinking that just a few months ago that hand had been a flat webbed thing inside its uterine sac, but through some ingenious mechanism just the right cells at just the right time had died so that these fragile little fingers could take form. And, yet, as Betsy had insisted, beyond the embryo living cells were not part of the same mechanism. That beyond the womb, our cells weren't programmed to die—just age. No death clock ticked within this little bundle of life.

He closed his eyes to clear his mind of all that. He had become too bound up with seeing people in terms of their cells and DNA. Bound up with thoughts he should not consider.

When he opened his eyes again, he beheld his new-born son at Wendy's breast. It was the most beautiful moment in his life.

Later that evening, after Jenny had left and Wendy had gone to sleep, and all the hospital was quiet, Chris stood outside the nursery window and watched his son sleep, wondering what placental dreams went through his tender little brain. It crossed his mind that the last time he was in a hospital was eight years and three months ago when Ricky had died. He had held Wendy's and his son's hand then, too.

Then his mind was full of death.

Now it was aswirl with forever.

Because of the epidural Wendy had slept most of yesterday afternoon, so Jenny had managed to get in a couple hours shopping. Along with her luggage she had two large bags of stuff she'd bought for Abigail from FAO Schwartz. She had spent another fortune. It was bizarre the way Jenny had taken to her own new motherhood—a near-maniacal compensation. When Chris asked how Kelly was getting along, she offered a chirpy "Just fine" which ended the discussion. Yet she talked about Abigail all the way to the airport and showed him a stack of recent photographs. "I'm so much in love with her," she confessed, "it almost scares me."

Probably scares her too, Chris mused.

Because Wendy would be discharged later that day, he returned to the hospital. But the moment he entered her room he sensed something was wrong. Her face had that strained look that even the painkillers couldn't mask.

His first thought was the baby. Yet he was peacefully curled up in her arms. And it couldn't have been complications from the delivery or Wendy wouldn't be dressed and sitting in a chair with Adam. A new bouquet of flowers sat in a vase on her table.

"Is everything all right?"

"Everything's fine." Her voice was flat.

"You don't look it. Who brought the roses?"

"Betsy Watkins."

"That was nice of her."

"Yes, it was."

There was a gaping silence that seemed to suck the walls in.

"Wendy, what's the problem? And don't tell me 'nothing' because I can see it in your face."

Wendy looked up at him. "She said that she proposed calling in an ethical review board, but you were opposed."

Instantly he felt defensive. "I don't know what she's trying to prove, but she had no right to say anything. And we don't need an ethical review board."

"She asked me to convince you to put a hold on the project until one could be set up."

"Wendy, you're not part of the equation. This is Darby business, not a family forum."

"What you're doing is dangerous."

"Can we talk about this some other time? You've just had a baby, for God's sake." He got up and went to the window.

"It has everything to do with the baby," she said angrily. "You're obsessed with this, Chris, and it scares me."

"I'm not obsessed, just busy."

"No, *obsessed,* and you've been like this for months. I feel as if I'm married to you by remote control. I don't see you anymore, and when I do you're distracted all the time."

He sighed audibly. Betsy had gotten to her with both barrels, and she wasn't going to let up. "I'm just swamped, that's all—neck-deep in setting up protocols and all."

"Chris, what you're doing scares me."

"I'm doing what all of medical science does—

including every doctor and nurse in this hospital. My goal is no different."

"Medical diseases are not the same."

"Not the same as what?" he shot back. "Death is the ultimate medical disease—100 percent fatal."

"I mean viruses and bacteria. They come from the outside. Death is built in."

"So is Alzheimer's." The moment the word hit the air, he wished he could retract it.

The effect was instant. "Is that what this is all about?"

"It's too late for Sam."

"I'm not talking about saving Sam. I mean you."

Chris made a move to leave. "I've got to do the paperwork to check you out."

"Chris, you know what I'm talking about."

He flashed around. "No I don't, Wendy," he said. "Corny as it is, what we're doing is in the name of science and humanity, nothing less." He put his hand on the door handle to leave.

"Think of him," she said. "Think of how you'd relate to your son if he grows up to be older than you. Think about the day your child dies of old age and you're still going strong at forty-two." Her eyes were huge. Like Jenny's when crazed.

"Wendy, what the hell are you talking about?"

"You're thinking of taking it yourself."

"Jesus, Mary, and Joseph!" he exclaimed. "That's the most ridiculous thing I've heard you say." His reaction was exaggerated not in anger at Wendy but at himself for appearing so transparent. "This is scientific inquiry of the highest order, not a Robert Louis Stevenson story."

"Promise me you won't."

"You can't be serious."

Tears filled her eyes and splashed onto the baby. "For his sake, promise me you won't. Promise me!"

"I don't believe this!"

"Promise me."

Chris stood at the door unable to move, transfixed by the desperation in his wife's voice. "I promise," he said.

Then he opened the door and left, wondering if she really believed him. Wondering if he really believed himself.

He returned later to drive Wendy and the baby home. She was still sullen. They put Adam into the crib for the first time in his life. And for the second time in their lives a newborn little boy slept in their home.

Wendy was exhausted, and after Adam went down, she went to bed and was out almost immediately. They did not discuss Elixir again.

Usually Chris drank a couple beers at night to settle his brain for sleep. But tonight he wanted a fast buzz. So, he poured himself some vodka over ice and felt the heat spread throughout his head. On his second glass he slipped into the nursery to look at his son. The small table lamp fashioned in a big red and yellow clown's head lit the room in soft glow. Adam was asleep on his back, his head to the side, the tip of his finger in his mouth.

Chris raised the drink to his eyes and studied it for a moment. The vodka was clear and colorless. Like Elixir.

Obsessed.

She was right.

And not just scientific inquiry.

Right again.

His mind turned to Sam, and he felt a deadly logic nip him. Wasn't he becoming more forgetful? Sometimes fumbling for words? Sometimes stumbling on pronunciations? Sometimes forgetting the names of colleagues' spouses? Forgetting what month it was? Forgetting to book the Caribbean?

Wendy had said it was distraction. Distraction, stress, anxiety. What anybody experienced when riding command. Sure.

Then from the sunless recesses of his brain shot up a couple bright red clichés:

Like father, like son.

The spitting image of his dad.

And soon, coming to a theater near you, he thought sickly: *The drooling image of his dad.*

The room seemed to shift, like that moment of awareness with Iwati by the fire. What if it were beginning—the great simplification—the convolutions of his brain puffing out in micro degrees? He could read the signs—forgetfulness, confusion, repetitive gestures. Those moments when his brain felt like a lightbulb loose in its socket.

Nerves? Distraction? Stress? Maybe. Maybe not.

He could see a doctor, but at his age there was no definitive test. Not until it was too late—when you looked in the mirror and you realized what a frightening, unfamiliar thing your face was.

Sure, he was only forty-two, but Alzheimer's could work its evil early. The doctors had said that Sam had an unusually virulent case. *Accelerated* was the term. If it had already started in himself, there was no known cure. No salve for the terror and the horror. Nothing but nothing.

Except, perhaps, Elixir. It preserved brain cells too.

Chris swallowed the rest of his drink, and calculated the dosage necessary for a 170-pound man.

12

The morning was appropriately cold and raw. It was the day Jimbo would die.

Phase One of the testing had been completed. With no standard procedures to guide them, Chris and his team had worked out the minimum dosage–to–body weight ratios to maintain a steady state for the animals—levels where chemistry and behavior plateaued, where test-culture cells replicated indefinitely, and where Elixir maxed out, the excesses passing through their systems unabsorbed.

Phase Two was withdrawal—the stage everybody hated because it meant sacrificing animals they had become attached to.

First to go had been Fred, age twenty-three. They had weaned him off Elixir for a period of two weeks. At first, the effects were imperceptible—loss of appetite and lethargy. Then one day he curled up in a corner, occasionally whining in pain. He remained that way for two days, then died. The postmortem indicated kidney failure. A twenty-one-year-old female named Georgette was next. After two days she came down with a high fever. After a day of fitful shakes, she lapsed into a comatose sleep and died of heart failure. The only noticeable sign of senescence was that her heart had swollen by 30 percent. Four more animals were sacrificed—all dying within a few days, all by causes attributed to age: kidney failure, heart failure, brain strokes, liver dysfunction. Except for slight withering, most showed no overt signs of senescence.

The night before they withdrew Jimbo, Chris visited him alone. He was the oldest monkey and the one whose death Chris dreaded the most. Over the months, he had come to love him like a favorite pet. More than that, Jimbo was a kind of soulmate—an alter self across the evolutionary divide.

His cage was three times the size of other singles—a special senior-citizen perk. Chris found Jimbo curled up on an old L. L. Bean cushion. Because he was a light sleeper, he awoke when Chris approached. He moved to the bars and pushed his fingers through. Chris locked on to them and wondered if Jimbo was aware of the wonderful changes that had taken place in him over the months. Did he know he was younger, stronger, more alert? Did he remember being old? Could he gauge the difference? Chris hoped so, but thought probably not. Self-awareness and awe were capacities unique to humans.

"You're a miracle, big guy, and you don't know it."

Jimbo gazed up with those flat black rainforest eyes. Chris's heart squeezed. "Sorry, my friend."

His mind shifted to a room in Rose Hill Nursing home in West Hartford where last week Chris held the fingers of his father who lay confused by most everything in his waking day. There was more self-awareness in an old rhesus monkey.

Chris fed Jimbo his last supper, then went home and cried.

The mood was somber the next morning when Chris and his team had gathered. Quentin Cross showed up uninvited. As with the other animals, two video recorders would capture the entire process—which they estimated would take four days. Following that, an extensive post-mortem analysis would be done on his vital organs.

Elixir was administered to the animals' systems through minipumps connected to refillable implants under the skin. These worked best because needles were traumatic. Jimbo's last refill would have been at nine A.M. Based on the other animals, signs of degeneration were not expected to show for at least twelve hours.

It was a little after one when Chris got a call from Vartan that Jimbo was acting oddly. He could hear his shrieks even before he reached the lab. All the others had assembled around the cage. "He's experiencing some kind of trauma," Vartan said.

Jimbo was at the top of his climbing structure, trembling and clutching it with both hands. His eyes were full of terror and he was shrieking as if plagued by phantoms.

"He looks possessed," Betsy said, watching in frightened awe.

When Jimbo spotted Chris he fell silent, gaping at him, his ears flattened against his head, a terrified grin on his face, his lips retracted so his huge canines were fully exposed. Then, without warning, he flew at Chris with a shrill screech. Had there been no bars, Chris was certain Jimbo would have torn open his face.

Suddenly Jimbo dropped to the floor and began running in circles, defecating and making yakking sounds nobody had heard before, his tail up like a female presenting out of sheer terror. His face was a scramble of expressions, running the gamut of fight/flight programs. He came to an abrupt stop. His eyes, large and opaque, settled on Chris. His mouth opened in a huge O as if comprehending some gross truth.

The next moment, he began to convulse. He flopped to the floor among his own waste matter. His limbs began to twitch as if he were being electrocuted. Then, slowly at first, his face and torso began to wither, the fur buckling as if there were too much of it to cover him. Betsy let out a gasp of horror as Jimbo's skin lumped and crawled as if small creatures were moving under it. She rushed to give him a mercy-killing shot, but stopped, realizing it would make no difference. Jimbo was dead by the time she filled the needle.

What happened next defied belief, but made horrifying sense. Without the prophylactic protection of Elixir, the telomerase genes in the cells of Jimbo's body suddenly switched on, triggering a mad cascade. Multiplying at lightning speed, cancer cells oozed in bright red tissue mass from the orifices of Jimbo's body—ears, nose, mouth, and anus. From his penis a thin red worm extruded out of the urethra, coiling onto his belly. Simultaneously, a pulsing gorge swelled out of Jimbo's throat and enveloped his head.

Within minutes, cancer cells made up for months of forced dormancy. Cells that continued to grow and multiply long after the animal had died flowed like lava across his limbs and torso until any semblance of his original form was lost to a grotesque and throbbing red mass.

When it was over, Betsy turned to Chris and Quentin. "Are you satisfied now?" she shouted. "What we are doing is wrong, and that hideous spectacle was a warning. This is bad science. *Bad!*"

She then turned and left the lab.

DECEMBER 11

"What do you mean a *technical snag*?"

"Well, a kind of . . . you know, side-effect."

"What kind of side-effect?"

Quentin was sweating, but trying to remain cool.

"Well, the stuff kills the animals in withdrawal. I don't understand it—something at the DNA level."

Vince Lucas listened without expression and sipped his tea. He was dressed elegantly in a gray flannel sport coat, white shirt, and silk paisley tie. A fat gold Rolex peered out from his wrist. With his slick black hair and tan, he looked like an Italian movie star.

"We're working on it, but unless we eliminate it, it'll never be marketed."

They were sitting in the lounge of Boston's new Four Seasons Hotel. Seven months from now Quentin was scheduled to pay Vince Lucas the first $2 million he owed him for his loan—and his life—the same amount to be paid the following July 1. That was on top of the $5 million he had already wired Antoine for the apricots. Nine million dollars in debt and nothing to show but some hideous monkey carcasses.

"But I think there's something we can do."

Vince looked at him with those unreadable black eyes. "I'm listening."

"But it's not legal."

"Now we're home."

The waiter came with a second Chivas. Quentin took sip then explained. "I'm thinking a deep-pocket clientele would pay serious money for an endless supply of Elixir. People who like their privacy."

"Howard Hughes is dead."

"I mean your Consortium."

The suggestion hung in the air. Vince sipped his tea patiently.

"Well, I'm thinking that maybe you and Antoine can approach them with the idea . . . a chance to live indefinitely, and what they would pay for it."

Vince lay his glass on the table. "The Consortium is not a club for rich hermits," he said. "What happens when the kid who used to drive your limo meets you twenty years later and he's forty-five and you're the same? You tell him you're taking some secret youth potion?"

"By then we'll have worked the bugs out, and the stuff would be on the market. I mean in the meantime. Like, you know, now."

Vince thought that over. "How long to get the bugs out?"

"Three years, four the most."

"Sounds like a trap, if you ask me."

"How's it a trap?"

"Say the Consortium is interested. They'll want a guarantee they can still get the stuff without any hitches or sudden price inflation."

"We'll give them written guarantees."

"Enforced by what authorities?"

Quentin looked at him without an answer.

"Another thing: Say you run out of raw materials again, or the Feds find out you're dealing in illegal pharmaceuticals and shut you down. What happens to your clientele? It's not like some junkie's supplier runs dry and they can tap another. People want peace of mind."

"We can work out some foolproof trust."

"No such thing." Vince removed a single almond from the dish of nuts and chewed it, all the while turning something over in his head. "You say Elixir still works on the primates as long as they get a constant supply?"

"Yes."

"Before you go looking for takers, you might want to see if it works on real human beings. Otherwise nobody's interested."

"That's the problem. We can't just walk into a clinic and ask who wants to volunteer for a longevity study that ends in death."

"Volunteers can be appointed."

Quentin looked at him blankly as the words sunk in. "I see."

"The real problem is at your end—getting people to make the stuff without the FDA finding out."

"Subcontractors," Quentin said. He had already worked that out. Outside jobbers would manufacture the compound—and nobody would know its purpose, and nobody would ask questions. And no worry about protocol.

Vince nodded as Quentin explained. "What about your lab people? Any problems there?"

Quentin finished his drink and ordered a third. "That's something I think we should talk about."

Adam blew a bubble, and Wendy laughed joyously.

It was two days before Christmas, and she was bathing him in the kitchen sink, thinking how full of love she was for her baby boy, who was giddy with laughter as she rubbed the washcloth across his pink little body. It was a small moment among the millions of her life but one she wished she could freeze forever.

She knew, of course, the notion was silly. If you could freeze such moments, how would they remain blissful? Joy was an experience defined by contrasts to lesser moments. Besides, there would be others.

As she dressed Adam for bed, she felt Elixir coil around her mind like a snake. At moments like these, she understood its allure.

She could hear Chris's words: *"The trouble with life is that it's 100 percent fatal."*

And: *"I've never died before, Wendy, and I don't want to learn how."*

And: *"Think how many books you could write if you had another fifty or hundred years. You could be the Dorothy Sayers of the twenty-first century.*

There was almost no escaping it. One night a few weeks ago, they watched a rerun of *The Philadelphia Story*. Before a commercial break, a young, handsome Jimmy Stewart turned to twenty-two-year-old Katherine Hepburn and said, "There's a magnificence in you, Tracy that comes out of your eyes and your voice and the way you stand there and the way you walk. You're lit from within. . . ." While Chris got up for another beer, he wondered aloud how painful it must be for the eighty-year-old Hepburn, now wrinkled and palsied, to see herself in reruns. She probably didn't watch them, he concluded. Wendy's response was that Kate Hepburn was supposed to grow old and die. Painful as it was, she had no doubt accepted that. As we all must.

It was a good response, like her usual caveats about tampering with Nature, or her old standby: " *'Death is the mother of Beauty.'* "

With Adam in her arms, Wendy felt that the Stevens line never made better sense. Such moments were beautiful because they *didn't* freeze. Besides, all the animals had died from withdrawal, which meant it would be years before human testing, maybe never. She could only hope.

The telephone rang, jarring her out of the moment. Her first thought was Chris. He was at a two-day conference on cell biology in Philadelphia. But it was Quentin Cross.

"Chris said you were having trouble landing accommodations in the Caribbean."

"That's what happens when you make plans at the last minute," Wendy said. "Everything's been booked for months."

"Well, coincidentally, we've got a time-sharing condo at La Palmas on the east coast of Puerto Rico that's free for the first two weeks in February, if that interests you. Margaret and I go down every year, but with Ross's retirement and all the things going on, we're going to have to pass this time around. But you guys can go in our place," he said.

"Are you serious?"

Quentin chuckled good-naturedly. "Yes, and it's on us, free of charge."

"Oh, Quentin, I'm speechless. How generous of you!"

"The only catch is that you have to book with the

airlines today. I hope you don't mind, but, just in case, I took the liberty of making reservations in your names. All you have to do is call Eastern and confirm. But it has to be today. What do you think?"

"My God, yes, we'll take it!" Wendy said. "And thank you, Quentin. Thank you so much. Wow!"

"Well, think of it as a little token of appreciation for what Chris has done for us—and you, for standing by him all the way."

Thrilled, Wendy thanked him again. After she hung up, she called Eastern and confirmed their reservation, thinking, How considerate of Quentin. Maybe Chris had misjudged him.

13

Every morning at five, Betsy Watkins would drive to the Cambridge Y and swim fifty laps in the pool before going to work.

At forty-eight years of age, she would do her regimen in forty leisurely minutes, letting her mind free-play, while her body kicked into autopilot, guided by the lane lines.

At that hour, especially in the winter, the place was nearly empty but for the lifeguard. By six-thirty a few people would dribble in. But this morning with a sleeting rain, she did her laps alone.

As she swam, she thought about the new position she was taking at the National Cancer Institute in two weeks. She would have started the day after Jimbo's death had Chris not pleaded for her to delay her departure so he could find a replacement. She agreed on the condition that no more animals be sacrificed. Chris swore to it, and no more animals were withdrawn.

At the NCI she intended to study how tabulone deprived cancer cells of the telomerase enzyme, which was not the interest at Darby. And before she left, she would approach Ross again in hopes of getting him to agree to a watchdog agency coming in to monitor the development of Elixir. Quentin was dead set against that, but

Ross would appreciate the need for the assurance of ethical practice and accountability. Prolongevity was frontier science fraught with frontier dangers.

On lap forty-four, she thought about her approach to Ross should he stonewall her. It was not beyond her to let the FDA in on what they were doing.

She also thought about Chris—how he was a good man and fine scientist torn between ethical considerations and a near-personal appeal of Elixir. His wife held the opposite sentiment, yet they seemed very much in love. Betsy would miss Chris and those wonderful two-tone eyes.

On lap forty-five, she looked up to see the lifeguard step out for a coffee refill. She flashed the okay.

On lap forty-six, at midpool, she noticed some movement out of the corner of her goggles. Another swimmer was in the other lane moving toward her on a return lap. A man wearing a white bathing cap, snorkle and fins. Betsy preferred swimming unassisted.

On lap forty-seven, she felt a sudden blow to the top of her head. The pain was blinding, and instantly she slipped into thrashing confusion, sucking in water and feeling arms embrace her legs like an anaconda and pull her down. A flash of the white cap. Under the pain and choking anguish was utter disbelief. She was being attacked underwater.

On what would have been lap forty-eight, her mind cleared for a split second. She saw the bottom of the pool rise up, while her diaphragm wracked for air and her arms flapped against the grip.

On lap forty-nine, bubbles rose up around her . . . so many bubbles . . . and panic filled her chest . . . and the weight on her leg . . . so heavy . . . all so heavy and dark, and her lungs burning for oxygen against the water filling her throat . . . and a face in a mask . . . eyes staring back at her . . . and the glint of chrome from a SCUBA regulator . . . black hoses and bubbles . . . the leaden weights of her limbs . . . her mind filling with dark water . . . and she kept swimming . . . swimming . . . toward a man with two large black eyes . . .

On lap fifty, she was dead.

14

Vince Lucas handed Quentin a Chivas on the rocks as he stepped inside his Hampton estate—a building that the designers had fashioned after Monticello.

Dressed in an elegant double-breasted suit with a white shirt and white silk tie, Vince led Quentin inside where a large crowd of people spread throughout the rooms. At the far end of a large and opulent ballroom, a jazz combo played. Waiters and waitresses in black and white worked their way through the crowds with champagne and hors d'oeuvres.

Quentin kept his briefcase gripped in his right hand as he made his way. Every so often he would spot someone he recognized from magazines and television—athletes, entertainers, New York politicians.

At the rear of the building, under a glass ceiling, lay a serpentine pool in small groves of palm and other tropical plants—all fed by fountains and waterfalls that emanated from rock-garden formations leading off to a poolside bar at one end. It looked like a jungle-movie set. Several men and women cavorted in the water while patio guests sat in lounge chairs as waiters moved about with drinks and food. In the distance through the rear glass wall spread the vast black Atlantic, whitewashed by a full December moon.

Quentin had a drink and met some people, then at ten o'clock he was taken to a back room where they entered a private elevator that took them two flights down to a sub-basement where the sounds of the band and revelry could not be heard. They made their way down a corridor with several rooms including a mirrored gym full of exercise machines. At the end was a heavy oak door that Vince unlocked.

Quentin stepped into a room full of men and women around a huge oval conference table—people he had seen upstairs, some from the island.

"Long time no see." Antoine Ducharme.

Quentin shook his hand, thinking that if it weren't for Elixir Antoine would have eliminated Quentin and his family. Now they were partners again.

They chatted for a moment as the place settled down. Quentin asked how Lisa was, and Antoine made a rueful smile. After the bombing of Apricot Cay, she had left him for another man. "The flesh is weak," he added cryptically.

On the far wall was a screen for the slide and video projectors. They had discussed the proceedings several times, yet Quentin's heart was doing a fast trot. Some 30 billion dollars sat around the table. He knew very little about individual Consortium members except that they embodied an exclusive international coterie of power brokers—financiers, foreign government officials, sheiks, retired oil execs, and the like—people whose word could send ripples throughout the stockmarkets around the world or incite international incidents. An untouchable elite who got where they were by being consummate opportunists. And here they were assembled for the ultimate conquest.

Vince's job had been to assemble them with just enough bait. Quentin's job was to sell them the goods with everything he had. And he was well prepared. He stepped up to the small lectern and described Elixir, taking the group through the various stages. He showed them slides of medical charts and procedures, and a video of the mice and the monkeys. The crowd was amazed at the before-and-after scenes of once infirm elderly primates suddenly jumping around as if transported back in time. Quentin explained how the animals could go on indefinitely. About the consequences of withdrawal, Quentin was forthright—or nearly so. As with any patient dependent upon medication, the animals would eventually suffer adverse symptoms leading to death. He did not go into detail.

What sold the group was the video that Antoine had brought.

Vince dimmed the lights, and the screen came alive. The locale was not immediately clear, but several people were shown sitting in a room. Most were black. All of them were in their seventies or older. At first it appeared to be a hospital, but a quick pan of the camera revealed barred windows. An off-camera male spoke in a crisp Caribbean accent. Each of the eight patients wore a first-name tag around the neck. A large woman sat in a wheelchair. They were all dressed in white T-shirts and shorts to reveal their physical condition.

The narrator asked each patient to walk across the room. Three men were bald, one with a full white bush. Some had missing teeth. Skin was loose and wrinkled, eyes discolored and rheumy. Two women were quite frail; one large white woman could barely walk for arthritis and remained in her wheelchair. The rest hobbled a few times around the room as best they could. Two used canes. "Very good, very nice," said the narrator.

To document the dates, the camera zoomed in on that day's *New York Times*. The first day was December 16. The patients were told to sit again. Without showing his face, a man in white injected a clear liquid into each patient's arms. Before the fadeout, the voice asked each how he or she felt, and all mumbled that they were fine.

The screen went to black for a moment, then lit up on a tight focus of *The New York Times*.

December 30. The same featureless room. The same elderly group in chairs against the wall. The same clean white outfits. Some stared blankly, a couple smiled. At first, nothing seemed different. But as the camera moved, subtle differences were discernible. The dark wrinkled man named Rodney seemed a bit more alert; his eyes were clearer and more open. He was also sitting straighter, as were two others. When asked, the frail woman named Francine said she felt better than the last time.

January 11. Same room. Same group of eight. But what summoned a response from the Consortium was the appearance of Alice, the fat, wheelchaired woman. She was on her feet and shuffling around the room. When asked about the arthritis in her feet, she said that her feet were "much happier." Likewise, the others circled the room with posture more upright and greater agility. Ezra and Hyacinth, who had previously used canes, now walked unassisted. The camera tightened on their faces which looked smoother and tighter. According to the narrator, each was feeling considerably better, more energetic. Two also remarked that their memories had improved.

January 19. This time their spirits were visibly high. Chatting and laughing, the eight of them walked their circles with smooth, steady gaits—including Alice, now with a cane. She had lost weight, and her face was thinner, her eyes wider. The camera shifted to Robert arm-wrestling with Rodney, the others cheering them on.

January 27. The group of eight was in the middle of the floor dancing to a reggae tape. The transformation was astounding, and the Consortium gasped in astonishment. In a matter of six weeks, each patient had regressed a decade or more. All laughed and swayed to the music, including Alice, who was on her feet unassisted, her hair neatly brushed, her face made up and smiling brightly.

When Vince flicked on the lights, the place exploded in cheers. One Frenchman asked where he could get a liter of the stuff tonight, and pulled out a checkbook. Others had the same response.

Quentin was peppered with questions.

Somebody asked about the fate of the patients, and Antoine said that they were being well cared for, and secure—an answer that satisfied the Consortium. An answer far from the truth.

By the end of the meeting, Vince was taking orders for Elixir treatments at $2 million per year.

Around midnight the conference room cleared out, leaving Vince, Quentin, and Antoine to themselves.

Vince removed the video cassette from the projector. "By the way, your Betsy Watkins had an unfortunate accident this morning."

"What a pity," Quentin smiled.

"And the other problem is being taken care of as we speak."

Quentin felt a rush of relief. All was going so well. In a matter of weeks, they would be in full swing, all obstacles removed. Elixir would be sub-contracted to pharmaceutical firms outside New England, distribution would be handled by Vince and Antoine's people, and international bank accounts would be opened for proceeds. In a handful of years, Elixir would be their billion-dollar molecule.

"Are you familiar with the novel *The Picture of Dorian Gray* by Oscar Wilde?" Antoine asked.

"No," Quentin said.

"How about the short mystery story 'The Facts in the Case of M. Valdemar' by your own Edgar Allan Poe?"

"Not really."

"Too bad. It's a wonderful tale about a man put into

a state of hypnosis at the moment of death, prolonging his life for months. The fun is when he's snapped out of his trance. In less than a minute he rots away into a liquid mass of putrescence."

Quentin looked at him blankly for an explanation.

From his valise Antoine pulled out another video and slipped it into the projector. "Watch, my friend."

Blue sky filled the screen. Slowly the camera pulled back to reveal an ocean horizon, boats floating in the misty distance. The camera canted to reveal Lisa posing at the bow of the *Reef Madness*. She was just as Quentin remembered her—stunningly beautiful with a gleaming smile and long tight body. Dressed in a baseball cap and a white one-piece suit that fit her like damp tissue paper, she could have been a supermodel posing for a calendar spread. The small rose tattoo on her right shoulder glowed like a medallion in the sunlight. She was laughing and poking a still camera at whoever was taping her.

The scene suddenly shifted to the same barred featureless room of the first video. It looked empty until the camera panned to a darkly clad figure in a wheelchair. Somebody off-camera said something, and the figure raised its head.

"Jesus Christ!" gasped Quentin.

It was Lisa. She was withered and stooped. Her hair was a wispy white film across her scalp, the skin of her face like weathered parchment. Her mouth was open to labored breathing, her lips chapped and split, most teeth missing. One eye was a gaping milky ball, the other eye a jellied slit.

Quentin's hope against hope was that it was trick photography or some fancy theatrical makeup job. But it was real. And it *was* Lisa—he could make out the rose tattoo. They had conditioned her on Elixir from the same batch that Quentin had stolen some weeks ago from the lab for the elderly patients. Somehow Antoine had injected her either against her will or with the promise of immortality, then withdrew treatments so she would rot.

Enjoying Quentin's reaction, Antoine paused the video on a closeup of her miserable face. "Some things don't age well, especially a cheating heart."

15

I think she was murdered," Chris said.

"Murdered!"

Chris and Wendy were driving to the Burlington Mall to finish shopping for their trip. Adam was asleep in his car seat.

"But who would murder her? And why?"

"I'm not exactly sure, but the line of questioning suggested foul play. I guess they're waiting for the medical examiner's report and following some leads."

Chris had been at a seminar on cell biology at the Heritage Hotel outside of Providence when Cambridge detectives showed up. They questioned him for nearly an hour, wondering why he had left the house at five that morning for an hour's drive to a conference that began at nine. He said he wanted to beat the traffic and have a leisurely breakfast to review the literature.

"What leads?"

"I don't know, but they asked if Betsy had any known enemies. All I could think of was Quentin."

"Quentin? That's ridiculous."

"Maybe not. Once he let slip that some people would pay dearly for Elixir as it is. I think he was sending up a trial balloon to see how I'd react."

"What did you say?"

"That I was opposed to the idea—that it wasn't meant to be the drug of choice for the elite. That's when he retreated, claiming he wasn't serious. But I wasn't convinced. I think he was testing me. He does things like that."

"Why would he take such a chance? He'll be CEO next month."

"Because he's gotten the company into debt up the yin-yang. And because Quentin Cross dreams of building empires, no matter what they're made of."

"That's absurd."

"Maybe, but I think I'm next."

Wendy turned to him. "Chris, you're scaring me."

"And they're scaring me. I think they want me out of the way like Betsy. She was a loose cannon. She threatened to expose Elixir on moral grounds. If she suspected they were considering blackmarketing it, she'd sound the alarm. And that's why they want me out of the way."

"He was just talking through his hat."

"Quentin doesn't talk through his hat. Then out of the blue comes this Caribbean offer—two weeks in a fancy seaside condo with a car and a boat all for free. And all the buddy-buddy stuff about what a terrific time we're going to have down there, and how great the diving is right off the beach."

"How about he was just being generous?"

"How about he's just too anxious to get us down there? He called this morning from New York to say we shouldn't feel bad about missing Betsy's funeral because the company will hold a memorial next month."

"I still fail to see the problem."

"Wendy, it's too good to be true. Quentin is a sly opportunist driven by self-interest, not magnanimity."

"Frankly, hon, I think you're being very ungrateful. He said his friend Barcello offered it to him, but with Ross's retirement and the holidays he couldn't get away. So he passed it on to us."

"Nice coincidence, except I checked. First, there is no

diving off the Las Palmas beach—the nearest reef is thirty miles.

"Second, I called a realtor down there about the condo, and there is no Barcello Mendez proprietor, and nobody who's ever heard of him or Quentin Cross. Then I called the number he gave and got an answering service for something called Fair Caribe Exchange, Ltd. which it turns out is headquartered in Apricot Cay—the same island our apricots were from."

"So?"

"About a year ago, Apricot Cay was bombed by U.S. Navy planes because the place was a big-time cocaine center. The point is Quentin was negotiating with traffickers of illegal substances—people who resolve problems by eliminating them."

"How do you know all this?"

"Ross Darby." Chris pulled the car into the parking lot of the mall. "Wendy, I think this trip is a setup. I think the people he's involved with killed Betsy and are planning to do the same to me down there. Maybe both of us."

"If they really wanted to get rid of you, why send you all the way to Puerto Rico?"

"To distance my own death from Betsy's—and Darby Pharms. To make it look like another terrible tragedy for hapless tourists."

"Then why don't you go to the police?"

"Because I have no hard evidence, just a lot of bad feelings. Besides, I'd have to explain Elixir."

She looked at him in dismay. "You seem more interested in protecting Elixir than yourself. Or us."

"I'm interested in protecting us and it."

"By doing what?"

"That's what I want to talk about," he said, "but it'll mean making some changes."

•   •   •

A little before one the next morning Chris entered the rear of Darby Pharmaceuticals. He hadn't used it since New Guinea, but his pistol was stuffed into his belt.

He neutralized the alarm system, then slipped into the main lab. Against the far wall was a locked file cabinet with all the notes ever assembled on Elixir, arranged according to years—from the earliest days of the flower synthesis up to yesterday's notes on the animals. The complete scientific records: chemistry, pharmacology, biology, toxicology—full details of the various procedures, printouts, analyses of purity, spectral data, animal medical histories. Down the hall in another room was a bank of red fireproof cabinets containing duplicate files.

It took him over an hour to remove every last note from both cabinets and load them into two steamer trunks in the van he had rented under a false name. When he was through, there was nothing left from which the company could ever again reproduce the Elixir molecule.

He then went to the lab and removed every one of over two hundred ampules of Elixir from storage and a backup two-liter bottle. He even removed the silastic implants and subcutaneous tubes from each of the animals. What clenched his heart was the knowledge that within a few days they would all die, some horribly. It pained him, but before he left he gave each a lethal injection of phenobarbitol.

He then drove to Logan Airport where he parked in the central lot. He took a cab to Belmont, the town next to Carleton, and walked home in the dark to avoid leaving record of his return.

It was nearly five A.M. when he entered the house. The place was dark and quiet. His car was parked in back. Wendy woke when he entered. So far, so good, he said. But she looked traumatized. She couldn't believe what they were doing, but he had convinced her that it was their only option.

At ten minutes to six, right on schedule, the limo

Quentin had hired pulled up the driveway. The driver loaded their luggage in the back. They had brought with them several heavy suitcases. Wendy got in with the baby. She was in shock. Chris sat beside her with one hand on hers, the other on the pistol in case the driver tried anything funny. He didn't.

At six-forty, the limo pulled up to the Eastern gate. The place was swarming with buses and cars. Several tour groups were departing within an hour of each other. Theirs was scheduled for eight o'clock. Chris tipped the driver, then found a redcap to take the luggage inside. Through the windows Chris watched the limo pull away, making note of the plate number in case it circled back. It didn't. The man was just a hire.

While Wendy went to a coffee shop with Adam, Chris brought the two heaviest cases to the men's room where in a stall he wiped each clean of fingerprints, then checked them in lockers. Each contained unopened sets of dishes for weight.

The ticketing area was a swarm of people. The check-in line was long, and he fell in at the rear, his heart pounding. He didn't think anyone would keep tabs on them here. Still, he kept his sunglasses on and his base-ball cap low.

As he moved closer to the counter, he spotted a couple with a little girl among the standby passengers. He then slipped out of line and went to the bank of pay phones on the far wall. He punched a bunch of numbers then grimaced noticeably as if hearing bad news.

When he returned, he called the standby couple aside. Under their parkas, they were dressed for warm weather, including the little girl who had already slipped into shorts.

"Look, I've got a bit of a problem," Chris explained to them. "My wife and son and I were scheduled for this flight, but I just learned that we've had a medical emergency at home. My father's in the hospital," he said, hating using Sam as their excuse.

"I'm sorry to hear that," the man said.

"The point is we can't go to Puerto Rico and have to get out of here fast. So, instead of turning in our tickets, I figured you folks can have them at standby prices. There are three of us and three of you, and I don't know where your names are on the list, but there're maybe twenty others going standby."

Chris would have gladly given them the tickets at no cost, but that would have raised suspicion.

"That's very nice of you," the woman said.

Beside her the little girl pulled at her dad. "Does it mean we can go?" she asked hopefully.

Her father looked leery, though the wife was as anxious as their daughter to be on the plane for a Caribbean vacation.

Chris pulled closer to the man. "Since you don't need passports in Puerto Rico, you can fly under our names and not have to worry about getting seats. Once you're there, you're yourselves again. The charade's over."

The man didn't take long to decide. He pulled out a checkbook. "How much?"

The tickets had sold for $1,050. "Make it for seven hundred."

"Geez, that's quite a bargain."

"That's also a long line, and we've got to get out of here," Chris said.

Chris handed the man the tickets with the names C., W., and A. Bacon.

When the man was certain they were legitimate, he wrote out the check which said Thomas and Karen Foley, from Brockton, Mass. Chris thanked him.

Glowing with gratitude at what a deal he had, Foley pumped Chris's hand. "Thank *you*, and I hope all works out okay for you and your family."

"Me too." Chris said. *God, me too!*

•   •   •

They rode in pained silence for a long while.

Chris tried conversation, but Wendy didn't respond. She just glared out the window, occasionally shaking her head in disbelief. He could almost read her mind. On the road were people doing normal, ordinary things—going to work, shopping, driving the kids around. Families off to visit friends or relatives. Not running for their lives. And she was thinking that in three weeks they were supposed to have a publication party for *If I Should Die* at Kate's Mystery Book Shop in Cambridge. At the cusp of the most wonderful time of Wendy's life—motherhood and the first step of a writing career—they were heading for the frozen backwoods of the Adirondacks. It was grossly unfair. And Chris's heart twisted with guilt. His only hope was that once settled into the cabin they would work out a plan of action—maybe consult lawyers—and she would come around.

In the rearview mirror he peered at Adam in his car seat and innocent blue snowsuit. And behind him two steamer trunks full of eternal youth and death.

What have I gotten you into, little man?

Wendy had no idea what they were transporting. He had told her only that he had removed some personal stuff from the lab, not robbed the place clean.

It wasn't until they stopped outside of Albany for lunch when she asked about the two trunks hidden in the rear. It was then Chris told her the truth.

Wendy exploded. "First we fake an airline trip, now it's grand larceny. We're fugitives from the law, goddamn it. Why did you bring this stuff?"

"So it wouldn't fall into the wrong hands."

"I don't care about that, Chris. I care about us."

"So do I, but I told you what they were planning."

"You have no proof they were going to blackmarket it."

"Betsy's death is proof enough."

"That could have been a random killing—some lunatic. Damn it, Chris, I'm not living this way. I'm not living in hiding. You promise me you'll go to the police, or I'll call them myself."

"Honey, please calm down."

"Don't 'honey' me. Give me your word, or I'll call them, so help me God!"

"Okay. Give me a couple days to think it out. Please."

"Two days, that's it. Then you are going to take us back home and go to the police."

"Okay."

"Swear on it."

And for a split second he heard Iwati. "I swear."

A little before six they arrived at the old hunting lodge. The place sat deep in the woods off a logging road on the shore of Black Eagle Lake. Except for the headlights of their car, there was no sign of life anywhere. Just impenetrable black.

The property was still registered under Wendy's maternal grandmother who had bought it in the 1930s. With the mortgage long paid up, it was not easily traceable to Chris and Wendy should they have to hole up for a while. The nearest winterized house was over a mile away, and the nearest town, Lake Placid, twelve miles. Every summer Wendy's parents brought her and Jenny up from their Albany home. Because of the drive from Boston, Chris and Wendy rarely used the place. Jenny and Ted never did.

Unfortunately, the driveway had not been plowed, so they had to trudge through deep snow to reach the house.

Once inside, Chris turned up the heat and made a blazing fire in the fieldstone hearth. The old television still got good reception from a station in Vermont. They found some wine and canned food, and Wendy settled by the fire under a blanket. Meanwhile, Chris set up a makeshift crib for Adam in a bureau drawer. He changed and fed him and had just put him down when he heard Wendy scream in the other room.

In reflex, he pulled the gun and bolted into the living room, half expecting to see somebody coming through the window. Instead, Wendy was sitting straight up, her hands pressed to her mouth, eyes fixed on the television screen and huge with horror.

"It blew up. Eastern flight 219. It blew up!"

The news anchor was describing the explosion: ". . . had been on route from Boston to San Juan when it went down about 120 miles off the coast of Savannah, Georgia.

"Although there were no witnesses, the plane disappeared from radar at about 10:20 this morning. Wreckage and bodies had been strewn over a large area, indicating to authorities that the plane had exploded before crashing.

"Initial speculation is that the aircraft was hit by lightning. A large coastal storm continues to hamper search-and-rescue operations. So far, there have been no reports of survivors. . . ."

To the right of the announcer was a map of the mid-Atlantic coast with a star in the water indicating the site of the crash. Suddenly the map shot was replaced by another still photo.

"Those poor people," Wendy said. "If it weren't for us—" Suddenly she gasped.

On the screen was a picture of Chris.

"Killed in the explosion was Dr. Christopher Bacon, his wife Wendy, and their young child.

"Just hours ago, Boston police issued a warrant for his arrest in the death of a coworker, Betsy Watkins, whose body was found yesterday in a pool at a local YMCA. According to authorities, police had questioned Bacon earlier in the day and released him. But following a medical examiner's report issued later, it was concluded that Watkins had been struck on the head with a heavy object before drowning. Physical evidence was found linking Bacon to the murder scene. . . ."

The caption across the bottom of the screen read: MURDER SUSPECT DIES IN AIR CRASH.

Wendy said something and the announcer carried on with the story, but Chris just stared into the flickering glare of the screen, thinking what a brutal new shape the universe had taken.

16

"You didn't say you were going to blow up the plane," Quentin said. "You killed 136 innocent people. You were supposed to do it on the island—just him, nice and simple. Like with Betsy."

"It was Antoine's idea." Vince said. "He calls the shots."

"That guy's an animal."

"You might want to keep that opinion to yourself."

Quentin was at a pay phone outside a gas station on Route 2 in Concord about three miles from his house. It was Sunday morning, and after a few calls back and forth, he had connected with Vince Lucas at another pay phone someplace on Long Island. It was how they communicated without worry of taps.

"Innocent people die every day," Vince explained. "It had to look like an accident, so nobody asks a lot of questions. If he showed up with a bullet in him, the authorities would be looking for a third party and two unsolved murders from the same company in the space of a week. Which means they'd be wondering if it was an inside job and thinking about you. This way, there are no loose ends."

Quentin hadn't thought about that, but Vince was right.

According to the news, the water was nearly a mile deep with little surface wreckage to determine the cause. The lead theory was a lightning strike. As one commentator had said, commercial jets were built to fly through storms, but a direct hit by a couple million volts could do it. Of course, all it took was three volts from two double-A batteries, a timer, and two pounds of Simtec plastic explosives in the cargo hold below the central fuel tank. And two baggage handlers working for Antoine.

"Now you and your people can move ahead with the stuff, all nice and clean," Vince said.

"Yeah, nice and clean. You took out all the Elixir, too."

"What's that?"

"He had it with him. All of it, including the science notebooks."

"What are you telling me, Quentin?"

"I'm telling you that Chris Bacon cleaned us out. He took every goddamn drop of Elixir, and every goddamn page of notes on how to produce the stuff. The son-of-a-bitch was skipping the country with the whole show. He probably had made connections in San Juan to South America or Europe, wherever. They were on the plane with him. His wife, his kid, and Elixir."

"How do you know it's not all back at his house?"

"It's the first place I got the police to check."

The silence was cut by the hush of the open line. That and the clicking of Quentin's heart in his ear.

"You mean you don't have the formulas to make the stuff?"

"That's what I'm telling you."

"Don't you remember how to do it? All those scientists you got, and nobody knows how to do what they've been doing for a fucking year?"

"Vince, it's not exactly a recipe for baking bread. There are hundreds of complicated steps and procedures. He must have planned it for weeks. Jesus! Do you believe it? We set him up for Betsy, meanwhile he robs us blind."

"What about backup copies of the notebooks?"

"He took those too."

More silence as Vince absorbed the implications. "And where exactly were those backup copies?"

"In the fireproof locker I showed you."

"Two sets of notebooks containing the formulas for endless youth just fifty feet from each other?"

"More like a eighty or a hundred feet," he muttered, and suddenly he felt a hole open up. "Besides, those are reinforced steel fireproof lockers. I mean, they were perfectly safe. You could torch the place and they'd be fine."

But Vince found no solace in that. Fireproofing was not the problem. "What about off-site copies?"

"Off-site copies?" The hole opened wider and Quentin slipped to his waist.

"Copies in safety deposit boxes in banks or your home safe. Second backups in case the place blows up, or some asshole decides to clean you out?"

"Well, not really. It's not company policy. . . . I mean, we never had a need to, you know. Nobody ever steals project notebooks. Our people are very, you know . . . trustworthy . . ." He trailed off, wishing he had a place to land, wishing he could edit out the last thirty seconds of the conversation. Wishing he had never said anything about the missing notebooks.

"Didn't you once tell me that he didn't like the idea of marketing the stuff on the side?"

"I guess I did."

"Didn't you once say you were worried he might try to take the patent and run off on his own?"

"Yeah, but I wasn't really serious. I mean, he wasn't really the type. Didn't have the balls for a heist, and all. . . ."

Silence.

"Vince, look I'm sorry. Tell Antoine we'll pay everybody back their deposits. That's no problem. They'll get their money back. Please tell him everybody will get what they're owed."

"Money's not the issue."

"What is?"

"Longevity."

"Sure, of course. I know, I've lost that too, believe me. Jesus, the son-of-a-bitch. But, you know . . . what can I say?"

"Nothing," Vince said. "Not a fucking thing."

And he clicked off, leaving Quentin standing there in a raw winter wind as cold as eternity.

If Jenny caught the evening news, she would be hysterical. So Wendy drove to a pay phone on highway 87 outside of Lake Placid to avoid leaving records at the cottage. Chris would have gone, but his face might be recognized. He was already thinking like a fugitive.

With the snow it would be two hours before Wendy returned. Meanwhile, Chris removed the trunk containing the Elixir to a small chamber in the cellar where Wendy's parents had stored wine. The room was locked and well insulated. The thermometer read 20 degrees, which was fine, since Elixir could be kept frozen indefinitely without decomposition. The two-liter container he left in the refrigerator upstairs because freezing would split the container. The rest was kept in two hundred-and-twelve ampules fixed with rubber septums for injection needles. Because tabulone was highly active in low concentrations, Chris estimated that he had enough Elixir to keep a single rhesus monkey stable for two thousand years.

A little after two, Wendy returned wrung out. She had reached Jenny.

"What did you tell her?" Chris asked.

"That the police reports were wrong, that you were framed for Betsy's murder."

"How did she take it?"

"How do you think she took it? She was shocked, confused, and horrified," Wendy explained.

"Does she know we're here?"

"Yes." Wendy was so weary that she leaned against the fireplace mantel to keep from slipping to the floor. Her face was colorless with defeat. "I told her we took off when you suspected a plot to get you too." Her voice sounded like a flat recording. "When she finally calmed down she offered to help us."

Chris nodded, thinking how Jenny might be able to do that. "Did you tell her why?" he asked cautiously.

"No, I did not tell her about Elixir." Even her exhaustion could not mask the sarcasm in her voice.

"You did the right thing," Chris said, knowing how hollow that sounded. She didn't care a damn about keeping the stuff secret.

Wendy pushed away from the wall. She wanted to go to bed. "So, what are we going to do?" She asked. "They found your snorkle stuff in the locker room."

"That was planted. It was a setup. I was halfway to Providence at the time."

"And what evidence?"

Chris took her by the shoulders. "Jesus, Wendy, you don't think I killed her, do you?"

For a split second, she appeared to struggle with her answer. "No, but the police do."

"I can't document where I was until later in the day." He had driven straight to Providence and breakfasted on complimentary donuts and coffee in the hotel lobby, then settled in a corner of the deserted bar to look over the seminar material undisturbed. He had spoken to no one, and left no receipts. He had no evidence; nobody could place him there that early.

"Then you have no alibi. It's your word against theirs."

He took a deep, shaky breath. "I'm sorry," he whispered, and pulled her to him. Wendy lay limply against his chest. It was like cuddling somebody who had died.

For a long moment Chris held his wife, thinking that this might be the first time in seventeen years that Wendy had ever regretted her marriage to him.

Over the next three days, the crash slipped from lead story. When the weather cleared the NTSB dispatched helicopters and a coast guard vessel to search for bodies and debris.

The mood in the cottage varied from abrasive silence to panic. On some level Wendy blamed Chris for the upheaval of their lives, irrational as she knew that was. Because she had opposed Elixir from the beginning, the latest twist only served as proof that the project was a curse. For seven years Chris had chased Nature to her hiding place, and now they were stuck in these godforsaken woods, exiled from their old lives and the ordinary world. And it had happened at the peak of renewed joy for her. But she resolved that, no matter what, they would fight this, for she would not bring up her baby in hiding.

Chris spent the next few days listing lawyers' names from telephone directories and doing chores. He chopped and split wood. There was an old chainsaw in the cellar, but he feared the noise would draw attention.

Wendy, meanwhile, did the food shopping at a supermarket in Lake Placid. She wore a ski cap and sunglasses even though nobody would know her. But it struck her how even the most mundane chore was fraught with anxiety that somebody would look into her face and recognize an accessory to murder.

She paid for everything in cash which Chris had withdrawn from accounts before they left—over $17,000. They had been listed as dead, so Wendy began to think of herself as nonexistent—a woman with no credit cards, checks, social security number. Or name. It was almost funny. She was a blank of herself.

Luckily, there was plenty of clothing at the cottage. And the utilities had been paid through June by a trust fund, again untraceable. The propane tank was over half full. They could survive for several weeks if need be, though Chris promised to contact a lawyer by week's end, then turn themselves over to the police.

But that wouldn't happen. Thursday night after Adam was down, they watched the evening news. The lead story was the crash of Eastern flight 219 once again. But this time it was not Chris's photo on the screen but a family portrait, and not theirs.

". . . Relatives of the Foleys claimed that they were hoping to fly to Puerto Rico on standby. Authorities now believe that Thomas and Karen Foley had purchased their airline tickets for themselves and their young daughter, Tara, from Christopher Bacon."

The Foley family photo was replaced by that of Chris.

"According to authorities, security cameras captured Bacon talking to Foley and his wife. . . ." In jerky black-and-white Chris could be seen huddled with the Foleys, then disappearing into the crowd.

"Meanwhile, friends and relatives have not heard from the Foleys. Nor is there any trace of them in Puerto Rico, leaving investigators to conclude that they were aboard flight 219 to San Juan, and the Bacons were not.

"In a bizarre twist to the story, an all-points bulletin has been issued for Christopher Bacon and his author wife in the death of Betsy Watkins and now the more serious charge of sabotage. According to the NTSB, preliminary analyses of debris show evidence more consistent with a bomb than lightning. Quoting an unnamed spokesman from Darby Pharmaceuticals, the FBI said that Bacon not only had the expertise to construct such a bomb but had apparently stolen the necessary chemicals. . . ."

"Quentin!" Chris shouted. "He set us up."

Wendy let out a cry of despair. On the screen was a photo of Wendy and Chris from a Darby Christmas party two years ago.

"As for the whereabouts of the Bacons, police are not saying much about leads. However, the FBI has entered the case placing the Bacons on the Ten Most Wanted List . . ."

"My God," Chris said. "How much worse can it get?"

* * *

FEBRUARY 5
THE WHITE HOUSE

Ross Darby leaned toward the president. "Ron, he didn't do it. He wasn't the type."

"That's not what they're telling me at the Bureau. They're saying he planted a bomb to fake his own death."

Ross and the president were sitting alone in the Oval Office on facing sofas. Of all the visits he had made here over the years, this was the first time Ross did not feel the august thrill of history.

"I know what they're saying, but I also know this guy. I hired him. He's a dedicated scientist, not a mass murderer."

"Well, then, who did it?"

Ross felt a prickly sensation in the back of his neck. "I don't know."

"Well, they've got the best people looking for him."

"That's what I want to talk to you about," Ross said, and he described the Elixir project while Reagan listened intently.

Ronald Reagan tipped his head and smiled. "Boy, could I use some of that."

"So could the republic," Ross said. "Consider the

economic impact. Health care for the aging baby-boomers could bankrupt the government in twenty years. If we work out the bugs, Elixir could prevent that."

Reagan thought all that over. "How close are you?"

"Maybe a couple of years, but the problem is that he took it all with him. Cleaned us out of all the science and the compound itself."

"How come?"

"That's what I'm not yet sure about, but he's out there someplace with the secret of eternal youth."

Ross's guess was that Chris had acted on fears for his own life. What bothered Ross was Quentin. He was too anxious to pin the murder and sabotage on Chris. A man wanted for murder does not steal the world's hottest pharmaceutical secrets to set up shop elsewhere. First, he'd need unlimited resources to reproduce Elixir. Second, he'd be nabbed in no time since his face had been broadcast around the world. Besides, it wasn't in Chris's character.

Maybe Quentin's.

"Ron, I'm asking that you do what you can to bring him in alive. If you think your drug war is bad now, this would be Armageddon if the stuff fell into the wrong hands."

When they were finished, Reagan called Buck Clayman, FBI Director, and asked him to use every means necessary to bring in Christopher Bacon unharmed. It was a matter of national security.

"What does this mean for you?" Reagan asked. "Aren't you retiring next week?"

"I'm putting that off. He left us pretty high and dry with debts up to here."

The president walked Ross to the door. "Has this stuff been tried on people yet?"

"Not yet, but the effect on primates was incredible."

"Well," smiled the President, "I know a couple of higher primates who'd happily volunteer."

17

---•---

Every morning Quentin would drive his daughter to the Sunny Vale Day School about a half-mile out of Lincoln center. He would then proceed down Main Street which narrowed to a lovely tree-lined road that took him to Route 2 and Darby Pharms just off of the Lexington exit. This morning began no differently.

He had just dropped off Robyn when a school van closed on his rear, flashing its lights. In the mirror the driver waved him over. Quentin pulled into a clearing. Maybe Robyn had forgotten a book or something. Or maybe his rear tire was low.

The man came up to Quentin's door. He was wearing sunglasses and a parka.

"Is there a problem?" Quentin asked.

Without answering, the man swung the door open. Before Quentin knew it, two other men pulled him out of the car and hustled him into the van.

"What's going on? Who—who are you people?" They strapped him in place. "Where're you taking me?"

Nobody answered him.

The driver turned the radio to an oldies station. While the Bee Gees sang "I Started a Joke," Quentin peered out at Lincoln's Norman Rockwell–like center with its country store and white steepled church and red brick library—and he thought how this was the ideal little suburban town where nothing ever happened, and that this was the last time he would see it.

Quentin had never laid eyes on these men before, but he knew why they had been sent. He just didn't know how they'd do it. His only wish was to pass out or have a cardiac arrest first.

For half an hour they rode through back roads until the driver, talking into a radio phone, turned down an abandoned lane lined with dark evergreens. Soon the trees gave way to a frozen marshland. Quentin's eye fixed on a section of ice that had not frozen over, where reeds stood up. He thought about how cold that water was and what the ice looked like from underneath.

The door slid open and Quentin was pulled outside. He was cold and numb, hoping it would be quick. The men rubbed their hands and waited. The man with the sunglasses removed a pack of gum and thumbed out a stick for Quentin. A few chews of Juicy Fruit to make him feel better about being shot in the head and dumped into a frozen swamp.

Then from nowhere came a fluttery sound as a small helicopter dropped to a nearby clearing. The pilot Quentin didn't recognize. But the passenger was Vince Lucas in muffler phones. If they wanted him dead, they would have done it by now.

The cockpit door opened and Juicy Fruit rushed Quentin inside behind the pilot, then pulled beside him. A moment later they were over the treetops and heading full throttle toward Boston.

Quentin settled in place. He didn't know why, but he was going to be spared.

As they approached the spires, the pilot cut over the North End. But instead of tilting toward Logan, he pulled to a thousand feet over the bay to open water. After a spell, Vince poked the pilot who nodded and zipped up his jacket. Then Vince put his hand on Quentin's door latch and began to jiggle it.

My God! Quentin thought. They were going to push him out. Everybody was harnessed in but he. They were going to bank hard at the same time Vince would throw open the door so Juicy Fruit could push him out.

It all happened with such a blur that Quentin could barely process the final moments: The pilot's hand pressing the steering mechanism, Quentin's body suddenly shifting to the door, his hands grasping for something to block the fall, the bright blue sea rising up in his face, the sudden plunge that sent his organs up his throat, the sudden frigid blast. The long agonizing scream in a final expulsion of air . . .

The chopper landed with a thud.

Very little had registered in Quentin's mind: Not Vince double-checking the lock on Quentin's door, nor the pilot's protest about a Cessna appearing from nowhere and sending them into a sharp turn, nor the fact that they had landed on the heliport of an eighty-five foot ocean cruiser, nor the fact that he had wet himself. All that registered through Quentin's gasps was the face staring at him through the hatch that Vince had swung open.

Antoine Ducharme.

Ross knew very little about computers, including the fancy new system installed a year ago. When he wanted to check financial records, he turned to Quentin to whom Accounting and the Legal Department answered directly. But Quentin was out, so he called his secretary Sally to access the quarterly earning reports for the last two years on his own terminal. She wrote out the access codes and called up the files.

Ross scrolled through tables of numbers and spreadsheets. He took note of certain figures, particularly losses in accounts with foreign pharmaceutical houses. Because Sally might say something to Quentin, he went to Accounting to check backup files with Helen Goodfellow, a confidante whom Ross had hired long before Quentin married his daughter.

She was riffling through folders when she remembered something. "Actually, they're not here. Mr. Cross took them. He was working on those personally and had a deadline, so he just gave me the numbers and said it was okay to sign." She looked at the empty file slots. "I guess he forgot to return them."

"I see," Ross said. "Helen, I'd appreciate it if you didn't mention this to Quentin. He's got a lot on his mind right now."

"Certainly, Mr. Darby."

At 10:30 Ross dialed the number for Werner Ackermann, president of Alpha-Chemie in Geneva, Switzerland where the time was 4:30 in the afternoon. They had been associates for years.

Luckily Werner was in. Ross made small talk, then said, "Werner, I have a favor to ask. Our records are a little off." He explained something of the problem. "I'm wondering if you'd check the first- and second-quarter earnings last year and let me know what you have for a net loss on the R-and-D report." Twenty minutes later Werner called back with the requested figures. Werner asked if things were good, and Ross lied.

All project accounts were under Quentin's control. That may not have made good business sense since it left no checks and balances. But, after all, Quentin was family. What shocked Ross was that checks for over $3 million had been written to two corporations in the Caribbean: Global Partners Inc. in Grand Cayman and Fair Caribe, Ltd. in Apricot Cay.

"Either you're part cat, or that Elixir stuff's for real." Vince popped a wedge of honeydew melon into his mouth.

They were aboard Antoine's new yacht, a huge sleek craft named *Regine* after Antoine's mother. The interior was larger and more elegant than that of the late *Reef Madness*. But, like its predecessor, there were bookshelves stocked with mystery hardbacks. Quentin imagined Antoine moving from port to port making drug deals between P. D. James and Sue Grafton.

"They say he's hiding someplace," Antoine said. "Which means he has Elixir and the notebooks. Is that what you think?"

"Yes," Quentin said. "Absolutely."

Outside a cloud bank closed in from the west. There would be snow that evening. Quentin wondered where Antoine would sail to next. He was like a phantom, appearing and disappearing at will. He seemed to have unlimited power and resources.

"How long has he been working for you?"

"Fifteen years."

Antoine wore a forest-green fisherman's net sweater, but his face still sported a tropical tan. He leaned forward. "I am going to explain something to you in very simple terms, Quentin." The intensity in his eyes took Quentin back to that night when with the same heat of expression Antoine had held forth about loyalty and trust just moments before Marcel was hurled to his death. "Every man has one major mission in life—one that he dates the calendar from, understand? A turning point in the progression of his days—the point after which nothing will ever be the same again, and all things that came before are forever gone. Like birth and death, it happens only once. Do I make myself clear, Quentin? Do you understand?" Antoine's face had a rigid fixity. His eyes were like laser beams focussed to score the message on the back of his skull.

Quentin felt parched with fear. "Yes, I understand."

"A mission with no margin for error."

Quentin glanced at Vince Lucas, who stood against the windowed wall of the cabin dressed in black glasses and black leather, looking like the allegory of death from some medieval painting. "I understand."

"A mission whose stakes are beyond mortal. This is yours, Quentin Cross: To find out the names of this Doctor Christopher Bacon's intimates—friends, relatives, his wife's friends and relatives, where they go on vacation, what they do for hobbies and recreation—anything and everything and anybody that could lead us to him. Check your files, talk to your people. Do what you need to do to find him because everything you hold dear in life depends on it. *Comprende?*"

"Yes."

If the police weren't all over Jenny yet, they soon would be—interrogating her and Ted, tapping their telephone, reading their mail, tailing their every move.

From a call box in Lake Placid, Wendy phoned Ted's work number in Kalamazoo and made arrangements for Jenny to call her from a public phone as they had the other night.

It took nearly half an hour for Jenny to find a phone booth where she would not be noticed. When they finally connected, Wendy got right to the point: "I know what the news reports say, but it's all a setup," she explained.

"So, why don't you go to the police?" Jenny asked.

"Because we have no proof that Chris was out of town when Betsy Watkins was killed, nor that he didn't check a bomb on the plane." Security photos placed him in the crowd with a shoulder bag not shown in the shots with the Foleys. With Quentin's help, the media had already convicted Chris for murder and sabotage. "Jenny, we were meant to die in that explosion. It was meant for us, I'm telling you."

"That's awful! But who on earth would do that to you, and why?"

"I don't know. I don't know. Chris thinks it's his boss Quentin Cross and some criminal element he's tied up with."

"I don't believe it," Jenny said. "Why would he do

something like that? I mean, this is unbelievable."

"That's another story," Wendy said, wanting to deflect the subject, wanting not to yield to the panic that she heard in Jenny's own voice. "It's not worth getting into. But we need your help."

"The reports said something about stolen company property."

"That's not the issue."

But Jenny would not let go. "Well, did Chris steal something from them? That's what they're saying."

"Jenny, I'd rather not discuss that. Please, I need help, not an interrogation."

"Wendy, I'm on the other side of town in a different telephone booth from the last time. Nobody's in sight and nobody's listening in."

"That's not important—"

Jenny cut her off. "If you want us to help you, I'd like to know just what we're getting ourselves into. It's only fair."

Exasperation was beginning to fill Wendy's chest. But Jenny was persistent, and she had every right to be. "It's something to do with a secret new drug."

"But everybody knows about the cancer drug. It was on the national news months ago."

"Not that."

"Something else?"

"Yes."

"You mean you won't tell me."

"I'm sorry, Jen, but I promised Chris."

Wendy could hear Jenny's hurt mount in the silence of the open line as she wondered why she and Chris were putting company confidentiality ahead of family—especially when that company was out to destroy them.

All her life Wendy had tried to protect Jenny from pain because of her medical condition and her fragile state of mind, and because she was a bird with a broken wing who could not handle crises but whose life was a concatenation of crises—from a troubled childhood, to jilting lovers, to the death of her first husband, to her daughter Kelly's mental problems, to a second marriage to a man who verbally abused her. Not to confide in Jenny at the moment would simply confirm her suspicion that she was inferior or untrustworthy or incapable of handling critical matters.

Yet, ironically, Wendy was calling to ask for Jenny's help at the worst crisis in their lives. Still, she refused to explain the cause. And Wendy hated herself for it, but she had sworn to Chris not to make mention of Elixir.

"I don't like it, but we're going to hole up at the cottage, I'm not sure how long," Wendy said.

"So, I suppose you're asking for money." Wendy could hear the resentment in Jenny's voice.

"No, we have money. What we need are fake IDs—driver's licenses and social security cards." With them, they could get a post office box, open bank accounts, and apply for credit cards, even passports. "I'm just wondering if you could do that for us through Ted's contacts. We can pay whatever it costs. But we need them to survive."

Ted owned a car dealership, and years ago he had run into some trouble with the law for illegally selling cars overseas. She was hoping he still had contacts who could get them bogus credentials.

There was another long pause as Jenny let Wendy's request sink in. Finally she snapped. "I see—you're asking us to break all sorts of laws that could send us to prison for years, but you won't explain why. All because little sister can't keep a secret, right? Because she might blab to the neighbors or tell the police. But just call her out of the blue for fake IDs, and she's right there like an old dog ready to please."

"Jesus, Jen, it's not that at all," Wendy pleaded. "I hate this more than you know, but they're after us for mass murder. And there may be unknown killers gunning for us. We have nowhere else to turn, and you're my sister."

"Yeah, the same sister you can't bring yourself to trust."

Wendy couldn't believe how Jenny was twisting this around. "If I didn't trust you, I wouldn't be calling you, for God's sake."

"Then, for God's sake, what are you holding back? Unless he really did kill that woman and blow up the plane."

"Damn it, Jennifer, Chris is innocent! He's constitutionally incapable of murder, and so am I, period!"

After another moment of silence, Jenny said, "Well, you can understand my suspicions."

Wendy had scolded her like a child and she could hear the woundedness in Jenny's voice.

Clearly it was important for Jenny to know what her sought-after collusion was rooted in. Wendy looked around her, feeling her resolve crumble. She was at a callbox at a small strip mall just out of the center of Lake Placid. Cars and people were moving about their daily business. Nobody cared about her. Nobody eavesdropped. Nobody knew she was on the FBI's Top Ten List. And Jenny was right: Nobody had tapped these lines.

She just hoped that Chris would understand. In a low voice, she said, "It has to do with an anti-aging substance Chris discovered." While Jenny listened intently, she explained in the barest details, emphasizing the fact that its very success was the cause of all the bloodshed.

"And he took it with him?"

"Yes."

"It's at the cottage?"

"Yes."

"Oh my."

When Jenny seemed satisfied with the explanation she said she would talk to Ted.

"Thanks."

Before she hung up, Jenny had one final question: "Does it work on people?"

"It never got to that stage," Wendy said.

When she hung up, she felt drained and guilty. Yet, curiously, she experienced some relief at having told someone, of getting it out. It was like lancing a boil. She just prayed that her revelation would go no farther than Jenny. She had promised as much, but Jenny did have her spells.

Wendy walked up the street to a market to buy food and hair rinse. She moved down the aisles envying other customers who did their shopping without worrying about police photos. The simplest things in life were suddenly fraught with mortal terror. What kept her going was the illusion that it was all temporary—that life would return to normal so she could raise her son in the open. Jenny had suggested getting a lawyer. But that was risky. Even in the outchance they were exonerated in court, unknown killers were still after them. And living in a police-protection program would be worse than jail. Their only other option was to remain in hiding.

So, at forty-two, the mother of a newborn and the author of the forthcoming mystery novel *If I Should Die*, Wendy Whitehead Bacon bought herself a Cover Girl hair kit to bleach-strip away the first half of her life.

18

Quentin left the *Regine* filled with relief that he was still breathing—a realization that produced in him an odd sense of obligation to Antoine. By the time he pulled into his slot at Darby, he knew he would kill to find Chris Bacon and Elixir.

On his desk was the usual pile of work and call slips. He pushed that aside and on his computer he looked up personnel records on Chris Bacon—original letters of employment, transcripts from grad school, letters of recommendation—anything that would yield names of relatives, associates, and the like.

Because of all the sensitive records, Quentin had installed lock-check softwear that would signal if anybody tried to access his files, giving the password of the intruder. As he logged in, a box lit up on his monitor: UNAUTHORIZED ACCESS. Shocked, he tapped a few keys, and the screen lit up with ROBYN.

Ross's password. Startled, he tapped a few more codes.

Shit! Ross had called up files of financial transactions from last year. If he cross-referenced, he would discover payments to Antoine.

Quentin collected himself, then called in Sally.

"Yes, he wanted to look over some of the last year's

quarterly reports. So I gave him the access codes."

Quentin felt himself turn rigid. "I see."

"Will that be all, Mr. Cross?"

"Yes, thank you."

Sally left, and a few minutes later Quentin walked down the hall to Helen Goodfellow's office in accounting. "Helen, Ross came by earlier today for some files," he said, trying to maintain a tone of casual interest. "Do you recall which ones they were?"

Instantly she turned defensive. "Ross?" she said, pretending to rummage through her memory.

Quentin bore down on her. "Yes, Ross. Sometime this morning."

"Well, yes, I guess he did come by, now that you mention it," she said. "But, gosh, we handle so many files all day than I can't say which ones they were."

Helen, who was in her early sixties and not looking to retire for another five years, did not equivocate well. Her face had darkened as she was struggling to maintain her composure.

Meanwhile, in his mind, Quentin saw himself in the cabin of the *Regine* with Vince hanging over him like some carrion bird.

"Helen, the efficiency and operation of this office falls under my responsibility, including the handling of its files—which, I need not remind you, are very important and confidential. In turn it is your responsibility to be certain that such files are not casually passed about. Is that clear?"

"Certainly, Mr. Cross," she said, hearing the suggestion that she could be replaced by a younger woman with better recall.

She then moved to the cabinets and went through the motions of trying to determine which files had been removed. "Ah, yes," she said after a brief while. "I believe it was Alpha-Chemie."

Quentin was barely able to squeeze out a thank you. Ross knew.

Back at his desk, Quentin sat in numb realization, half expecting Ross to come storming in for an explanation. But that didn't happen. Ross had left early without dropping by.

An hour before closing, Sally came in to say that Ross had telephoned to ask that Quentin drop by his house that evening.

For the rest of the afternoon, Quentin attended paperwork and made calls, while in the back of his mind a notion took form. While it was still soft, he took and squeezed it like clay, kneading it, examining it from different angles, pressing here, poking there, molding it until by the time he left, the thing had shaped and hardened like a brick.

After the last employee had left, Quentin let himself into the restricted area of the storage room and into a vault accessible to only a handful of people. It was where they stored highly sensitive compounds such as cocaine, heroin, lysergic acid, and other psychotropic drugs—some in purities approaching 100 percent.

At the rear of one shelf he removed a small glass vial. He slipped it into his pocket and left.

Ross lived on prestigious Belmont Hill in a handsome brick garrison on two woodsy acres set back against tall oaks. It was the home he and his late wife had purchased when the company began to flourish some years ago.

Around nine o'clock, Quentin pulled up the long driveway. Ross watched him get out of the Mercedes, thinking how this would be the last time he would be dropping in like this. After tonight, all would be changed. Sadness undercut Ross's anger and disappointment. After Quentin's marriage to Margaret, Ross had come to look upon him as the son he never had. Yes, he had suffered from pie-in-the-sky ventures that had cost them dearly. But Quentin was bright and aggressive and capable of acting with prudence, Ross had told himself. Now he was a crook.

Ross met him at the door, unable even to feign a smile. He led him into the living room where a small fire burned. A bottle of scotch sat on the bar with a bucket of ice. Quentin helped himself. Ross sat by the fire with a brandy. Since his heart attack five years ago, he was restricted to one drink a night.

"Refill?" Quentin asked. Ross handed him his empty. Quentin's eye twitched. "Police say they're following leads. Wendy's got a sister in Michigan someplace."

Ross sipped his drink quietly.

"We're trying to reconstruct assays on the compound from old notes, except it's like trying to build a car from memory."

"That's not why I called you," Ross finally said. He got up and put another log on the fire. "I'm asking for your resignation, Quentin."

"My resignation? You've got to be joking."

"I'm not joking. I want you out by Friday."

"Why, for god's sake?"

Ross handed him printouts of downloaded files. "Over the last year you transferred 3 million dollars of earnings from overseas clients to corporate accounts in Caribbean banks—bogus outfits with nothing more than an account line. My guess is that you used the funds to pay off your drug pals from Apricot Cay. I'd like to believe it's not true, but the evidence is sitting in your lap." Ross looked down at him and simply asked, "Why?"

A long moment of silence filled the room as Quentin struggled to fabricate explanations. But he had none. Finally he cleared his throat and said in a soft voice of defeat, "They threatened to kill Robyn if I didn't pay."

"You could have come to me. We could have gone to the authorities. We could have done something. God Almighty, Quentin, you had options other than fraud and theft."

"You don't understand."

"No, I don't, because you violated everything that's important—your family, career, your future, your sense of self."

Quentin silently stared into the fire. There was nothing else to say. Next week Ross would begin an outside search for a replacement. Quentin stood up. "I'm sorry about this, Ross."

"You're sorry! Is that it? Is that all you have to say? No explanation why you embezzled money from your own family's company to pay off drug barons? A company I nearly killed myself to build? A company that was going to be handed to you, to build for your own child and grandchildren? Nothing more than a little 'sorry about this,' as if you'd spilled your drink?"

Quentin locked his eyes on Ross's and his face shifted as if something large and dark had passed behind it. "I guess not."

Ross sighed as if his heart were breaking.

Quentin started toward the door then stopped. "I'd appreciate it if you would not tell Margaret. It's my problem, and my job to tell her."

Ross nodded. He had not told her. Nor did he want to. It would be like delivering a death warrant. And he was already at the edge of despair. Seventy-four years old, at the threshold of retirement, and facing the biggest crisis of his life. "One more thing," Ross said. "They're saying that the plane was sabotaged. Do you know anything about that?"

Quentin slammed his glass down. "No, goddamn it! And you're not going to pin that on me, too."

"I'm not pinning it on you, but you've been dealing with the kind of people who don't think twice about killing others."

"Well, you're wrong, Ross. Dead wrong! That was your golden boy, and when the cops bring him in they'll fry his ass."

Quentin left and slammed the door behind him, leaving Ross standing there with tears in his eyes and feeling very old and tired and desperately missing his wife. He turned off the lights, and went upstairs and took a double dosage of Xanax to help him sleep. At his age, sleep was a reluctant friend.

He settled in bed and felt a warm mist fill the pockets of his brain, blotting out the last look on Quentin's face before he stormed out the door—a look that said he was lying.

Tubarine chloride is a salt derived from the curare plant found in humid tropics of South America. A woody shrub (*curarea toxicofera*), the plant's bark is used by the Jamandi Indians of Brazil and the Kofans of Ecuador and many other tribes as the chief ingredient in the poison of their blowgun arrows. Known simply as tubarine, the chloride is mixed with sterile water before being injected. An overdose causes respiratory failure, which begins with a heaviness of eyelids, difficulty in swallowing, paralysis of the extremities and the diaphragm, a crushing substernal pain, and ends in circulatory collapse, and death. The effect is immediate—within ten to twenty seconds—and the drug remains in the body only a brief time after expiration. Unless there is suspicion otherwise, death appears as a heart attack.

In his pocket Quentin carried a capped syringe containing five cubic centimeters of tubarine, enough to send a bull elephant into cardiac arrest.

He drove around replaying the meeting with Ross until he had worked up the necessary resolve. Then he headed back to Belmont Hill.

Ross's house was black. And being that it was a weekday, the street was dead with no traffic or midnight strollers.

Quentin pulled into the driveway and slipped on the surgical gloves. Because Ross had trouble sleeping, he had come to depend on Xanax. He also had drunk at least two glasses of brandy, making a dangerous combination.

Using Margaret's key, Quentin slipped in through the kitchen. The only sound was the hum of the refrigerator. Because the place was old, the floors creaked as he made his way to the front stairs. There he slipped off his shoes, then climbed, stopping with every step to listen. Nothing but the occasional creaks of the house settling. He was nervous but resolute. There were no options, he reminded himself.

"A mission with no margin for error."

"A mission whose stakes are beyond mortal."

Elixir was the one thing separating him, maybe even Robyn, from the grave. Something Ross could never appreciate.

The bedroom door was open, and the light of the clock radio cast a green glow on the hump of Ross's body. It would have to be quick and precise. Fortunately the upstairs had wall-to-wall carpet which allowed him to move with catlike stealth.

Ross lay on his back, the only comfortable position given his lower lumbar problems. From the fluttery sounds, he was in deep chemical sleep.

For a moment Quentin watched the man and cleared his mind of all but his resolve.

no margin for error

Quentin snapped on the light. Without waiting for a reaction, he spread open the lids of Ross's right eye and rammed the needle of the syringe high into the white of the eyeball above the iris, pressing the plunger all the way in.

By reflex Ross's head snapped to the side as he let out a hectoring cry. So as not to tear the eyeball or pop it out of its socket, Quentin let go, horrified at how the needle stuck in Ross's face and flopped as he screamed and convulsed. Ross's hands rose to grasp the syringe but froze in the air, paralyzed from the shocking pain.

Quentin threw himself full-body onto Ross, pinning

his arms and legs to the mattress. Ross continued to shriek as his face contorted in agony and his head flopped about with the needle still buried in his eyeball.

Die, goddamn it! Die! Quentin screamed in his head.

Tubarine was rated six out of six on the scale of toxicity. It was supposed to work within twenty to thirty seconds. Ross was supposed to experience total paralysis—total muscle depression. Instead, he was still struggling, his mouth moving, and his lungs still pressing out long hideous squeals.

Then he remembered the Xanax—alprazolam, a muscle relaxant like tubarine. Over the years, Ross had built up a tolerance intensified by the alcohol. *Christ!* This could go on forever.

To stop the awful cries, Quentin clamped one hand onto Ross's mouth and pulled the needle out with his other—only to find himself inches from his eyes, one huge and gaping, the other spurting ocular fluid. Through his gloved fingers he felt Ross groan. It was maddening. His muscles were supposed to be useless by now. Yet his legs still twitched and his pelvis rose in an obscene parody of sexual intercourse.

For what seemed an interminable spell, Quentin lay on top of Ross's body, until, at last, he felt it go into neuromuscular paralysis. His mouth slacked open and his upper torso relaxed, rendering his diaphragm useless and his lungs dead pockets of air. In reflex, Ross's head twitched to catch a final breath, then settled against the pillow, a final gasp rising from his throat—a corrupt miasma of brandy that passed into Quentin's own lungs.

As Quentin jerked himself off the body, the sudden release of pressure forced a plug of vomit to spasm out of Ross's throat and into Quentin's face.

Revolted, Quentin dashed to the toilet and scrubbed himself clean, fighting to contain the contents of his own stomach, aware that the stench was seeping into his clothes. He removed his shirt and lathered it until all traces of odor were gone.

When he reentered the bedroom Ross was staring directly at him, a thick pudding of vomit on his mouth. Quentin's heart froze as he expected Ross to rise up. But he was dead. Unmoving, unbreathing, unfeeling. His face blue.

Quentin wiped the liquid from Ross's offended eye which was red and swollen but which would shrink to normal by morning once the body fluids had settled. He then turned him onto his side to affect the sequence of events of a heart attack. Vomiting is a symptom, not the cause of death; by reflex a victim would try to keep his throat open. Given Ross's age and heart condition, Quentin was certain there would be no autopsy. The brandy glass in the sink and Xanax on the nighttable made the perfect scenario. Even if there were an autopsy, his body would manifest no visible signs that he died of anything other than natural and predictable causes. Which was why Quentin had targeted Ross's eye. The blood vessels would disseminate the substance throughout his system while the hole would be virtually invisible.

And in two days the obituary would read that Ross Darby had passed away at his home at the age of seventy-four, suffering a heart attack in his sleep, and leaving behind a grieving daughter, Margaret Darby Cross, and granddaughter Robyn, and son-in-law, Quentin W. Cross, who would assume the position of Chief Executive Officer of Darby Pharmaceuticals, Inc.

And God was in His heaven, and all's right with the world.

Quentin turned off the light and went home to bed.

19

By their third week, they had worked out a communications routine with Jenny. She would call every fourth night at a designated time from public phones in Kalamazoo to public phones around Lake Placid.

The good news was that Ted had made contact with a couple of street-wise guys who could get them phony licenses. It would cost two thousand dollars and they would need photos and signatures under new names. Jenny would drive out in a safe car to be swapped for Chris's rented van, which Ted would turn over to a chop shop. Before they hung up, Jenny mentioned that Wendy's book had been published to good reviews, and because of all the publicity it had made some local bestseller lists. "Too bad I'll miss the book tour," Wendy said grimly.

Four nights later Jenny arrived in a two-year-old Ford Explorer. In case she had been followed, Chris met her at a highway rest stop twenty miles away. When he was certain that nobody had tailed her, he led the way to the cottage.

Jenny had brought forms to sign and a Polaroid for IDs. In blackened hair and beard Chris would not be easily mistaken for the TV photos. And Wendy was now a blond and twenty-five pounds lighter than in her author photos.

Jenny had not been to the lodge for nearly fifteen years. Besides the remoteness, it was not her kind of place. Nor Ted's, whose idea of a getaway was Las Vegas.

"Better you than me," Jenny had said, looking around the old place.

"But we had some good times," Wendy reminded her, still amazed at the fact that Jenny had arranged for their new IDs and driven all the way out here by herself and undetected. Sometimes Jenny's reaction was so unpredictable that Wendy felt guilty for ever underestimating her. The element of danger seemed to have given Jenny new resolve. Perhaps new motherhood had created a greater sense of family, sharpening her protective instincts.

"Between the snow and mud, the bugs and mice, this place would drive me crazy. But," she added, "I supposed it's a good place to raise kids. They'd be far from all the rot out there. Unless, of course, you got one of those awful satellite dishes. Gosh, the stuff they're showing on television these days. No wonder kids are so screwed up."

Following dinner, they settled by the fire while Jenny showed them photographs. She had brought maybe two dozen—all of Abigail at Christmas dolled up a variety of different outfits and sitting among mountains of presents. "She's getting so big," Wendy said.

"Too big. Her babyhood is just flying by."

"How's Karen doing?" Chris asked.

"Karen? Who's Karen?"

"Your other daughter," he said, suddenly feeling a chill of embarrassment.

"Kelly."

"Kelly," he said, and slapped his forehead. "What's the matter with me?"

I'll tell you what's the matter, a voice inside whispered. *It's happening: Your brain is dying.*

Wendy shot him a look of concern. She knew what he was thinking.

Like how you forgot where you left the axe this morning, and how you have to make lists to remind you of things, and how you put the milk in the pantry and the cereal in the fridge the other day, and how simple head calculations you now have to do on paper, and those moments of disorientation when you step into the next room.

Wendy had said it was stress and anxiety, but he knew better. He could almost feel clusters of brain cells clot and die.

His eyes dropped to the photo of Abigail and thought how he would never see his son grow up. How he would never know Adam as a boy or young man. How in two years, if he were still alive, he would look at Adam and not know who he was from all the other alien faces in the world. Like Sam.

A particularly virulent form of Alzheimer's.

He'd rather die first than put Wendy and Adam through that.

"She's better, thank you," Jenny continued with an exaggerated singsongy voice that said she had nothing else to say about Kelly. "But would you believe it that in just five months Abigail will be two years old? I'm going to have a big party. Which reminds me." Without missing a beat, she pulled a bright red package from her bag. "Belated Merry Christmas."

Wendy unwrapped it and froze. It was a copy of *If I Should Die*. She studied the cover and dustjacket copy and photo. Then she put the book in a desk drawer and left the room without a word.

Perplexed, Jenny looked at Chris. "I didn't mean to upset her."

There was one thing Chris hadn't forgotten. March third. "Tomorrow was to be the publication party."

But the gaps in Jenny's thinking had less to do with pathology than thoughtlessness, Chris concluded.

"Oh, I forgot. Well, it's not like you'll be living in hiding forever. You're getting yourself a lawyer, right?"

Chris tried to shake his mind clear. "We're working on that."

For a moment they both stared into the fire which sputtered and flamed vigorously.

"So," Jenny said finally, "tell me about this Elixir stuff. Does it really work?"

Chris wished Wendy hadn't broken down and told her. "On lab animals it does."

"What does it actually do?"

"It appears to protect them from diseases associated with aging."

"Like what?"

Like Alzheimer's.

Like Alzheimer's.

Like Alzheimer's.

And he saw Methuselah whipping through complicated mazes as if wired.

"Arthritis, cancer, heart disease."

"Oh my, that's wonderful. And somebody thinks it's good enough for people." She rubbed a kink in her neck. "Frankly, I could use a little of that myself. Ted, too. He's pushing fifty."

Chris could hear Wendy upstairs in the baby's room. It was feeding time. He could also hear the ticking of the old grandfather clock in the corner. In a year he could be brain-dead.

"Is it possible to see what the fuss is all about?" Jenny asked. "The Elixir stuff?"

"There's really nothing to see."

"Christopher, I'm not going to tell anybody," she said with mock hurt.

Jenny had driven seven hundred miles with hot IDs for two fugitives at the top of the FBI's Most Wanted list, so he could not in good faith refuse her. "It's just that we've been walking a tightrope up here."

Jenny got up. "I understand perfectly. You're under a lot of stress."

Chris nodded. *Stress*.

He got up and led her downstairs to the wine closet. He unlocked it and pulled out one of the trunks. Two hundred and twelve ampules had been packed like glass bullets in styrofoam.

"Oh my," Jenny said. She removed one and held it up to the light. "And this can keep you alive indefinitely?"

"It it appears to have some such effects on monkeys." He played coy to discourage questions, but she was impervious. Being a former nurse, she wondered how they had figured out the proper dosages to give the animals. Chris explained it was trial and error until they determined that a fifteen pound monkey was could tolerate 10 milligrams.

"So, for a 150-pound man it would be ten times that, right?"

"I guess."

"So, how long could one of these keep a monkey going?"

"About ten years each."

"That much?"

"It's very concentrated, so it would have to be cut with saline. I'm getting cold," he said, and made a move to leave. The questions were making him uncomfortable. So was the pull of those ampules.

But Jenny disregarded him. "Is it just one shot and they go on and on?"

"More like once a month." He wanted to go back upstairs.

"And if they don't get their monthlies?"

"They die."

"I see." She held up the ampule. "Do you ever get tempted yourself?"

He felt the skin across his scalp prickle. "Nope."

He made a move to close the trunk when Wendy

called down from upstairs. He stepped outside the closet to hear her better. A moment later he stepped back in. "One order of zinfandel," he said.

"I second the motion," Jenny chortled, and stepped outside while Chris hunted for a bottle.

He went to secure the trunk, but Jenny had already done that. For a moment it puzzled him that she had taken such liberty. And he would have said something, but she was already on her way upstairs. Just like Jenny: driven by presumptions and tidiness.

Chris locked the door and headed up, thinking about how good the wine would taste. Maybe he'd have just half a glass. If his brain cells were dying, what the hell difference would a little wine make?

The next morning before she left, Chris asked Jenny if she would call the Rose Hill nursing home in Connecticut to check on Sam's condition. She agreed and he gave her the number and some instructions. A little after ten, Jenny drove off in the van. In her handbag she carried the photos of Wendy and Chris and sample signatures. Also, two ampules of Elixir.

On their eighteenth night, Chris drove to a call box outside a fire station in Rumford. The street was dark and deserted. A little after nine, Jenny's call came through. But after a few seconds he could tell something was wrong. Had the authorities cornered her? Did she and Ted fear they were getting in too deeply? Was it a money problem?

"Chris, I'm sorry. It's your father. He's dead."

"Oh no."

"I did just as you said: I identified myself as an assistant prosecutor from Massachusetts. . . ."

"When did it happen?" Chris asked.

"Ten days ago. They said his remains were cremated,

which was the home's policy when next of kin couldn't be located. I'm sorry, Chris."

He felt the grief well up in him, but he pushed it back. "Thank you, Jenny." He hung up and headed home, concentrating on driving under the speed limit.

He arrived at the cottage around eleven. Wendy and the baby were in bed. But he knew he would not be able to sleep. He knew he would have to confront the full force of his grief and guilt. So he sat on the couch and turned on the television.

One of the channels was playing *The Wild One* with a lean, young Marlon Brando swaggering about the screen in tight jeans and a hurt truculent look. Today he was a three-hundred-pound bald and wheezy mound of fat draped in black tunics to hide what time had done to him.

Chris watched the movie with the volume off. The only sound was that of the sleeting rain against the windows. With his glasses off, the picture was fuzzy. But that made no difference, because all he could see was Sam lying in his bed, a pathetic shriveled shadow of the man he had been, dying in an institution made up of hands and feet and mouths moving without sense.

Chris knew that Sam hadn't had long, that his organs would give out as he languished in a vegetative state. But what ate at Chris was that he had not had the chance to say goodbye. That life had turned so bizarre he could not even risk visiting his father one last time.

Blankly he stared at the TV and proceeded to drink a six-pack of beer, one can after the next—brain cells be damned—until his head was a throbbing mass and the geometry of the room took a non-Euclidian slant and the fuzz on the screen sharpened into shapes and forms that pulled him in.

Green. The black and white had turned a dazzling green. He was walking on a vast lawn between Sam and his mother Rose. They were at Campobello, Hyde Park, New York. He could see it with brilliant clarity—the great white house with the high windows. The massive white marble tombstone of FDR. Then he was rolling on the lawn and his seven-year-old legs were cool from the grass. He was wearing navy blue pants with black-and-white saddle shoes and a Brooklyn Dodgers baseball cap.

"Hey there, slugger!"

Then grass shifted and became a dirt diamond at Goodwin Park in Hartford, and Sam was at the pitcher's mound with a bucket of baseballs and Chris at the plate with his Louisville Slugger. Sam held up a clean white hardball. "What do you say we give this one a run for its money?" And Chris swung with all his might and cracked the ball up to the clouds.

The next moment Sam was climbing aboard the dive boat on a reef off Boroko on the southern coast of Papua New Guinea: his body still lean and bronze, joking about the giant grouper that had spooked him, handing Chris a triton shell. Chris held the shell up to his eye imagining he could see around the curves spiraling forever inward . . . until he was peering through a window of the nursing home where he spotted Sam in the bed. . . .

Chris climbed through the shell window thinking how odd it was that Sam was sleeping in his navy blue jumper shorts with a white polo shirt and socks and saddle shoes. But Sam's face was not tanned and full, but thin and dry and spotted with age. His hair was a wispy cloud across a sad pink skull. He breathed in short raspy starts through a raw toothless mouth. So that he wouldn't injure himself, Sam's hands had been bound to the sides of the bed. Chris untied one and pushed up the sleeve of his johnny. The arm, strapped with an IV needle, was like a stick covered with old wax paper. Sam looked like a mummy of himself.

"Dad? It's me, Chris."

Sam stirred but he didn't open his eyes. He didn't know Chris's name. He didn't know his own name. Chris removed the syringe from his pocket and inserted it into the IV and pushed the plunger.

It didn't take long. Sam's eyes opened. He looked confused and frightened and Chris's heart slumped. "Dad, it's me, Chris."

Sam nodded and closed his eyes. When he opened them again he smiled. "Hey, slugger, where you been?"

As if by magic, his face had tightened and smoothed out, his lips plumped up and skinned over, and his eyes lit up. From under the sheets he produced a bright new baseball. *"What do you say we give this thing a run for its money?"*

You betcha!

And Chris woke up.

His shirt was damp with sweat. His head thrummed painfully and his mouth was sour with beer. The television was still on: Young-buck Brando was mounting his chromed stallion.

Chris clicked off the TV, then stumbled into the bathroom and threw up. When he returned to the living room, his eyes fell on a framed photograph of Sam and Rose and Chris in box seats at a Washington Senators game. Chris must have been thirteen.

Suddenly Chris felt grief press up from the pit of his soul like a geyser. He grasped the photo and slipped to his knees to let it come. And it did. He collapsed onto the photo and dissolved into deep wracking sobs—the kind that came with no inhibitions, that rose up in black fury. Chris wept for his father. For his mother. For Wendy and Adam and himself. For the loss of it all. He wept until his eyes stung and his chest was no more than an aching hollow cavity.

"What do you say we give this thing a run for the money?"

Chris's breath stopped short. For an instant he felt totally sober.

No need to act surprised. It's been there all the time, a few layers beneath the skin of things. Like some strange organism with a life of its own, every so often sending up signs of life. Little fetal kicks and rolls, getting stronger by the day. What finally took a jab at old Dexter Quinn.

Chris pulled himself up. His legs felt wobbly like a newborn colt's. But he felt a sudden sense of purpose. Dexter was desperate, he told himself. He had had a bad heart and knew he would die soon. That was a one-shot thing. *But not me. Got flagons of the stuff—last a hundred lifetimes.*

Chris started to giggle but burped up a bubble of acid.

You're twisting things, buddy boy, another voice cut in. *Pulling out of the hat every rabbity reason for taking a leap off a cliff in the dark, hope against hope that you'll end up in the land of milk and honey. The problem is you're fucking drunk. That's right: Gassed, blotto, smashed and filled with guilt and grief up the yin-yang. You're like the guy who convinces himself he's got this special alcohol-resistant radar unit inside his skull that will lead him home in the rainstorm no matter what, but who slams into a tree only to spend the rest of his life in a coma, curled up like a shrimp.*

But another voice whispered, *"Hey, slugger, what do you say we give this thing a run for the money, Huh?"*

Don't want to end up like Dad, now, do we? he asked himself.

Uh-uh, no way!

But what if you miscalculate?

Impossible! He had worked out the dosages long ago.

And what if it doesn't work?

Iwati never lied. *". . . on the soul of Jesus."*

What about Wendy and Adam? What do you tell your wife?

That could be worked out, he reasoned. She could take it too.

And what if it works and forty years from now your kid wonders why you both look the same age?

Chris was in no mood for speculations. Forty years from now: He'd worry about that when they got there. This was *carpe* the *diem* while you still had some *diem* and brain cells left to guide your hand.

You're crazy drunk and reasoning through a point-eight blood alcohol level. You saw what happened to—

Suddenly his mind hit a void.

He balanced himself against the fireplace and stared into the dying embers, concentrating with all he had to remember the name of that old rhesus monkey. He could see the animal's face. He could see him jumping around the cage like a juvenile. How could this be? He had worked with the animal daily for months.

Jesus! Two syllables. Two bloody goddamn syllables. *Think.*

Simba. Rumba. Rambo. Jumbo. God Almighty! Help me remember that monkey's name.

It's the beer, he told himself. You're just drunk.

Bullshit! You know what's going on. Just an inch behind your hairline whole clusters of neurons are turning into gumballs. That's right, you're beginning your little bump down Alzy's Lane. Sure, it's bright up at this end, but watch the dark close around you as the rest of your brain sludges up so all that's left of Dr. Christopher Bacon is something connected to a catheter.

He shook his head and the fugue gratefully ceased. Silence.

He stared into the dying hearth for a long moment.

Then a little bright node sphinctered open at the core of Chris's consciousness, and moving on some crazy autopilot he followed it out of the bathroom and through the living room, stopping once to remove the small black pouch from the desk drawer, then proceeding down the hall to the cellar door which he opened, and then he flicked the light switch and quietly walked down the stairs, feeling the musty chill of the cellar air and the hard concrete floor that led toward the thick oak door with the large steel lock whose combination Chris couldn't recite but which his fingers knew, spinning through the right-left turns until the tumblers made that gratifying click that let the door swing open so he could grasp the pull chain of the overhead light which lit up what to the untrained eye was a wall of wine bottles behind which sat two trunks that opened with the keys around his neck.

For a long spell he stared at the rows of clear glass ampules—212, each capable of sustaining a 170-pound man for three years.

Two ampules were missing.

That couldn't be. Maybe he had miscounted when he packed them. God knows that was possible given the condition of his mind. But at the moment he could not have cared less.

He opened the pouch and removed the alcohol pads and syringe.

"Hey, slugger, what do you say?"

His mind dipped as he thought of Wendy upstairs asleep, Adam beside her. But he snipped off those thoughts.

For old time's sake, huh? You, me, and one-point-eight ccs.

Home run, Chris thought, and shot up.

He felt nothing.

Even if there were initial effects, his senses had to compete with seventy-two ounces of beer. Besides, the lab animals did not display any effects until the fourth day. So he staggered up to bed and slept a dreamless sleep until eight the next morning when he woke to a fifty-megaton hangover.

Wendy was downstairs with the baby. He could smell coffee and toast. With his head thudding painfully, he got up and took a shower and passed the day trying to detect any effects from the drug. There were none.

None but the anxiety that gripped him like claws mid-morning when he realized what he had done. There was no turning back. The substance was in his system seeking a stabilizing level which he would have to maintain or risk deterioration. After two short weeks of treatment, withdrawn mice showed aging signs beyond their time. After three weeks, their steps shortened and they died prematurely.

The stuff had immediate genetic effect. He was already dependent. Worse, he would have to tell Wendy because soon he would manifest effects that he could not predict.

Over the next few days he had momentary panic attacks. Yet, on some level, he felt a perverse relief that all other options had been eliminated. He never let on to Wendy and filled his time with chores. Meanwhile, Jenny had come up with the names of three dead people from the Midwest whose social security numbers Ted was having transferred to bogus licenses and other IDs.

On the sixth day, Chris started to wonder if Elixir was working because he still couldn't detect a reaction. On the seventh day it hit like a storm.

He was alone in the attic fixing a leak, when he felt a strange buzzing sensation in his head, as if a hornet were trapped in his skull. Rapidly the hum seemed to light up the frontal lobe of his brain with a strange alertness.

He steadied himself against a beam to gauge the effects. His heart pounded and his arms tingled. Rapidly a sensation of lightness filled his body as if he had undergone a transfusion of helium.

He took off his glasses, feeling a craving for air. As he moved to a vent window, a giddy sensation rippled through his genitals and loins. Suddenly he wanted to move, to go outside and run, leap, jump—anything to release the energy percolating throughout his system. He pushed open the vent and sucked in the cold mountain air.

The view was splendid—the frozen lake, fringed with high dark pines, and in the distance the mountain range with a bank of brooding clouds. A deer was at the lake's edge where the ice made a window.

As he watched the animal drink, it occurred to him how sharply focused the scene was. Everything stood out in stereoscopic clarity. It was shocking because his glasses were dangling from his neck. "My God!" he whispered.

Every day since ninth grade he had worn glasses. Twenty-eight years of nearsightedness that grew worse with age. Not only was the lake in perfect clarity, but the mountain range, too—as if he were peering through binoculars. He turned around and the attic interior was sharp even in the dim light. It was almost magical. He slipped his glasses on, and everything turned blurry.

His muscles hummed to move, so he bounded downstairs. Wendy was fixing a toaster oven, and Adam sat in his car seat babbling. Chris slipped on his pullover and said that he wanted to get some air. Wendy had no immediate chores for him, so he left.

The temperature was 28 degrees, but he felt hot. With his watch cap pulled low he broke into a stiff run. For four miles his legs pistoned him powerfully to the main road. He stopped barely winded and humming to run more. It was astounding. Like old Jimbo running around the open pen.

Jimbo. The name popped up as soon as he went for it.

That was another thing: His mind felt acute and strong. No holes or shadows.

He ran back to the cottage. While Wendy was preparing dinner, he went out back and chopped more wood. After several minutes she came out with a cup of coffee. "You doing your Paul Bunyan impression?"

"Mountain air. Nothing like it," he chuckled. He took

the coffee, thinking that it was Wendy's first gesture of reconciliation since they had arrived a month ago. He wondered how long before she finally forgave him, if ever.

"How much more do you plan to do?"

"Another half hour, why?"

"Just didn't want to see you wear yourself out." A small firelight flickered in her eyes. Something he hadn't seen for weeks. She smiled. "I was hoping you'd save a little for me."

"Tell me you don't mean moving a bureau."

"No, but take a shower first." She took his hand and they went into the house.

Chris showered, and when he came out Wendy was naked in bed and under the covers. A fire was burning in the bedroom fireplace.

Chris lay beside her. "It's been so long. Is it still done the same way?"

"Let's see if we can remember."

They did.

When it was over, they lay still and listened to the fire cracking in the hearth. In a few minutes, Chris brushed his lips against hers. "I love you, Wendy."

"Thanks," she said.

"Thanks?"

"I love you, too."

For a second he thought he would cry, having resigned himself to living their lives at prickly odds, their love hardening to anger and hurt. But he didn't cry. Instead, he kissed her mouth and slipped down to her breasts. He then kissed a long slow line down her body until he was nestled between her thighs, moving his mouth over her pubis until she was arching herself against his face and groaning deeply again. He slid up and entered her again, feeling another full surge of passion.

"What's gotten into you?" But she closed her eyes and groaned in pleasure, not really expecting an answer.

Fires of spring, Chris thought and slipped his hands under her, raising her bottom until he was deeply engaged and moving in slow deliberate cadence again. Wendy closed her arms around him and they moved in unison until they came together for the second time.

Chris rolled onto his back. For long slow minutes they lay embraced, the only sound being their own breathing and the fire. They dozed off for a few minutes until a log cracked.

Wendy yawned and stretched, her warm breasts falling against his chest, one leg innocently entwining his. Chris felt himself stir again, and before he knew it he was fully erect under the blanket.

"That was nice," she whispered.

"Was?" and he pulled her onto him.

"You've got to be kidding." She reached down and felt him. "I don't believe it. You get a battery implant or something?"

Chris grinned. "Love-starved."

"It's only been a three weeks."

"Three weeks, four days, and two hours," he said. "But who counts?"

"Thank God it wasn't three months."

Had Adam not wakened, Chris would have gone a third round.

20

He didn't like the idea of Wendy going alone. But after six weeks cooped up in the cottage she jumped at the opportunity to get away. Jenny had called to say their IDs were ready, and Wendy would pick them up in person in Detroit.

Because Jenny and Ted were under FBI surveillance, they couldn't travel. And Wendy looked less like her media photos than Chris did his. At the Detroit bus terminal she would retrieve the material from a locker put there by a trusted employee of Ted's. They had worked out the plans in detail. Nonetheless, Chris was worried. It was the first time they would be apart.

On a Wednesday morning, with Adam in his car seat, Chris dropped Wendy off at the station in Lake Placid.

"I hope you guys will be all right," she said. She held Chris's hand tightly and cuddled the baby.

Chris kissed her. "We'll be fine," he said. "We've got so much wood to chop, you'll be back before we know it."

Wendy gave Adam a dozen kisses. "I'll call from Detroit." She brushed back the hair from Chris's forehead and studied his face. "You look good, by the way. Your skin is nice and smooth, and your eyes are clear. Must be all that exercise."

Chris gave her a lecherous grin. "Just what you give me lying down, pussycat."

She chuckled lightly. "That's another reason I'm going—just to recover."

Chris watched her go into the station. He waited in the car while she purchased her ticket. Already, he was missing her.

As the bus filled up, he glanced in the mirror. She was right: He did look better, although Wendy hadn't picked up half of what he saw. The crowfeet tracks around his eyes had begun to fade. Incipient liver spots on the back of his right hand had disappeared. His hair was thicker. And it wasn't all the wood-chopping—his body had hardened into that of an athlete ten years his junior. His deltoids bulged and his forearms looked like small hams—nothing wielding an axe would do. In fact, the changes were almost frightening. Like some kind of *Twilight Zone* experience—looking into a mirror with a yesteryear reflection staring back.

Even more remarkable were the interior changes. He felt more agile, stronger, and, yes, more sexual. In a word, *younger*. And, most important, he could swear that his mind was sharper—that his recall and memory had improved. He'd even bet that his IQ was higher. His only wish was that he could share it with Wendy. But the time was not yet right. When they settled down someplace safe in their new identities.

The long bus rolled out of its bay onto the street. Wendy was at a window waving at them. Chris waved back and uttered a silent prayer. *God, send her safely back to me.*

Later that day Wendy called to say she had made it safely to Detroit and would meet him Friday night at the station.

The two days passed and Chris took care of Adam and did more chores.

He also took his second shot. It still puzzled him that

two ampules appeared to be missing. His only explanation was that he had miscounted that night at Darby.

" *'Frere Jacques, Frere Jacques, dormez vous? Dormez vous . . . ?'* "

Jenny changed Abigail's diaper while she sang to the music box. The silver metal plinkings filled the air like bubbles.

"That's French, and someday I'll teach you, but for now we'll do it in English. 'Brother John, Brother John . . .'" She held a foot in each hand and danced them in the air as she sang and her daughter wiggled and giggled. " 'Ding, ding, dong.' Can you say that, 'Ding, ding, dong?' "

"Donk, donk."

"That's it, that's it," Jenny laughed.

It was the only moment of peace the whole evening. Before Ted stomped out of the house for his card game with the boys, they had had a big fight. He didn't like how much they had gotten themselves involved with her fugitive sister and her husband. "Their faces are all over the networks," he had shouted.

"She's my sister."

"I don't care if she's the Virgin Mary. If they find out we helped them, they'll put us away for twenty fucking years."

She hated him when he got loud and vulgar. She hated how his face contorted and turned red, and the filthy language that flowed out of his mouth like raw sewage. "Will you please lower your voice? The baby can hear you."

"The baby, the baby. Is that all you think of? We supplied bogus IDs to the most wanted criminals in the fucking country, and you're worried about the baby waking up. Jesus!" He jabbed a finger at his forehead. "Sometimes I think you're not all there."

Jenny deflected that. "Well, it's not the first time you've done something outside the law."

They both knew what she was talking about. In the late seventies, the Internal Revenue Service had caught Ted for tax evasion and sentenced him to three years in prison. Jenny also suspected that he had something to do with a car-theft ring that exported stolen luxury vehicles to Europe and the Middle East.

"You bitch. You just don't let go, do you? The dog shits once, and you just keep rubbing his nose in it."

"Will you *please* stop swearing. She'll hear you."

"Jesus!" he shouted in frustration. "Now I know why that kid of yours is such a flako." He grabbed his keys and left the house, slamming the door behind him.

She heard him drive off, thinking how for years Wendy had complained that Chris was never home. How Jenny envied her that. She loved it when Ted was gone. He knew nothing about the sensitivity of children—how impressionable they were. That was the problem with men. They created a vulgar and dangerous world unfit for the babies they sired.

Jenny ran upstairs. All the shouting had aroused Abigail. "Don't cry, my little angel, don't cry," she cooed, as she took her in her arms. "Daddy's been bad, but he's gone now. And Mommy's right here."

Jenny dimmed the light and sat in the rocking chair while the music box tinkled softly in the background.

"Don't cry, my little beauty, don't cry. Mommy's going to be your mommy for a long long time," she said, and her eyes fell on the two glass vials sitting on the nightstand.

On schedule, Wendy called Friday morning to say that she had a complete set of new ID's—licenses, birth certificates, and social security cards. Their names were Roger and Laura Glover, and their son was Brett.

He liked the names but couldn't process the fact that

when she returned they would no longer be known as Christopher, Wendy, and Adam Bacon. It was too much to hold onto.

In fact, Chris's mind was having problems holding much of anything. His metabolism had kicked into turbo. It was like being on amphetamines nonstop. He could not focus. Were it not for Adam, he would have gone for a long burning run. Instead, he put the baby down and made a mental note that there were three things he had to do that night—three MUST-DOs: Check up on Adam. Pick up Wendy. Take his next Elixir injection.

If another treatment made him even more hyper, he'd take some Xanax—what Ross Darby once recommended for insomnia.

He shot out back to the pile of tree trunks. The night was clear and frigid, the sky pinpricked with a million stars. Low on the horizon of trees rose a fat white moon. Over the last week he had moved to the chainsaw. The sound traveled, but there were too few winter residents about to take notice. Besides, he got a lot more wood cut. It was also much more exciting. He pulled the cord, and the saw growled into action.

In the light from the deck he worked the saw, cutting logs until he had a huge pile. He did that for an hour until his hands felt fused to the machine—as if the muscles of his arms had grown over the grips and up the blade of the rotor, its high-whining barbs powered by the heat of his own blood and blotting out all awareness but the raw pleasure of grinding through the timbers and spitting up dust and smoke and filling his head with a gratifying roar.

He chainsawed until he ran out of gas, then refilled it and continued cutting, knowing in the back of his mind that he had passed into some crazed auto-mode.

Someplace deep down a voice whispered of things he couldn't forget—*three* of them.

Adam.

He snapped off the saw and bolted back into the

house. The baby was in a deep sleep still. "Good," he whispered, and shot outside again.

A flick of his arm, and the chain screamed into action, and he cut until the motor choked out again.

You're forgetting something

Adam's fine, he told himself. So he refilled the tank and pulled the cord to action.

Something else. Wendy. Pick up Wendy . . . Where, though? Where was Wendy?

Bus station.

Lake Placid.

The thoughts came to him in little periodic bursts. Bursts that were getting farther apart. *Lake Placid.* Plenty of time.

time

What time?

He put the saw down still idling and ran into the house and checked Adam. His eyes passed by the clock, but nothing registered. Not the fact that it was 9:45 and he was supposed to be on the road by now.

Back outside he revved the saw then screamed through another ten-foot trunk of oak until he had neat fat logs in a pile.

forgot something else

time

Adam

something else

He turned it off the chain saw and looked around as if expecting somebody to step up with a cue card. He walked toward the lake. The surface was a brilliant sheet dusted with diamonds. It was a magical scene, and for a long moment he just stood by the banks taking it all in, his head still buzzing from the saw.

Without thinking he plopped onto the ground. He was sweating profusely, his shirt icy against his skin. He rubbed the cold metal band of his watch. In the moonlight he noticed the small hand on the eleven, the long one on the three. But it didn't register because he felt faint.

He got up hoping that movement would help. Guided by the moonlight, he began walking but instead of heading toward the house he moved into the woods without thought. Deeper into the thick he stumbled until he was totally disoriented and feeling fainter, driven onward in hope of remembering just what he had forgotten to do.

Wendy.

He braced himself on a tree. "Where's Wendy?" he said out loud.

Coming home

"Have to get Wendy. Almost forgot."

You forgot something else

He turned and saw the moonlight through the trees and he felt his body jolt.

"It was horrible. He just shriveled up like that."

"Oh, God, no. Nooooo . . ."

He stumbled toward the moon, thinking it was the warm bright lights of home, with Wendy inside and Mom and Dad and baby Adam all by the fire. And a big bed.

and in the big bed was . . .

gotta get back before it's too late.

not enough time.

gotta take my shot.

no, not the insulin

ELIXIR

ELIXIR

He saw the bed, open and clean white glistening sheets so wide and smooth. . . . I want to go home. Not feeling good. Body sore. Hurts me.

me hurt

He flopped on the bed and spit out a tooth. The tip of his tongue found the gaping hole. He put his finger inside and felt another wiggle. His teeth were breaking off in jagged pieces. It was horrible. They filled his mouth and he spit them out.

His head ached. He pulled off his gloves and ran his fingers across the scalp. Large clumps of hair came off in his hands. His head felt cold. He was going bald by the second.

In the moonlight he saw his hands.

His hands, they screamed with pain, and before his eyes they shrivelled up to small knobbed things. He brought one to his face. It had gotten tiny and dark. His fingers hurt, but he barely felt the pain. His face felt totally unfamiliar. It was full and flabby, the creases too deep, the flesh under the chin too loose, the neck too thin. It was like touching somebody else's face. And his head all smooth with thin fuzz in the back.

Then the pain erupted. And he suddenly saw himself from above, lying on the bed of snow in a clearing, his body convulsing with agony as he began to shrivel up and die—like Methuselah and Jimbo—

Like Dexter Quinn—

Like Sam—

But then the pain stopped and he felt his mind slow down as if under rapidly dimming power—a thing old and weary and barely able to process the few sad moments left, wishing it would get itself over with, wishing he could for one last time see his wife (*don't let her find me like this*), sensing himself going down a long spiral stairwell, not bumping his way step by step but moving smoothly because he couldn't walk since his feet were all gnarled and twisted which explained why he was slouched up in a big metal chair with wheels on the side locked in place and on this special escalator that corkscrewed down toward a small ball of white light at the bottom that grew larger and brighter as he descended, his poor eyes fixed in horrid fascination on the glow which in no time became a dreamy white light, not hard or harsh, but like fog lit up from within—a warm incandescent blankness that closed around him like a shell, the interior growing dimmer and quieter until all he registered was the soft raspy sigh of his last breath before the long long night closed down on him.

Three

But at my back I always hear
Time's winged chariot hurrying near;
And yonder all before us lie
Deserts of vast eternity.

—Andrew Marvell, "To His Coy Mistress"

21

THE PRESENT
DEVIL'S LAKE, WISCONSIN

The kid with the blond ponytail under his cap was good.

He was from Pierson Prep where they had an experienced team and a dedicated coach who trained his wrestlers as if they were heading for the Olympics.

Wally Olafsson had watched the kid's last match earlier that afternoon. He had pinned the captain of Appleton Tech in a mere thirty-nine seconds. He wasn't too tall, but he was well-built, fast, and balanced. Worse, he knew some fancy moves Wally's son, Todd, hadn't experienced before, including a cunning reverse cradle. Unfortunately, Todd was facing the kid for first-place finals in the 135-pound weight class for the region. If Todd won, he'd go home with a two-foot-high trophy. If he lost, he'd take second and a fourteen-incher.

It was after seven, and the gym was packed with wrestlers and spectators filling the stands and pressed five deep around the three mats where the matches had been running continuously since ten that Saturday morning. Parents with cameras were squatting on the edges, hooting and hollering for their boys.

Wally sat high in the stands so he could get an overhead zoom of Todd through the video cam.

All around him were wrestlers—young hardbodied

Zeuses smelling of Gatorade and testosterone. The heat of their presence took him back to his own high school days when he played varsity baseball at Buckley High in Urbana. Now he was fat, bald, and grossly out of shape. His joints cried out just watching the boys twist each other into crullers. Yet, there was a time when he, too, was lean and made of hard rubber. But, sadly, at fifty-seven, Wally Olafsson had decided that he was beyond physical fitness and had settled into middle age ripeness. George Bernard Shaw was right: Youth is a wonderful thing; too bad it's wasted on the young.

Because Marge had moved to the other side of the state with Todd after their divorce, Wally saw his son wrestle only at these weekend tournaments. And this was the biggest—a three-state regional. Wally could barely steady the camera as Todd faced off with the kid in the green Pierson tights. First place would mean everything to Todd.

The ref blew the whistle, and instantly the Pierson kid dropped to a predatory crouch, dancing to keep Todd at bay. It was the same strategy he had used in his last match—start low, jig a few seconds, then springing to take his opponent off guard and pulling him down like a cheetah on a gazelle.

Tiring of the sparring, Todd made a move to get the kid in a headlock. But he missed. And the Pierson boy flew up, catching Todd around the shoulders and pulling him down on his back with a hard thud. In a reflexive squirm, Todd rolled onto the kid's back which through the viewfinder seemed like a smart move but proved fatal—a ploy the Pierson kid had used on his last opponent. In a lightning flash, he whipped his right arm around Todd's neck, turned 90 degrees to his body, and pressed his back to Todd's front, brilliantly arching him into a reverse cradle. The ref dropped to the floor, and a moment later smacked the mat with the flat of his hand. It was over. Todd had been pinned in fifty-seven seconds.

Instantly, the Pierson crowd exploded and jumped in place. Wally's heart sank as he zoomed in. The disappointment on Todd's face was palpable. He shook hands with the Pierson kid who pulled off his cap and waved at the crowd.

In the split instant as the kid turned full-face into the camera, something jagged through Wally's consciousness. It was too fast for him to process the experience—like trying to recompose a television image after the set had been turned off. But something tripped his mind.

He climbed down from the stand and cut through the crowd, hoping to console Todd who sat on the bench with his head in his hands. He muttered a few words of consolation, but Todd wanted to repair on his own.

The big green Pierson team was on the far side of the gym. Although Wally was toxic with resentment, he decided to congratulate the winner. He also wanted to dispel something he had picked up through the viewfinder.

He cut behind the gallery until he spotted the blond ponytail, then aimed the camera. The kid was taking slaps and high fives from teammates. Wally thumbed the zoom button until he had a tight shot on the kid's face. He was handsome, with a tight muscular jaw, finely etched features, a thin straight nose, high forehead. Somebody put his arms around him in a bear hug, and Wally froze.

The man in the blue sweatsuit and baseball cap was clearly the kid's father—the same build and facial structure. What stopped Wally's breath was not the strong resemblance to his son but to somebody else . . . the guy who lived upstairs from him at Harvard back in 1970.

Christopher Bacon.

A thrill of recognition shot through him. The last he had heard, Chris had taken a job at some chemical lab around Boston. He must have relocated.

Wally cut through the crowd for a closer look. The man turned. Except for the dark beard and long hair, it was Chris Bacon.

Sweet Jesus, the guy had kept himself in good shape. Through the zoom, he pulled the man in all the way and hit the record button.

If it was Chris, he must have had some plastic surgery—lots of guys did these days—because he didn't look any older than he did in grad school when Chris was doing a post-doc in biochem, and Wally, a doctorate in economics. They had both been freshman proctors at Pennypacker House, Chris on the second floor—a corner room, and the center of all-night bull sessions.

In a flash, Wally was back in Cambridge: in that room, at the Wursthaus in the Square, clinking glasses (and under the warm glow of the alcohol swearing "Friends for life!"), partying at tight Garden Street apartments, protesting Dow Chemical recruiters on campus, storming Harvard Square over Nixon's carpet-bombing of Hanoi, getting maced by Cambridge cops after Kent State, Harvard-BU hockey games, double dating at the Orson Welles Cinema, and the *King of Hearts* marathon in Central Square. . . . (What was his girl's name? Brenda . . . ? Wanda . . . ? No . . . Wendy. That was it: *Wendy*.)

As Wally peered through the zoom, it all rushed back as if he were looking at a kinescope through a time warp.

While he told himself that the guy just looked like a young Chris Bacon, that he was somebody else completely, Wally felt himself flush with emotions, as if trying to hold onto a make-believe moment—not wanting the guy in the viewfinder to be anyone other than Chris Bacon of 1970. It was irrational and pathetic, but for one shimmering moment Wally slipped through the lens to a greener day.

A buzzer went off, and he was back in the gym.

He moved to the wall where the elimination matches were posted. On the 135 weight-class sheet, Todd's final opponent was listed: BRETT GLOVER, Pierson Prep.

Glover, not Bacon.

Wally's heart sank. *Not Chris Bacon, but, God, what a resemblance!*

He made his way to the knot of green uniforms. "Great job out there."

The Glover boy thanked him.

At the same time, the boy's father glanced over his shoulder. And Wally's mind jogged in reflex. *Chris Bacon*!

"That was my son he just pinned." His held out his hand. "Wally Olafsson. By the way, you look very familiar."

"Roger Glover," he said. "I don't believe we've met before." But something flitted across his eyes.

"You didn't, by any chance, do a post-doc at Harvard, did you?"

"Nope."

". . . or date a girl named Wendy?"

"Sorry, wrong guy." Glover made a move to get away.

Too young—tight smooth face, no wrinkles, no eye pouches, no paunch overhanging his belt, no thinning hair or receding forehead. None of the assaults of time and gravity that made Wally look his fifty-seven years.

But Mother of God! It was uncanny—like looking through a tear in the time-space continuum.

The wrong guy, Wally told himself.

(Those eyes. Something about those eyes.)

wrong guy

coincidence

"Guess not." Wally apologized. "Your son knows some good moves. Hell of a wrestler. Congratulations." He mumbled, feeling foolish.

Glover nodded and turned his back.

But Wally was transfixed, his mind still stuck on details long forgotten. Like stumbling on your first Little League glove decades later, amazing how it all comes back—the leathery smell, the way the shiny rawhide ends curled, the company logo magically incised on the wrist strap, your name proudly lettered in ballpoint. Little lost oddities that rush into place at first glimpse. The same with faces. The set of the mouth, the widow's peak, the way the nostrils flare, the slightly asymmetrical eyebrows.

Coincidence, he told himself.

(The eyes.)

Just a resemblance.

As Glover moved off with his son, Wally could not suppress a dumb impulse. "Hey, Chris!" he shouted.

The man did not flinch or even peer over his shoulder.

A childish test, and the guy had passed, leaving Wally wondering what he would have done had the man looked back.

Imperfect memory, Wally told himself, *born out of nostalgia and an aging mind. And I made a thundering asshole out of myself to boot*.

Later that evening after he had driven Todd back to his mother's place and returned home, Wally lay in bed and replayed the encounter over in his head, fixing as best he could the look that flitted across Roger Glover's eyes at the moment he saw Wally.

Yes, it was fast and nearly imperceptible, but for one split instant Wally would have sworn that what he saw in Roger Glover's eyes was recognition.

"He recognized me."

"How do you know?"

"I introduced myself as Roger Glover, but he called me Chris as I walked away. He didn't believe me."

Laura's expression froze. "What did you do?"

"Nothing. I kept walking."

"Then he'll conclude it's a case of mistaken identity."

"Let's hope."

They had considered plastic surgery, but back then his face was too recognizable to risk walking into a surgeon's office. Nor could he leave the country with their photographs at every immigration checkpoint. So he had dyed his hair, grown a beard, and wore tinted contact lenses which combined with the initial rejuvenation created a sufficient cover until Brett reached the age to ask questions. By then they had moved to Eau Claire where nobody knew their faces. Chris kept the beard and hair, but put away the tinted contacts.

What Chris had not counted on was stumbling into somebody from his deep past. And, yet, it was a possibility that had sat in the back of their minds for thirteen years.

He stood at the mirror touching up his beard and sideburns with whitening makeup. Laura was in her nightgown ready for bed, her face glistening with her nightly cold cream. "Besides, you look half your age even with the gray."

"That's what bothers me." In college his hair was sandy, not black, and he didn't have a beard.

"Honey, it's been thirty years. I can barely remember what my roommate looked like from college, let alone some guy downstairs," Laura said. "Christopher Bacon is dead, so is Wendy."

After thirteen years that was the virtual truth.

All they had wanted was to become normal people again—to blend into the scenery, to remake themselves so nobody thought twice. So, early on they had engaged in regular psychodramas, playing out the deaths of their former selves until they were nearly convinced they had always been the Glovers. For hours on end, day after day, they recited their new names, dates of birth, and social security numbers like mantras, writing them out until they were second nature. They always addressed themselves as Roger and Laura, resorting to sneak tests until they had conditioned away all the old reflexes. They even took trips to Wichita and Duluth to visit the neighborhoods and schools of Roger and Laura. It was difficult, but like immigrants desperate to learn English, they eventually strip-mined their old identities until they fell for the artifice.

"I know that. But Wally Olafsson doesn't," Roger said. "I look more like I did in 1970 than 1988."

Silence filled the room as they considered the risks.

"I'm not about to drop our lives and go into hiding again," she said. "I'll stop him first if he tries anything. I swear to God I will."

Roger could feel the heat of her conviction. They had been wrongly convicted by the media of monstrous crimes, and nobody had risen to their defense. Nobody! Short of murder, Laura Glover would not allow Brett's life to be upset. It was what a dozen years of meticulous fabrication and maternal love had produced—a good, happy life for their son and the protective instinct of a mother bear.

Roger folded his makeup kit. "Laura, Wally was an old friend."

"So was Wendy Bacon," she said, and snapped off the light.

The dark silence of the bedroom took Roger Glover back. Back before his wife was Laura Glover, mother of Brett Glover and owner of Laura's Flower Shop on South Street in Eau Claire, and he was Roger Glover, co-owner.

Chris Bacon did not age and die that night in the Adirondack woods. On the contrary, Elixir not only had frozen his cellular clock but created restorative effects that had stabilized at a level where even with the beard he looked no more than thirty—twelve years less than his age when he first injected himself, and twenty-five years less than the number of years he had been alive. And the reason why his body did not waste away and his mind did not gum up was diabetes.

It took him some time to work out the logic, but he concluded that the tabulone steroid had attached itself to a hitherto unknown receptor in his cell makeup—one of the dozens of "orphan" receptors whose purpose science still did not understand. As Betsy Watson had long ago explained, once attached the new shape caused the manufacture of a protein which turned off the telomerase aging effects. It had also turned off other inhibitors that disrupt normal regulation of enzymes so that one would fast-forward die once off tabulone.

But being a diabetic meant that the extra glucose in Chris's system somehow signaled biochemical changes that activated the enzyme even without tabulone. In other words, some combination of tabulone and Chris's diabetes rendered the receptor active for long periods without the need for regular boosts. Apparently the same was true for Iwati, also a diabetic—which explained why he didn't need frequent shots, just an occasional smoke.

That was why Wendy had not found a shriveled, freeze-dried mummy in Chris's clothes when she returned from Lake Placid that night all those years ago. And why after three days of Chris's disorientation and fever, she had managed to nurse him back to health. In time he had worked out a treatment schedule, discovering that he could go as many as three months without a booster. Fortunately, his body signaled when it was time. Just in case, he wore around his neck an emergency ampule that was hidden in a simple tubular gold case with a tiny spring-release button. It looked like a piece of jewelry, but contained a three-year supply of Elixir.

At fifty-six years of age Roger had plateaued at the health level of an athlete half his age. His blood pressure was 110 over 70; his cholesterol hovered at 160; and he had 10 percent body fat. Essentially Roger Glover *nee* Christopher Bacon was immortal. The only way for him to die was accident, murder, or suicide.

Of course, he had told Laura what he had done—how in a drunken moment fraught with grief and terror he had injected himself. As expected, she reacted with disbelief and anger. There was no turning back. Her first concerns were the unforeseen complications—potential cancers from messing around with his DNA and hormones. Those fears faded when in time he had stabilized. Besides, he felt extraordinary. Gone were arthritic twinges in his back and knees. Gone also were those frightening lapses in recall and memory.

Laura, however, refused to join him. Every instinct had told her Elixir was wrong. Nonetheless, the temptation reared its head higher as the years passed. It was there where she applied makeup to her face each morning. It was there every time she considered the porcelain smoothness of Roger's skin, or felt his hard-body vigor and sexual heat. Or when she considered the impossible anachronism they became by the day. It was there in his entreaties, in sometimes desperate reminders that she was prone to lumps in her breast.

Yet Laura held firm because of Brett. It was bad enough they would someday have to explain Roger. One freak parent was enough.

Because she kept in shape, nobody knew her exact age. They both looked about forty—Roger painting himself older, Laura painting herself younger. The problem was that Laura was fifty-five and Roger was biologically nearly half that. In ten years she could pass for his mother. His encounter tonight only brought that home.

"We're the same people," Roger said. He put his arm around her, hoping she'd sidle up to make love. As always he was primed, but she wasn't interested.

"But we're not the same."

There it was, he thought, the one sure measure of the distance separating them. With so much anguish and grief they had shared over the years, he wondered if he could go it alone when the time came. She would never agree to take Elixir as long as Brett was young, but he hoped that in time she'd change her mind—and before she was elderly. He loved her too much to watch that happen. He also did not want to spend the next century without her. She was the only one who knew who he was.

Until tonight.

"How did it feel to see him?" she asked.

"Strange. I wanted to hide and embrace him at the same time."

While he had stonewalled Wally, the encounter had touched the old Chris Bacon, setting off eddies of bad feelings. Wally had been a good friend, a funny guy he had shared laughs and good times with. Denying him tonight had killed a chance to connect to a past that had nothing to do with Roger Glover. Yes, he and Laura had acquaintances and business associates; but there was a permanent divide that left them alone in an uneasy claustrophobia. It would be nice to connect with Wally again. But that was impossible.

The divide that was closing was Brett. They had told him nothing about Elixir or their past. Yet they were reaching the point of explanation. He was a bright, perceptive kid who believed his parents were in their late thirties. And they looked it. But he would eventually wonder why his father didn't age in family photos, and why he was younger than his friends' fathers. For the time being, it was still cool to have a dad who could sprint around the track and wrestle and who still got carded in restaurants. But the day would come when it would change: When Brett would close in on him. When they would appear like siblings. When Roger would be younger than his son.

It was a day that thus far had lain out *there*—in the general blur of tomorrow. A day they dreaded, because it meant sharing a secret not possessed by any other human being in the history of the species—or any species.

A federal warrant had estranged Roger from outsiders; Elixir had estranged him from his own blood.

But how do you tell your child that you will not age or die? It would be like announcing you were an alien: When the laughter died, you braced for the screams.

22

The eyes.

Wally shook himself awake. Like a Polaroid photo developing, it all came back in vivid color—and with it, the thing that had nibbled at his mind all night: Roger Glover had the same weird two-tone eyes as Chris Bacon.

And *that* was no coincidence.

Chris had been born with two different-colored eyes— one brown, the other green. It was a feature one does not forget. As he once said, looking at Chris Bacon was like looking at two faces superimposed. And he had joked how Chris had been born to see the world from an either/or perspective.

(*Hey, Chris, are you ambivalent?*
Yes and no.)

But why the denial? They were once close friends. He was an usher at Chris and Wendy's wedding and had given them a fancy piece of calligraphy as a gift.

Wally got up and went to the cellar and tore through boxes of memorabilia—stuff he hadn't looked at in years, stuff his ex-wife had been after him to dump. Stuff that always made him a little sad—old letters, concert ticket stubs, baseball cards, Woodstock photos, school newspaper pieces he had authored, record albums of the

Mamas and Papas, Joan Baez, the Beatles, Jefferson Airplane, even 45s of Buddy Holly, Elvis, and the Dell Vikings. Stuff that he just couldn't throw out.

It must have been an hour before he located the old album of photos taken at Cape Cod—of him and an old flame, Jane Potter, and Chris Bacon and Wendy Whitehead. Most were shot at a distance. Except for two—the group of them sitting on rocks with the water in the background.

The same facial structure and sinewy physique. Except for the lighter hair and sunglasses, it looked like Glover.

Back upstairs he poured himself some port and watched the short segment of video he had shot of the man who called himself Roger Glover. The resemblance was remarkable. Beyond coincidence. Maybe it was a younger brother of Chris. But identical twins weren't born twenty years apart. Even if it were a younger sibling of striking resemblance, why deny the name?

And if it were Chris, why deny an old friend?

What sent a chill through him was that Glover looked exactly like Chris Bacon in the photographs from 1970. It did not make sense. None of it.

For a minute he sipped his drink and let his mind run down some possibilities. Then he turned on his computer, got onto the Internet, and accessed a search engine. He typed the name CHRISTOPHER BACON.

Instantly he got a long list of old newspaper abstracts of articles from the winter of 1988, beginning January 30 with an obituary:

SCIENTIST MURDER SUSPECT KILLED IN PLANE CRASH
EASTERN FLIGHT 219 CLAIMS DARBY
MURDER SUSPECT

Four days later a *Boston Globe* headline read:

"FBI: BIOLOGIST BACON NOT ON PLANE"

Then the next day from papers around the nation:

MAN CHARGED IN MURDER MAY BE AIRLINE BOMBER
SCIENTIST TURNS MASS MURDERER
ALL-OUT HUNT FOR SABOTEUR BACON
POLICE AND FBI INTENSIFY SEARCH FOR BACON & WIFE
BOMB SUSPECT, WIFE, INFANT DISAPPEAR

Wally was trembling with disbelief as he clicked on one of the articles. Christopher Bacon had been accused of killing a coworker in his lab, then planting explosives aboard a commercial airliner heading for Puerto Rico. He didn't remember the incident because he and his family had been living in Japan at the time.

Wally scrolled down the articles. Following the sabotage, Chris had dropped off the face of the earth with his wife and infant son. As the years went on, the articles thinned out, occasionally producing pieces such as "Is Mass Murder Suspect Among Us?" and theories that Bacon and family had moved to Mexico or Canada. By 1991, the articles had stopped coming, the latest listing Christopher Bacon as the FBI's Number One most wanted fugitive.

Whatever the claims, these were crimes Wally could never imagine his old pal committing. Accompanying the articles was a color photograph of Chris and Wendy. It was grainy and had lost something in transcription, but recognition passed through Wally like a brick. Take away the black beard and it was the same man.

But it didn't make sense, since the Chris Bacon in the 1988 Internet photos looked older than he did in person. Older by a decade or more!

Wally didn't get it. He didn't get any of it.

Either Roger Glover was some astounding lookalike, or Roger Glover *was* Chris Bacon who had undergone a stunning makeover.

Confused and baffled, Wally downed the rest of his wine. Then he went back upstairs and went to bed, wondering what the statute of limitation was on the million-dollar reward.

"He's so big for his age," Jenny said.

"He's only a year younger than Abigail," Laura said.

In the photo, Brett was in his wrestling outfit, standing tall and straight, square-shouldered, his young body firm and rippled with muscles. The image filled Laura with love.

"He looks like Roger, except for the eyes." Brett had Laura's brown eyes. Both of them.

It was at these secret hotel trysts where she and Jenny shared family news. Today it was the Milwaukee Marriott just up the street from the annual flower show—Laura's cover for the rendezvous. Although Jenny was no longer under FBI surveillance, Laura still insisted on meeting surreptitiously—never in public, and never at each other's homes. This was their first meeting in four years.

Laura wished the rooms came with VCRs so she could show Jenny the tape of Brett's winning match from yesterday. Ironically, he had wanted to go out for basketball, but felt he was too short and signed up for wrestling reluctantly.

"How they change. I would never have recognized him."

Jenny had not seen Brett since he was baby Adam. Sadder still, Brett knew nothing of Jenny. Laura had told him that she was an only child of two parents who themselves were only children—like Roger. That he had no other family. Laura hated deceiving him, but if they announced he had other relatives, he'd want to visit them, and that could put the authorities on their trail. Plus it would open that awful can of worms. Not until he was older. Not until he could handle the entire, lunatic truth.

"I wish you'd brought pictures of Abigail," Laura said.

"Oh, you know these teenagers. She's camera-shy." Jenny hadn't brought photos of her for years. "She's something else, though, smart as a whip. We're studying French together." Jenny prided herself in being cultured, of rising above crass TV values.

"What a nice thing to share. Maybe you could take her to France someday."

Jenny smiled noncommittally. "That's another thing: She doesn't like to travel."

Laura saw Jenny infrequently, but she knew how devoted a mother she was, funneling all her energy into raising Abigail and schooling her at home. It was her way of making up for Kelly. Laura swore that without Abigail, Jenny would have lost her mind given the turmoil in her life. Nine years ago, she and Ted got divorced. It was a stormy breakup but she won custody of Abigail and a large settlement. Two years later, Ted was sent to prison for eight years for operating a car-theft ring. Then in 1993 real horror struck. Kelly, age twenty-nine, committed suicide.

It was impossible to gauge the effects by phone or a meeting every few years. But some weird denial had set in, because Jenny never mentioned Kelly's name again. She had moved to a suburb of Indianapolis with Abigail where she started life all over as a first-time mother.

Jenny flipped through photos nervously, distracted. Something was up. Laura had sensed the tension the moment Jenny walked into the room. Even in her voice when she called to schedule this rendezvous. Finally, Laura asked her point-blank what was wrong.

For a moment Jenny tried to dissemble. Then she blurted out, "I need help."

"What kind of help?"

"Elixir. I want some Elixir. Simple as that. I need some, and you can't say no."

The intensity of her expression startled Laura. "Jennifer, I can't do that and you know it."

"Laura, I'm fifty years old, and aging fast. Look at

me, I'm putting on weight and fleshing out. I'm feeling older and I hate it."

"So am I. That's life."

"But Mamma was my mother, too. I carry the same family thing for cancer, and you said that stuff prevents cancer cells—"

Laura cut her off. "You don't know anything about the stuff. It's forbidden. Everything about it is forbidden."

"But Roger—"

"But Roger nothing! Yeah, he doesn't age, but do you want to end up like him—cut off from your kid? From your friends? Living in a state of biological schizophrenia—graying your hair and not knowing who the hell you really are or what generation you're from? That's what it's like for him. That's what it's like for us, and I'll be damned if I'll let you do that to yourself."

What she didn't mention was what had happened to them as a couple. She still loved Roger, but their widening biological gap had set off a flurry of confused emotions—from sheer envy to anger to something akin to repugnance at the unnaturalness of his condition. Even sex was a perverse throwback experience—as if she were making love to Chris Bacon, the horny ever-ready grad student. Except she was a post-menopausal fifty-five and feeling like a cradle-robber. Elixir had thrown time and love out of joint.

"I can live with that," Jenny pleaded. "I'm willing to take the risk. Please. I'm begging you." She began to cry.

Seeing her weaken touched Laura, but she could not let the crocodile tears sway her. "You're not a hermit living in the woods, for god's sake. You've got a daughter to think of."

"That's who I'm thinking of," Jenny shot back.

"Then ask yourself what you'll tell her in ten years?"

"What about Brett? What are you going to tell him?"

Laura didn't answer.

Jenny made no effort to stop her tears. She was bordering on hysteria. "You have to help me. You have to let me have some. I'm not asking for much. Just a few ampules. You can't let this happen, after all I did for you—protected you, lied for you, got you passports and IDs. If it weren't for me you'd be in prison for the rest of your lives."

"And I'm very grateful. But Elixir is lousy with horrors."

"You don't understand," Jenny said.

"What don't I understand?" Laura shouted. "I've lived with it for fifteen years."

"But Roger's managed. He's fine. You've got the power to prolong life, and you won't give me a drop. Your own flesh and blood."

"Jesus, Jenny, live the years you have, and stop whining about the ones you don't have."

"I'm afraid of getting old. I'm afraid of becoming wrinkled and decrepit. You're my sister."

"It's because I'm your sister I won't let you." Laura put her hand on Jenny's. "And you're not old and decrepit, for god's sake. You're making yourself crazy. You look ten years younger."

It wasn't false flattery. Jenny did look younger. Her skin was smooth and shiny—the skin of somebody who took proper care and avoided sunlight. But more than that, she dressed young: not in teenie-bopper flash, but jumpers and flats and plastic beads. She looked like a Catholic-school girl.

"If I didn't know better, I'd say you were already taking the stuff."

Jenny looked at her with a start, then gathered her stuff to leave.

The tryst was over. And a disaster. For the first time they had fought over it. Yes, in phone talk Jenny would hint how she wished she could go on indefinitely like Roger—if only it were safe. What Laura had discounted as idle musings. But Jenny had meant it, and it shocked her to see how much festered below the surface.

Laura tried to hug her goodbye, but Jenny pushed her away and opened the door.

"I don't want you to leave hating me."

Jenny gave her an icy stare. "You don't understand," she said through her teeth. "You don't, don't, don't."

Laura watched her walk down the corridor to the elevator, thinking they were more like strangers than sisters. Thinking that Jenny's desperation went beyond fear of fifty. Something else was going on. She was over the edge. Maybe she'd recommend psychiatric counseling.

Laura stepped back inside and closed the door. She still clutched a photo of Brett. She stared at it for a moment, taking in his young colt beauty.

"What are you going to tell him?"

On Monday morning, Wally Olafsson walked into the resident agency office of the Federal Bureau of Investigation in Madison and reported his encounter the other night and what he had discovered on the Internet, producing the downloaded articles, photos copied from news stories gotten at the UW La Crosse campus library, the Cape Cod snapshots, and the video taken of Chris Bacon at the Wisconsin Regionals.

The complaint duty agent, Eric Brown, took notes as Wally outlined his past acquaintance with Christopher Bacon. On his computer, Brown checked the Bureau's database and located the outstanding warrant. He reviewed the charges, comparing screen file photos of Bacon with those Wally had brought and the video segment he ran on a VCR.

"There's a resemblance," Brown admitted, "but the guy looks on the young side. According to files, he should be fifty-six. This guy looks about thirty."

"He's not. He's my age." Wally suddenly felt self-conscious of his big fleshy head and bulging gut. "His kid must be about fourteen like my son, which means there should be over a forty-year difference between them. You saw the videos. They look like brothers."

"That's what I'm saying, Mr. Olafsson: You've got the wrong guy." Brown made a flat smile to say he's wasting both their time. "It's not Christopher Bacon, it's Roger Glover."

"I hear what you're saying, but I'm telling you, it's Chris. What convinced me was his eyes. You can't tell in the photos, but they're two different colors. I didn't remember until I got close."

"Sounds like you studied him pretty good."

"I did, and I'd bet my life it's Chris Bacon."

"Except he's about twenty-five years too young."

"Maybe he found good plastic surgeons. Criminals do that I hear." Brown's dismissal had put an edge in Wally's voice.

"Yeah, but when they want a change-over they get their faces restructured, not just a lid lift and tuck."

He ran the tape a couple more times. Glover had on a tight-fitting pullover that revealed a trim physique. "It's not just the face. Look at his body, and posture, the flat gut. . . ."

"Some guys preserve well," Wally said.

Brown, who was himself trim and about forty-five, glanced at Wally without expression. But Wally could read his mind: *If you're the same age, how come Glover looks like the poster boy for Geritol, and you're a middle-aged Tweedle Dum in wingtips?*

Wally made a sigh of impatience. "Look, instead of dickering around, why don't you just bring him in and do a fingerprint check? Isn't that what you guys do?" Wally stopped short of an "I'm-a-taxpayer" harangue.

"Yeah, when we have probable cause."

"Christ, man, look at the photos! How much more probable cause do you need?"

"We can't arrest someone because he vaguely resembles a fugitive."

"Vaguely!" He pushed a photo at him. "Shave the

beard and cut the hair, and these are the same goddamn guy."

"In your mind maybe, but he's got sunglasses on here, and the wire photo is fuzzy. And if he's the same guy, he's Peter goddamn Pan."

Wally felt his face flush. "Listen to me, Agent Brown. I'm not some jerk groupie of *America's Most Wanted*. I lived with the guy for two years. We were drinking buddies, we double-dated, we studied together. Roger Glover is Christopher Bacon. And if you don't do your job and investigate, you will be negligent in apprehending a federal fugitive wanted for mass murder."

Brown's eyes hardened, but he did not lash back. He gathered the photographs and stood up. "We'll look into it."

Wally got his briefcase and moved to the door. He felt wracked. Outside the window a light rain was falling. It was a three-hour ride back to Eau Claire. He'd stop on the road for a sandwich.

To clear the air before he left, he said, "Look, I'm sorry for the outburst, but this has put me on edge for the last two days. I just can't reconcile the guy I knew with these crimes. He was not some crazy or political fanatic. He was a good guy, a biochemist working to cure cancer. He wanted to save lives. It just doesn't jive."

Brown opened the door. "What can I say? People change."

"Did they ever prove he did it?"

"According to the files, he's the only suspect."

"Well, I hope to God I'm wrong."

Brown frowned. "You do?"

"Of course. We were old friends."

"Mr. Olafsson, if you hoped you were wrong you wouldn't be in here."

"I don't think I follow."

"The first question you asked when you called this morning was if the million-dollar reward still held. So much for auld lang syne."

23

At 12:10, Wally left the Madison FBI offices, and crossed the lot to his big gold Lexus—not the vehicle of a guy who had once had a golden mane down the middle of his back and who had headed up the Cambridge chapter of the SDS. But time had a way of changing things. A high-paying establishment job, a house in the heartland suburbs, and three decades of taxes would turn the pinkest radical into a Republican.

Driving a black unmarked Dodge Caravan, Roger Glover followed Wally north on Route 90 to his home in La Crosse. It was the same car Wally drove yesterday to the UW library where he photocopied microfilmed articles in the periodical room. After Wally left, Roger checked the reshelving box deposit: *The Boston Globe*, February 1988.

The parking sticker on the Lexus said Midland Investment Company, which confirmed in a telephone call that Wally was Senior Marketing VP. It was not a professional post that lent itself to personal visits to the FBI. Nor was it just a casual drop-in to see a friend—not at prime time on a Monday, and not on a five-hour round trip of 250 miles. Wally had come to file a report on Christopher Bacon.

It was a fear that he and Laura had lived with but

could never fully prepare for. If they did nothing, the authorities would show up at their doorstep asking for evidence that they were Roger Glover born in Wichita and Laura Gendron Glover from Duluth. They would want documents and take prints. While they had birth certificates, a deep check would reveal that Roger Glover and son Brett had died in a car crash in 1958, and Laura Gendron Glover had died in 1968, age twelve.

Fortunately, Chris and Wendy had never been officially printed. And even though their prints were all over their home in Carleton, Mass., there was no way of distinguishing them from each other's or those of the cleaning people, friends, and guests who had passed through their place.

As Roger drove back to Eau Claire he considered his options. The first was do nothing and wait for the knock at the door. The second was to turn themselves in as a demonstration of their innocence. Either choice would result in long public trials. Since the odds were against him, he could end up convicted. Even if he didn't receive the death sentence, it would, under the grimly ironic circumstances, be far more preferable than life in prison without parole.

There was also Brett. Even if Roger plea-bargained for a lesser charge, he could still serve time for fleeing federal and state warrants; Laura, too, as an accessory. That would leave Brett parentless—an unacceptable option. So was a witness protection program. Whoever had framed them could still be out there and still thirsty for Elixir.

The third option was flight. Over the thirteen years on the lam, Roger and Laura had devised contingency plans should they be recognized. They had established several different identities with different cars, business cards, bank accounts, and credit cards, as well as alternate residency in Minneapolis. Because Brett knew nothing about this, they would leave him with friends a couple times a year and, under their alias, would spend a few days at the condo and role-play with local business people and neighbors. It was schizophrenic, but it worked. It also made their return to the Glovers of Eau Claire like going home. The Bacons were a couple who died a long time ago.

The money for their alternate lives came from trust funds Sam had set up for Chris when he was in college. Before they disappeared, Roger had transferred the full content to a blind account. Several months after establishing residency in Eau Claire, he again transferred the funds into a new account—a little over $1,200,000— some of which they used to become the Glovers, the remainder of which he converted to cash and buried for an emergency getaway. That was his third option.

The fourth required a gun.

Roger was in the back room working on a funeral arrangement when an agent from the FBI entered his shop.

He knew the guy was a Fed because earlier that morning he had spotted him through field glasses sitting with another man in a green Jeep Cherokee with tinted glass across the street. His suspicions were confirmed when they later followed him across town on deliveries.

The man who looked in his thirties was of average build and dressed in jeans and a Chicago Bulls jacket. He did not identify himself. Nor was Roger surprised. Unless they had probable cause, he could not be arrested on resemblance to a fugitive. And unless they had an arrest warrant for Roger Glover, they could not bring him into custody. For the time being, he was safe. This was a reconnaissance check to verify any resemblance to file photos.

The agent pretended to examine the Boston ferns, but Roger caught him studying his face, knowing full well that his appearance was too young for a matchup. After several minutes, he brought a plant to the counter. Hanging conspicuously on the wall by the cash register was a large blowup of a smiling Roger at a surprise party three years ago. A banner hanging over his head said HAPPY 35TH BIRTHDAY. In the photo Roger was displaying a copy of an old *Life* magazine.

The man peered at it as he got his money out. "Looks like John Glenn in his space capsule."

"Yes, it is," Roger said brightly. "It was the issue that came out the week I was born."

The man nodded. "Must have been '62 or '63."

"Sixty-two."

"Nice birthday gift."

"Yes it is. Will that be it?"

The man nodded, and Roger wrapped the plant.

All throughout the transaction, Roger wore his tinted lenses and surgical gloves. When he finished, he placed the plant on the counter and removed the gloves. While the man fished for his money, Roger lathered his hands with lotion from a dispenser by the cash register. Then he slipped the gloves back on. "Chapped hands. A real drag in this business," he said and gave the man his change.

The man left, but not before he helped himself to a business card.

Through the windows Roger watched him go to the car and drive away.

He would tell his partner about how Roger had worn gloves because of a skin condition. They would have the pot and wrapping paper and business card dusted for fingerprints. It was possible his or Laura's could be on them, as well as those of any number of customers, assistants, distributors, and manufacturers. But they had nothing on file. The agent would also tell his partner about the photograph—how in spite of any resemblance, Glover was too young to be Bacon, even with the graying hair.

•   •   •

Roger did not go home that evening. Instead, he slipped out the back and let the air out of a tire of his van so it looked like a legitimate flat. He then cut through some back lots to a street several blocks away where he caught a cab. When he was certain he wasn't followed, he had the cab leave him off at a municipal parking lot where he had a rental spot for a black Jeep registered under one of his aliases, Harry Stork. He then left town without being followed, and drove for over an hour.

The house at number 213 Chestnut was a handsome modern structure with a two-car garage. A car was parked in one of the bays. The lights were on and the television pulsed against the curtains.

Roger drove up and down the road twice, then parked under a tree. He approached the house. In his right hand he carried a briefcase. In the inside pocket of his jacket he carried a Glock nine-millimeter pistol.

When he was certain there was nobody else inside, he stepped up to the front door. There was no peephole, just narrow side windows along the door. But the hat and scarf hid much of his face.

Roger rang the doorbell. In a few moments the door swung open.

"Hi, Wally. It's me, Chris Bacon."

24

Wally's face drained of blood. "I'll be damned."

"Can we sit down?" Roger asked. "We have a lot to talk about."

"Yeah, thirty years worth." Wally caught his breath and nodded. "Heck, I knew it was you the moment I saw you." He tried to sound neutral. "But how come I'm fat and bald and you look like you did back in school? Must be the genes, huh? Man oh man, don't you wish we were back there again?" He was struggling to maintain a casual reunion air.

Roger followed Wally into the living room but did not take a seat.

"Can I get you a drink?" He inched toward the doorway leading to the kitchen.

"No, I'm fine."

"How did you find me?"

Roger did not answer.

"Well, make yourself at home. I'm going to grab myself a beer. Jeez, it's good to see you."

Roger knew what he was planning—go to another room and punch 911. He put his hand up to block him. "Wally, I'd prefer if we talked first."

Wally stared at him for a moment. "That's what gave

it away. You're the only person I'd ever seen with two-tone eyes."

Roger smiled, feeling a flush of warmth for his old friend.

Hey, Chris, are you ambivalent?

Yes and no.

Wally's manner suddenly shifted. "Chris, what's this all about—this Roger Glover stuff?"

He was playing dumb, and Roger couldn't blame him. "Let's sit down and talk a bit, then you can get us the beers."

Wally moved to the couch, and Roger took a chair by the doorway. He lay his briefcase on the floor. The gun inside his jacket pressed against his ribcage. If Wally tried to make a run for it, Roger would pull it. Too much was at stake.

As they faced each other, it struck Roger how much Wally had aged. Most of his hair was gone except for an apron around the back of his head and a few strands plastered across his scalp. His gut bulged over his belt like a sack of flour. His shoulders were broad but thin like his arms from lack of exercise. His face was gray and fleshy and the skin was pocked on the nose and cheeks—looking like old melanoma scars. His eyes still held the reef-water blue Roger remembered, but they looked tired and unhappy. It was sad to see what the years had done to his old friend—a guy who had been lean and handsome like a young Alan Ladd.

"Wally, I have just one question, then I'll explain things."

"Okay."

"What did you tell the FBI?"

Wally flinched. "The FBI? What FBI? What are you talking about?" His sincere bug-eyes weren't convincing.

"Wally, I'm here to be straight with you. And for old time's sake I want you to be straight back. You visited the Madison office two days ago at ten-thirty and spoke for an hour and forty minutes with agent Eric Brown."

Wally looked nonplussed. More mock-shock. "He's an old friend."

"No, he's not."

"What the hell do you mean, 'No, he's not . . .'?" Now he was playing the indignation card.

"Because when I called your office later and told your secretary I was Eric Brown, she asked from what company. Any executive secretary worth her salt knows the names of the boss's old friends."

Wally tried to hold the indignation in his face, but it slipped.

"Furthermore, you photocopied some microfilm articles from *The Boston Globe* the other day. February 1988. And don't tell me you were checking old Beanpot scores."

After a long silence Wally said, "You seem to have all the answers."

"I want to hear it from you."

He looked scared. "What are you going to do?"

"Talk."

"And if I don't?"

"I think you should."

Wally wiped his mouth and stared at the floor for a moment. "The papers said you murdered a colleague and blew up a jetliner with a hundred and thirty-seven people."

"Thank you," he said. "Now let's get those beers, then I'm going to explain how I was framed for those crimes."

As they walked into the kitchen, Wally looked at Roger. "By the way, you look damn good for fifty-six."

"Because I'm not, and I'll explain that too."

They got the beers and returned. Then over the next two hours Roger told his story, leaving out very little. Without getting too technical, he explained how the tabulone molecule worked on the DNA sequence to prolong cell life. As documentation he showed Wally the old Elixir brochures from Darby and the videos of Methuselah and Jimbo.

Wally was astounded, of course, and asked lots of questions. Every so often he'd examine Roger's face and hands, amazed at their condition. At one point he even tugged at Roger's hair to see that it wasn't a wig.

"You've discovered the mother of all miracle drugs," he said. "But, man, I'm looking at you and seeing something that shouldn't be. It's goddamn creepy. If I were religious, I'd say you'd been touched by Jesus."

A long silence passed as Wally nursed his drink and let it all sink in. Finally, he said, "What's it like not to age?"

Roger smiled. "Mirrors no longer depress me."

"I've conquered that myself. I avoid them."

They both laughed. It was the same old Wally, the same self-deprecating wit. And it came back to Chris why he had been so fond of him. Yet, despite the renewed warmth, Roger reminded himself that Wally could still think him a killer.

"Why are you telling me all this?"

"Because I was framed. It's the truth, and I want you to believe it. I did not kill anybody."

"There's got to be another reason you're here."

Chris nodded. "I want you to go to back to the FBI and tell them that you were wrong. That you checked old photographs and it wasn't Christopher Bacon you had spotted, just a guy who resembles him. He's too young to be Bacon."

Wally listened without response.

"I want them off my tail, Wally. I've got a kid and a wife, and they don't deserve to be put on the run again. We have new lives and we want to continue living them out."

"Well, I guess my head is still spinning."

"I understand, but a lot of people have already died."

Wally's face hardened. "What does that mean?"

"It means that if I were a guy who blew up a hundred

and thirty-seven family people heading for vacation, I would have little compunction eliminating anybody else."

"You mean me."

"And your son. Instead I'm drinking beers with you in your living room."

"Aren't I grateful!"

"Of course, if you do it you'll be out the million-dollar reward."

"Well, there's that."

"A lot of money. Could make for a nice early retirement."

Wally's face darkened. Roger picked up his jacket, feeling the comforting weight of the pistol. He reached his hand into the right inner pocket, firmly gripping its contents. "I hate to spoil things, but so will this."

Wally made an involuntary gasp as Roger whipped out his hand and aimed it straight at him: A long glass ampule. "Elixir."

"What?"

"Elixir," Roger repeated. "Earlier you asked did it work for anybody. To my knowledge, two people in the world today. You could be the third. Compensation for forfeiting the million dollars: perpetual life."

Wally stared blankly. It was too much to absorb all at once.

"You don't have to make a decision now, but it has to be soon. They're watching us. I'm offering you an unlimited supply of Elixir to keep you alive indefinitely. In return, I ask that you retract your claim."

Wally contemplated the offer. They both knew he was the perfect candidate—divorced, lonely, overweight, aging all too fast, and looking at maybe ten years at best before he died.

"You don't have to take it, of course."

Wally rolled the ampule of tabulone in his fingers, studying the promise locked in glass. Outside the night wind had picked up, and someplace in the dining room a banjo clock chimed midnight.

"Run by me the side effects again."

"There are no side effects in the ordinary sense—just a rejuvenation surge that sets you back about ten years. It's hard to measure. But it takes place over six weeks to three months. Once stabilized, you would need injections infrequently—once every two weeks. Eventually, once a month. But once you start you can't stop or you'll die. That goes for me too."

"What about cancer cells? What if I've got a spot on my lungs or something in my liver?"

"The stuff holds them in diapause. They don't replicate but sit there, while normal cells continue to divide."

"So, it's like a kind of chemotherapy—the good cells grow while the bad ones are held in check."

"Something like that, except the good cells go on indefinitely."

"What happens when the Elixir stops coming?"

Roger could still see Jimbo dying, his body exploding in carcinoma gone wild. "You die."

"What about your organs—heart, kidney and liver? Don't they eventually wear out?"

"Theoretically, they shouldn't as long as you take care of yourself. And if they do, there are always transplants—every ten thousand miles or fifty years, which ever comes first."

Wally laughed. "As we kids say, 'Holy shit.'"

He got up for another beer. Roger escorted him, though he no longer expected Wally to go for the phone.

When they returned, Wally said: "You've lived unchanged for nearly fifteen years. Are you happy?"

Are you happy?

While Chris hadn't expected it, it was a legitimate question. But the answer was far from simple.

His impulse was to declare, *Of course I'm happy. Never aging. Never growing weary, depressed, infirm. Not watching your body fall apart. Never having to die.*

Being around to see all the great changes—manned rockets to Mars, nano-engineering, controlled fusion, a cure for AIDS. To go on indefinitely learning and doing the things you enjoy. To prolong your time with those you love. Hell! Who wouldn't be happy?

But it was more complicated than that. Yes, he loved his wife and son. They were the fundamental conditions of his life. But all that came at a price. When Chris Bacon took his first injection, they were on the run trying to become strangers. That was behind them now, but he could never go back to the man who wanted to live forever to do his science. Without credentials, he could never step foot in a lab again.

Likewise, Laura had abandoned her dream of becoming a full-time writer, nor could she go back to teaching without college degrees as Laura Glover. When that all came to an end bitterness and boredom set in. What saved them was Brett. His existence relieved them from the claustrophobia of their secrets. He provided them love and cause outside themselves. He kept them from depression and divorce.

While flower arrangements didn't do it for Roger, he threw himself into fatherhood, and not just the male stuff—baseball, wrestling, and fishing. He took charge of monitoring Brett's schooling, setting up piano lessons, doctor exams, shopping. To keep the rust off his brain, Roger tutored neighborhood kids in biology, chemistry, and math, sometimes performing simple experiments in a makeshift lab in his garage.

"Are you happy?"

But Wally wasn't asking about the joys of parenting and playing Mr. Wizard. He wanted to know if there was happiness in being stuck in the moment.

Roger still wore a watch and saw life in segmented chunks, shaped by schedules and deadlines. Yet, biologically speaking, time was what other people experienced. He was a mere spectator, living with clocks, but impervious to their movement. Except for Laura who got older and Brett who grew up.

Like an exile on an island in the timeflow, Roger was unable to determine which was worse—watching his wife drift off or his son pull toward shore.

"Are you happy . . . ?"

Roger knew what Wally meant. But he'd lie because, in part, he missed his old life and his wife and the tick of the clock.

"Yes."

"You're not bored with the sameness?"

"The alternative is watching yourself grow old."

"Been there, done that," Wally said. "So, it's like being thirty-something forever."

Roger had to admit to himself a selfish impulse to his offer. If Wally agreed, he would have someone else to share vast stretches of slow time with. Laura, of course, had no interest. "Yes."

"My God!" He again grinned in wonder at Roger. "If you can't lick 'em, join 'em," he said.

"I don't follow."

"Just that I've reached the age when it's finally hit me that this ride isn't forever. I'm beginning to think like an old man even though part of me still feels twenty-one. As a result, I find myself resenting the younger set because I'm not one of them anymore. I don't even go to movies anymore because nobody in them is over thirty. Worse still is TV which is a nonstop puberty fest. Christ, I sit here sometimes wishing there was an AARP channel. Instead, I rent Randolph Scott videos or listen to the Russian Five. Sure, laugh, but every morning I go to work expecting to find some kid who hasn't started shaving yet sitting at my desk. I'm telling you, we live in a culture that eats its old."

Roger smiled, recalling the familiar passion that thirty years ago had rallied protests against the Vietnam War. "I hear what you're saying, but it won't change your chronological age."

"But when they retire me I won't go home to die."

"No, you won't. But keep in mind that this is for real. It works, and there's no turning back. You will not age, yet your son and everybody else you care for will. In time, that will be a problem without precedents. Think these things over very carefully before you decide."

"I hear you."

Roger removed a new syringe from his shirt pocket. He put the needle through the rubber septum, extracted 1.2 ccs, and injected it into his own arm. "A booster shot. In three days I'll call you for your decision. If you accept it, you'll have an endless supply available to you."

Roger then asked for a candle and a match. He lit the candle and dripped some wax over the septum and had Wally press his finger over it as a seal. "I can't leave this with you, but if you decide you're Go, we'll inject you from the same batch just so you know that you're getting the same stuff. You can check the seal that it's not been tampered with."

"What if I reject your offer?"

"Then I will assume one of two possibilities. First, that you went to the Feds and called them off. Or, that you didn't which means we're still under surveillance. Since I cannot with certainty assume the best, I will consider my status and that of my family in peril."

"And . . . ?"

"And you'll never see a dime of the reward money."

"You mean you'd kill me."

Roger did not respond.

"You have a gun in there." Wally nodded at Roger's jacket. "I heard the thud."

"Yes."

"Look, Chris—sorry—Roger, I think you've been straight with me all night. I think what you've told me is real—at least as real as what I'm seeing. I also believe that somebody tried to screw you. I'll do what you say. I'll go back to the Feds and retract my claim. I swear on it for what it's worth since you'll probably follow me anyway."

Something in his manner said he was as good as his word. "You won't be able to reach me for the next three days," Roger said. "But I'll call you. If you decide on treatments, I'll give you instructions where we can meet to begin."

"How much of this Elixir did you say you had?"

"Enough to keep you alive until the middle of the thirty-seventh century."

Wally let out a squeal. "The thirty-seventh century? My God! But who'd want to live that long?"

"Probably no one, but it beats three score and ten."

"I'll say. But what if you get tired of living?"

"The treatment comes with a cyanide cap."

The next morning Wally drove to the Madison office of the FBI.

Agent Eric Brown was out of town at a conference and wouldn't be back for a week. An agent named Mike Zazzaro was taking Brown's calls. He knew about the case and had read the report. When Wally explained that he wanted to retract his claim, Zazzaro asked permission to videotape the interview for Brown. Wally agreed and signed a form. Then Wally took a seat beside a table sporting a Boston fern in a gold pot and explained his retraction.

"I made a mistake. It was the wrong guy. I went back and checked on some old photos and realized my error. Roger Glover is *not* Chris Bacon. There's a resemblance—what had caught me off guard—but it isn't the same man. Besides, he's about thirty years too young—you can tell that just looking at him. I don't know what got into my head. Early senility I guess. So I'm here to apologize for sending you guys on a wild goose chase, and I guess I should hope this Roger Glover didn't get into any trouble. Jesus, I should call him and apologize.

I met the guy for the first time a couple weeks ago at my son's wrestling tournament, and now I've got the government on his tail for mass murder. I feel terrible, really terrible. I mean, how do you apologize for that? He hasn't been arrested has he?"

"No."

"But he's still being investigated, right?"

"We're still looking into it."

"Well, that's got to end. He's the wrong guy. . . ."

Wally rambled on. Zazzaro asked him some questions, and Wally answered, trying to affect woeful regret. When he left, he felt drained, as if he had just pleaded for his own life.

He had.

Wally spent the next two days replaying the interlude with Roger/Chris in his head. It wasn't that he didn't believe him. On the contrary, he was convinced, and what did it was the video of the lab animals. He had Roger replay them several times to dispel any suspicions of trick photography. Wisely, Roger had documented each sequence by affixing that day's *Boston Globe* front page to the animals' cages, occasionally closing in on the date. Also, there was no switching of younger animals for older ones since they were nearly as distinguishable as people up close. Jimbo had a missing left incisor, a hole on his left ear, and a scar above his right eye—none of which could have been faked. Furthermore, the animals clearly became younger-looking and more vigorous as the newspapers became more current.

And, of course, there was Roger, or Chris. Every visible aspect of the man's being denied his chronology. Even the youngest-looking fifty-six-year-old man has some giveaway—wrinkles, hair, skin, flesh, musculature, posture, stiffening body movement—a feature or combination that verifies his fifth decade of life. Roger Glover had none.

At fifty-seven years of age, Wally Olafsson saw himself as a rapidly aging organism, living out the rest of his life alone. He was overweight, his cholesterol was 312 at last checkup, he had high blood pressure, he drank and ate too much, and he got no exercise. Much of his decline came with the breakdown of his marriage. His wife had won custody of Todd and moved two hundred miles away. Wally had a few male friends, but he did not feel desirable to women, especially younger ones. While he tried not to think about death, he envisioned his future as a featureless tunnel, constricting like an occluded artery.

Now, he had an option to push back the clock and jam its mechanism.

Suddenly he began to think young again. About getting back into life, in the words of the old Depends ad. He could join a health club, get into shape, maybe meet some nice fortyish women. There was golf—a game he had always wanted to take up, and a good way to enhance business contacts. (All he had for a social life now was a men's book group.)

And maybe he'd take up skiing again. He had hung up his poles ten years ago when he took a bad fall. Todd had been after him to return to the slopes, take refresher lessons so they could do something fun together besides an occasional movie or UW football game. He might even go off on one of those discovery vacations, an Earthwatch expedition. And with Todd—a father-and-son high-adventure getaway.

He didn't think too long-range—like how he'd explain to his son and friends why he didn't grow old. But it crossed his mind that he could make a killing on the stock market. He could sell out in twenty or thirty years and take on a new identity while investing his earnings for another twenty years. Keep that up for a while, and he'd be as rich as Bill Gates by the end of the twenty-first century. And still only fifty-seven years old, and looking thirtyish.

By Friday, Wally had made up his mind: He was Go on Elixir.

He would live his life all the way up.

He would make up for lost time. Would he ever!

At 1:30 on Friday afternoon, Roger called Wally at the office and instructed him to drive to the empty parking lot of St. Jerome's Roman Catholic Church on Preston Street where he would find a shopping bag behind the statue of the Virgin Mary. Inside was a cell phone.

Wally did as he was told and retrieved the bag with the phone. The lot was empty and nobody followed him.

At two o'clock, Roger called him with instructions to drive to the Silver Pines motel on Route 61 and to keep the line open all the way so that Wally could not make a quick call to the police before arriving. Roger was a man devoid of trust. Thirteen years on the run would do that, Wally guessed.

At 2:36, he arrived at the motel and entered room 217 with the phone line still open.

Roger was waiting for him, phone in hand. Wally's face was shiny with excitement. "What do you think?" Roger asked him.

"You know what Woody Allen said: 'I'm not afraid of dying; I just don't want to be there when it happens.' "

Roger smiled. "So, you're on?"

"Yeah, but on one condition—that I get my own supply to draw from."

Chris shook his head. "Nope, I can't do that."

"Why not?"

"The entire supply stays with me. That's the way it is."

"You afraid I'm going to blackmarket the stuff?"

"No, but if something should happen to you and it falls into the wrong hands, it could be duplicated. And that can't happen."

"Then I'm dependent upon you for my life."

"As I am with you. It's what'll keep us honest."

"Hell, Chris, I'm not going to turn you in. You were framed, and I believe you. I went back the feds as I said. There's no way I'd betray you."

"Maybe in a few years when things have settled, but for the immediate future, I will dole it out. And the name's Roger."

"But what if something happens to you—you know, you get into an accident, a car crash or something?"

"I'll leave instructions with people I trust to send you a key to a locker containing enough serum to last for centuries. That key and the serum's location will be sent to you if and only if I die by accident."

"Who are these people?"

"Blood relatives and trustworthy."

"What if you're caught by the feds?"

"Let's hope that I'm not. But if that happens and it's clear you had nothing to do with it, you'll be sent the key. On the other hand, if I learn you were instrumental in my capture or the capture of my wife or son, you'll never get any."

"Then what?"

"Then you'll die."

"Jesus, you don't trust anybody."

Roger grinned. "It's how I'm going to live to a ripe old age." He produced the ampule and lay it on the table.

Wally took a long look at it. He then picked it up and inspected the wax seal on the septum with his finger print deeply incised in it. It was clean and unbroken.

"Was the FBI convinced?"

"I think so. I gave it my best shot." Wally rolled up his sleeve.

"Before we do this, I want you to understand that if you tell anyone, I'll cut you off and you'll be dead in a matter of weeks."

"Gee, that's comforting."

They both chuckled, and Roger felt something pass

between them—an inviolable trust of his old friend.

For a second time Roger explained that the first shot would be of high concentration to be followed up in three days. Then three days after that, followed by a fourth shot on the tenth day. The idea was to build up a plateau in his system. In a few days he would begin to feel the first rush of rejuvenation. The follow-up shots would be administered at different motels. In an emergency—any unexpected side effects—he gave Wally the number of an answering machine whose messages Roger would check periodically.

Wally took it all in, then he opened his arm as Roger applied a tourniquet. He wore surgical gloves. In fact, he had arrived with them on so as not to leave prints.

Roger removed the protective wrapper from a new syringe then scraped away the wax seal. He inserted the needle through the septum and extracted four ccs of Elixir.

"Ready?"

"Forever and ever," he chuckled nervously. "Famous last words."

Then Roger injected the contents into Wally's arm.

"Now what?"

"*Now* we're friends for life."

The woman bounded like a gazelle.

She was a sleek, long-limbed creature whose silver Spandex highlighted the muscles and curves of her body. Her face and shoulders glistened with sweat, her eyes fixed on herself in the mirror as she pounded the treadmill in a strong, clean stride at eight miles per hour. She was pretty in a gamine kind of way with short, swept-back hair and sweatband. But she wasn't very friendly, projecting an air of cool superiority.

Wally had tried to strike up a conversation at the water dispenser, but she was too busy timing her pulse. When he said that he'd just joined the club and wondered if she'd explain the treadmill program, she reluctantly stabbed a few buttons and suggested he hire a trainer. Then she snapped on her headphones and proceeded to stretch elaborately, never once looking his way, but making certain he got to appreciate the full wonders of her body. When she was through, she jumped onto her machine and into a brisk run.

Meanwhile, in his new white shorts and tank top, Wally Olafsson looked like the Pillsbury dough boy waddling on the treadmill beside her. His joints squeaked and clanged as he slowly turned up the pace to a pathetic 3.5 MPH walk, hoping he could keep it up.

He had a mental flash of himself stumbling off in cardiac arrest as Wonder Woman continued to bound away, refusing to break stride to administer CPR and—God forbid!—mouth-to-mouth resuscitation.

At one point he caught her studying herself in the side-wall mirror, no doubt admiring what a perfect specimen of womankind she was—firm in body and mind, worshipped by men of all ages, the envy of the entire female breed. When she caught him smiling at her, she flashed a disdainful look and snapped her head forward.

Wally felt a fleeting pang of remorse. He was nearly inured to female rejection. Not only was he out of the league of young good-looking women, but he had convinced himself that they were a different species: porcelain goddesses whose siren smiles were reserved for Alpha males—those young studs bench-pressing half the building at the other end of the room. In her mind Wally was some fat bald middle-aged creep gawking up the Great Chain of Being.

But that was okay, he told himself. His body cells were humming with renewal. In the week since his first shot, he had dropped three pounds to 218. At this rate, he'd be down to his target weight of 180 in a few months. Except for high blood pressure, also correctable with diet and exercise, he was in general good health. He had never been to the hospital and only once sought medical care—for actinic keratosis, a condition besetting fair-skinned Scandinavians, which had been remedied with the removal of a few frecklelike papules on his forehead and nose, the consequence of too much sun as an adolescent.

Even though he was nearly as bald as a honeydew melon, Roger had said something about the possibility of hair regeneration. It had happened with lab monkeys. Even if not, he could always check out hair clinics. Wouldn't that be something—a head full of hair again? Why not? Miracles were happening in his body by the minute. He swore he could glimpse signs of lost youth in the mirror—the fading of the wrinkles around his eyes, fleshier lips, smoother complexion, the sharpening of his jawline. He looked better by the day. And, best still, he could feel it inside.

It had begun on the sixth day with an odd euphoric lightness as Roger had predicted. Then strange fluidy sensations throughout his muscles—sensations that peaked in nearly uncontrollable urges to move about, to exercise, to feel his blood race. Sensations that led him to his membership here at UltraFit, the *in* yuppie health club in La Crosse. Sensations that kept him marching to the oldies on his headphones, determined to turn his body into a temple of health.

For the first time in his adult life Wally Olafsson looked forward to the passage of time. For the first time in years he no longer had old-man thoughts. He couldn't wait to see what the next weeks would bring—how his body would harden and his face thin down. How his mind would sharpen. How his will to live would heighten.

As he jacked up the pace to 4.0, he could not help but be amazed at how a chance encounter at the wrestling tournament last month had brought him to this machine with a head full of tomorrows.

The plan was to meet at different motels over the next several weeks. They were entering the critical stage of stabilization, Chris explained. And timing was everything. Soon only a one-day window would be allowed before reversal patterns set in. This meant, of course, that Wally could not leave town nor be late for treatments.

On his headphones the Beach Boys were celebrating the special charms of California girls which took him back but without the old sad longing. He turned up the volume.

A few minutes later Wonder Woman got off her treadmill. "Have a good run?" he asked pleasantly.

She mopped her brow with a towel and guzzled some

chi-chi water from her bottle. "Always do," she said smartly, and walked away to join her Alphas.

Wally smiled to himself as he admired her chrome-plated buns in the mirror. *When you're old and gray,* he thought, *and covered with liver spots and hanging on a walker, I'll still be doing eight-point sprints, my child.*

"I'd say he's lying."

Mike Zazzaro had seen the tape twice already in the last few minutes, but Eric Brown punched the play button again. It was his first day back from the conference.

"Look at his face and hands. His eyes."

"I'm looking," Zazzaro said. "What about them?"

"The big innocent Orphan Annies," Brown said. "And the way his voice picks up. He's too loud, and his hands keep moving too much. He's all exaggeration. He protesteth too much." He switched to slow motion. "There: See how he wipes his mouth when he says it's only a resemblance?"

"Yeah?"

"An unconscious gesture, like trying to rub off a lie."

"A one-week conference on cult psychology, and you come back Sigmund Freud. Maybe he spit on his chin."

"He's faking."

"Eric, the guy's nervous and feeling like a horse's ass for fingering an innocent man. That's what's going on."

"Maybe, but I've got a hunch there's another agenda behind that guy's face."

"Like what?"

"Like fear. Like he's scared something will happen, or he's been threatened."

Zazzaro pushed his face to a foot from the monitor again. "He's embarrassed, not scared," Zazzaro said. "Besides, you saw his video of Glover. He's twenty-five years too young—plain and simple. The wrong man."

But that's what didn't make sense to Brown. He paused the tape on Wally Olafsson with his hands floating in front of him, his face full of remorse. When Brown had interviewed him, there was nothing ingenuous in his manners or expression. He looked convinced that Glover and Bacon were one and the same. In fact, he was belligerent about it. Now he's a bundle of nerves, insisting they call off the investigation.

"I know that face, the hairline, body movements, the gestures."

Zazzaro and Bill Pike had gone into the shop two days later. Pike drove the surveillance car. In his report Zazzaro had noted the birthday photo of Glover with the *Life* magazine that would make him thirty-eight, not fifty-six.

"What color were his eyes?"

"Brown."

"Both of them?"

"Yeah."

"He said one was brown, the other green."

Eric nodded, thinking that he could have been wearing colored contacts. But without due cause, they couldn't bring him in because no judge would grant a warrant on the possibility of tinted lenses.

Mike crossed the room and poured himself some coffee from the Braun machine.

"We get a good print on the guy?" Brown asked.

"Yeah. He had on the gloves when I went in, but Billy walked by earlier and saw him handling the fern pot bare-handed. Prints were all over it."

But there was nothing in the Bureau's database for either Roger Glover or Christopher Bacon.

"I have no opinion of this Roger Glover," Brown said. "But it's possible our friend Wally is a flake. He looks good on paper—marketing VP of Midland Investments, active in civic circles, on the hospital board, blah blah blah. But he could also be running around in his mother's undies and insisting the Midas Muffler guy down the street killed JFK."

"So, it's case closed."

"Not yet. I want you and Billy to stay on him a little longer."

"Come on, man. We've got a Net memo to check out the Fiskers. This is going to eat up our time."

Yesterday a directive from central headquarters in Clarksburg alerted all offices to keep watch over followers of a Maryland based group called Witnesses of the Holy Apocalypse. Ever since the millennium, they had gotten such alerts a few times a month. Most were just fire-and-brimstone preachings. But people in this group had ties with paramilitary organizations. The danger was that its leader, a Colonel Lamar Fisk, had a warlord mentality and exhorted his followers to take an active part in the battle of Armageddon. What concerned the Agency was that Fisk knew guns and preached violence.

"That can wait a day," Brown said, staring at the freeze frame of Olafsson in a broad gesture. "Just to get the bug out of my ear."

Because the case was thirteen years old, nobody was actively working on it. The Boston agent in charge had retired from service, which meant that it was Brown's case now.

"So, what do you have in mind?" Mike asked.

"Have the prints sent to Clarksburg for a hand check on the Bacon file. It's possible there might be some unidentified latents they can cross-ref with what you got."

"That could take months."

Because the Bureau did not database unidentified prints, the likelihood was small that any latent prints lifted from the Bacon's home, car, and office were in any evidence file. And if any were, it meant somebody in the West Virginia headquarters had to go ferreting through boxes and evidence bags in the warehouse, removing unidentified strays, recording and classifying them, then comparing what they had with those of Roger Glover on the fern pot. Mike was right. It would tie up lab people for weeks and cost thousands of taxpayer dollars, most likely for naught. Eric knew all that.

"All because of a hunch," Zazzaro said.

Brown made a what-are-you-going-to-do shrug.

Zazzaro shook his head. Then he mouthed the words: "THE WRONG MAN."

"Probably."

"TOO YOUNG."

"Probably."

"YOU'RE AN ASSHOLE."

"Probably."

26

"H appy birthday, Dad."

Roger opened his eyes to a large ice cream cake blazing with candles and inscribed in pink sugar script: *Happy 38 Roger.*

It was March 15, and, according to his birth certificate, Roger Glover's birthday.

He made a big happy face. "What a nice surprise!"

Their house, a modern two-floored structure, was built with a side-attached garage that led into the kitchen. The moment Roger had returned from work, Brett met him and made him close his eyes as he led him into the dining room with the cake in the middle of the table and streamers draped across the ceiling.

Brett and Laura broke into "Happy Birthday to You." When they were finished, Brett insisted that Roger make a wish and blow out the candles. He was enjoying himself, and Roger surprised well.

"I don't know what to wish for," he said.

"A million dollars would help," Laura joked.

"I tried for the last two dozen birthdays—it doesn't work."

"You could wish to live to a hundred," Brett said.

"Yeah, that's a good one."

Laura felt a small ripple of discomfort, but let it pass.

"In a few more years," Brett said, "there won't be any more room on the cake."

"Ho, ho, funny man." Roger blew out the candles.

Birthdays always made them uncomfortable, but they played along because they had taught Brett that family occasions were important. There would be gifts after which they would go out to celebrate at Gino's on Altoona Avenue. Roger's name was on the cake, but the party was really for Brett.

That was the most important thing, Laura told herself—the love of your son and your husband. It's what she drew from during moments when she couldn't sort out reality from masquerade, when she had to remind herself who they were or what time and space they occupied. On occasions like this, she felt a little like Alice stuck halfway through the Wonderland mirror—part of her in the ordinary world, the rest of her in mad makebelieve.

Roger took the knife to the cake. Its center was still frozen solid.

While it thawed, Laura handed him his gift. As usual, he teasingly drew out the moment. It was a small thin package, but he shook it to guess its contents. "New running shoes. No, golf clubs." When Brett complained, Roger finally unwrapped two CDs—a Creedance Clearwater album and the latest Bob Dylan release.

Brett made a face. "Dad, how come you like that old sixties stuff?"

"The Dylan's a new collection."

"Yeah, but he's an old hippie."

"So am I," he slipped, ". . . kind of."

"Thirty-eight's not old."

Laura forced a bright smile. "Brett has something to give you, too," she said, wishing this were over.

Brett then handed Roger his gift wrapped in paper covered with cartoon bouncing babies trailing balloons.

"Hey, nice macho paper!" Once again Roger weighed

and shook the box. "Not a CD. . . . Too small for a new car. . . ."

"Dad, we haven't got all night. Open it." He was more excited than his father.

But Roger continued teasing—feeling its heft, sniffing it, shaking it vigorously. "Tropical fish?"

"We have reservations at seven o'clock, and it's six-thirty," Laura reminded him.

"You guys are no fun." Roger finally removed the paper. Inside was a large framed picture of some sort with a wire attached for hanging. Still prolonging the foreplay, he kept the back side up and the picture face down so neither he or Laura could see it.

Brett was now percolating. "Daaad!" But Roger closed his eyes and turned the picture to his face.

"Dad, will you open your eyes? I'm starving."

"Does Mom know what it is?"

"Not a clue," Laura answered. "But I think it's you naked on a bearskin rug with a rose in your mouth."

"Gross, Mom."

"By the way, Gino's closes at ten," Laura laughed.

"Oh, okay," Roger said and opened his eyes.

His smile froze on his face. It was a blown-up photograph of him holding one-year-old Ricky in the back-yard of their Carleton, Massachusetts home.

"I found it in your old wallet in the basement," Brett said proudly. "I didn't tell Mom, but she gave me the money to get it enlarged. It's you and me. Like it?"

"Yeah."

"How about you, Mom?"

Laura stared at the photo, and felt her mouth twist into a rictus of a grin. "It's lovely."

She had forgotten the photo. Ricky at fifteen months, the summer of 1983. He was wearing Chris's cap and sunglasses so that his eyes weren't visible. But the shape of his baby face could be taken for Brett's and he was wearing red Oshkosh overalls like Brett's. In his hand was the red and black stuffed Mickey Mouse doll.

They had fled Carleton in such a fury that Laura was staring at the only photograph of Ricky they had seen in fourteen years. What ripped at Laura's heart was how Brett thought it was himself in Chris's arms.

"Do you like it?"

Laura held her breath and nodded. "Yeah." The syllable caught in her throat.

"How old was I then?"

"About a year and a half," Roger answered.

"And you were twenty-five. Don't get mad, Dad, but you looked a lot older back then."

Laura handed Roger the knife. "I think it's ready now."

"But how come your hair was lighter?" Brett asked.

"The sun," Roger replied, thinking fast. "I spent a lot more time outdoors. The sun bleached it out. Oh, good cake." He pushed a slice to Brett.

"And my hair looks brown in the photograph," Brett continued.

"Well, it got lighter as you got older."

"It did? I thought if you were born brunette you stayed the same, but if you were born blond your hair sometimes turned darker."

"Not always," Roger said.

"But who had blond hair in the family?"

"Your grandfather."

"So I got his hair?"

While Brett and Roger talked, Laura tried to lose herself in tidying up the table, removing wrapping paper, cutting more cake.

"Yes."

"What was his name?"

"Sam."

"Sam Glover?"

"That's right."

"And where's he buried?"

"Wichita, Kansas."

"Maybe on Memorial Day we can visit his grave."

"Uh-huh," Roger nodded. "We'll see."

"And who were my other grandparents? And where are they buried?"

But before Roger could answer, Brett said, "Mom, what are you doing? There are only three of us here. You cut eight pieces."

"Oh." She looked up stupidly and lay the knife down.

She felt crazy. Brett's questions and Roger's made-up responses were almost too much to take. Lies and more lies. They were poisoning their son with them. And the photograph sitting there on the table. Ricky laughing, his two bottom teeth poking up, and Brett thinking it's his teeth and his hair, his life. How could they tell him? How could he ever accept the truth or forgive them?

"At first, I didn't even think it was me," Brett said. "I also don't remember that Mickey Mouse doll."

"You were only a baby," Roger said.

"But I still remember Opus. And I still have him."

"I guess Mickey got lost."

"It's getting late," Laura said, but nobody paid her attention.

"But whose house were we at?" Brett continued.

"Friends'," Roger said.

"What kind of a car is that?"

It was then Laura recognized Roger's yellow 240Z in the background.

"It's a Datsun."

"What's a Datsun?"

"They're called Nissan now."

"It looks pretty old. What year is it?"

Laura looked to Roger for help. "I think it's a '72 or '73. My friend collected sports cars."

Brett accepted that. But with a shock Laura made out the license plate and the green-on-white Massachusetts registration. Wisconsin plates were yellow. Gratefully, that hadn't registered with Brett. But something else had.

"What's *Darby Pharms*?"

Laura felt as if she were sinking in quicksand.

"My hat. It says 'Darby Pharms.' I can just make it out, but they spelled it funny."

Roger squinted at the photo, pretending to make sense of the letters. "Oh yeah. But I'm not sure what that was exactly."

"Here, have some cake, honey." Laura felt desperate.

"Mom, you're crying."

She made a dismissive gesture. "You know me," she said with a forced smile.

"No, you don't like it," Brett said. His face began to crumble.

"No, I do. I love it. It's just I'm such a sentimental sap, you know. It's been so many years. You'll understand when you're a parent."

Brett's shoulders slumped. "You don't like it." His eyes filled up.

"No, honey, I love it. . . . I do, I really do," she insisted. "It's getting late. I better get ready." And she ran upstairs leaving Roger to console Brett, who stood there wondering what had gone wrong with his big surprise.

" 'Younger than springtime am I. Gayer than laughter am I, blah blah blah blah blah BLAH blah blah blah blah am I . . . with youuuuuuu.' "

Wally stepped out of the shower. It was March twenty-second, and he felt every bit of it.

He toweled off, then stepped on the scale. *"Yes!"* he hooted.

One hundred ninety-nine point four.

The first day of spring, and the first time in sixteen years Wally Olafsson had tipped in at a weight below two hundred pounds. That made it a twenty-one pound loss in six weeks. It was also the first time he could read the scale without his glasses, or sucking in his gut. Still naked, he bounded out of the bathroom and examined himself in the floor mirror he bought a few weeks ago.

It was happening: His belly had lost that explosive

bulge, his thighs had shrunk, and his neck had reappeared. No longer did he look like a giant pink bullfrog. Even the beer wings had begun to melt despite the suspicion that he had been born with beer-wing genes.

All the weight machine activity had given definition to his arms and shoulders. His breasts began to give way to pectorals, and, remarkably, he could make out the physique he had inhabited as a younger man.

Even more remarkable, he could fit into 36-waist pants—down three inches. In another month he'd be a svelte 34. And maybe by summer, a dashing 32—his college waistline. The speculation sent a thrill through his loins.

There is a God! And He/She dropped Roger Glover into my lap.

The best part was how he felt: confident, light-hearted, funny, and quick with the old wit. He had also stopped thinking old. In a word, Wally felt happy. Happy, as he hadn't known since the early days of his marriage to Marge. Or even earlier, because *this* form of happiness was the kind reserved for the young who drank life to the lees from bottomless cups. When friends and colleagues remarked how good he looked, he simply told them that he'd joined a health club and gone on a diet.

Of course, only Roger knew the truth—and Roger's wife. Wally wished he could see Wendy again; it had been thirty years. Roger admitted it would be fun to share old times, but it was dangerous. Even though the Feds had apparently called off the investigation, were they to spot the three of them whooping it up in a bar, they would smell a rat. You don't accuse a people of mass murder, then retract your claim only to become drinking pals.

Wally opened the window. Cool just-spring air flooded in. Amazingly, it even smelled different—the way it did when he was a kid. Elixir was like a transfusion of new blood. Heightened vision, brighter eyes, smoother skin, higher energy level. And a blazing libido.

"A couple more injections," he had told Roger, "and I'll probably grow another penis."

Last week Wally had leased himself a second car—a shameless look-at-me–red convertible Porsche Boxster. And next Tuesday he had his first appointment at a hair transplant clinic. He also put his lonely-guy divorce house on the market and planned to move into a city condo next month. And that afternoon he had converted three hundred thousand dollars in bonds to aggressive-growth mutual funds.

Life was good. And getting better by the day.

He got dressed. Although he had designs on the kinds of outfits old rockers wore to the Grammys—a black pullover under an unstructured black sportcoat—he needed to drop another few pounds. Soon enough, he told himself—Keith Richards, Paul McCartney, and Wally Olafsson.

Tonight he would suffer tradition in a dark pin-stripe by the Brooks Brothers. As a concession to impending youth, he shocked his white shirt with a here-I-come polychrome Jerry Garcia tie. The final touch was an expensive pair of slick black dress boots. He hadn't had a pair since the Roy Roger specials when he was nine.

When he finished, he looked in the mirror and in his best Jack Palance voice said, "Shane, this town ain't big enough for the two of us!" and he snapped off the light.

He headed out to the garage and hopped into the Porsche. He checked himself in the mirror then drove across town feeling like Tom Cruise in *Top Gun*.

They were going to dinner. Le Bocage, the fanciest new restaurant in town. He and Sheila Monks, aka Wonder Woman.

"So you like older men? Heck, you had me fooled."

"It was a bad day. I had just broken up with a guy and had sworn off the entire male race."

"You mean that densely wadded dude I used to see you with?"

"Yeah, that's him. Tory. After we broke up, he joined another club."

Tory: The beefcake Alpha with the baseball biceps, bumped by middle-aged-but-on-a-comeback Wally Olafsson. "If you don't mind me asking, what exactly came between you and old Tor?"

"His snowboard."

Wally looked at her blankly. "His snowboard," he repeated, as if taking an oath.

"Yeah, and his Roller Blades, tennis racket, golf clubs, shotgun, and mountain bike."

"This guy some kind of sports-equipment fetishist?"

Sheila chuckled. "Kind of. All we ever did was some form of athletic competition. He was a nice guy, but he was more committed to his hunting dog than me. When he joined a rugby team, I cashed in. I lacked the leather balls."

Wally smiled and sipped his champagne. Beauty, brains, and wit to boot. Sheila was the producer and host of a local cable TV program with dreams of moving to the networks. Her latest show was on the failure of America to adopt the metric system. It wasn't a barn-burner, but next week she was interviewing Mikail Gorbachev who was coming to UW Madison to accept an award.

"I know how corny this sounds, but, frankly, I prefer older men. Men in their forties."

Wally smiled. *Thank you, God.* December-May rapidly becoming November-May. It crossed his mind that if things continued with Sheila, they would eventually reach May-May.

Yikes! Then what?

But Wally was savoring life from moment to moment. And at the moment, it was very sweet.

"So how old are you exactly?"

Wally had expected that. Even though this was their

first official date, they grew friendly at the club and had gone for coffee. He looked about ten years younger. But he couldn't lie because if their relationship continued, she would meet his friends and son and learn his real age. If they became "serious," he'd have to explain the "cell plateau" down the road. Fifty-seven would shock; forty-seven would be a lie. Already he was sensing dilemmas.

As they sat there smiling into each other's eyes over champagne and trout amandine with white asparagus, Wally had to remind himself that although Sheila was a delightful young woman, there were many other delightful young women in the world—and so much time.

It was hard to comprehend, but Wally Olafsson's life was becoming an infinite moment.

Suddenly Wally saw himself from afar, sitting in this elegant room full of other couples sipping from each other's eyes, and it occurred to him just what a strange and wondrous thing he was becoming. They were mere mortals, while he was experiencing an apotheosis. He felt like an extraterrestrial sitting among them. No, like some kind of secret deity.

"Well?" Sheila said.

Wally giggled to himself. "I've never had a problem converting to metric."

She frowned. "I don't follow you."

"You asked my age."

"Yeah?"

"Twenty-nine Celsius."

Sheila laughed and dropped the subject.

27

S omething told Roger that he was being watched. Call it a sixth sense or psychic powers or conditioned paranoia, but he was like one of those delicate seismographic devices that picks up tremors just below the threshold of human perception.

It didn't go off very often, but when it did he knew it—like that time last month when the two Feds had put the shop under surveillance. They dropped out of sight a couple days later, probably convinced they were tailing an innocent all-American family going about its business of being unremarkable.

Now the needle was jumping again while he and Brett stood in a line of other runners at the registration table for the 7K Town Day Charity Race.

He looked around, trying to determine the epicenter. Lots of people milled about—runners, spectators, photographers—but nobody seemed to be paying them particular attention. No one but Laura who waved from the gallery at the start and finish line.

False alarm, he thought.

It had happened before in crowds. And this one was alive with nervous energy. Runners were jumping in place, pacing, stretching, getting in some last carbo kicks from PowerBars and O. J. Just the collective electricity of the mass, Roger decided, and got back to the moment.

As Brett exchanged his form for a numbered bib, Roger quietly admired his son. He had grown into a handsome, well-proportioned young man with sculpted musculature, a wasp waist, and hard round glutes. He looked like a young Greek god.

I love you, beautiful boy, Roger whispered to himself.

The registration form asked for the usual data: Name, address, past running meets, and the like. It also asked to check off your "Age Group" because at the end they gave out trophies for each category: Twelve to eighteen years, nineteen to twenty-nine, and so on. Like weight classes for wrestling. The idea was to keep victory relative and not embarrass older runners. But it always created a dilemma because he felt like a cheat—like Rosie Ruiz, who in the 1980s took the women's first place in the Boston Marathon until it was discovered that she had ridden partway on the subway.

Roger was riding Elixir. He checked the 30–39 box and was given a number.

Roger liked to run. On weekends he and Brett would do some miles on the track at Pierson. Brett once commented how cool it was to have an athletic dad. Lots of other kids' fathers were out of shape and did little more than return a baseball. But *his* dad could wrestle, ski, lift weights, and run a six-minute mile.

They did their stretches and took their places. There were maybe three hundred runners. Because it was a charity race, the protocol was a matter of etiquette. The faster runners were up front, while kids and older joggers took the back field.

Brett and Roger took places about three or four deep from the front string, made up of members of the track teams from North and Memorial High and the UW campus as well as people with no body fat and all legs who took town races very seriously.

At the gun, the front wall bolted away, Roger and Brett stayed in the field just behind, keeping up a steady and comfortable pace. This was for fun, so there was no need to push themselves.

The weather was cool and overcast, perfect conditions for the race which would make a large circle from the head of Carson Park, along the river and down some streets, then back to the starting point.

By the end of the fourth kilometer, many who led the pack had fallen back, letting Brett and Roger through. Older runners felt the distance and the younger ones lacked the stamina of a steady high pace. In fact, Brett himself was becoming winded. So Roger slowed down.

As they passed the sixth kilometer mark, the feeling was back—like a magnetic tug at the rear of his brain. Roger looked over his shoulder. A few runners were scattered behind them—a young couple in identical running outfits. A wiry black male. Two white women. All looking intensely absorbed in their running.

His attention fell on a white male. Number 44: A tall guy, in his twenties, who wore a headband, white tank top, and blue shorts and who held steady about ten paces back. He had been pacing Roger and Brett since the beginning.

Then it came back. At registration. Roger had first dismissed it as idle curiosity. But suddenly Number 44 did not seem like just another runner gauging the competition. He was studying him and Brett. Roger caught his eye—an eye made for watching—but he looked away. From all appearances he wasn't struggling. He could easily take them, but held his place instead.

Then Roger remembered something else. Earlier he had spotted him milling about the registration area with an older man in a windbreaker and shouldering a camera with a telephoto lens. Roger didn't like cameras, especially ones with big zooms.

They rounded First Avenue to River Street with less than a kilometer left. Brett was tiring, so Roger cut his pace even more.

Immediately 44 pulled ahead with a hard glance.

Roger felt better. He wasn't a cop after all, just a runner with an attitude. Trying to give you the Evil Eye. Whatever it took to psyche down the competition.

Brett didn't like Roger dropping his pace. "Keep running," he cried. "Don't slow down."

Roger shook his head. "I'm fine."

"No. Do it!" Brett was struggling, but he wanted Roger to open up.

"You sure?"

"*Yes!*"

But he didn't want to leave Brett behind.

Brett must have read his mind because he gasped, "Burn him, Dad. Burn him!"

That was all Roger needed. *For you, Brett*, he whispered, then kicked into a sprint that no other fifty-six year old could possibly summon—and very few thirty-eights.

In a matter of seconds he closed the gap on 44. Someplace behind him he heard Brett let out a howling "Yahoo!"

At about a three hundred meters before the finish, Roger pulled to approximately five paces behind 44, so close he could see the shamrock tattoo on his right shoulder.

Roger kept that up for several seconds as he readied to pull away. Then he moved until he was neck-and-neck with the guy about ten feet on his left. Ahead the road was wide open. They ran in formation like that for awhile. A couple times the guy looked over to Roger. Roger hooked eyes on him, and in that flash something passed between them. Roger didn't know what it was, nor did he care. All his concentration was on that bright yellow finish line a hundred meters ahead.

Cheers from the huge gallery rose up as a small knot of local track stars crossed the finish line first.

At about sixty meters, Roger pushed his throttle to the limit. Straining with everything he had, he moved past 44 without a glance and pumped down the road to the fat yellow finish, crossing a dozen paces ahead.

The crowd went wild not because they knew Roger, but for his breakaway. From over a hundred meters they had watched the two run in perfect stride until Roger made his stupendous sprint to the finish.

Laura ran out to Roger as he panted and stumbled around to catch his breath. She embraced him and gave him some water.

He knew it was irrational, what he had just done— yielding to testosterone. But, Jesus, it felt good to take that guy.

Standing on a bench in the Park across from the finish, Agent Eric Brown shot off two dozen frames from the Nikon with the black zoom and motor drive as Roger flew across the yellow line and into the cheering crowd.

He takes a cup of water from someone. He bends over to catch his breath. He raises a pained face to the sky. He takes a hug from his wife, who looks older than he in the zoom. He dumps a cup of water over his head. He towels off. He downs more water. He high-fives his son. He gives a wave to Bill Pike when he crosses the line.

And Brown caught it all.

"Olafsson's right," Pike said when he finally made his way to Brown. "The wrong guy." He was still panting and mopping his brow with a towel.

"Yeah, but for thirty-eight, the bastard can run."

"Tell me about it." Pike's face was drained and his lungs still burned. "I don't know what his secret is, but he must have rocket fuel for blood, is all."

"Roger, I'm sorry to call you at the shop, but it's extremely important."

Jenny tried to disguise the desperation in her voice, but he heard it.

And, yet, he still turned on her harshly. "If it's about the orchids, m'am, I can't help you. They're not available."

That was their code word. Whenever they discussed Elixir on the phone, her sister and Roger had referred to it as the "orchids."

It was so unfair, Jenny thought. So unfair. And Laura was to blame. She had poisoned his mind. Her own sister! "But you must," Jenny pleaded. You have to. If you don't—"

"I'm sorry, m'am, I can't help you," he said, and hung up.

For a startled moment Jenny stood there with the dead phone to her ear. He had cut her off because he was afraid their lines were tapped, which was why he never even addressed her by name.

But that was ridiculous after all these years. Roger and Laura had new lives, and Jenny had moved out of Kalamazoo years ago. Even Ted didn't know where she and her daughter were living.

Jenny put down the phone, thinking how selfish and inconsiderate of him. Her own brother-in-law. And after all she had done for them.

The music still wafted down from Abigail's room. Thank goodness she hadn't heard the conversation.

Jenny felt the panic grip her again. The last injection of serum could not hold her much longer. Any day now she could begin to change. Laura had said it was awful what happened to the monkeys.

What will happen to me? Jenny's brain screamed. They said you turned old and died in a matter of hours. It was too horrible to contemplate.

I can't leave her like this.

"Mother!" Abigail called from upstairs.

"Yes, darling?"

"How do you say *kangaroo* in French?"

"I don't know," she yelled, "but I'll look it up."

As she made her way for the dictionary, Jenny looked at her face in the mirror. "God, help me," she whispered.

"It's the second time this week she's called. She sounded a little crazy," Roger said from the bathroom.

As usual, Wendy was in bed propped up with a book. It was what she did every night before going to sleep.

Jenny had turned fifty a few months ago, and Wendy knew it had hit her hard. She had called them several times about Elixir, to the point of begging. Having been a registered nurse, she assured them that she could administer needle injections to herself, that she would be no problem to them at all, that they could even Federal Express a few vials to her. But they had flatly refused.

Roger snapped off the bathroom light and headed for the bed. He had touched up his beard and grayed his sideburns.

"She wasn't just irrational," he continued. "The way she talked. Her tempo was all off. She took long pauses before responding. I wasn't even sure she got what I was saying. At one point she called me Mr. Bigshot and threatened not to be my friend anymore. It was like talking to a child."

Laura didn't want to get into more Jenny-bashing. "She's been through a lot," she said.

"But I don't think she'll let it go. She sounded almost threatening."

He got into bed beside her.

Tonight Laura was reading a mystery novel. For years she had avoided the genre because they reminded her of her own lost career. Ironically, her fugitive status had made *If I Should Die* a best-seller years ago. She had thought about getting back into writing under a pseudonym, but there were too many risks in going public. They still lived in fear of seeing recognition flicker in a stranger's eyes. Also, some hawk-eyed reader might picked up on quirks of style and connect her to Wendy

Bacon. So, sadly, she had abandoned her passion and became just another reader.

Roger reached over and pulled the book out of her hand and gave her a kiss. He had that goatish look in his eye. He rubbed his hand down her thighs.

"Not tonight." She could see the disappointment in his face. Brett was already asleep in his room, so that was no excuse. She just didn't feel like it. She gave his hand a conciliatory squeeze. "I'm sorry."

"Not as much as I am."

There was a time he would have protested—when they were both younger. When they were biological equals. But he had become resigned to rejection. These days they made love just a couple times a month.

He took her face in his hands. "I love you, you know."

"I know," she said. She still liked hearing that, but she no longer took refuge in the words. "And I love you. Tomorrow night, I promise."

Roger nodded. "Sure," he said and kissed her lightly on the mouth.

She dimmed the light and lay quietly against him for several minutes. The silence was charged with bad feelings. Several times when they were out she'd catch him looking at younger women. And how could she blame him? Even though she kept up aerobics, ate right, colored her hair, used vitamin supplements and all the hot anti-wrinkle creams on the market, a quarter century of biology separated them. Technically, she could be his mother.

"We don't have many more years left for this," she said.

"Left for what?"

She wished he wouldn't play dumb. "For charades."

"Do we have to get into that now?"

It scared him when she brought it up because the inevitable was happening—to her, not him. Between fake identities and the makeup, he had almost fallen for the artifice. Once a few years ago she had let the roots of her hair grow out, and he was shocked at all the gray. He had nearly forgotten she was growing old.

"Well, when exactly do you want to talk about it?" she asked.

"How about tomorrow night after jumping on each other's bones?"

"Roger, when are you going to face the obvious? I'm fifty-five years old. In four years I'll qualify for senior citizen discounts."

"You're in great shape."

"No, I'm not. I'm older and heavier. I don't have your energy level, nor your sexual hunger. I've changed. I've slowed down."

"That's bull. You're fine, and you look terrific."

"Roger, will you please stop it?"

"Stop what?"

"Stop patronizing me. Stop this *pity* sex."

"It's not pity sex. I want to make love to you."

"No, you want to make love to Wendy Bacon."

He started to protest, but fell flat. He looked away, but she could see the tears in his eyes.

She felt the tears well in her own eyes. She took his hand. "I'm sorry, but it's not like it was."

After a long moment's silence, he said, "You have an option."

"That's not an option, and you know it."

"Don't you like being alive? Don't you want to be with me?" For a second, he looked like a little boy begging his mom for understanding.

Laura sighed. Yes, she felt the temptation. More than her sister or any other woman alive, she heard the siren call every day. But she had made herself a promise long ago.

"How about when he's older?" He was still holding out hope that when Brett matured she would give in. "In seven years he'll be twenty-one."

"And I'll be sixty-three."

Already their sex was bordering on the bizarre. In

seven years it would be sick. She'd feel like a cradle-robbing old hussy, and he'd have to fake it.

"But you'd retrogress to fifty or younger."

"You mean Laura would be as young as Wendy."

"If that's the way you want to look at it."

"Maybe I won't want to be."

"But maybe you will."

They were silent for a long spell, and Laura felt the old anger burn itself through the sadness. Roger had brought this upon them himself. In a monumentally stupid act he had injected the stuff into his veins thirteen years ago and forever infected the very fabric of their lives. While she understood all the forces that had driven him to that act, she could never forgive him. More than anyone else alive he was able to foresee the consequences but had chosen to disregard them instead. And while she felt pity and compassion for him, there were moments she hated him for what he had done.

"Laura, I need you. I don't want to go this alone."

Laura closed her eyes and remained silent. She knew the panic he was beginning to feel. Aside from Wally, who still remained on the sidelines of things, she was the only person in the world who knew who and what Roger was. She was his sole intimate. His life had come to a standstill, and the future appeared some vast and empty stretch. It might take another thirty years for her to die. Toward the end he might even care for her like an aged parent. But after she was gone, could he go on without her? Could he live alone with his secret? Would he take another lover?

With Brett in her life, these considerations were no longer priorities. She didn't say this, of course. Nor did she mention a third option that had crossed her mind: divorce.

Brett was still too young. He was crazy about his father and splitting up would scar him permanently. Nor could he comprehend the rationale: not for the lack of love, but time.

When he was older, she told herself. After they had explained all the other awful stuff.

"Laura, promise me just one thing," he pleaded. "That you'll keep open the option—okay? Maybe after Brett's off and on his own?"

She sighed. "I'm out of promises," she said and turned off the light.

And as she lay in the dark, she wondered at the extraordinary muddle of their lives.

God Almighty, how was it going to end?

FBI HEADQUARTERS, CLARKSBURG,
WEST VIRGINIA

Eileen Rice was only half-conscious at how the coffee had turned cold in her cup. She was too lost in what she had discovered on her computer monitor.

The image was of partial loops with a count of eleven ridges on a bias from the triradius to the core of the inner terminus. Her best guess was the right index, although that made no difference since the morphologies were identical across the digits.

What set off the alarm in her head was the nearly full loop found on the latent print coded "Mark (4)-137-left II."

On the split screen, she enlarged the image and clicked on the base print. With the pivot ball, she rotated the axes until they were in alignment. Then she tapped a few keys and brought the two images into superimposition.

A perfect match.

The image on the left was the print lifted from the Carleton, Massachusetts premises in 1988. It was the same print found on household objects including a coffee mug at the same premises. The image on the right had been lifted seven weeks ago from a flower pot in a shop in Eau Claire, Wisconsin.

It had taken that long because it was an old case and no prints were on file in the database. That meant Eileen had to conduct a hand search of all the latent prints from door handles, clothing, and household items included in the evidence files. And because of their recent move to new headquarters, boxes of old cases had been misplaced. Eventually she found dozens of different prints, scanned and entered them into the database, then classified and compared them to the nine different latents found on the Eau Claire fern pot, wrapping paper, receipt, and business card which also had to be scanned and classified.

That meant running over three hundred comparisons, carefully tabulating each elimination. Also, of the 43 million individuals in the National Fingerprint File/Interstate Identification Index, none matched any prints in the case.

But identifying the prints was not Eileen Rice's problem. With the mouse, she clicked the terminal to print out the matching prints—one for her own files, and one to the terminal of the field office in Madison, Wisconsin. She then picked up the phone and dialed the number of Agent Eric Brown.

Wally didn't quite know how to ask her.

It had been so many years since he had last dated—twenty-five, counting two years of cohabitation, nineteen of marriage, and four of celibate divorce—he wasn't quite sure how it was done. This was their sixth formal date and they had not yet been sexual. How exactly did you word such a request to the Now Generation?

"Say, are you feeling romantic?"

Or: *"Gee, Sheila, you know it's been a hundred and four days since we met, and we've exchanged six hello-and-good-night kisses. It's all been nice and innocent, but isn't it time we moved to Phase Two?"*

Or: *"So far this has cost me twelve hundred and thirty-nine dollars, and I still haven't scored yet. What about it?"*

Or simply: *"Want to fuck?"*

They were driving back from a movie in Wally's Porsche with the top up because it was unseasonably cold. But the stars were out, the traffic was light, and the cotton was high.

And Wally Olafsson felt as happy as Tinkerbell.

It was especially momentous since that morning he had dropped below the 185-pound mark into territory he hadn't known since college. He was also down to a thirty-four-inch waist and 15½ shirt. Even more remarkable, his hair had started growing back. Somehow the tabulone stuff had restimulated the follicles, producing a new golden growth that had covered a once-vast dead zone. It looked like fine silk, like that of a newborn's hair. Already an inch long, he had actually fashioned a part. He told Sheila that he was taking hair-growth stimulants.

"You look like a different person."

"The same Wonderful Wally, just less of him."

"You should patent that diet you're on. You could make millions."

"You can't put willpower in a bottle, lady," he said in his best John Wayne. In the mirror he patted his new hair, still in disbelief. *God, it felt good to be alive!*

"If I didn't know better, I'd say you were getting younger."

Gulp! he thought.

"I mean it. It's amazing."

"It's you, my dear. You bring out the boy in me." Then he broke into a few bars of "You Make Me Feel So Young."

"Bull! It's ninety minutes a day on the StairMaster and old Menudo tapes you've been hiding."

He laughed happily. "Aw, she saw through my cover."

"So, how old did you say you were?"

It had become a game: He, the coy older companion; she, the insistent young inquisitor.

"Why is knowing my age so important?"

"Just curious. Besides, it's women who don't tell how old they are, not guys."

"I'm liberated."

"I'd say forty-four."

"Forty-four!" He slapped his chest in mock horror.

She laughed. "Okay, forty . . . maybe thirty-nine."

"That's better," he sniffed.

"You're going to hate me, but when you first joined the club I thought you were about sixty."

He made a sharp swerve of the car.

She chuckled again. "Surely, I erred, but you know what I'm saying—the weight and the hair."

"Yes, I do," he smiled. Tomorrow he would meet Roger for his next shot—the first of three large dosages spaced a day apart. The high critical period, Roger had said. "I'll make a deal with you."

"Try me."

"I'll tell you my age if we can let the evening extend beyond a simple *bon soir* at your doorstep."

"Wally Olafsson, that's bribery."

"Or sexual harassment, depending on how badly you want to know my age."

She smiled and thought about it for a few moments.

In the rearview mirror he fixed his hair again and noticed the same big SUV behind him, its headlights like twin suns bearing down on him. These days every other car on the road was some kind of sports utility vehicle. He felt like an immigrant in his Porsche.

As he flipped the mirror to night mode, he felt Sheila's hand rest on his leg.

"Your place, or mine?" she asked.

The rush of joy returned Wally from the mirror. The

big Jeep Cherokee could have driven over his car and he wouldn't have noticed. "Which is closer?" he gasped.

She laughed and gave him a great big kiss on his part. "Yours."

28

---·•·---

Roger had just turned down Margaret Street for his next delivery when he spotted a green SUV two cars back.

He couldn't see the faces of the two men, but it looked like the same Jeep Cherokee. If it was, then this was no casual surveillance. They had come up with evidence and had a warrant to take him in.

His first thought was Laura. She was shopping for food and a present for Brett whose graduation from Pierson middle school was in three weeks. He pulled out his cell phone. It would be a call he dreaded almost as much as getting caught.

The SUV kept a couple cars back. Traffic was light on the main roads so he could hold them in the mirror. If it was the Feds, they had come up with something. Something Wally had nothing to do with. He was far into treatments and having too good a time playing New Age Playboy. Something else.

On the floor sat a cooler containing four dozen ampules of Elixir. Since the day the Feds first dropped by, he had stashed the supply in the Igloo under a layer of ice, some insulin, and a couple cans of Pepsi. Another thirteen dozen ampules were in the freezer of their Minnesota condo. Except for the three year supply in the emergency tube around his neck, the remaining supply was buried miles from here. The Igloo went wherever he did, just in case. Even a man on death row is allowed his medicine.

Roger made two turns through the heart of town. And they stayed on him.

He slammed the wheel with his hand. *This was not supposed to happen.*

He punched Laura's number on the cellphone. They each had one registered under aliases. In thirteen years this was the second Red Alert. The first was a false alarm. God, that this was another.

He heard her voice, and muttered a prayer of thanks. "Where are you?"

"In the car. I just finished shopping."

"Where are you exactly?"

She told him the street. "Why?"

"I'm being followed. I think it's the Feds."

"Oh, Jesus, no."

He tried to keep his voice even, soothing. "Laura, don't panic. It may not be the real thing. But just in case, pick up Brett."

The first place the Feds would check was their house. They'd ask around and one of their neighbors would remember that Brett had a game at Pierson. He could hear her fighting the terror. "Laura, do you understand? Get Brett and head for the condo."

No matter how measured he kept his tone, the mention of their safe house made it more real. Their condo was in Minneapolis, a hundred miles from here.

"Laura, do you understand?"

He heard the catch in her voice. She took a deep breath to steady herself. "Yes. I'm okay. I'll get him." The thought of Brett being left parentless had steeled her resolve. "What about you?"

"I'll be there tonight."

"Tonight? Why tonight?"

He wished she hadn't forgotten. "I told you, I'm meeting Wally in Black River Falls."

If it weren't critical mass, she would blast him. From the start she had resented his treating Wally, even if it meant buying him off. She resented the very sight of the ampules. It was what had gotten them into this nightmare twenty years ago.

Before he hung up, he said, "Laura, we'll be fine."

But she clicked off.

For a moment, his mind was lost in the silence of the open line—a silence crackling with frightened disbelief that it was happening again. What they code-named the Awful-Awful. But all he heard was fear and anger.

The light at Fenwick turned yellow, and Roger floored the accelerator. The van careened across the intersection and made the first left down a side street. The Jeep must have pulled out of line and run the red light, because it appeared in Roger's mirror about a hundred meters back.

He took three more turns then crossed the river and headed for the airport. The Jeep stayed with him several cars back.

He cut to an access road, weaving his way through traffic, then pulled into an industrial park consisting of rows of warehouses separated by long driveways where trucks pulled in for deliveries. Because it was Saturday, there was no traffic in the complex.

The streets were potholed from all the trucks, yet the Jeep barreled after him as if on the Interstate.

Ahead, Roger spotted the familiar yellow sign that hung over the narrow alley separating Triple E Sheet Metal from DeLaura Display.

He floored the accelerator until he was maybe a hundred feet short, then slammed the brakes and cut the wheel, sending the van into a screeching slide that flung him into the alley. Luckily it was clear, so he floored it. A couple moments later, the Jeep turned in behind him.

The alley was wide enough for a single truck. Behind it lay a spacious lot with trucks and half a dozen cars including a 1992 dark blue Toyota Camry which he stored for just such a contingency.

At a point near the alley's end, Roger slammed on the brakes and cut the wheel, sending the van into a sideways rest. Even if the Jeep decided to ram through, the van was too heavy for a single shot to clear. It might also incapacitate itself.

Roger grabbed the cooler and bolted across the lot to the Toyota.

He heard no crash as he sped out the rear exit. But he could see the agents run after him in frustration. The one with a cell phone to his ear he recognized. Number 44 from the Town Day Race.

He was a fed, after all!

Roger had only a few moments reprieve before every cop car in a twenty-mile radius was alerted, so he raced across town to the municipal lot off Jefferson where he kept the black Blazer registered to Harry Stork. Over the years he had rehearsed these runs, hoping in his heart of hearts not to hear the curtain call. In the glove compartment was a stage makeup kit including mustaches, wig, and glasses.

In less than ten minutes, he was on the ramp to highway 94. Every atom of his physical being urged him to turn north to Minneapolis. Laura would be in a terrible state trying to make things seem perfectly normal to Brett. It was the worst possible time to be separated.

Yet, he knew what he had to do and turned up the south ramp that would take him to the Best Western Motel in Black River Falls to give Wally his stabilizing shot.

Laura was on the way back from the grocery store when she got the call.

As rehearsed, she drove to a city parking garage where they kept a dark blue Subaru Outback registered under an alias. The police would be looking for her in a maroon

Volvo. If this was the Awful-Awful, her face would be all over the media which meant she couldn't walk into a grocery market within hundreds of miles. So she unloaded the groceries from the Volvo, then raced out of town to Pierson.

Years ago she had pledged to stay with Roger all the way. But things were different today. They weren't the same people. If it weren't for Brett, she would turn them in and dump all the serum but what Roger needed.

She approached the school, frantically hoping not to find the place jammed with flashing blue squad cars. It wasn't. But if the police were after them, she had small window before they showed.

The parking lot was full of cars for the game. As she pulled in, she felt under her seat for the box containing a loaded .38-caliber Smith and Wesson. Roger had taken her out to the woods to practice shooting until she felt comfortable. It made no sense to have a gun if you didn't know what to do with it.

She parked at the far end of the lot and slipped the gun into her shoulder bag, praying it wouldn't see the light of day. She cut through the cluster of small buildings to the playing fields. The good news was that the white Pierson team was at bat. The bad news was that Brett, number 33, was on second base.

A large boisterous crowd filled the grand stands and spilled along the baselines. Laura was active in the Pierson PTA, so she recognized many people. But the game was tied with two outs, so nobody paid her much attention as she cut behind the crowd. Brett spotted her and nodded.

Coach Starsky and his assistants were clustered by the Pierson bench. She didn't know how long before the sides retired. If there were hits or walks, it could go on for another twenty minutes. She waited, with her heart pounding, under a tree, thinking that she might suffer cardiac arrest if she didn't get Brett out of here.

The batter was walked, and she nearly screamed in

frustration. The next batter took two balls then cracked the third high to center field. Thank God, it was caught.

While Brett trotted off the field, she approached Starsky, telling herself it had to be sure and quick.

Starsky, a guy in his late twenties, was barking batter lineup when he saw her. "He's having a great game." He nodded toward the scoreboard. "Three of those runs have his name on them."

She tried to look delighted. "Look, Star, I'm sorry, but I'm going to have to take him out."

He looked at her in disbelief. "What?"

"It's a medical emergency. Roger. He's in the hospital." She began to choke up.

Starsky's face fell. "Oh, jeez, I'm sorry. Yeah, sure. Jeez, I hope he's going to be okay. Christ, he's so young."

Brett came over.

She took a deep breath knowing how rotten this was. "It's Dad. He's in the hospital. We have to go."

Instantly Brett's face darkened. "What's wrong with him? What happened?"

"I think he'll be okay, but we have to go."

Thankfully, Brett didn't protest. "Sorry," she said to Starsky.

"Jeez, good luck. Nice game, Brett."

Laura hustled him toward the parking lot. She could feel the eyes rake her. People were thinking that it had to be pretty bad to pull him out of a game. She hated herself for the sham. She hated depriving him of the glory. This was a high point in his young life. And in a few short hours the television would blare out the story that he had been pulled from the game because his parents were mass murderers disguised as just-plain-folk Laura and Roger Glover.

She led him to the Subaru. Brett was fighting tears and asking her for details. "In the car," she growled.

They were nearly at her car when a police cruiser pulled into the lot. Laura nearly started screaming. But it turned the other way. She fumbled in her handbag for the keys. Her hand was shaking so badly, she could barely get the key into the lock.

Suddenly the cruiser pulled directly behind the Subaru.

"Mom, whose car is this?" Brett asked loud enough for the cop to hear.

Goddamn you, Brett.

"Hey!" the cop shouted.

Laura froze. In the next minute their lives would change forever. Laura slipped her hand in the bag and gripped the gun, still not looking at the officer.

The cop called again, and Laura flicked the safety off. She knew she would shoot him dead if he tried to stop her. She knew that as sure as night followed day. It made no sense and somewhere down the road she'd wish she had exercised better judgment, sorry she hadn't settled on a less brutal alternative. But at the moment she was operating on pure mother-bear adrenaline, thinking only of saving her son from a life of foster homes.

"Mom, it's Mr. Brezek."

"You pulling out?"

Gene Brezek was the father of ace pitcher Brian, and Brett's good friend. Laura gasped a yes.

"I just got off duty," Brezek said. He still had his uniform on. "Who's winning?"

"Tie six-all," Brett said.

Brezek moved the cruiser so she could back out. "How come you're leaving?"

Laura was still fumbling with the key. "Not feeling well."

"Get a new car?"

She nearly said a rental, but caught herself. Rental cars all had coded license plates. "A friend's."

"Where's Roger?"

She opened the door without answering and let Brett in. In any second his radio would start squawking an all-points bulletin for their arrest.

"Hope you're feeling better," Brezek said, giving up on friendly chat.

She nodded and backed out, concentrating on not hitting anything or squealing away.

"Why did you say I wasn't feeling well?"

It was like Brett to pick up on a lie. They had made honesty a centerpiece in raising him. Trust is what kept families whole and healthy.

She pulled the car out of the grounds and took off up the road away from town.

"You lied to him, Mom."

"It was too much to get into. We've got to go."

"Mom, you're doing sixty. The sign said thirty-five."

They were on a residential road heading for the highway. She didn't know how long before the police showed and Brezek learned that she'd gotten away under his nose. Her only hope was that he didn't notice which way she headed from campus. She cut her speed.

"What's wrong with Dad?"

"Chest pains."

Another lie, but their lives were infested with them.

"Where is he?"

"In the hospital."

"Memorial's the other way."

"Another hospital."

"There are no other hospitals this way. You're heading for the Interstate."

"Minneapolis."

"Minneapolis? That's a hundred miles from here."

"He was on business there."

And another, she told herself. But at the moment survival was all that mattered, not truth. That might come later when she heard from Roger. If it turned out to be a false alarm, they could stall a few more years.

If it was the Awful-Awful, her son's life as he knew it was over.

•　　•　　•

The meeting was set for two P.M. Wally was on the highway by noon and heading for their rendezvous.

He had awakened that morning a little before nine with Sheila beside him. The real measure of attraction was gauged by how you felt about that person in the morning—before the mouthwash, shower, and brush worked their wonders.

And she had looked beautiful asleep—the small perfectly straight nose, long feathery eyebrows, a ridge of tiny freckles across her nose, full pale lips, shiny brown hair pooled on the pillow like liquid chocolate. He wanted to kiss her awake and make love again. But he felt out of phase. Maybe it was all the champagne they had drunk. And the fact he had gotten only five hours sleep. They had made love four times until Sheila fell asleep from exhaustion.

Wally stepped into the bathroom. He felt lousy and looked it. The bloom was missing from his face. His eyes were glassy and red. Maybe the alcohol. Maybe he needed the stabilizing shot.

After a long shower, he felt a little better and made coffee and breakfast. By the time he drove Sheila home, the slump was back. But he took refuge in recollections of the night. And what a night it had been.

They had driven to his new pied-à-terre high on a bluff overlooking the Mississippi. He had moved in three weeks ago after the furniture arrived, including a king-size bed and an elegant entertainment unit that housed a state-of-the-art sound system. For the occasion he had on ice a bottle of Grand Dame Veuve Clicquot.

It had started on the white leather couch in the dim light of the living room overlooking the boats on the river, and rapidly proceeded to the bed in the next room, leaving a Hansel-and-Gretl trail of clothing.

He could still see her sitting on the bed with her legs up to her chin, waiting for him to select a CD from the rack. And while he did, all Wally could think was *Thank you, God. Thank you, God.*

Sheila had jokingly suggested Ravel's *Bolero* as in the movie *10*. Wally didn't have that, thinking that there was a time when "Old Man River" would have been his speed.

"Will you settle for *'The Sabre Dance'*?"

"My God, what am I in for?"

Sheila's musical laugh still chimed in his heart.

This was heaven, he had told himself, and he put on some vintage Sinatra which seemed about right. Sheila agreed.

And somewhere in the middle of "In the Wee Hours of the Morning," she put her arms around Wally's neck, and he knew he had found forever.

Around one-thirty, he pulled into the parking lot of the Black River Falls Best Western Motel on Route 94. As usual, he had made the reservation once Roger had called in the time.

As with all previous meetings, Wally phoned from the room to Roger's safe number and left a cryptic message signaling that he had arrived without notice. To kill time, he inspected himself in the bathroom mirror. He still looked like the image of himself from maybe twenty years ago, although tired, pale, and a little full-faced. Excessive consumption and debauchery, he told himself. The scourge of a Puritan God.

He lay on the bed and closed his eyes, thinking of Sheila Monks. Also Barbara Lopez, the new marketing manager at work, Cyetta McCormick, the condo agent who sold him his place, Julie Goodman, whom he had met at the Black Swan last month, and Barbara Fleishman, Todd's foxy English teacher.

All single, all available.

So many women, so much time.

At 1:50 the telephone rang. Paranoid that he was, Roger always called to check that all was well before arriving.

Wally answered, but there was nobody there. Just the sound of the open line, then a click and the dial tone.

An hour later, and Roger still had not shown, nor called. It was not like him to be late. They had met nine times over the last three months and he had always shown up at the agreed hour.

By four o'clock, Wally had grown anxious and was feeling worse. Roger was two hours overdue, and timing was critical.

Wally's mind raced over the possibilities. Maybe he had hit traffic—but on a Saturday? Or his car could have broken down. Or maybe there was an emergency in his family.

Or maybe he suspected a plot to trap him.

Then an even darker thought shot up: What if Roger had decided not to show? Sure, get him dependent on the stuff then abandon him when critical—a convenient way to eliminate the one person who knew his secret. But why? Did he suspect Wally would leak? Was he afraid he might tell Sheila or his son?

But Roger wouldn't do that. Not his old pal. Their bond was too special. Friends for life.

But, what if?

Wally was nearly breathless with panic when he heard a knock at the door. A rush of relief shot through him as he leapt off the bed and threw it open.

"What the hell . . . ?"

Standing there were Agents Eric Brown and Mike Zazzaro. They walked in and closed the door, Zazzaro keeping his body against it.

"Who were you expecting?"

"Who said I was expecting anybody? And what the hell you doing following me?"

"Mr. Olafsson," Brown said, "we'd like you to come down to headquarters."

"What for?"

"We've located other photographs of someone we

think is Christopher Bacon, and we'd like you to identify them."

"I thought we cleared that up weeks ago," he protested. "It was all a mistake. Ask him." He nodded at Zazzaro.

"I saw the tape, and frankly, we think it was Bacon you saw."

"I don't believe this."

"They're one and the same man, as you'd said," Zazzaro replied. "So we're asking that you come down to the office."

Things were backfiring horribly. Roger had probably picked up their tail. "You mean you're calling me a liar?"

"We didn't say you were lying, but if you are you could be covering for him."

"Covering for him? That's bullshit." For good measure he added, "If you're so interested in who Roger Glover is, why don't you go ask him?"

Zazzaro flashed a look at Brown, and Brown took the question. "He's missing, and that's another thing we want to talk to you about."

Wally suddenly felt faint. "Missing?"

"So are his wife and son. I won't go into details, but they appear to be evading apprehension. We found that telling. We also found it telling that two days after you filed your original complaint you showed up to retract it."

Wally was nearly frantic. The clock radio read 4:22. The window was shrinking by the minute.

"We have fingerprint matches. They're the same man."

Roger was on the run, which meant he could be anywhere in a three-hundred-mile radius. *JESUS CHRIST!*

He had to get these guys out of here so he could call in a message. "Maybe the prints just look alike."

Brown sighed. "They're identical."

"But he's too young." It was all Wally could think to say.

"If you have knowingly been in contact with this Christopher Bacon, you'd be liable to charges of aiding and abetting a fugitive of a federal crime which if convicted is punishable by life in prison."

"Now I've heard enough." It was a last-ditch effort at righteous indignation. "This is pure bullshit. You have nothing on me. Even if it is the same guy, you can't threaten me with a federal indictment. I know my rights. You've got nothing on me. Nothing."

"So far we haven't."

"What the hell does that mean?"

"We're not threatening you. We're simply asking you to come down to answer some questions."

Wally felt himself heat up. "Do you have a warrant for my arrest?"

"No, but—"

"But nothing!" He shot to his feet. "Get out of here," he said and opened the door. He hoped that someplace out there Roger was keeping watch—that as soon as they were gone he'd appear.

But the agents did not move.

"Get out, goddamn it. You have no right to detain me. *Get out.*"

And before he could stop himself he grabbed Zazzaro's arm and pushed him outside. When Brown tried to restrain him, Wally lost control. He swung at Brown, belting him on the side of the head. With a chop to the neck, Zazzaro brought Wally to his knees and slapped cuffs on him. "Now you have no choice, asshole."

Wally let out a cry of agony. "Please let me go. You don't understand."

They pulled him to his feet. "You can explain it to us at the office."

The FBI agency office was in Madison—three hours away.

* * *

They arrived around nine-thirty.

Because there was no holding cell on the premises, they had summoned a U.S. marshall's car to take Wally to the Madison County jail where he would officially be booked for assaulting a federal officer. As Brown explained, he would be held for the next two nights until sometime Monday when he would be taken to the courthouse for formal arraignment.

That could mean a minimum of forty hours before he'd be granted a bail release. Possibly days before he was free to see Roger again.

While he waited for the car to arrive, Brown said he could call his attorney. They uncuffed his hands to dial, while Brown remained in the room.

The wall clock said 10:20.

It was almost funny how the ironies piggybacked each other, he thought. Here he finally had a chance to leave a message at Roger's safe number, and it was on an FBI phone with an agent just ten feet away. Even if he left a cryptic code, the call would be traced with all their fancy technology, and wherever it was, authorities would swarm down on Roger like vultures on a zebra carcass.

Instead, Wally called his attorney, briefly explaining the situation, telling him to meet him in court tomorrow.

They drove him across town to the U.S. Marshall's office where he was uncuffed and locked in a single cell with a toilet bowl, sink, and bunk. He took to the bunk.

He let his mind drift to Todd. Would he ever see his son again?

He thought of Sheila. At long last he had emerged from the oppressive despair of the last years to discover love, happiness, and a state free of the universal condition of mortality, only to find himself cut at the knee on the very threshold of paradise.

It *was* funny.

He blanked his mind, trying to determine if he were

entering any form of withdrawal. Except for the itchiness of the bedding and a headache, he felt nothing unusual. Nothing but fear wracking his bowels.

Fear which an hour later began to make him drowsy. His hope was that the judge would dismiss charges as a spontaneous misdemeanor and release him. Then he could contact Chris and arrange a quick rendezvous.

Chris/Roger. Where was he?

Evading apprehension.

He could be in Mexico by now.

The cell was quiet and sometime a little after midnight, still not registering any problems, he fell into a deep sleep.

He was awakened the next morning about seven by the guard delivering his breakfast. He still felt weak and only nibbled on the wedge of toast.

By midmorning, his arms and legs were beginning to ache. He also had developed a strange sensation in his head, like a migraine but in the frontal lobe.

By eleven, his skin began to itch even worse, as if he had come down with a case of the hives.

Sometime before noon, the guard came in to tell Wally that his lawyer, a Harry Stork, wanted to see him.

The name meant nothing to Wally. His lawyer's name was Michael Craig. But Wally said to show him in.

Wally waited on his cot with his head propped up on the pillow and stared through the bars while he scratched his arms and chest, his eyes fixed on the security camera over the barred door.

The sound of footsteps made his heart quicken. A moment later the guard unlocked the door. "Fifteen minutes," he said, and let in Harry Stork.

It was Roger.

"It's about time," Wally protested. "I'm paying you bastards good money."

"You're not my only client who spends his weekends in a cellblock."

The guard left.

"Harry Stork?" Wally whispered.

"Don't ask."

"Christ, you have a name for every occasion."

"Something like that."

"What's happening to me?"

"You'll be okay," Roger whispered.

Although this was a low-security holding cell, they had a ceiling mounted security camera for suicide watch. And Roger felt it gawk at him.

The guard had frisked Roger thoroughly and checked his briefcase. But he had missed the syringe and vial of Elixir which were wrapped in gauze and wedged into his crotch under his underwear.

Somehow with his back turned Roger had to unzip his fly and reach into his pants and extract the packet without drawing attention. He tried not to imagine what his movements would look like from the rear, but if the guard were watching the monitor he would become suspicious.

"I feel like hell," Wally whispered. "Weak, blurry vision, itching all over."

"We'll get you back."

Roger pretended to converse softly while Wally lay on the cot with his head propped up. He looked jaundiced. His eyes were out of focus and glassy, and his mouth was white and dry. His fingers were trembling. He was in pain. But he had to hide it or they would call in a doctor. What he needed were the four cc's of what rested uncomfortably in Roger's pants.

He had to be quick.

With his back to the camera and pretending to huddle, Roger undid his fly and slipped his hand into his pants. With a clean motion he pulled out the packet, and unfolded the contents. There was no time to swab Wally's arm and tap for his vein.

He pulled the cellophane wrapper off the syringe with his teeth and in one clean motion, stabbed the needle into the septum, sucking out all 4 ccs of fluid.

Somebody shouted something, and Roger froze. Sudden commotion from down the corridor.

Shouting and the sound of feet. The guard. Jesus! He had been watching the whole time.

"What the hell you think you're doing?"

The guard was at the door, fumbling with his keys. Roger glanced to see the man throw open the door and charge at him with his baton raised.

"What the hell you doing? What've you got there? You guys shooting dope?"

But Roger didn't stop. He dove at Wally to plunge the needle into him, hoping to hit flesh and not end up on a rib or collarbone before the baton came down on his skull.

But that never happened. The guard caught his arm and slammed him into the wall. The syringe flew out of Roger's hand.

Then Roger felt the baton smack the back of his knees, instantly folding him. Then a vicious blow across his shoulders that pancaked Roger to the floor.

A moment later he heard a sickening crunch as the guard's foot came down onto the needle. It was the only needle he had.

Wally let out with a cry—the kind of sound an animal makes when it's been treed for the kill.

The guard pulled Roger up by the shirt. His pants were wet from the puddle of Elixir on the floor.

As the guard went for his cuffs, Roger chopped him on the windpipe. Instantly he fell backward and landed on the toilet bowl, gasping for air.

The cell door was still open. Roger looked at Wally and held open his hands to say there was nothing he could do. He had the emergency supply around his neck but no way of getting it into Wally's bloodstream.

The expression on Wally's face said that he understood. "You tried," he whispered. Then he noticed the guard catching his breath. "Go! Go!"

Roger had only a moment before the guard was on his feet and calling for help. It sickened him to the core to leave Wally but he was in no condition to run.

The guard stumbled to his feet when Wally reached for the keys and tossed them to Roger who bolted through the door, locking it behind him.

Before he dashed out, Roger gave Wally a last look. "Sorry."

Wally shrugged weakly. "All rock and roll while it lasted."

The guard reached for a remote control switch on his belt. Before he could trigger it, Wally rolled off the cot full-body onto him.

By the time the alarm went off, Roger was out the front door and into his car, feeling as if his heart would break.

They moved Wally to another cell in the basement of the building. He did not let on how bad he felt. Even if they brought him to a hospital, they could do nothing for him. The antidote for his condition lay in a dried up puddle on the floor upstairs.

He slept most of the afternoon. At suppertime a different guard brought him a tray of food. He didn't touch it. When the guard asked if he was feeling okay, Wally nodded that he was fine, just tired. The guard asked if he wanted to call anybody—his lawyer, friends, wife— but Wally grunted no. He just wanted to be left alone to sleep.

In a semi-dozing dream state, he imagined Roger had returned, this time disguised as a guard and quietly giving him his stabilizing shot. So convincing was the dream that he fell into a deep peaceful sleep. And for several hours, nobody again disturbed him. Sometime the next morning, which was Monday, he would be taken to the Madison courthouse for arraignment. Then he would be released on bail.

A little after midnight, Wally shook himself awake from an awful dream of being eaten alive by lice. He woke up clawing his face and ears. He pushed himself up. His whole head felt inflamed and swollen including his eyelids, which were so thick he could barely open them. And when he did, his vision was fragmented, as if looking through cracked lenses.

Worse, his ears were filled with a high-pitched tinnitis that over the minutes became louder, as if somebody were turning up the audio.

Soon the sound was unbearable, condensing into hot filaments of pain shooting through his brain; yet he could not stop it with his fingers. It was coming from inside his skull—as if a million insects were filling his head with mad music.

What's happening to me?

He heard himself yell, but it seemed to come from somebody else.

In his mind he floated high above the cell. He banged his head so hard against the ceiling that he was sure his skull was crushed. But it wasn't, nor did the chittering stop. Nor did he pass out as hoped.

He dropped to the floor screaming. Blood trickled over his brows and into his eyes from where the skin split. He rolled around the floor as a strange hot pain twisted the muscles and tendons of his limbs, throbbing in agony as if turned on a rack. Voices yelled at him.

"Cut the fucking noise."

"The sumbitch woke me up."

"Somebody shut him the fuck up."

His brain was a noisy animal thing that couldn't hold awareness. He'd focus on a thought, and suddenly it was gone as if holes were opening up in his brain like bubbles in cheese.

Help me.

For an instant, he was in his dorm suite at Pennypacker, playing bridge and drinking a Haffenreffer because it was the cheapest stuff at the package store, and when you're low on cash a good beer is whatever you can afford. And the Beatles were singing "When I'm Sixty-four," and Wendy and Chris were dancing naked, and Sheila was sitting on his lap kissing his new hair.

Somebody opened the window, and hot yellow pus poured over the sill.

His mind screamed, *Help me. Chris gotta help me*.

Lungs filled with wet air. He was having trouble breathing, flushing out the sacs. As if the old tissue had lost its suppleness.

Drown. You're going to drown.

He rolled to his side and spit up stringy fluid. His lungs were filling up. He couldn't get air.

More yelling.

Then hands were on him. Turning him. Wiping his forehead.

"It's only superficial. Put a Band-Aid on it."

"Chris? That you?"

"What he say?"

"He wants to know if you're Christ."

"Yeah, J. Christ himself at your service."

"We get a screamer once a month, which is why we got this."

Somebody pulled his arm and pushed up his sleeve.

"His buddy came in yesterday and tried to shoot him up. Bopped Clint in the throat, and this one held him down while needle man got away. Want a little fix?" he asked Wally. "Well, here you go."

Wally could barely feel the prick of the needle.

Thank you, Chris . . . Roger.

He heard his mouth mumble something.

"What he say?"

"Thislicksa?"

"He wants to know if you lick it."

"Yeah, lick this, pal."

Jab.

"A lick sir?"

"Yeah, a lick, sir, and a promise, buddy boy. Now go to sleep."

"Frensfalife."

"Yeah, friends for life. You'll feel better in the morning."

Monday morning came six hours later.

Outside a cold sun rose over the horizon and sent shafts of light through the window of the guard's office.

The Monday day deputy was Lenny Novak. On the docket filled out by Clint Marino, a weekend night guard, was the name of the men being held. In cell number four was one Walter P. Olafsson, age fifty-seven, brought in two nights ago for assaulting a federal officer. He was to be taken to the courthouse in the center of town by 9:30 where he would be arraigned.

Every morning Lenny would slip in a breakfast tray. He was a new guy who made an effort to say good morning to the inmates. At cell three, he said, "How you doing this morning, Tom?"

Tom shuffled to the tray slot. "Be doing a lot better if that asshole didn't keep me awake half the night." He nodded to the cell on the other side of his wall.

"Happens sometimes. The walls close in, and they flip out."

Lenny pushed the cart down to the next cell. "Hey, Mr. Olafsson, breakfast." And Lenny pushed the tray into the transfer slot.

No response.

"Time to get up. I'm taking you to courthouse at nine."

Nothing.

Lenny called again. Still no response. Not even a stir. It must have been the sedative they'd given him.

He checked his watch. It was 7:38. He had to be fed and ready to go in little over an hour.

"Hey, pal. Rise and shine."

Nothing.

Because Olafsson was sleeping on his side against the wall, Lenny could not see his face.

He took out his keys and unlocked the door, automatically dropping his hand onto the handle of his baton. It was an unnecessary precaution in this case, because the guy was probably still dopey from the shot. Lenny put his hand on the man's shoulder and shook it. "Come on, guy, time to get up."

Still the man did not stir.

What hit Lenny first was the odor. A sweet sick smell of dead meat. An instant later it registered that Lenny had felt no heat from the man's body.

In one smooth movement he tore off the blanket and pulled the man onto his back.

The man was dead, all right. Lenny's first thought was that he had the wrong prisoner. The docket said the man was supposed to be Caucasian. But this guy was black.

He flicked on his pocket flash. "Jesus Christ!" Gooseflesh spasmed across his scalp.

The man's head did not look human. It was twice the size of normal and covered with dark red lesions. The eyes were swollen balls. His nose looked like a huge deformed black potato covered with lichens. One exposed ear had doubled in size—a fat ragged leaf with dark liquid running out of the canal.

What nearly stopped Lenny's heart was the realization that those scaly lesions were moving. No trick of the light—the skin on the man's face—if you could call it skin—was actually rippling as wet new growths continued to bud off from the man's flesh like some alien organism.

The next moment, Lenny was bounding down the hall for the phone, concentrating all his might to hold down the scream pressing up his throat.

29

L aura tried to conceal her panic so Brett wouldn't think Roger's condition was critical. Yet she did a feeble job of it.

When he turned on the radio, she snapped it off, fearful there would be a police report on their escape. Brett protested, saying he would keep it low, but she refused. When he asked what the problem was, she exploded. " 'No' means *NO!* I don't want to listen to the damn radio, okay?"

A moment later she apologized. He had never seen her so anxious.

"Mom, tell me the truth. Is Dad going to die?"

She looked at him. His gorgeous tawny eyes were so wide with fright that she nearly burst into tears. *So damn unfair.* "No, honey, he's going to be fine. It's probably just muscle spasms. They're doing tests."

It was the best she could do. To elaborate would thicken the lie and make her feel worse. Her objective was simply to minimize his fear.

He didn't respond, and she wasn't convinced he believed her.

Someplace near Hudson on Route 94, she pulled into a gas station to fill up. Before the attendant stepped out,

she stuffed a twenty into Brett's hand and dashed into
the restroom.

Inside she dialed Roger. The sound of his voice filled
her with relief.

He was just approaching Black River Falls. She told
him how she had picked Brett up and the excuse she
used to get him out of the game. He listened, then trying
to sound calm, he told her that it was the feds and he
had gotten away in his safe car.

When they clicked off, she threw up into the toilet.
The Awful-Awful had begun.

"Whose house is this?"

"A friend of Dad's."

"What friend?"

"Nobody you know. One of our growers. He uses it
for business associates when they're in town."

Brett seemed to buy the answer. Laura thought grimly
how good she was getting at deceiving her son. She
could now do it by reflex.

But there was no way she could tell him that it was
their place or he'd want to know why they never mentioned it or brought him before. She also couldn't pass
it off as a rental or he'd wonder why Roger didn't save
money and get a hotel room. They had always treated
Brett with respect, so he trusted that they held few secrets and never dissembled. He accepted her explanation
without question.

When eventually he learned that the last thirteen years
had been a grand lie, she wondered if he'd ever trust
them again.

She also wondered how long she could maintain the
illusion before cracking up.

The condo was located on the west end of Minneapolis—a five-room place in a large, anonymous complex
occupied by young business couples. They had selected

it because its residency included few retirees who might be around all day to keep tabs on them.

"Why can't we see Dad?"

An expected question, and she was ready. "Visiting hours aren't until tomorrow."

"Aren't you going to call the hospital at least?"

He was still in his baseball outfit. She looked at her watch. "In a few minutes. Why don't you take a shower and I'll get dinner ready, okay?" Reluctantly Brett agreed.

She waited until he was in the bathroom and the water was running to call Roger again. He was still in his car but now on his way to Madison. But the news was bad.

Through field glasses he had watched federal agents escort Wally from the motel to a waiting car. Either he had put up resistance or the Feds had dug up incriminating evidence. Whatever, he was in custody and probably on his way to be booked and jailed until arraignment next week.

Laura groaned. "What are we going to do?"

"Hold tight."

"Hold tight? Brett's worried sick you're in a hospital bed."

"I'll be back tomorrow."

"What are you going to do?"

"I want to see where they're taking him. He needs his next shot."

"And what do I tell Brett?"

"That I'm okay and will be home tomorrow."

"He's scared."

"Let me talk to him then."

"I hate this."

"Me too. Put him on."

She tapped the bathroom door then handed Brett the phone. "It's Dad, but you'll have to make it short."

A few minutes later Brett handed her the phone back. "He sounds pretty good," and went back to showering.

Laura closed the bathroom door. Another lie well done.

When Brett was out of the shower and dressed, he looked around the rooms. The place lacked any personal character reflecting real inhabitants. It was furnished with generic sofas, chairs, and tables sitting on beige wall-to-wall carpet and displayed reprint art on the walls. It could have been Motel 6, but it was the best they could afford. The bureaus and closets contained a few items of clothing, some with tags still on them.

While Brett explored the place, Laura put together some dinner. She felt better since Roger had eased Brett's mind. But she wished he were here because being so far made her feel all the more vulnerable.

Was this how they would be living again—in hiding? And how were they to explain that to Brett? He had finals next week and was to graduate middle school in three, then go to overnight camp in the Dells with Brian. How could they tell him that all that was over? That he would never see his friends or go home again? That his parents were not who he thought they were?

Roger's attitude was that they would manage. He had withdrawn $65,000 cash the day he first spotted the tail just in case. They had more money buried with the other half of the Elixir supply. They could move to places far from urban centers. It meant sacrifices—changing their names again, buying more IDs, home schooling, and disguises. But Brett was young enough to adjust.

"Chris, we're not the Unabomber family," she had said.

"The alternative is life imprisonment for us and foster homes for Brett. Which would you prefer?"

She was halfway through cooking the pasta when Brett appeared at the kitchen doorway.

"Feel better?" she said looking up.

He was still in his uniform because it was the only

outfit he had. But his hair was wet from the shower and his face was shiny.

He held a book in his hand. "Is this you?"

Laura nearly fainted on the spot.

If I Should Die.

The copy Jenny had given her years ago. She had forgotten it was on a shelf in the other room. Brett was staring at the black and white dustjacket photo.

Of all the nightmares Laura had lived with, this was the one she had dreaded the most. They had thought about making up a story about Roger stumbling upon a bank robbery one day, and how because he had seen the face of the man who killed a teller, they had entered a witness-protection program and taken on new identities.

Brett's eyes shifted form the photo of Wendy Bacon to Laura, reading the author's bio on the inside. She knew she could not mouth another lie. "Yes, it's me."

Confusion clouded Brett's eyes. "But it says Wendy Bacon."

Laura felt the press of tears but tortured her face into a smile. "Well, honey, that was the name I used back then."

"Back when? When did you write it?"

She took a deep breath and put her arm on his shoulder. This was not how she wanted to break it to him. "A long time ago."

"It says, 'Ms. Bacon makes her home with her husband and son in Carleton, Massachusetts.' " He looked up at her for an explanation.

"That's where we used to live."

"But you said I was born in Kansas."

"We moved."

Brett glanced back at the photograph. "But you look so different. Your hair. . . ." The look in his face was utter bafflement. "The license plate said Massachusetts in Dad's picture I gave you."

"Why don't we sit down inside and I'll explain."

She walked him into the living room. Brett did not

take a seat, but stood facing her with the dustjacket photograph of a brunette Wendy Bacon beaming out into the world from a simpler time.

Laura cupped his face in her hands. "Honey, I first want to say that we love you very much, and that it was because we love you—"

"Mom, cut the crap!" He dropped the book on the table. He looked scared. "It's Dad. He's dying, or something."

"No, that's not it. We're both perfectly *fine*. You just talked with him. He'll be here tomorrow. Believe me."

"I thought he was in the hospital." There was a frantic look in his eyes. "Where is he?"

She took a deep breath. "Madison."

"You lied."

"Honey, you asked about the book—"

"I don't care about the dumb book. What are we doing here? What the hell is going on? Where's Dad?"

"I'm telling you Dad's in Madison. And he's not in a hospital. I swear to it."

Brett wiped his eyes. He didn't have a clue.

It was obscene. *This is the worst moment of my life*, she told herself.

"Honey, there are some things we've not told you, so I wish you'd sit down—"

"I not going to friggin' sit down!"

"Okay," she said trying to find a center. "I'm going to start from the beginning, and everything I'm going to tell you is the truth, I swear to God. I swear on my life."

He looked scared.

God, give me strength.

"Long before you were born, we used to live in Massachusetts where Dad had a job as a biologist. About twenty years ago, he went to Papua New Guinea where he discovered a very rare flower that . . ."

And she told him the story.

At first, Brett didn't believe her, thinking it was some roundabout tale to say how Roger had picked up an exotic disease that was killing him. When it was clear that she was not making it up, he sat in stunned bewilderment.

"But Dad's hair is turning white."

"Because he uses makeup."

"No, he doesn't," he protested angrily.

"Brett, I know how scary this all sounds, but he's perfectly healthy. Elixir keeps him from aging. The only problem is that there were some bad people who wanted to get hold of it and sell it illegally—people who blew up that airplane so we would be killed; but because we weren't on it, they blamed it on us."

Brett's eyes filled up. "What's my real name?"

"Brett's your real name."

"But you said I was born before you took off and got new IDs. When you lived in Massachusetts." His voice was trembling.

"We had named you Adam, but after seven or eight months we . . . you were . . . Brett." She just couldn't tell him that Brett was the name off some dead boy's Social Security card.

"Adam what? What's my whole name?" he demanded.

Laura summoned every last bit of strength to keep from breaking down. "Adam Bacon."

"What?"

"Adam Bacon."

"Adam Bacon?" He spoke his birth name for the first time in his life.

"But that was only while you were a baby."

"I'm adopted. That's what this is all about. You adopted me and my real parents want me back."

"No, no, that's not it."

"Yes, it is. That's why I'm short."

She felt the absurd impulse to laugh. "Brett, honey, I've told you the God's honest truth. You're our son. I gave birth to you. Please believe me. You can see your resemblance in Dad, the shape of your face, your eyes and features . . . and you're not short."

Brett looked as if he were suddenly trapped in a whirlpool and grasping for low-hanging branches. "How old am I? For real," he shouted. "How old am I?"

"You're fourteen. You'll be fifteen in November. You were born in—"

"That's not me in the photograph I gave you, is it?"

"No . . . it was your brother who died before you were born. His name was Ricky."

"I knew that wasn't me, but you said it was. You lied. *You lied!*"

Before she could explain, he jumped to his feet and cried out, "I don't believe this." His face was flushed and beginning to crumble.

"I know how hard it is coming at you all at once—"

He turned toward her, his face wild. "Dad's a freak," he cried. "He's a freak. He can't grow old like everybody else. He's a freak, and you're criminals."

Laura came toward him with arms, but he recoiled. "Don't friggin' touch me!" he screamed. "I don't even know who you are."

"I'm your mother. I've always been your mother."

Frantically he looked around the room again as if for the first time. "We're going to be put in prison. Dad's probably already in prison."

"You just talked with him. He'll be here tomorrow."

Then Brett snapped his head toward her again looking at her as if she were alien. "How old are you? *The truth!* How old?"

She knew this would scare him even more than Roger's condition—that his mother was suddenly fifteen years older than he had believed. "Fifty-five. For real."

She barely got the words out when he dashed into his room. The door slammed like a gunshot through her heart.

Inside she heard the muffled sounds of him crying into the pillow.

•   •   •

Roger returned late the next night in sleeting rain. For the last week, unseasonably cold air had poured down from Canada and turned spring into winter.

After leaving Madison, he had driven to a wooded area and waited until nightfall for his drive to Minneapolis.

For most of that day Brett had stayed in his room, sleeping on and off, refusing to interact with Laura. He was in bed when Roger arrived.

The look on Roger's face made Laura shudder.

"Wally's in jail," he said. He knew that she could not care less about Wally at the moment. He was somebody from thirty years ago. He was somebody associated with Elixir.

But she bit down on all that. "Is there anything you can do?"

"I tried." And he told her.

"You could have been killed."

"I couldn't leave him."

"What does that mean?"

"It means he's going to die if he already hasn't."

"Oh, God. Can't something be done?"

"No."

"But he's your friend. You got him into this. You got him on the stuff, now he's dead or dying."

"Look, I feel shitty enough about this. I did what I could. And don't talk to me like I'm some dope peddler."

She walked to the window. A hard white moon sat in the eastern sky setting the last of the storm clouds in motion. "I'm sorry," she said. "I'm just scared."

"So am I."

"What do we do?"

"Nothing." It wasn't a good answer, but for the time being the condo was as safe as anywhere. Until that changed, they could hole up for a couple weeks, with

Brett doing the food shopping and running errands. It was *their* faces that would be all over the media, not his. "How much did you tell him?"

"Everything."

He nodded. "I suppose it's best."

Silence filled the room.

"Roger, I want us to turn ourselves in. I told you that I would not go on the run again. I will not put him through this."

"Would you prefer Brett grow up with his parents on death row?"

"You don't know that. We might get off. Even so, Brett can live with Jenny."

"Jenny isn't emotionally stable enough to handle another teenage kid."

"She is his aunt, after all. And it's better than moving from place to place in the middle of the night. Think of him."

"I am thinking of him." Once the media got hold of this, the same people who bombed the plane could get back on their trail. People more interested in Elixir than justice—people who could use Brett to get to it. "We stay here for a week or two, then move out."

"No, we're going to find a lawyer."

"And put our fate in the hands of the judicial system?"

"It's better than what we've managed on our own. We're innocent, and we just need to find the right people to believe us."

"We can't prove a negative."

"Their job isn't to prove Quentin and his people are guilty. It's to make a case that we're innocent. And they have no evidence that links us to explosives."

"For thirteen years we've fled prosecution, stolen property, forged credentials, and violated every mail-fraud law on the books."

"They can't execute us for that."

"No, but they could give us life in prison. Wouldn't that be the ultimate irony?"

"If you don't do this I will."

He looked out into the black and thought about it. "It could mean a witness protection program—new names, new locale, new identities."

"What else is new? But at least we won't jump at every cop car."

"That's if we could make a case."

"We have no other choice. He's not growing up undercover."

She was right: Brett needed his parents, but more than that he needed the semblance of a normal life.

"And what about the stuff?"

She looked at him in dismay. "I don't care about it. Take what you need and dump the rest."

"I meant the scientific benefits."

"There are no scientific benefits!"

He said nothing.

"We have to get out of here," she said. "Even if nobody noticed, I'd go nuts cooped up like this."

"For a few days till things cool down. Then we move out and find some good lawyers."

"And what do we do for a place to stay?"

"There's always Aunt Jenny's, after all."

30

I don't know how he died. I've never seen anything like it before. It was like hypertrophic melanoma accelerated a hundred times."

"In English," Eric Brown said.

"Skin cancer gone wild." Ben Friedman was Madison's chief medical examiner. "There was squamous cell carcinoma all over his body and tumors in his stomach and intestines. It was like he exploded in cancer."

"The guard said his head didn't look human, that it was twice the size and covered with growths."

Friedman shook his head in total bafflement. "I don't get it either," he said. "My best guess is a speeded-up form of Werner's syndrome."

"What's that?"

"A chromosomal defect that causes people to age abnormally fast and die before they reach forty. Except this guy appeared to have aged literally overnight."

"You're saying that's impossible."

"I'm saying that whatever happened to him has to my knowledge never occurred before. Besides the wildfire cancer, his body was riddled with diseases associated with advanced aging—arteriosclerosis, malignant neoplasms, osteoporosis, cataracts, liver and kidney morbidity. If I didn't know better, I'd say the man was in his ninth or tenth decade of life."

Brown had laid out the fingerprint matches of Wally Olafsson taken when he was booked the other day and after he died. "It's the same man, birthdate February 13, 1943."

"That's the impossible part," Friedman continued. "Because that would mean that in a matter of hours his body experienced a total and cataclysmic decline. Just how beats the hell out of me."

"What about one of those cell-eating bacteria?"

"Negative. Besides, no known bacteria is that virulent."

"How about some unknown bacteria?"

"Bacteria doesn't work that way." He glanced at a photo of the dead man's head. "This guy died from some monstrous genetic catastrophe."

Ben Friedman's bewilderment sent a cold spike through Brown. He was an unflappable professional who in three decades had seen every grisly form of human death. He was a man who was beyond shock. And now he was at a total loss.

But medical anomalies were not Brown's charge. "Any evidence he had been in contact with Glover?"

"We questioned his colleagues, ex-wife, and girl-friend. Nobody ever heard of Roger Glover," Zazzaro said.

According to the Glovers' neighbors, they were nice normal people. They had a son, Brett, a terrific kid. They owned a flower shop. Nothing unusual. No known relatives. And no friend named Wally Olafsson.

"And they disappeared into thin air."

But the fact that Glover had led them down an alley to a getaway car was a well-thought out emergency plan. The bastard was clever, Brown thought.

"I don't know how Olafsson died or if it has anything to do with Roger Glover," Zazzaro said, "but the son-of-a-bitch knew we were after him. He knew we had connected him to Eastern 219. Why else the chase? You don't set up an elaborate escape just to shake tailgaters."

"I want a cross-reference to anything connecting Glover, Bacon, Olafsson, the wife and kids," Brown said. "Keywords, names of places, people, birthdates, anything."

Zazzaro nodded. "We checked the house. Looked like they left at a moment's notice. Closets were full of clothes. Toothbrushes still in the rack in the bathroom. Books in the kid's backpack. Empty suitcases in the cellar. He must have spotted the tail and called his wife."

That was Brown's guess too. The Pierson baseball coach had said she appeared anxious to pull the kid out of the game. Something about her husband at the hospital. They checked and, of course, no area hospitals had a listing for either a Roger Glover or Christopher Bacon. "Anything connecting them to the Bacons?"

"Not yet, but we're still going through letters, old bills, stuff like that. But we found this." From an evidence bag Zazzaro held up a pouch. "Hair coloring— blond for the wife, black for him. What's interesting is, the small jar is theatrical makeup paint. White. For his beard and sideburns."

"Why make himself look older? With a thirteen-year warrant on my head, I'd go the other way, like the wife."

"You'd think," Zazzaro said. "What also doesn't make sense is that the black hair dye and white paint were stored in a box on the back shelf of his closet, but the Clairol was on a shelf in the bath. Like he was hiding the fact he colored his hair."

"Women can spot these things in the dark."

"I mean from the kid."

"It doesn't make sense," Zazzaro said.

According to files, Christopher Bacon was fifty-six years old. And in his shop Glover told Zazzaro that he was born in 1962 which would make him thirty-eight. Why, wondered Brown, would a fifty-six-year-old man posing as a thirty-eight-year-old need aging makeup? Mike was right: None of it made sense.

"How old does the wife claim she is?" Brown asked.

"Thirty-eight."

Brown checked the shots he had taken of her at the Town Day Race. She could pass for thirty-eight, although in a couple closeups she looked older. He slid one to Friedman. "How old would you say she is?"

The phone rang and Zazzaro took it while the others talked.

Friedman studied the photo for a moment. "Mid-forties."

"How about thirty-eight?"

"Possibly, though time's not been generous with her." He studied the other photos. With a pencil he pointed things out. "Look at her neck here. The skin shows creases and folds of an older woman. I'm not saying she is, but it's one giveaway. That's why women with face-lifts wear scarves. You can stretch a seventy-year old face like Saran Wrap, but it'll be sitting on two inches of chicken skin."

Zazzaro jotted something down then hung up. "We got a background ID," he said. "Roger and Brett Glover of Wichita, Kansas died in a car accident in 1958. Laura Gendron Glover, age twelve, died ten years later. Three bogies."

"Big goddamn surprise," Brown said.

Friedman picked up the photographs of Roger Glover and Christopher Bacon and studied them. "And this is the same guy?"

"We got a print match."

Friedman held them side by side in the window light. "I see the resemblance. But if it's the same guy, how come this Roger Glover looks younger than Christopher Bacon?"

"I don't know how come," Brown snapped. "And I don't give a damn. But I want these photos printed and flashed everywhere in the universe. We're going to get this son-of-a-bitch no matter what."

31

At the bottom of the front page of *The Boston Globe* was a photograph of Roger Glover made from the video shot by the late Walter Olafsson. It was in color and slightly fuzzy, though recognizable. Beside it sat the familiar 1988 media photograph of Christopher Bacon. The caption read: "Same man? FBI claims that Roger Glover of Eau Claire, WI, is Christopher Bacon, a 'most-wanted' fugitive who allegedly blew up Eastern flight 219 in 1988."

On an inside page where the story continued was an additional photograph of Glover doctored by FBI artists to resemble the original of Christopher Bacon. The hair had been electronically cut and lightened and the beard removed. The men looked identical.

An all-points bulletin had been issued in the midwestern states for Glover, who was believed to be armed and dangerous.

The morning television led with the same story. The comment raised most was how Roger Glover appeared younger than when he was Christopher Bacon nearly fifteen years ago. The consensus was that Bacon had undergone facial surgery.

But Quentin Cross knew otherwise.

Sitting in the president's office of Darby

Pharmaceuticals, Inc., he felt the old billion-dollar fantasies quicken his heart again.

Even after all these years, the company had not fully recovered from Bacon's sudden disappearance. For five of those years Quentin had gone into great personal debt paying off Antoine and Consortium investors. Even more capital was lost trying to duplicate Elixir from memory.

By 1991, he had given up trying to locate Bacon, assuming he had moved to a foreign country or died. He had also abandoned all attempts to reproduce the compound.

Until that morning.

The news was like a transfusion.

Besides all the financial promise, Quentin at fifty-one was feeling the ever-sharpening tooth of time. And Christopher Bacon had defied time.

But locating him would be impossible on his own. Especially with an army of Feds after him.

Quentin got up and walked around his suite. It had been years since he had thought about Antoine Ducharme. The last he knew, the man owned a string of health clubs and other legitimate businesses. He probably still trafficked in narcotics, and had an assumed identity. Quentin had no idea where he was or what name he went by or if his real name was even Antoine Ducharme. The man lived a layered existence.

But Quentin did have an old telephone number. It had probably been changed long ago. His heart racing, he dialed.

Remarkably, he heard Vince Lucas's voice. "Your old buddy's been spotted," he said right off.

"That's why I'm calling."

"You on-line?"

He was concerned about phone taps.

"Yes."

"Good, turn it on, I'll find you."

Quentin went on-line. In a matter of minutes Vince

sent him an e-mail. *What do you have in mind?*

Quentin wrote back: *I think we should resume our former plan.*

Sounds good. A's already got people working on it. We'll keep you posted.

Quentin was amazed. They didn't miss a beat. *A.* Antoine. Still in power. Still in command. And he had come to the same conclusion about Bacon's condition.

Quentin tapped the keys: *He'll need to be tested. Call.*

A few minutes later Vince called from a cell phone. "What's this 'tested' stuff?"

"If his system has stabilized, we'll need to know his body chemistry, the dosages, side effects, stuff like that."

"You mean, you want him alive?"

"Yes! Absolutely. Nothing must happen to him or his wife if she's on it too."

They had to understand that this went beyond making the stuff for high-rolling clients. It was a quest for godhead. Christopher Bacon was the most valuable specimen in the universe. Once found, they'd strip him down to his atoms.

AIR FORCE ONE

President John Markarian remembered the bombing of Eastern 219, but knew nothing about Elixir.

Before departing for a speech in San Diego, aides had dredged up memos from the Reagan White House and spoken to members of that administration intimate with the efforts to locate Christopher Bacon.

As he listened to a summary of the report, his thoughts were not on the efforts to solve the first case of domestic sabotage in recent times, but the implications of the serum.

"Do people really think he had something?" he asked an aide, Tim Reed.

"Apparently Mr. Reagan did." Reed handed the president a report of the meeting between Ross Darby and Reagan.

The language was not very technical, but detailed enough to convince Reagan that Bacon had manipulated the DNA sequences to stop the cellular clock.

When he was finished, the president was shown that morning's *Washington Post* with the side-by-side wire photos.

"It's the same guy," he said.

"Which would you say looks younger, sir?"

"Except for the white hairs, the guy with the beard."

The aide nodded. "That was taken four months ago, the other in 1985."

"No retouching?"

"None."

"Is Darby still with us?"

"No, sir. Coincidentally, he died in his sleep of cardiac arrest a few days following his visit."

"What are we doing to find Glover?"

"Everything possible."

"And alive and unharmed."

"We'll try."

While the Republic rolled by thirty-seven thousand feet below, the president's mind considered the same implications that had fascinated Ronald Reagan. Given recent medical advances, the populace was growing older. The downside was the ballooning of the age-related diseases. He envisioned a great graying future of Baby Boomers on walkers and in wheelchairs, collecting social security and Medicare checks that totaled in the trillions.

Already, more than half of federal spending—beyond defense and the interest in the national debt—went to pensioners in some form. In ten years when the last of the boomers had retired, more than half of the next generation's taxable income would be used to pay the costs. By 2020, the nation would go bankrupt. It was a crisis too monstrous to resolve for any administration.

However, Markarian speculated, if this Elixir actually prolonged life for a decade or two, it could solve the Social Security crisis and save the nation. If people lived longer, they would work well beyond sixty-five, which would mean a phenomenal reduction in health care as well as a greater tax base.

Of course, the Reagan report mentioned mice living six times their lifespan. Nothing about humans. So his speculations were demographic fantasies.

Yet his mind kept coming back to how much younger Roger Glover looked today than fifteen years earlier. Was it possible the guy had tried it on himself? Sounded like something right out of some sci-fi tale.

But it got him thinking about hereditary averages, averages that suggested John Markarian had about ten years left. Were he to serve a second term, that would leave him three wee years to write an autobiography, work on his golf game, and spend time with his grandchildren.

As he stared out the window into endless blue skies, all he kept thinking about was "biological retrogression" and how he wanted to see this Christopher Bacon/Roger Glover guy up close and personal.

The large white jet touched down a little after one in warm California sunshine. The president and his entourage were picked up on the tarmac.

When he was settled into the limo, Tim Reed slipped beside him to say that CNN and had just announced that an unnamed former employee from Darby Pharmaceuticals was spreading rumors that Christopher Bacon had discovered some kind of "fountain-of-youth" drug.

"Great! Now everybody and his cousin will be gunning for him."

"We can squelch it."

"You can try like hell, but it'll be like getting toothpaste back into the tube. What I want is to bring this Roger Bacon guy in."

"Glover. Roger Glover."

"Whatever. But get him. It's like having Jesus on the loose."

By the time he reached his suite atop El Coronado, the television was blaring nonstop reports of the anti-aging drug.

By early evening, the networks were airing testimonies from unidentified former employees of Darby about animals living far beyond their lifespan, even rejuvenating.

Countering the rumors were biologists who claimed that prolongevity breakthroughs were highly unlikely. Such advances were decades away, unless, of course, Bacon and his group had made some truly miraculous discoveries. Even then, the scientific world would have known about it. Great discoveries don't happen in a bell jar.

One geneticist said he wished he knew what the compound was. "We've known about the telomerase enzyme for years. But if what you're saying is true, then he's found the silver bullet."

Another researcher declared that such a discovery would be the greatest in human history.

One religious leader went so far as to claim that Elixir would make possible a new order of human existence— something akin to the angels.

But others took a darker view. A spokesman of the Witnesses of the Holy Apocalypse, a fortyish-year-old man identified as Reverend Colonel Lamar Fisk, proclaimed that if Elixir could prolong life indefinitely, it would be a sign that Judgment had arrived, closing the long cycle that began with the Fall and to end with the Savior's return. When asked what that meant in human terms, Fisk happily proclaimed that the world would end in conflagration.

"This would not be a war between Arabs and Jews, Serbs and Muslims, black and whites," he said to the camera. "But a war between those who live forever and those who die. This is the handiwork of the Antichrist himself."

Then he lapsed into passages from *Revelations:* " 'Woe unto the inhabitants of the earth for the devil is come to deceive you with false miracles . . .' Only through Jesus Christ the Lord shall men live forever."

Markarian hit the mute button on the remote. "Didn't take them long to plug in the old equations," he said to Reed. "They yapped the same lines when Galileo discovered sunspots and Morse invented the telegraph."

"Except he's no harmless Luddite. His sermons are heard on a hundred different stations."

"Where did the 'Colonel' come from?"

"Desert Storm."

The scene shifted from Lamar Fisk to public opinion polls. According to the announcer, a survey conducted that afternoon showed 79 percent of those questioned would take the Elixir were it safe; 14 percent said they wouldn't; the remaining 7 percent had no opinion.

In another poll, only 9 percent said there was no government coverup, while a whopping 81 percent said they believed the government was not telling the truth.

One man even speculated that the original project was intended to grant prolonged life only to "the chosen." It reminded him of *Dr. Strangelove* where only top government officials, military brass, and scientists were allowed into bomb-proof shelters. "The public be damned."

Somebody else complained about how the government always kept secret "the really good stuff" like Roswell, New Mexico, and Area 51.

Markarian shook his head. "This makes one yearn for Oliver Stone."

"When asked again today about a government cover-up, the president flatly denied the claims, saying that the media is to blame for the wild rumors. 'Democracy survives on honesty, not deceit,' the president said."

The scene switched to a reporter in Lexington, Massachusetts, trying to get a statement from Quentin Cross, president of Darby, on way to his car.

Cross acknowledged that Christopher Bacon was a former employee wanted for murder but that there was no substance to the Elixir rumors. "It's all nonsense. We never had any fountain-of-youth drug." And he got into his car and drove off.

"Get somebody on this guy," Markarian said.

"We already did. He knows nothing."

HILTON HEAD, SOUTH CAROLINA

Antoine Ducharme checked his watch.

He knew it was around six-thirty because the news was on and the sun was slanting on the sea. He also had a finely tuned internal clock that was always within a few minutes of the actual time.

He lay down the mystery he was reading. He had loved mysteries ever since he was a boy in Marseilles, where he exhausted the library's collection of Georges Simenon. It was how he now filled his time when he wasn't at one of his health clubs or at the computer.

He clicked up the volume on the television.

"A goddamn feeding frenzy," Vince Lucas said.

"And it's going to get worse."

They were sitting in the entertainment salon of his estate located on a bluff overlooking Caliogny Bay. Called Vita Nova, the stunning structure in stone and glass enjoyed hundreds of feet of ocean frontage. Out the window spread the Atlantic, behind them a lush garden grotto with flowers in outrageous bloom. Beside the gazebo he had constructed a waterfall that filled the backyard with a cascading rush. The place was his own private little Eden.

Antoine was wearing a green workout suit that he had designed himself for his HealthWays Clubs, a large chain spanning eleven states. He had selected green because it was the color of nature and money.

At sixty-one, he would not go gently into that long night. So, he maintained a vigorous workout schedule and abandoned old eating habits for a miracle Hawaiian diet consisting of taro, poi, and seafood. He had also bought himself an industrial-strength juicer with which he made all sorts of healthful concoctions. At the moment, he was sipping a seaweed-broccoli-mango cocktail.

Vince flicked off the television. "We'll be stumbling over every law agent in the country."

"What do we know about the wife's sister?"

"Divorced, daughter age sixteen. Her ex got out of Marion Federal last year. She moved out of her place in Kalamazoo."

The Glovers could not have managed to disappear without her help. "But you don't know where."

"We're working on it. We figured it's the Midwest still." He picked up a sheet of paper. "We've got nearly a hundred Jennifer Kaminskys in a four-state area we're running down."

"So are the feds, if they haven't already found her."

And when they did, they'd wring her dry. The difference was that the authorities were bound by democratic measures in arriving at the truth. Antoine wasn't.

He walked to the sliding glass door and pressed a button so that it hummed open.

Fresh cold sea air rushed into the room before he closed the door again.

He loved the sea. He had lived by it all his life in France, and then in the Caribbean. It was in his blood, which was why he could never settle in Chicago or Las

Vegas or any inland locale. He needed that view, its constant rhythm, the fishy brine.

Since the news of Glover had broken, Antoine had played the videotape of the elderly Jamaicans rejuvenating. He almost wished he hadn't because it heightened his urgency to find the compound. And toward that end he had summoned every resource at his command including technicians who could worm their way into banks and corporate databases.

But the wife's sister Jennifer had eluded them.

He looked out across the shimmering blue, thinking how he possessed more than any mortal being could make use of in a lifetime. He owned estates on Hilton Head, Jamaica, and Corsica. He owned every mode of transportation. He owned an array of businesses plus a percentage of the cocaine coming into North America from Columbia. At last count his net worth was over 2.8 billion dollars. He had the fortunes and power of King Midas.

There was nothing in the material world that he did not have. Nothing he needed. Nothing he envied in another man, now or ever.

Except one.

It was 6:55, but he checked anyway. "I'd like to meet him face-to-face, this Roger Glover."

"How come?"

"I want to meet the man who stopped wearing watches."

The media confirmed his parents' story. But, under-standably, Brett was still in shock.

For two days he did not talk to them. He felt betrayed, even a little scared. They were not the parents he had thought they were. Not the parents who had brought him up. They were Wendy and Christopher Bacon who were sought by the FBI for mass murder. They had lived a dozen years of make-believe.

At one point Brett asked Roger point-blank, "Did you blow up that plane?"

"No, we did not."

"Then who did?"

Laura had been through this with him the first night, yet Roger felt compelled to let Brett hear it from him. "I think a guy named Quentin Cross had something to do with it." He explained who he was and told him about Betsy's death and the drug connection.

"But why didn't you tell the police?"

"We never got the chance. We were afraid we'd be next, so we took off. Then they bombed the plane we were supposed to be on and blamed it on us. Now we had the police and bad guys after us, and no one to turn to. You were just a baby, and our only concern was keeping you safe."

Roger did his best to assure him of the truth of his words. But past truths did little to ensure a future.

What helped Brett come around were the TV news reports. Before his eyes perfect strangers made horrific pronouncements about his parents—pronouncements that had nothing to do with the mother and father who had raised him lovingly for fourteen years. When Quentin Cross denied reports of an eternal youth drug but claimed that Christopher Bacon had committed murder, Brett exploded. "That's a lot of crap, you friggin' idiot. *You* did it."

The outburst was music to Roger's ears.

Brett was also impressed to hear Wendy Bacon described as a "promising new mystery author" and Chris as a "brilliant scientist."

When one geneticist said that Bacon might have discovered "the silver bullet" of human mortality, Brett gave Roger a pat on the shoulder. "Way to go, Pop!"

The center still held, Roger thought, at least for the moment.

On the fifth day, following Roger's suggestion, Laura called Jenny who now lived in Prairie, Indiana. "Jenny, we need help."

"Help. What kind of help? I don't have any money, if that's what you mean."

"We need a place to stay for a few days."

Instantly Jenny was flustered. "A place to stay? You don't mean here? That's impossible. Why do you need a place to stay?"

Jenny hadn't heard the news, which would have been incredible but for the fact that she didn't own a television or radio, nor, apparently, did she read newspapers. "The police are after us."

After a pause, Jenny said, "I see, but, frankly you're asking an awful lot. I mean, really! Besides, it's far too small here for all of you."

There were only three of them, but she was afraid of getting involved again, Laura guessed. And that was understandable since she was the single mother of a teenage girl. To harbor known fugitives could send her to jail. "I understand. I'm sorry to even ask, really, Jen. It's just that things are getting pretty dicey."

"Well, I really hate to say no," Jenny added. "Don't you have any friends someplace?"

"No."

"I see. Well . . ."

Jenny was not good at dissembling, nor was she good at thinking fast when confronted with crises. As expected, she was flustered by the revelation, and Laura could hear her struggling.

"If it means that much to you," she began, then seemed to catch herself. "But if the police find out you're here . . . well, that would be *awful*. I mean, we'd *all* be caught and sent to prison."

"You're right. Forget it," Laura said, not wanting to put a guilt trip on Jenny. "Really. It's okay. We'll be fine, I mean it." And she said goodbye and hung up.

"So what happens now?" Brett asked.

While the condo complex was fairly anonymous, somebody would soon wonder why the perfectly healthy teenage kid from C7 was running errands and not in school. And where were his parents?

"We'll hole up here for maybe another week," Roger said. "In the meantime, we'll look for a good lawyer. Do you think you can take a few more days?"

"Yeah, but what about you and Mom?"

"What do you mean?"

"You can't grow old like Mom."

The Gordian Knot, thought Roger—what lay at the core of it all. The one inevitability they did not want to ponder. Laura would not yield, and Roger's condition was irreversible. Their heads would not grow old on one pillow. Someday she would die, and he would go on without her indefinitely and unchanged. The prospect tore at him.

The signs were already visible—age lines in her face, loosening flesh, slowing down. And, worse, beneath the skin of things, disaffection had crossed with resentment. They were pulling apart.

Brett sensed none of that. But when Laura came into the room, he asked, "Are you going to take Elixir?"

"No, honey, I'm not." She said that as if announcing the sky is blue.

Brett's eyes filled up. "Why not? I don't want you to die."

She took his hand. "Brett, I'm not going to die, at least not for a long time. Meanwhile, you'll grow up and go off on your own like every other kid."

She had a knack for making things sound so normal. Brett thought about her words. He was not consoled. "How come Dad took it?"

"It was a mistake," Roger said. "I wish I hadn't. I wasn't thinking clearly at the time. I did a stupid thing. What's important is that we're still a family, and we're going to be a family for a lot of years. And right now we need you to be strong so we can beat this rap."

Brett stared at Roger for a long moment with an unreadable expression. Then he said, "What's so stupid about living forever?"

Eric Brown had hoped that Sally Johns, the Glovers' shop assistant, knew of relatives or friends who might put them up.

She didn't. She also never heard mention of a vacation home or favorite getaway. She had no idea where they went. Nor could she dispel the shock at the claims.

"He tutored kids in the back room. He had a blackboard and used the plants for show-and-tell. The kids loved him. And she was great—friendly and warm—and did fund-raising for the schools. I can't believe it."

Brown scribbled on his notepad. It was the same report he had gotten from neighbors: boringly nice people. Not even a fucking parking ticket.

Zazzaro stepped into the room with his cell phone. "Ben," he said and handed Eric the phone.

Brown moved to the far side of the room.

Four days ago, Ben Friedman had requested a priority cross-check of files at the Center for Disease Control in Atlanta regarding the death of Walter Olafsson. An extensive autopsy revealed no odd biologies. However, the CDC did have in its files a similar case of death by accelerated senescence dating from 1986 in Canton, Ohio.

"A sixty-two-year-old male named Dexter Quinn," Friedman said. "You'll be interested to know that, according to the Office of Social Security, Mr. Dexter Quinn from 1970 to 1986 worked as a biologist for Darby Pharmaceuticals of Lexington, Massachusetts."

"Oh my."

On the evening of the sixth day the cell phone rang.

Brett was in the shower while Laura and Roger were going through attorney names from photocopies of the Boston directory Brett had made at the local library. It made sense to seek counsel at the epicenter of their case.

They looked at each other anxiously. Only two other people in the world knew that number. And Wally was dead. Roger picked up.

It was Jenny. Thankfully, she remembered to use a nontraceable phone they had bought her years ago.

"I've thought over your request to stay," she announced with odd formality, "And I think we can help you."

"Well, that's very nice of you, but are you sure?"

"Yes, I'm sure."

"You know that the authorities are looking for us," Roger cautioned.

She must have bought a newspaper because she said, "I know that. But you'll be careful not to get caught driving down."

"We'll do our best."

"You have to," she said with forced solicitude. There was a long pause as she muttered something to herself. "It's just that I need a favor in return."

"What's that?"

No sooner were his words out, when like a half-glimpsed premonition he heard her say, "The orchid medicine. I want you to bring me some when you come."

Christ! She had reduced it to barter. "Jenny, we've been through this before. You know I can't do that." He tried to be gentle with her so as not to scare away her offer.

"You can do it if you want to."

"But I'm not going to."

"Then you can't stay here!"

"Then so be it."

He heard her voice change pitch. "Don't you hang up on me, Christopher!"

He didn't know if she had called him that out of hostility or if she was just out of it.

"If you don't bring me some, I'm going to call the police. And I know where you are."

Roger took a deep breath. They didn't need this. He looked over to Laura. "She's threatening to call the cops unless we bring her some Elixir."

"Shit!" Laura grabbed the phone from him. "Jennifer, what the hell is this all about?"

There was a long gaping silence. For a moment she thought Jenny had hung up, except she could hear some odd sound in the background. A tinkling, like broken glass. "Hello?"

Then in a strange girlish voice Jenny said, "Laura, I need my medicine. And I'm not taking no for an answer."

She sounded crazy. "Jenny, we've been through this—"

But Jenny cut her off. "I know where you are, and if you don't bring it, I'll have to tell them. I have their number right here. Minneapolis Police Department." And she rattled off the number.

"I don't believe you're doing this, Jen. I don't believe you'd betray us."

"It's you who's betraying me," she said in that weird singsongy voice.

Laura had never heard her sound so desperate. She had obsessed so much that she had pushed herself over the edge. "Jenny, listen to me, you haven't called them yet, have you?"

"No, but I will. So you better be here tomorrow with it. I'm not fooling."

"Please wait a moment, and don't hang up." Laura put her hand on the mouthpiece and glared at Roger. "We'll have to bring her some. She means it."

Roger nodded and threw his hands in the air to say "promise her anything."

"Okay, we'll be there," Laura said. "But, Jennifer, don't you dare call anybody, or we'll be arrested and you'll never get it. Do you understand?"

"Yes, but you better be here, or else I will." Then she gave her address. "It's a pink house with green shutters." And she hung up.

Laura dialed her number, but the power had been turned off. "What do we do? She sounds nuts."

"We don't have much of a choice."

All Roger could think was that Jenny would be the last person in the world to entrust with Brett.

Jenny lived five hundred miles from Minneapolis by Interstate. Under normal circumstances, the trip would take about ten hours.

But circumstances were anything but normal. Roger

Glover alias Christopher Bacon was everybody's prime
fugitive, which meant he'd have to take back roads and
drive at night to play safe. The round trip would take
days, and there was no way he would put that distance
and time between him and Laura and Brett. They were
in this as a family. They'd go together as a family.

The plan was to stay with Jenny for a night or two
and give her a few ampules and a syringe.

Of course, they didn't know what a safe dosage was;
nor would they know what to do should she have a toxic
reaction. Too much could kill her; too little could cause
her severe damage. And Jenny was damaged enough.
Laura could not live with that. The only solution was to
fake it.

So, before they left, she filled six ampules with saline
solution. Jenny would never know, and when she caught
on weeks later, they'd be working out their defense. Besides keeping her quiet for a few weeks, the visit would
give Jenny the opportunity to meet Brett in the event
their defense failed. They made no mention of this to
Brett. It was too unthinkable.

After leaving Jenny's place, they would continue east
and find the best lawyers they could buy.

"It's hard to believe anybody would take us on,"
Laura said when they were alone.

"Even Timothy McVeigh had a lawyer," Roger said.
"Besides, we have a bargaining chip." He patted the
emergency vial under his shirt.

"Going to try to bribe a judge like Wally?"

"Laura, I didn't bribe him, and you know it. He had
the option not to go on it." Then he added, "Like you."

They explained to Brett that for a day or two they were
going to visit Laura's sister Jenny who lived alone with
her sixteen-year-old daughter. And that while they were
being processed through the judicial system, he would

stay with them. But that wouldn't be for a while. Maybe weeks.

They would take Laura's Subaru and another set of IDs—Peter, Ellen, and Larry Cohen.

"Dad, when it's all over, you going to go back to your old names again?"

"We've been Roger and Laura for so long, it might be kind of confusing. What do you think?"

"Yeah. I don't have to change to Adam, do I?"

"Of course not."

"No offense, but it sounds kind of dumb—you know, Adam and Eve. Running around naked and naming the animals. I'd rather stick with Brett."

"Besides, no one named Brett would be caught dead in a fig leaf, right?"

"I'm glad you see my point."

Laura wore a dark wig and tinted glasses, also tanning lotion which turned her a few shades darker. Meanwhile, Roger shaved off his beard and cut his hair to a whiffle. He looked eerily young. So much so that Brett commented, "You could be my older brother," and looked away unnerved.

Roger also carried cotton absorption wads—the kind dentists used—to be packed in his mouth to alter the shape of his face when they stopped for tolls and gas.

In the middle of the night they loaded the car undetected.

Amidst suitcases of clothes sat the cooler containing chopped ice and two hundred vials of frozen Elixir serum. The remaining supply and notebooks were miles from here, buried nearly a decade ago. And with them, one hundred and twenty thousand dollars in cash.

Before they left, Brett asked to see a sample, so Roger removed the emergency supply from around his neck. He snapped open the tube and extracted the long glass ampule.

Brett held it up to the kitchen light. He had heard about it all week, but this was the first time he had actually laid eyes on what all the world was howling about.

"Looks just like water," he said and handed it back to his father without further comment.

They left just before midnight.

Using secondary roads, Roger calculated the trip would take about seventeen hours. Jenny had insisted on their arrival tomorrow afternoon—as if she held them to some deadline.

As the lights of the condo disappeared in the mirror, the thought circled Roger's mind that there were hordes of people under that black sky who would do anything to lay hands on them. Anything.

To help Laura and Brett doze off, he put on a tape of "Swan Lake" and turned the volume low.

Laura was too anxious to sleep, although Brett spread out on the rear seat with his pillow and a blanket. In the mirror Roger had flashes of that night thirteen years ago when in another car and under different names they drove northward to Black Eagle Lake. Another night, another flight of fear.

By the time they reached Faribault, Laura was asleep against headrest. And Brett was a long lump under the blanket.

At this hour traffic was sparse. Even though U.S. 35 was indirect, it avoided Madison and any police checkpoints.

It was odd, but being on the run made Roger feel closer to Laura than he had in a while. They were doing something together, as a family, bizarre as it was. At one point, she woke up and took his hand. Nothing was actually said in words, though the gesture warmed him. He needed to believe in them still, and in her love. Yet, when he tried to imagine their future, it came up blank.

Someplace in the middle of Odette's transformation into a cygnet, Brett sat up.

"Dad, what would happen if I took Elixir?"

The question came out of the dark like an icepick. He was about to answer, when Laura cut him off. "Don't even think about it," she said, suddenly awake. She spun around to face him. "Everything we've ever warned you about the dangers of drugs—this is far worse. One shot and your body is instantly dependent. And if you go off it, you die a horrible death."

So startled by her reaction, Brett chuckled. "You're just saying that."

"Only because it's true. We told you about the animals."

"Can that happen to you, Dad?"

"Monkeys and humans have the same reaction."

"Has it ever happened to anyone?"

"Yes, but no one you know."

"Then why did you take it?"

"I told you it was a mistake."

"But you'll live forever, right?"

"Not forever. Just longer. But it was still a mistake."

"If you could go back, would you do it again?"

It was like Brett to hammer away. "No, I wouldn't."

"You're just saying that."

There was no reason for Roger to play up his regret or Brett would pursue that. "I'm not. It was wrong."

"How about when I'm older?"

"Brett, you've got a long life ahead of you. You don't need the stuff."

"But someday . . ."

They were caught between minimizing and maximizing the dangers. "We can't think that far ahead."

"But you're going to live a long time, why not both of us? You too, Mom."

"We've already been through this, Brett," Laura said. "I'm not going to take it. And you're not going to take it. It's unnatural and dangerous, simple as that. End of discussion."

But Roger could hear the turn of Brett's mind. Laura had protested too much. "Brett, listen to me," he said, summoning his best voice of fatherly reason. "If you took it now, you would never get older. You would never fully grow up. You would never age but stay fourteen for good. Is that something you'd really want?"

There was long silence.

"Well?"

"Maybe."

"I don't believe this."

President John Markarian turned up the sound on the TV console in the Oval Office. Tim Reed and two other aides had come in to inform him of the latest. With them was Kenneth Parrish, director of the FBI.

As feared, Elixir rumors had snowballed and were barreling down on the White House like an avalanche.

On the screen were videos of laboratory mice and rhesus monkeys.

"What you're seeing are the same animals, just a few weeks apart," the commentator said. "According to former Darby employees, the animals had been treated with Elixir, a secret compound that allegedly had the capacity to prevent aging." The screen split with a BEFORE and AFTER caption under each.

"Sources who had once worked at the Darby labs claim that treated animals on the right had actually rejuvenated over the period."

The split screen gave way to another pair of still photos, that of Christopher Bacon and Roger Glover.

"Speculation holds that Dr. Bacon may have used the serum on himself . . ."

On the president's desk sat faxes and e-mails from scientists, religious leaders, and government officials from around the world demanding to know if the rumors were true, and, if so, to share the secret with the rest of the human race. There were also entreaties from the heads of AARP frantic for the government to find this Christopher Bacon and his secret of prolonged life.

Everywhere White House disclaimers were rebuffed. One commentator declared the Oval Office might be either the stupidest place in the world or the most deceitful.

The television scene shifted to anti-American rallies in Cairo.

How the hell do people mobilize so rapidly? Markarian wondered.

People were toting signs proclaiming "Death to America" and "Markarian is Saten." And "Elixir is Devel's Potion." "Elixir—American/Israeli Plot." And "ELIXIR: Genetic Imperialism."

"Middle East spokesmen view Elixir as a threat to international peace," the reporter continued. "One diplomat warned of possible military conflict unless the U.S. admits to hording the compound and makes it available to all people . . ."

The scene shifted to a fiery preacher addressing a congregation from a church pulpit in Baltimore.

"Meanwhile, here at home, religious leaders are calling for calm while others see Elixir as a Pandora's box. In the words of Reverend Colonel Lamar Fisk, the anti-aging drug is a 'hellish violation of the dominion of God.' "

" 'Ye know neither the day nor the hour wherein the Lord doth come!' " Fisk shouted. " 'And in that hour when the seventh seal is broken the armies of the lord will lay waste the evil that is Babylon . . .' "

The camera panned devoted followers as they howled and hit the air with fists and sticks.

"Goddamn field day for the nutcakes," Markarian said.

"Except this one's dangerous," said Parrish. "They're Heaven's Gate with fangs."

"Meaning what?" Markarian asked.

"Meaning they're not going to pop suicide pills and wait for the flying saucers to whip them away. This Fisk guy has warlord mentality. He preaches that they'll take an active part in Armageddon. A lot of wham-bam, and while they get beamed up to heaven, the rest of us fry."

"Nice religion."

"What's scary is that he knows guns and preaches violence. He's also charismatic and uses mind control and physical abuse to keep followers in line. He's like Charles Manson and David Koresh rolled in one, except he hasn't broken the law yet. I'm just worried when he does."

"What's the latest on Glover?" the president asked Parrish.

"Every airport, bus terminal, and train station in a four-hundred-mile radius around Eau Claire is covered. Highway patrols have been beefed up. We don't know what they're driving because he seems to have a fleet of vehicles. Or he's stealing one after another. But the local police are checking all leads."

"You mean you haven't got a clue."

"I'm afraid not."

"We're already frying."

33

Roger did all the driving, kept alert by adrenaline. They ate in the car and stopped only for fuel and rest rooms. He preferred the self-serve stations to avoid attendants.

But there were no self-serves in Fairfield, Iowa, and they were on empty. Roger pulled into a Mobil station. A guy about twenty came out and put in twenty-four dollars worth of gasoline.

It wasn't until it was time to pay that Roger spotted the hand-written sign in the window: "SORRY. No Fifties or Hundreds."

Big bills were all they had left, which meant having to pay by credit card. Roger was not too worried the attendant would recognize him out here between endless corn fields, especially in his disguise. But he had not counted on an overdue balance.

The kid returned from inside to say that payment was denied.

While Brett slept and Laura tried to doze off, Roger got out of the car and returned the card to his wallet then pulled out another.

But as the guy headed back into the station, Roger suddenly realized that the second card was made out to Peter Cohen, while the first said Harry Stork.

If the attendant was alert, he'd catch the discrepancy and wonder why two names. If he reported it, that could prove disastrous since Harry Stork was the name Roger had used as Wally's attorney—a name that was surely in the police network. In fifteen minutes every road within fifty miles would be blockaded.

Roger had about ten seconds before the guy reached the credit card machine.

If he jumped into the car and took off, the kid would pounce on the phone. If he did nothing and the kid caught on, there'd be a flag on the field. Even if the discrepancy were missed, there would be an American Express record of Harry Stork traveling east into Illinois.

Roger dashed into the office and snatched the card from the kid's hand just as he was about to run it through the machine.

"Hold it, but I'm overdue in payments on that too. You know how it is." He flapped a fifty in the kid's face. "I know it's against company policy, but it's all I've got, and it's real." He held the bill up to the light to point out the water mark and the hidden thread. "See? can't duplicate that."

The kid inspected the fifty, then looked at Roger, wondering if that beaming smile was the front of a fast-talking counterfeiter.

"And, I'll tell you what. For being such a good guy, you can keep the change."

"You serious?"

"You betcha."

The kid inspected the bill in the light again, thinking about the twenty-six dollar tip, weighing that against the manager finding a fifty in the till. The tip won.

"Thanks, mister," he said. And Roger was out the door before he could change his mind.

For the next couple miles his insides felt like gelatin. He was losing his grip, he told himself. That was a double slip-up—pulling the wrong card, and not keeping up with account balances. He should have been more careful.

What made it worse was that Roger Glover had now gone the way of Chris Bacon—right to the top of the wanted lists. So had Harry Stork. He was down to three different cards—under three different aliases, different addresses, different birthdates. Christ! He was beginning to wonder who the hell he really was. Peter Cohen? James Hensel? Frank D'Amato?

He rode into the graying light feeling schizophrenic.

A few hours later, they stopped at a truck stop where Brett bought them breakfast. They ate in the car then took turns using the rest rooms. Roger was dying for a hot shower. They all were.

At about ten, Laura called Jenny to double-check directions. Laura could hear the relief in Jenny's voice that they were only a few hours away.

But when she said they were bringing Brett, Jenny's reaction turned bizarre.

"Oh, no. That won't do. No visitors. We can't have visitors."

Laura didn't want to spell out the importance of their meeting, not with Brett in earshot. "What's the problem? You said we can stay for the night."

There was a pause as Jenny muttered something inaudible. Then she seemed to find herself. "Some other time. Abigail is sick in bed, and the doctors said no visitors because her resistance is low to infection."

"What's wrong with her?"

"Ooops. I have to go," Jenny declared and hung up.

So Brett wouldn't suspect anything, Laura continued to fake conversation. "I see, well I'll drop by myself then. I hope she gets better soon. We should be there about three. Bye-bye."

Roger looked at Laura for an explanation.

"Abigail's sick."

"So where we going to stay?"

"I don't know."

Around two-thirty they reached the driveway of number 247 Farmington Road, Prairie, Indiana.

Roger drove by, then circled back looking for signs of police. The nearest house, about a quarter mile away, looked dead. But that didn't satisfy Roger. He found a back road behind Jenny's place to check for signs of a stakeout. There were none. It was farming country consisting of open fields of low-growing corn and wheat, and devoid of human life.

Roger pulled into the driveway. From a distance it looked like a Jenny place—a neat little farmhouse in pink and green located at the end of a long drive set back in some trees from the main road and miles from the festering social diseases of big-city America.

But up close, shutters were broken, shingles were missing, half the chimney had lost bricks, and the paint had faded to a yellowy flesh color and was peeling badly. The place looked diseased. The lawn hadn't been cut in weeks. Yet, beside the garage was a small power mower—one that looked manageable by Jenny or a teenage girl.

The plan was for Laura to find out what the story was with Jenny while Roger drove Brett to a store for provisions. If there was a problem, they had a police scanner and cell phones. Jenny was irrational, but not enough to blow the whistle on her own private savior.

Roger pulled up to the front door. All the shades were drawn. No sign of Jenny. No sign of life.

Laura got out and went to the door. A small handwritten note on the bell said OUT OF ORDER. Another said NO SOLICITORS.

Taped to the door was an envelope on which in small fastidious script was the name "Wendy."

Furious that Jenny had posted her name, Laura tore

open the envelope. Inside was a note in tiny meticulous handwriting done in pink: "Please leave orchids in mailbox. Good Luck."

That was it? Laura thought. Drive sixteen bloody hours with every law enforcement agency on their ass, and what Jenny wanted was for them to drop the stuff off then beat it. Find a motel someplace or hole up in a cornfield. No way! If Jenny was dumb enough to plaster her name up, what else would she pull?

Laura banged on the door.

Nothing.

And standing in the open like this only heightened her anxiety. She waved for Roger and Brett to wait in the car, then went around back.

The kitchen door was also locked. But one window was open and the screen was up a few inches so she could get her fingers under it.

Laura slid up the window. Then she went around front and waved Roger and Brett off. Around back again, she climbed inside.

The immediate impression was how dark and lifeless the place was—like a house whose occupants were away on vacation.

Although the curtains were drawn, the small kitchen appeared tidy. It was done in white and pink. Magazine pictures of kittens were magneted to the refrigerator. Also some baby photos.

On the table sat a bowl of overripe fruit with some tiny black flies buzzing around it. Beside the bowl was a small pile of mail. On the top sat an electric bill addressed to Jennifer Phoenix, 247 Farmington Road. Under that were other bills and some toy catalogs all made out to Jennifer Phoenix.

Jennifer Phoenix?

Laura was shocked. Jenny had changed her name and never told them. How many years had it been? And why?

Feeling a hum of uneasiness, Laura moved to the dim

front foyer to call upstairs when she glanced into the living room. Her heart nearly stopped.

It was decorated for Christmas.

By the fireplace sat a large artificial tree fully decked with bulbs, icicles, and lights. Opened presents lay in boxes on the floor. By the fireplace sat a large pink dollhouse, its rooms neatly laid out in miniature furniture and figures. It was a vague replica of Jenny's own house. The fireplace mantle was decorated in colored candles and artificial pine and big red Santas. Over the mantle hung a pastel portrait of Abigail as a young child.

Across the foyer, the dining room was decorated for a birthday party, but it must have been from a while ago because some of the colored streamers criss-crossing the ceiling had come loose and most of the balloons had deflated. A partially-eaten cake sat in the middle of the table around which were several chairs, all but two occupied by large stuffed bunnies, bears, and kangaroos.

A sick chill rippled through Laura.

From the second floor she heard a faint sound. A tinkling, barely audible.

She moved toward the stairs and froze. She had heard it before. The same high metallic plinkings, almost like windchimes.

Music. Background sounds in their last telephone conversation. *"Frere Jacques."* The tune was *"Frere Jacques."*

An irrational sense of dread gripped her as she began to climb the stairs. The music box Jenny had bought in Boston years ago.

"Her first Christmas present."

A few more steps, and she could hear Jenny singing softly.

". . . Morning bells are ringing. Morning bells are ringing. Ding, Dang, Dong. Ding, Dang, Dong."

She reached the door.

Inside Jenny said: "Now in French . . ."

" 'Frere Jacques, Frere Jacques, Dormez vous? Dormez vous? . . .' "

The door was decaled in cartoon animals. A porcelain plaque in big happy letters said ABIGAIL'S ROOM.

A second voice sent a shard of ice through Laura's heart. A voice small and thin and singing along with Jenny.

Laura swung open the door.

" '. . . Sonnez les matines. Sonnez les matines. Din, Don, Din. Din, Don, Din." '

Jenny looked up, her face in a radiant smile. She was sitting in a rocking chair holding a small child.

In a telescoped moment of awareness, Laura registered the silky blond hair, the brown liquid eyes, the ruddy porcelain cheeks. The pink flowered dress from the photos.

"We're singing in French," Abigail proudly announced.

Horror surged through Laura. The room was a mausoleum of little girlhood: Bunny wallpaper, pink lace curtains, stuffed animals, dolls, a big pink toddler bed, pillows mounded with stuffed kittens and Raggedy Anns. A white decaled bureau with ballerina figurines and the big red music box that filled the room with its soulless ditty.

"Ooooo, look," Jenny sang out. "It's Auntie Wendy. How nice. And she brought you your medicine."

"Jenny!" Laura gasped.

"Oh, of course: And *this* is Abigail. I forgot how long it's been." Jenny beamed.

"Hi, Auntie Wendy. You look like your picture," the child said. She opened a small photo album from the shelf. "Your hair is different, but it's very flattering. I like it better." Her pronunciation was perfect.

"We have lots of pictures," Jenny piped in proudly.

"Do you know how to speak French?" Abigail asked. Laura's mind scrambled to land on something that made sense: The girl was somebody else, not Jenny's daughter.

No, Jenny had adopted another child but had not told her for some reason.

No, it *was* Abigail, but she had some growth disorder—some awful disease that had stunted her limbs.

"Well, do you?"

Laura made an inarticulate sound and shook her head.

"Well, I do." And she rattled off a string of words, none of which registered. "And Spanish." And she said something in Spanish. "I haven't learned to read yet, but Mommy says that's for older children. Don't you think I'm old enough to read?"

"Now, let's not be silly," Jenny said. "You're always in such a hurry to do this and that."

There was nothing in Jenny's manner that betrayed the appearance that she was anything other than a sane, willful, and rational woman going through the motions of indulging her toddler daughter.

"You must forgive me," Jenny said. "We're not used to company, so we don't have extra chairs."

Laura's eyes fell to the table beside the bed and bit down on a scream. On it sat a syringe and an empty ampule of Elixir. Roger had said some were missing but had blamed it on faulty memory.

"Jenny, what did you do?" Laura whispered.

But Jenny paid no attention. "Just as well," she sang out. "We were just getting ready for our nap, weren't we?"

Her voice had the musical lilt of a woman at ease with her life.

Laura looked for signs that she was playacting for the child's sake, that beneath the conditioned facade of a mother's loving patience lay some awareness. That Jenny knew what she had done to her daughter.

There were none.

"Can't I stay up, Mommy? Please?"

Nothing was as it seemed. Jenny was out of her mind.

Her daughter was a sixteen-year-old in a toddler's body. Roger was frozen at a half his age.

For a moment Laura felt as if her own mind would go, that without warning she would hear a sickening snap and all the freakshow horrors would be perfectly normal.

"It's already past your bedtime, Little Miss."

"But I want to stay up. I never get company."

"You have lots of company." Jenny waved at all the stuffed animals.

"I mean *real* company."

Abigail looked at the wall clock. "Oh, Mommy, it's time for my medicine."

The clock was a big plastic pocketwatch like what the White Rabbit toted to Wonderland. Except the numbers were reversed and the second hand was running backward.

Good God! The child had memorized positions of the hands without a clue.

"Now give Auntie Wendy a big kiss good night." Adoringly Jenny watched the child climb off her lap.

Abigail's body was tiny, like an anemic dwarf, with newborn skin and hair, but with older movements. She looked like some alien replica of a human child. She opened her arms, but Laura didn't want to touch her.

"How old are you?" Laura asked, her voice rasping.

Jenny tried to cut her off. "No more chit-chat, please. Time for bed."

"Six."

"Six?"

"Almost seven. Then I can go outside."

"Why can't you go out now?"

"Enough, enough, you two," Jenny sang out. "Time for good little girls to go bed."

"Because I'm sick," Abigail answered.

"What's wrong with you? How are you sick?"

"I'm sick, that's all. But Mommy says the medicine

will make me better. And then I can go to Boston. Do they speak French in Boston?"

Jenny got up. "Now I'm getting cross." She picked Abigail up and lay her on the bed to change her diaper. "If you don't mind," Jenny said and shooed Laura out of the room.

The door closed, and Laura leaned up against it with her eyes pressed shut. All her instincts were keyed to be as far from here as she could possibly get.

"You fucking bitch!"

Laura's eyes snapped opened.

A man stood before her with a gun at her face.

"What the hell did you do to my daughter?"

"Ted?" She barely recognize him.

"You made her into a freak." He jammed the gun under her chin.

"I didn't know," she gasped.

"She's the same age she was ten years ago. The same fucking age. She never grew up." His expression shifted as he studied her face. "She gave her your shit then kept her locked up in here for ten years. And nobody knew. Nobody. The neighbors thought she was a widow living alone. She never let her out of the house. Never."

All Laura could do was shake her head.

"She's never seen another kid." His voice cracked and tears began rolling down his face. "How did she get it?"

"She took them."

She explained how Jenny must have stolen some ampules years ago when they were at the cottage in the Adirondacks.

Ted listened and lowered the gun. "It took me a year to find her. I didn't know where they'd moved. She once said she liked the name Phoenix, so I checked the listing. For a whole year." His body slumped. "She still remembers me. Just like before I went away. She should be sixteen years old."

From inside Abigail was protesting something.

Ted put his gun inside his jacket as Jenny stepped out.

She looked at him, and the grin slid off her face and her eyes instantly hardened. "I told you her next visiting hours were tomorrow, not today. Doctor's orders."

Ted looked at Laura. "She's out of her mind."

"Mommy, is that Daddy?"

"Now she heard you," Jenny snapped. "It's time to take her medicine." Then she turned to Laura. "The refills, please."

"Mommy, I want Daddy to give me my medicine. I'll show him how to do it," she shouted.

Laura fumbled in her shoulder bag for the packet of ampules.

"Please, Mommy? Daddy hasn't seen me since I was five."

"Just this once," Jenny said and opened the door. She made a face at Ted. "Make it brief," she snapped.

Abigail was propped up on her bed with her dolls and holding a hypodermic needle. "Then Daddy can tell me about the army."

Jenny led the way, and through the closed door Laura heard Abigail. "Don't cry, Daddy. It doesn't hurt at all."

Laura was trying to decide what to do when her cell phone rang.

It was Roger. The police were coming. He didn't know how they got tipped off, but his scanner had picked up a dispatch call for number 247 Farmington Road. She had to get out immediately. He'd pick her up in a minute.

Ted had called, she told herself. Yes, he had called the police to get help for Abigail.

Laura shot down the stairs and ran outside just as Roger pulled up. Roger flung open the passenger door. "Whose car is that?"

"Ted's. Roger, we have to give her the real stuff," Laura cried. It was packed in the trunks buried in the back of the van.

"Hurry up," Brett shouted. "They're right behind us."

"No. She gave it to Abigail."

Roger looked at her not knowing what she meant. *"Get in!"*

"She gave Elixir to Abigail. We have to give her more."

But Roger disregarded her and pulled her into the passenger seat.

They could send her a supply, she told herself as she closed the door. Yes, they'd mail some ampules from the road. Laura locked the door. The only problem was that she didn't know when her last injection had been.

They were just pulling away when from inside the house three sharp sounds rang out.

"Omigod!" Laura screamed. "Nooooo!" She started to open the door but Roger pulled her back and screeched out the drive and onto the main road. "Go back. For God's sake go back!"

Laura was still screaming as the police in several vehicles turned into Jenny's driveway and poured into her house.

"He killed them. He killed them."

Antoine lay the book on his lap and looked out the window of his Lear jet.

He was two chapters from the end, and he still could not figure out how the protagonist was going to slip the peril. That bothered him because he had always prided himself in second-guessing authors. Only Agatha Christie could throw him. This one was a close second. So far.

"Finished yet?" Vince asked.

"Another twenty pages."

"You can knock it off while they refuel."

Vince double-checked the sheets of specs downloaded from the various databases they had penetrated. He passed a copy to Antoine and the other men in the cabin.

Antoine studied the material. They had narrowed it down, but it was still not enough to pinpoint them. There was a missing element, and timing was critical.

The aircraft descended into the Atlanta airport where they would refuel for the trip to Indianapolis. The unseasonable cold front had left a blanket of snow in the northeast but, gratefully, they would not be heading that far north.

Such bizarre weather for this time of year, Antoine thought. While meteorologists pointed to La Niña, El Niño's cool sister, one religious quack went so far to proclaim that it was "the wrath of God"—the same man who claimed that Roger Glover was the "hand servant of Satan" and Elixir "the Devil's brew."

While the authorities were hot after the Glovers, they did not have the data that sat in Antoine's lap. Data that but for one detail would point to where they were heading.

He checked his watch though he knew it was about four-fifteen.

4:09. He was losing his touch. Age, he told himself. It was mucking up his internal clockwork.

The plane landed.

While the ground crews filled the tanks, Antoine sipped his wine and finished his book.

He reread the last few pages in keen delight. A very interesting twist, he thought. Ingenious, in fact. He had not seen it coming at all. Not at all, even though, of course, there were enough clues—but nothing trite like planted buttons or pipe cleaners. It was in the character of the protagonist herself. So obvious, in retrospect: The yearning for the past. Like Dorothy in *The Wizard of Oz*. Three clicks of her heels.

Character, he told himself. And what is that, but the illustration of incident? And what is incident but the dramatization of character? Henry James, that one.

Antoine licked his lips the way he did when he got excited and picked up the phone to explain to the pilot that there was a change in plans. They would be heading northeast after all. And prepare for a descent in the snow.

34

The Glovers were about three hours into Ohio when the story came over the airwaves: a double murder and suicide that shocked the small farming town of Prairie, Indiana. Information was still scanty, and authorities were not disclosing the names of victims until notification of next of kin.

Laura snapped if off. "Next of kin," she repeated, her voice ragged from crying. "We're next of kin."

Roger said nothing. Gratefully, the hysteria was gone.

Earlier she had been so frantic to turn around that getting caught meant nothing to her. Even if she couldn't have saved them, Jenny was her sister, and Abigail was still her niece. She had to be there, she demanded. She had to be certain their bodies were cared for properly, that they would get decent funeral and burial arrangements—if for nothing else, to draw closure to the madness. Besides, they were responsible for their condition.

"Laura, if we go back, we'd be arrested." Roger had said. "We could also be implicated in their deaths."

"I should have known," she said. "He had a gun. It's why he came. I should never have left."

"He might have killed you, too, Mom," Brett added.

But Laura did not respond to him. "My family is dead," she cried. "Look what we did to them."

For miles she said nothing else but lay her head against a pillow and receded into a silent grief. Every so often she'd weep quietly.

Exhausted, Roger drove on.

More than anything else, what ate at him was what all this was doing to Brett. First, the terror of his parents wanted by every law enforcement agency in the country. Then the horror of Jenny and Abigail's murder. Adding to that was how spent Roger and Laura were. She had always been a brick and he, the voice of reason. Now they were tottering on the edge of defeat.

When they passed signs for the Interstate to Pennsylvania, Brett asked, "Where're we going?"

"Upstate New York," Roger said.

"Who's there?"

"Nobody, I hope. But there's a safehouse we used to live in," and he told Brett about the cottage on Black Eagle Lake. "Think you could handle living in the woods for a few weeks?"

"Sure. It'd be like going to camp."

Brett was putting things in a good light, as if this were some backwoods adventure. And Roger drew some encouragement from that. Brett was at an age when he was expected to assume some responsibility for their fate. Likewise, his opinion and strength of purpose mattered.

Unconsciously Roger fingered the tube around his neck.

The religious loonies had called him the Antichrist. At first he had been humored by the absurd accusation, but as he drove on it struck him how those claims made some kind of sense. Rather than new life, every human and animal he had touched with Elixir had suffered afflictions that were almost biblical.

They passed through Ohio and the northwest corner of Pennsylvania and into the western end of New York state.

While Brett slept through the night, Laura dozed fitfully or just gazed numbly out the window. She said very little.

Roger had thought about stopping at a motel for the night, but that was too risky. Besides, he wouldn't have slept, given the news.

According to the radio, anti-government protests were growing everywhere. People were demanding the White House come clean with the coverup. Others wanted Elixir released to the public. Meanwhile, a siege had taken place at the U.S. embassy in Cairo by fundamentalists. Some people were dead and hostages were being held by a group of men who had declared a holy war against the U.S. for "genetic imperialism." And Roger was its evil leader.

But his demonization did not stop there. Jewish cabalists to Christian millennialists saw Elixir as a sign that the Messiah would descend and wind things up. To some, Roger was simply a neutral harbinger. To others he was the devil incarnate.

There were other stories. One was a followup report about the murder/suicide tragedy in Prairie. Roger tried to turn it off, but Laura heard it and stopped him. She had been hoping against hope that it was somebody else's tragedy.

"We now have confirmed reports that the victims were a middle-age divorced couple, Theodore Kaminsky, age sixty-three, and his wife, Jennifer, age fifty. Jennifer Kaminsky is the sister of Wendy Bacon, alias Laura Glover, wife of biologist Christopher Bacon who . . ." The announcer went on to explain the bizarre twist that linked the crime scene to them.

But what summoned a gasp from Laura was the end of the report.

". . . As reported, there was a third victim who had died later at County Memorial Hospital, but authorities have still not been able to determine the age or identity because of unusual condition of the victim's body. According to Prairie police, it appeared to be a very elderly woman dressed in children's clothing."

"Oh, God!"

"What happened?" Brett asked, waking up.

Laura looked toward Roger, her face bloodless. She tried to talk but couldn't.

"A news report about Jenny," Roger explained. Then he took a deep breath. "What Mom didn't tell you was that Jenny had given the stuff to her daughter to keep her a child."

"What? How come?"

"I'm not sure, but I guess she felt like a failure with Kelly. Whatever, when Abigail died she must have aged."

"You mean she turned really old?"

"Yes."

"Is that right, Mom?"

But she didn't answer him. "Pull over," she said to Roger. "I want you to pull over."

They were on a country road of farms. It was mid-morning and traffic was sparse, and a cold rain fell. "Why?"

"I want you to take what you need, and dump the rest. Please."

She had that wild, desperate look in her eye that for a moment made Roger think he was looking at Jenny.

"Mom, calm down."

"Stop here."

"Laura, I think we better talk this over first."

"Roger, I beg you. Take what you need and destroy the rest."

"And what will that do?"

"It will spare others." Her voice was oddly flat, her manner controlled. But he knew she was at the edge, that if he refused her she would crack. "There's a clearing there," she pointed.

Roger pulled onto a soft shoulder by a field of corn.

"Let's talk this over," he said.

"There's nothing to talk over."

He knew what she was thinking: The substance had killed everything in her life. The world was threatening to explode. She wanted it eliminated. She didn't care how he did it—dump it off the next bridge, smash the vials with a rock. She just wanted the stuff to be gone from existence.

At the moment, Roger cared nothing about the world or even going on indefinitely any more. What was certain was that he could not ask her to hole up for a few weeks in the cabin. Either she would go mad or take Brett to the police herself.

He stared through windshield, the only sound filling the car was that of the rain pattering dismally on the roof. He thought for a moment.

"Okay, but give me twenty-four hours. Then I'll get rid of it. I promise, no matter what. You can do it yourself."

She turned her head toward him. "Twenty-four hours? Who knows where we'll be in twenty-four hours, or who might get hold of it?" She took his arm. "Roger, please do this for me." Her eyes were pooled with tears again. "Please."

"Give me a moment," he said and from his jacket he pulled out the cell phone and a portable tape recorder from the glove compartment. When he was properly connected, he called Information in Washington, D.C. When he got that, he said, "The White House, please."

"What are you doing?" Laura asked.

"Cutting a deal."

"What kind of a deal? What are you talking about?"

"Trust me."

Laura looked at him blankly.

"Dad, don't do anything dumb."

"I've already done that."

Several transfers later and minutes of waiting for a live operator, he announced who he was and asked to speak to the president.

"I'm sorry, the president is busy. If you would like to leave a message, one of his aides will get back to you." She said that as if common citizens called all the time to be put through to the Oval Office.

"Listen to me," he growled. "This is Roger Glover, formerly Christopher Bacon, aka Jesus or Satan depending upon your spiritual persuasion. If you don't recognize the name, turn on your goddamn television."

There was a long pause. Then, "One moment, please."

Two more transfers and he was switched to man who claimed to be the Deputy Chief of White House Security and who asked, "Why exactly do you want to speak to the president, Mr. Glover?"

Exasperated, Roger said: "Because he's the biggest man in the world, and I have the biggest drug in the world. Now do you want to continue haggling, or should I call AARP?"

Two more clicks, and another long wait, then Roger heard the familiar voice. And his heart jogged in his chest.

"This is John Markarian."

Roger nodded to say he got through.

While Laura just stared at him in numbed disbelief, Brett's eyes saucered. "Friggin' cool, Dad," he whispered.

"Mr. President, this is Roger Glover."

"How do I know you're Roger Glover?"

"Because anybody else would have given up trying to get through." To convince him, he outlined some details about Elixir that only the president had been made privy to, including Ross Darby's friendship with Ronald Reagan.

"Okay, what can I do for you?"

"It's what we can do for each other."

Roger explained that he, his wife, and son were ready to turn themselves in and release to the proper authorities the entire supply of Elixir and the scientific notebooks on its manufacture.

The president listened, then said he was pleased to hear that. Then Roger proclaimed his innocence in the murder of Betsy Watkins and the sabotage of Eastern flight 219.

"What I can do for you is help dispel all the mystical garbage that's been flying. And beginning with the fact that I'm still mortal.

"But the important thing, Mr. President, is that Elixir stops cancer cells from growing. It turns off their genetic switches. And one of the side effects is prolongevity." Briefly he explained that and the senescence limitations.

The president listened intently. "A chemical that prevents cancer while prolonging life indefinitely has astounding implications for health care and the economy, I need not tell you."

"I'm familiar with the hysteria," Roger said. "That's another reason why the compound must be monitored." Then Roger listed his conditions for the surrender of themselves and the serum.

So far, it was their word against the authorities' that they were innocent of the charges. But Roger did request a presidential pardon for fleeing prosecution and immunity for Laura and Brett. The president agreed. As for his defense against the charges of murder and sabotage, Roger requested the best legal representation. He also asked for witness protection for Laura and Brett. The president agreed again.

Finally, he asked that the entire supply of Elixir and scientific notebooks be turned over to the medical research arm of Public Citizen with the caveat that it be used exclusively in oncology studies, not human prolongevity. Roger did not personalize, but he warned that the potential dangers were unimaginable.

He glanced at Laura who nodded approval.

"But that's what all the excitement is all about," Markarian responded.

"Mr. President, the nightmare possibilities far exceed those for human cloning which, as you know, is also banned. I must have your consent to nongovernmental regulation, or I will destroy the substance."

"Oh, don't do that."

"I need your word."

"Well, I'll do what I can to aid your requests."

"Including a federal ban on prolongevity studies." He had phrased that as a statement not a question.

Markarian sounded hesitant. He no doubt viewed Elixir as the centerpiece to the economic salvation of the republic.

"Mr. President, imagine your grandchildren growing older than you. Or a child six years old forever."

There was a pause as the president pondered the scenarios. "I see. Well, it will have to meet with the approval of the House and Senate, of course, but I'll do what I can. I give you my word." Then he said that he would turn their surrender over to Kenneth Parrish, Director of the FBI. "So where are you?" the president asked.

"I'm as anxious to end this as you are, sir, but I can't tell you that just yet."

Roger said that he wanted another twenty-four hours before surrendering themselves and Elixir. They did not want the authorities storming their quarters on their last night together for a while. Around 8 A.M. tomorrow, Roger would call to name the exact time and place. And he insisted that it take place in an orderly fashion.

"After I hang up, Mr. President, I'm calling the editorial offices of the *New York Times*, the *Washington Post*, and the *Boston Globe*, as well as the editorial headquarters of all the news networks."

"Mr. Glover, I see no point in turning this into a media circus. This is a matter of national security."

"Something about keeping democracy honest."

The president chuckled. "You've been listening."

"Yes, and two more things. First, I'm taping this conversation. Secondly, I'm calling from a phone that cannot be tracked."

"You've thought of everything."

Roger then asked the president for a direct number to reach him tomorrow. Markarian rattled off the telephone numbers of Ken Parrish and the Oval Office.

Roger repeated them as Laura jotted them down.

He then thanked the president.

When he hung up, Brett slapped him a fiver. "Awesome, Dad. Friggin' awesome."

He looked to Laura for a response. Her face had softened. "That was smart," she said and squeezed his hand. "I just pray it works."

Me too, he thought.

As they drove on, Roger played the tape he had made.

When he got to his request for a ban on the substance, he thought he heard something hiding in the hedges just behind the president's pledge—a shadowy speculation that Roger recalled had once danced for him many years ago.

Eric Brown was thinking about bed when the fax came through from the Indianapolis field office. It was the Medical Examiner's report on Abigail Kaminsky. He made a copy for Zazzaro, and they read it over another pot of coffee.

It was seventeen pages long and thick with medical lingo, but he absorbed the essentials—and they made his skin stipple.

She was small like a child, dressed as a child, but looked like an aged woman.

After pages discussing discrepancies between photographs of the child at the scene and her condition, the report concluded that the victim was physically and mentally retarded, and, thus, had been treated as a young child by her parents. As for the condition of her corpse, medical examiners drew a blank. Abigail Kaminsky Phoenix had died three hours after being shot through the chest, but in that time she had experienced an anomalous mutation of genetic material that resulted in hyper-accelerated senescence. "Causes, unknown. Pathology, unknown."

For a long moment Brown stared at the concluding paragraph.

"You thinking what I'm thinking?"

"Walter Olafsson," Zazzaro said.

"Yeah."

You didn't need to be a Nobel laureate to connect the three cases. Jennifer Whitehead Kaminsky Phoenix was the sister-in-law of the man who invented Elixir; Walter Olafsson was the man who first reported him; and Dexter Quinn once served as his assistant at Darby Pharms years back.

"But why give it to a kid?"

"Beats me."

So far they had seen photos of four individuals on Elixir—the three who died had turned into genetic monsters. The other had rejuvenated.

"This is bad shit," Brown said. "Very bad shit."

Brown could not get his eyes off the autopsy photos of the Kaminsky girl. "Christ, she looks like one of those Egyptian mummies in a Little Bo Peep dress."

35

They arrived at Black Eagle Lake around six that night.

Roger did not head directly to the cottage but for the dirt access road across the lake to a sheltered spot in the trees.

He didn't think the authorities could trace the property to them. Twelve years ago, Roger had purchased the place under an alias and took over paying the taxes by cashier's checks. Unless Jenny had leaked, there was no way the feds could know. Nonetheless, he insisted they watched for signs of a stakeout.

The weather was cold, and this far north there was snow on the ground and more in the forecast.

They waited until sunset, watching the cabin through field glasses. An elderly couple, probably renters from one of the other waterfront places, was fishing from a boat on the lake. But that was the only movement. No planes or helicopters. No SWAT team vehicles.

Night fell, and the only lights came from a summer place half a mile down shore. Otherwise, the lake was an opaque black.

When they decided it was safe, they drove to the cabin. Roger wore his pistol in his belt.

The place was dark and lifeless. They had not been

back in nearly a decade. In the headlights it looked the same, but for some missing shingles. Still sitting in the front yard was the old fountain Laura's father had put in when she and Jenny were kids. It had once been electrified so that water poured out of a vase held aloft on the shoulders of a naked boy. The figure was long gone, and the pool was a shabby basin full of rotted leaves and icy water.

As he pulled the car up, Roger felt like ghosts of their own past returning. In thirteen years they had come full circle.

The key still worked, though the door needed to be shouldered open.

The inside looked untouched from the last time they were here. No signs of a break-in. No vandalism. Nothing out of place. Just cobwebs, dust, and damp frigid air that smelled of neglect. For a second Roger ticked off a fantasy of restoring the place to its original cozy charm and living out their days here. But that wouldn't happen.

The good news was that the electricity and water still worked. The bad news was that the refrigerator did not. That meant he would need to find a cold safe place for the ampules.

While Brett and Laura unpacked their clothes, Roger found one. Then he fired up the furnace to give them heat and hot water for three long showers.

Laura brought Brett to her old bedroom. It was musty, but neat. Laura had packed fresh linens, and while Brett took a shower she and Roger made the beds.

When they were through, she collapsed against his chest. "Almost over," he said.

"Thank God."

He kissed her and held her in his arms for a long time.

Laura showered and got ready for bed while Roger lay down with Brett. It was a ritual that went all the way back to his first big-boy bed. In the early days, they would read to him and chat before he dozed off to sleep.

Roger lay down next to his son and wondered how many more nights they had left.

"Remember what my favorite book was?"

"I sure do, I read it often enough. *Jack and the Beanstalk*."

They had bought him a large hardbound edition, intricately illustrated. The pictures that fascinated Brett the most were of the giant chasing Jack, and the last page showing Jack walking hand in hand with his mother toward a castle, the golden egg–laying goose waddling beside them.

"What happened to Jack's father?"

"Maybe the giant got to him for stealing his treasure."

"But Jack got him back in the end. Must be kind of neat to have a goose like that. I'd have him lay eggs forever."

There was a moment's silence and he heard Brett sniffling.

"You all right?"

"Yeah. I'm fine." After more silence Brett cleared his throat. "The one thing I didn't like about that story is that Jack's father never made it back."

"It's just a story."

Brett reached over and touched the tube around Roger's neck. "What's going to happen, Dad?"

"We're going to turn ourselves in tomorrow. And they'll use the Elixir for cancer research."

"I mean about us. How can we keep going?"

Roger leaned over and kissed Brett on the forehead. He could smell the lavender shampoo in his hair. "Love is how we go on, not youth potions."

A few moments passed in silence. "Brett, if something happened to me, do you think you'd be okay?"

"What do you mean?"

"I mean, if they put me away for a while. . . ."

"How long?"

"I don't know, probably not long. But if we end up

with a dope for a lawyer and I got, say, five years, do you think you could take care of yourself and Mom?"

"Yeah, I guess."

"Just what I figured."

Brett said nothing.

"I love you, big guy."

"I love you too."

Long into the dark silence Roger held his son's hand until Brett fell asleep.

When he got up, he checked on Laura in their bedroom.

The light from the hall spilled onto her sleeping figure alone in the bed. She was wearing his old Legion T-shirt from when he coached Brett's Little League team a few years ago.

For a protracted moment he watched her sleep. He wished she were still awake. He wished he could hold her one more time.

He wished he could turn back the clock to that night thirteen years ago when in a fit of fear and self-pity he stumbled down to the cellar and shot himself up.

He wished these things because he knew the day would come when Laura would wake up one morning and over breakfast would announce that although she still loved him she thought it best they live separately because they no longer could fake living by the same clock.

Roger pushed down the sadness and closed the door.

He was exhausted but too wired to sleep. So, he went downstairs and stretched out on the couch.

After a few minutes he flicked on the television just to fill the place with noise. They could still get only a couple stations.

At first he thought it was a movie. People were running in the street, fires were burning, guns were popping in the background. But it was breaking news.

". . . stopped firing. I can't see them from where we

are," the announcer said, "but the embassy appears secure again." The scene shifted back to the anchor. "Once again, the siege of the American Embassy in Cairo is over. But not before four people were killed and several others injured.

"The incident began late last evening when Islamic fundamentalists held a rally decrying the alleged youth-serum Elixir as a U.S.–Israeli plot . . ."

Roger sat shocked before the screen. He hadn't even handed it over yet, and the world was insane on rumors.

"Earlier, leaders demanded that the American government make the alleged youth–miracle drug available to all people of the world or risk a Holy War.

". . . In response to the spreading unrest, security has been beefed up at U.S. military bases overseas as well as American-owned corporations involved in genetics research.

"Meanwhile, Quentin Cross, president and CEO of Darby Pharmaceuticals in Lexington, Massachusetts, continues to deny his company's past involvement in Elixir. When asked earlier about the now-infamous videos of laboratory animals rejuvenating, he said that the tapes were fakes produced by disgruntled former employees." The scene shifted to Quentin Cross rushing to his black Mercedes in the Darby parking lot.

"How could they have faked the change in the animals, and the front page of *The Boston Globe*?"

"You can get old newspapers from the library," Quentin said, hustling to his car. "And monkeys all look alike."

"What about how young Roger Glover looks?"

"How am supposed to know? Maybe he knows some good plastic surgeons," he said and drove away.

"Meanwhile, in a White House press conference the president pledged an all-out effort to apprehend Roger Glover, who has so far eluded law enforcement officials in spite of an intensive search."

Roger got up to turn off the set, when something the announcer said stopped him.

"The call for a 'Holy War' is not just coming from the Middle East. The most ominous threat came from a hitherto unknown group calling itself the Witnesses to the Holy Apocalypse."

The scene shifted to a still of Lamar Fisk preaching to his followers.

"According to Professor Dennis Hadlock of the University of Connecticut, an expert on religious cults, such extremist groups view the Elixir serum as the beginning of the end." The camera switched to Hadlock. "Even if Elixir represents an actual scientific breakthrough, to the apocalyptic way of thinking it's blasphemy, a false gift from the devil. A grand lie, and the supreme sign to many that Judgment Day has arrived."

"What are the other signs?" asked the reporter.

"Well, for the Rapture-ready, they're all around us. There's the weather, for one. In the winter it was floods and mudslides reaching biblical proportions in California. Likewise the devastating drought in Africa and recent volcano eruption in central New Guinea. Closer to home, the strange arctic weather that's killing the spring. For those looking for them, these are sure signs of God's wrath. Not to mention the growing global chaos over this. The real danger is—"

Suddenly the scene cut back to the anchor. "We just received word from Cairo that an agreement has been reached and that the hostages will be released momentarily. We're switching live to the U.S. embassy . . ."

Roger watched as several men emerged with assault rifles on the rooftop of the embassy. On the street below Egyptian troops were shielded behind barricades. Smoke rose from piles of tires and burnt out cars.

"From this vantage, we can see Ambassador Boyle and seven staffers being escorted by their captors. They appear to be awaiting the U.S. helicopter. . . ."

Another camera pulled in the large helicopter gunship

approaching the embassy. While the blades whirled, the captors released the seven staff members who ran to the opening where U.S. soldiers helped them aboard.

When the last was aboard, the captors waved the chopper to leave, holding behind the ambassador, still in handcuffs.

The camera closed in on the lifting craft when suddenly the captors opened up with machine guns and grenade launchers. Instantly the rear end of the helicopter exploded, sending the vehicle into a tipsy angle toward the ground.

"Oh my God!" cried the announcer.

At the sound of the explosion, the group of gunmen cheered. Then as the camera closed in, the leader led the ambassador to the edge of the building, shot him in the head with a pistol, and pushed him off the roof.

Sickened, Roger snapped off the set.

"I have become death."

36

LEXINGTON, MASSACHUSETTS

I don't know how the videos got out. It's been thirteen years. People steal things," explained Quentin Cross. "No one's left from the old lab. They're all gone—some retired, some dead. I don't know how they got out."

"It was still careless," Antoine said. He was calling from his Lear jet. "You should have had those locked in your vault."

"Duplicates were made. What can I say?"

"The important thing is, can you still reproduce the compound if you had samples?"

"Of course we can. You know that."

It had taken years to pull themselves out of the debt Chris Bacon had left them in, but Darby had a first-rate laboratory with all the necessary technology to determine molecular composition of most compounds. And what they lacked, they could buy.

"All we need is a few cubic centimeters and we can make the stuff by the gallon," Quentin said.

"What about the technical staff?"

"We have the right people."

"People we can trust, not just clever technicians?"

"Trust can be bought. All you need is enough capital."

He could hear Antoine chuckle. "You're getting cynical in your old age."

"I have every reason to be," he said, tasting the sourness in his own voice. "Do you have any idea where they are?"

"I have ideas, yes."

Vince had boasted about an extensive computer network and ace hackers who could infiltrate the file systems of major corporations, departments of motor vehicles, local hospitals, the Social Security Administration, even a few banks. "If you've got a pulse, we'll find you," he had said.

"May I ask where?"

"You may, but I'm not going to tell you. Your job is geniuses and test tubes. Stay well, my friend. *Bon soir*."

Quentin hung and recalled why he disliked Antoine. He was a slick, arrogant thug. Other people were just rungs on his ladder. But that was not why Quentin needed him. His Consortium was an aging lot of multimillionaires who were hankering for the promised land.

And they needed him and not just to reproduce the stuff. He had people ready to get their hands on the body fluids and brain tissue of Roger Glover to see what made him tick.

It was a little after nine when Quentin got off his office phone. For the last six days, Darby Pharms had been crawling with media and protesters. Twice he had to call the police to break up fights between factions trying to break inside the plant.

He had even hired armed security guards to patrol the premises night and day. That and an enhanced monitoring system had cost him thousands.

But it would be worth it when they brought Glover in. And it wasn't just a cash cow come home. Every time Quentin looked at the photo of Robyn on his desk he saw in the glass the reflection of a tired middle-aged man, grown heavy in body and spirit, and weighted by the same dull routine of running a midsize pharmaceutical company. Perhaps it was a decade of struggling to get back on his feet, but he had lost his old belly fire. He missed those days when they were scrambling about for their great bonanza, pushing out walls and buying fancy staff and equipment. No, it wasn't the old man he missed. Ross was a prick who dismissed his ideas as pipe dreams, who never showed him respect as an equal. The only reason he had made him CFO was to keep the company in the family. The old bastard had deserved to die. No, what Quentin missed was a younger Quentin, so full of dreams and fight and years.

What passed for belly fire these days was the yearning to get his hands on Chris Bacon for what he had done to those dreams.

He glanced at the clock. Maybe there was hope still.

As he gathered his stuff to leave, Quentin noticed the red security light flash silently on the far wall.

His back had been turned to it while talking to Antoine, so he had no idea how long it had been flashing. It had gone on and off all day, but with the full security contingent to hold back the crowds there was no reason for alarm.

Motion sensors that rimmed the building had apparently picked something up earlier but had not been cleared.

Quentin cut to the security office across the hall. He flicked a switch to light up a panel of twelve surveillance monitors which gave him a full sweep of the property in real light and infrared. Maybe it was a stray dog or raccoon, because the lights showed nobody anywhere around the building.

The security guard sat conspicuously out front in a black vehicle. He would drive around the grounds through the parking lot periodically.

Another light flicked on.

Movement in the storage room at the rear of the building.

That was odd. At night, the security guards patrolled

only the outside of the building. Even during the day, that area was a restricted zone of high-security substances. Also, that end of the building was a cinderblock-and-steel structure essentially impregnable. There were no windows, and the only doors were the service bay for trucks and a single entrance made of steel and wired to an alarm. The only way inside was a battery of keys or an infantry tank.

Quentin left the office area.

He walked down the long corridor to the storage area. With his keys, he let himself inside. The heavy steel door closed behind him with a loud snap of the lock sliding into place.

The place was dim but for the night lights. And quiet. The only sound was the soft hum from the air circulation system.

Quentin slowly walked past the long aisles where they stored thousands of chemicals in bottles and boxes. The heels of his shoes snapped on the clean cement floor.

Nothing out of the ordinary.

Overhead he spotted the security cameras and motion sensors that lit up red as he moved by. In the security office the silent red lights would be blinking wildly.

Because the place was so tightly sealed, there was no way an animal could have gotten inside. Unless it was a pigeon that had strayed in through the delivery bay during the day. That had happened occasionally. But he could see none. If it were perched in the rafters, they would have to get it out tomorrow or the red lights would never go off.

With his key Quentin let himself into the restricted area set off behind a thick steel mesh. Against the back wall was the dark vault of specialized compounds.

He checked behind the vault and the various shelves. Nothing. He also opened the vault to be certain nothing was missing. In the rear he removed a small brown jar containing tubarine chloride. He looked at it, thinking of Ross and that bastard Bacon.

Clink.

Quentin froze in place, the tubarine clutched in hand.

Clink. Clink.

Quentin turned.

There was somebody behind him, on the other side of the steel grating. A man wearing a black Minuteman Security uniform.

"You startled the hell out of me," Quentin said. "H-how did you get in here?"

The man did not answer, and his face was shadowed by the brim of his cap.

"I asked you how you got inside the building."

Clink.

"I'm the president of this company. I hired you people. Will you please answer me?"

Clink. Snap.

"What are you doing?"

The man had padlocked shut the door with his own lock.

Quentin crossed to the grating. "What are you doing? Take that off. Let me out of here."

The man said nothing.

Quentin closed his fingers through the steel mesh and shook the gate. It was fastened shut. "Let me out of here. I own this place. This is my company. Who do you think you are?"

The man raised his head so that the security light caught his face.

A familiar face.

A television face.

"You're going to hell, sinner."

Reverend Colonel Lamar Fisk.

It was his people who had camped out on the grounds outside for the last week. The fanatics with the signs calling for Armageddon.

"Who the hell do you think you are coming in here like this?"

"Who?" Fisk's eyes were perfect orbs. "A soldier of

the Lord is who. You've bitten into His forbidden fruit for the last time."

"What the hell are you talking about?" Quentin shook the door again. "Let me out of here. Let me out of here."

Fisk did not respond but glared at him with such an intensity that Quentin backed away.

He then shot to an emergency phone on the wall near the vault. He raised it to punch 911 but could not get a dial tone. The line was dead.

Fisk raised his hand. "And I heard a voice from heaven saying, 'Blessed are the dead which die in the Lord from henceforth,' " he shouted. The veins of his neck stood out like thick cords of rope.

From behind Fisk half a dozen others in black uniforms appeared. One held a torch in his hands.

No, not a torch. A Molotov cocktail.

"What do you think you're doing?"

But Fisk moved back to the others. The man with the torch passed the flaming bottle to him. Then in a booming voice that reverberated in the steel chamber, Fisk raised his torch hand high and bellowed forth:

" 'And I saw the beast was taken and with him the false prophet that wrought miracles before him with which he had deceived them that had received the mark of the beast and them that worshipped his image. And they were both cast alive into a lake of fire.' "

Then he threw the torch toward Quentin. With a shattering whoosh, the floor erupted in a spreading pool of orange flame.

In the light Quentin saw two men rush into the interior of the building, to the labs and offices. A moment later he heard loud explosions.

It was then the remaining men let fly incendiary grenades into all corners of the storage chamber and down each of the aisles.

Quentin screamed as if his throat were shattering.

But he was drowned out by the sound of the grenades

and exploding chemicals, the rage of flames, and the wailing alarms.

In mere moments, the place was a thick vortex of smoke and fire. All along the shelves containers of chemicals blew up, spreading more flames and noxious fumes until the chamber was a roaring toxic inferno.

Inside the security cage Quentin shook the gate and howled until the smoke choked his lungs and filled his eyes with killing heat, and he fell to the floor, his fingers still clutching the small brown jar of tubarine.

37

According to the thermometer outside the kitchen window the temperature was 30 degrees the next morning. Fresh snow covered the yard. The lake remained unfrozen, however the water in the old fountain was iced over and pillowed in white.

But a warming trend was in the forecast. In a few hours the world would be green again. In a few hours the place would also be swarming with police and media people with vans surmounted by radio dishes. And by early afternoon it would be all over, Laura told herself. There was a strange roundness to it all. The saga had been born in the wilderness half a world away, and it would end in the wilderness of her old backyard.

Laura had gotten up before Roger and Brett. She made some coffee to get her heart going. She felt lousy and she looked it in the mirror. The skin of her face was a loose gray dough and her eyes were puffy. She had slept soundly until about four o'clock when she woke up with a bolt of panic at the bargain Roger had cut with the president.

It had crossed her mind yesterday, but she was so wracked with horror and grief that the realization had not registered. But two hours ago it hit her. In the effort to save her and Brett, Roger had signed his own death warrant.

He came down a little before seven.

Laura gave him a mug of coffee. On the television in the living room the "Elixir Unrest" story continued. Over the last few days it had become so prominent and widespread that CNN created its own graphics and crash chords.

Laura sat next to Roger and took his hand.

The news was worse than last night. Another rash of bombings of American corporations in foreign countries. More cries for a holy war. "An Elixir Jihad," someone had called it.

What particularly shocked them was the story of the torching of Darby Pharms and the death of its president. Some lunatic fundamentalist group had claimed responsibility. The same group that proclaimed Christopher Bacon a false prophet attempting to conjure the devil.

Meanwhile, a huge rally was scheduled in Washington that day at noon in protest of the government coverup. All efforts by the White House to downplay Elixir had failed miserably. A whirlwind of madness was whipping across the world, and it had Roger's name on it.

Laura turned off the set. "What's going to happen to you when you turn it over?"

"I guess I'll be given a regular supply to keep me going. Probably administered by some medical clinic wherever we end up."

She knew that even without the notebook protocol, the compound could be broken down into its molecular constituents which meant that it could be duplicated. All one needed was a lab and good organic chemists. "You won't be safe."

"Why not?"

"People will be after you as long as you live."

He had used the compound as a bargaining chip, but

she knew it meant more anxiety. As long as he was on the stuff, they would remain forever prey to every maniac wanting a sample. Just as bad, he would be the number-one infidel on top of every religious crazy's hit list.

She squeezed his hand. "It scares me."

"But we'll have federal protection."

His answer was too pat and resolve was missing in his voice. It would be the first time the compound was out of their hands. The agreement was for Public Citizen to assume full responsibility for the compound. But who knew where that could lead? If some got out, it could be like one of those renegade nukes from the old USSR floating around on the black market.

"I pray we're not making a mistake."

"We're not," he said.

But she didn't believe him.

About seven-thirty Laura woke Brett. While he got dressed, Roger put the call to the White House.

They were expecting him, and instantly he was transferred to the office of Kenneth Parrish. The rendezvous was to be one o'clock at the Black Eagle Lake lodge. Roger gave the location. Then he placed calls to the major television networks as well as *The New York Times*, the Associated Press, UPI, Reuters, and CNN.

One o'clock. That gave all parties over five hours to assemble. The last remaining step was unearthing the solitary backup stash of Elixir.

They packed a few things into a duffel bag. Roger stuffed his pistol inside his jacket.

When Brett came down, he asked, "So, what are we doing?"

"First, you're going to have a good breakfast," Roger said. "Then we're going to visit a cave."

•   •   •

The call to Eric Brown's home phone came while he was in the middle of his morning shower.

His wife handed him the portable. It was Assistant Deputy Director Richard Coleman in Washington. Brown dried his hands and face and took the phone.

"We got him," Coleman said. "He's in upstate New York."

"What was the break?"

"He called the White House direct to cut a deal."

"Shit."

"Yeah, well, can't always corner them at the 7-Eleven. The legal stuff will be worked out, but the long and short is that they're turning themselves and the Elixir in for immunity."

"Couldn't get better leverage."

"Yeah, the fountain of youth."

Coleman said that an agency jet was waiting for Brown and his men at the Madison airport. They should be airborne within the hour. The rendezvous was at one P.M. and it would take three and a half hours to touch down at Lake Placid, New York, where a car would be waiting.

"And what happens to the stuff?"

"That's what we've got to talk about, Eric. We're up to our earlobes in religious crazies, so we're asking you to act as liaison to the FDA."

"You mean courier the stuff to Washington?"

"We'll have a chopper waiting for you in New York."

He knew it was out of line to ask but he did anyway. "Why exactly do you need agency courier service?"

There was a slight hesitation before Coleman responded. "It's possible there may be a conflict with Glover over the exact disposition of the stuff. His stipulation is that it goes directly to Public Citizen."

"What's that?"

"One of those consumer medical advocacy groups. I guess he's trying to keep it out of federal control."

"But that's not the plan."

"Eric, I'm only reporting the news, not making it."

"Sure." It was not Eric's place to dispute government agenda. "Dick, I don't know if you saw the autopsy photos of Olafsson and the Kaminsky kid. The meddies don't know if the victims overdosed, underdosed, or what, but the stuff did a number on them."

"I saw them, and the old animal videos," Coleman said.

"Then you know what I'm saying."

Elixir wasn't exactly the Ebola virus, but what bothered Brown was that Glover knew the downside of the stuff better than anybody else. He wanted it quarantined even though it had turned him into some kind of modern-day Methuselah.

"Yeah, I know," Coleman said. "I also saw the shots of Glover. He looks like an Olympic athlete."

"Right."

"One more thing," Coleman added before hanging up. "The Glovers are carrying an audio tape he made of his conversation with the president. Retrieve it and any backups."

"You mean unofficially."

"Correct."

When they clicked off Brown finished his shower, trying to dispel the uneasy flutter in his gut.

A ndrea's Cave was located in the hills on the far side of the lake about a mile from the cabin. Roger parked the car in a clearing in the woods and the three of them hiked for maybe twenty minutes to the cave.

Although its interior was commodious in places, the entrance was no gaping mouth but a passage constricted by boulders and covered with scrub that made it invisible until you were on top of it.

The cave was known to the locals, and was listed in spelunker's guides. Because of its remoteness and lack of distinguished formations, the place was not a draw. But to the Whitehead girls who came up every summer from Albany, it was a magical place—the entrance to Middle Earth, a Kraken's den, the home of one-eyed giants—a great hideaway just a bike ride from their family cabin. It was also where, nine years ago, Laura and Roger buried the Elixir notebooks and a two-liter container of the serum.

They led Brett inside. The interior was dark and raw, and much colder than outside. They could see no signs of recent disturbance. The ring of stones of their old fire was still in place.

As if in some old pirate tale, they had a hand-sketched map pinpointing the location. Because the soil was full of large rocks, it had taken Roger hours to bury the two polyvinyl chests. But it would be easier coming out.

Using an army shovel and hand pick, he and Brett dug while Laura made a fire with some newspaper and kindling. The smoke curled up but did not fill the place because further inside was a natural vent that acted as a chimney. It was also Laura and Jenny's secret escape hatch.

It took them maybe half an hour to clear the containers, each constructed of rugged polyvinyl and sealed with stainless-steel locks. They were intact, and still sealed.

For the first time in nine years Roger used the key. The lock gave easily. And he snapped open the first container.

The large jar still sat in the plastic foam mold—and still full. Remarkably, the seal of the box had kept out all moisture so that the original Darby Pharmaceuticals label was as crisp as the day it went under. The container was the original motherlode from the production lab and once destined to be subdivided into hundreds of glass vials and ampules for freezer storage.

Roger held it up to the light.

"How much is that good for?" Brett asked.

"For one man, about a thousand years."

Brett's face lit up. He pressed his face toward the container. "Wow!" he said. "A thousand years from now people would be living like in *Star Trek* I bet, flying around to other planets and stuff. There probably wouldn't even be any cars. People would just teleport themselves around." He lowered the pitch of his voice. " 'Beam me to Brian's house, Scotty.' Awesome! Probably wouldn't even have to go to school, just plug your head into some kind of machine and you'd know everything."

Laura sat on a stone breaking twigs and tossing them onto the fire. She said nothing, but Roger could feel her uneasiness as Brett's mind reeled at the possibilities.

Roger snapped open the second container.

The entire collection of Elixir notes he had consolidated into four thick folders. Buried with them and bound in plastic was $120,000 in fifties and hundreds. Survival money in case it got to that.

Brett looked at the money. "Cool."

While Roger thumbed through the notes, Brett wandered off to explore the cave with his flashlight.

For several minutes they sat silently as Roger let himself roll back through the years when he had pursued Nature to her hiding place, as Laura had said. How when the ink on these pages was still wet he had believed without doubt in the rightness of that pursuit.

He glanced up from the pages only to find Laura staring at him across the fire. In the capering light, she looked so far away, but he could make out the sadness in her eyes. She made a flat smile but said nothing.

In the dark Roger heard Brett poking around. He checked his watch. Maybe it was time to get it over with, he thought. He had given the police and media five hours, but Albany was only three hours by car, and, of course, they'd arrive early. They were probably beginning to assemble while they sat here. He glanced down at the Elixir notes for the last time. On the open page was a funny little cartoon he had drawn of Methuselah in a muscle-man pose. It was dated December 13, 1986. His sixty-sixth month, and Wendy's forty-second birthday.

He closed the notes. "What do you say?"

"I guess," Laura replied. But she didn't make a move to leave. She reached her hand across the fire for his. "Sorry," she said.

Her hand felt warm. He gave it a squeeze, then began to close the containers.

"That won't be necessary."

• • •

Laura gasped. The voice came from behind them.

Three men had appeared from nowhere, one holding a light on them, the other two, raised weapons.

The older man dropped the beam onto the glass container. "You saved us a great deal of difficulty." He spoke in a lilting French accent.

The others said nothing but trained their weapons on Roger.

"Who are you?" Laura said.

They didn't look like religious fanatics. Nor police. One of the gunmen, a guy about fifty with slick salt-and-pepper hair, was dressed in an expensive fur-collared black leather jacket.

"Doesn't matter who we are," he said in unaccented English.

"What's important," the Frenchman continued, "is who you are and what's in your little treasure chest which we will unburden you of, thank you very much."

Roger started to move away with the bottle, but the American jammed the barrel of his gun into Laura's ear. Roger went for his gun, but the second gunman jabbed his pistol to the top of Roger's head.

The Frenchman removed the pistol from Roger's hand and passed it to the American. "No silly heroics please," he said, and gently he took the jar from Roger's hand. He smiled charmingly. "So, this is what all the noise is about." He peered into the clear liquid. "Half the mortal world would love to have this in its veins, the other half in the sewers."

While he talked, Laura flashed Roger a look and tipped her head toward the cave's interior.

Brett.

He was deep in the cave, and for some reason the men did not seem to know.

But if he heard the voices, he'd come stumbling out.

Roger made a silent prayer that he'd sense the danger and find the chimney vent. Just follow the trail of smoke, and keep his light low.

The Frenchman raised the torch to their faces. "I must say it is very exciting to see you in person. Very. You are world-famous. And so well preserved. *Quelle merveille! I* feel like Ponce de León."

"What do you want?" Roger asked. He tried to speak loud enough for Brett to hear.

Don't come, his mind screamed. *Get out.*

"What do I want? You have to ask? I want what you have in this jar."

"You followed us," Roger said.

The Frenchmen frowned at the statement. "We didn't have to. But we found your car."

The men had emerged from the entrance, Roger thought, which meant that they had not been hiding in wait for them. So they did not know about Brett.

"How did you find us?" Laura asked, picking up on Roger's cue. They would stall for Brett to catch what was going on and get away.

The Frenchman cradled the jar in one arm and with the other and pulled something out of his back pocket.

He smiled broadly. "I read your book." In his hand was the paperback edition of *If I Should Die.*

Like a schoolteacher, he opened the book to a page mark. " 'Ceren Evadas.' It's where your 'plucky' little sleuth hides in the end from the villains. Ceren Evadas— the make-believe little hideaway that she and her sister invented when they were children—safe haven from the bad guys, yes? And where she takes off to at the end. Andrea's Cave. It took me some time to figure it out then find it, but even cave hunters have websites.

"Then we cross-checked your ISBN number with the Library of Congress and learned that your maiden name was Whitehead and that you were born in Albany, New York. Our guess was that you had another childhood home up here, but we found no records. But the big clue was that you put your cave in Black Eagle Lake, Ohio. That confused us at first because there is no Black Eagle Lake, Ohio. Nor did it make sense to have a summer home in Ohio while living in Albany. Then we discovered a Black Eagle Lake, New York, and an Andrea's Cave. And *voila!* The two lines cross—and here you are.

"A good thing the police aren't better readers."

Neither his cultured manner nor accent diminished the primitive menace of the man. As he spoke, he kept licking his upper lip like an animal, finding chilling amusement in how he had cornered them.

"They say that one should write from what one knows. Perhaps that is not always the best strategy. But, I suppose, all you famous authors are narcissists, no? Every tale is an autobiography of sorts. So impossible to escape the self or the longing to go home again." He looked around. "I must say that you described this to a *T*, as you Americans say."

"Who are you?" Roger asked.

He peered down at Roger with that same smug grin. "The shark in your fountain of youth, my friend."

"Fair Caribe," Roger said. "Fair Caribe. You're the guy from Apricot Cay."

"Maybe *you* should write the detective stories."

"You were going to blackmarket it," Roger continued. "Quentin's little dream of getting around the FDA—sell it to high rollers."

"So disrespectful to speak ill of the dead."

"Without him you'll have to find another lab. Or somebody who knows how to make it."

"You may be immortal, but you're not indispensable," the Frenchman said. "That's not our interest."

The American in the black jacket tapped his watch to end the foreplay.

"You're right," the Frenchman said and nodded for the second gunman to fetch the empty box for the jar.

But Roger blocked their move. "Then what is your interest?" All he could think of was stalling as long as possible for Brett to escape. His eye fell on the machine pistol.

"Are you really so concerned?" the Frenchman asked.

"Yeah."

The American clearly wanted to get it over with. "Antoine."

But Antoine disregarded him. "I have no care to capitalize on your little miracle, if that's what worries you. My life is full. I have all I can ask—all but more time to enjoy it. *N'est-ce pas*? Now I've got that."

This was how it would end, Roger thought. Shot to death in a remote cave by nameless gunmen. The perfect crime: Elixir gone, and Number One and Two fugitives mysteriously murdered.

"You have what you want. Just leave us be."

"It's not that simple, my friend. To live indefinitely, one must be invisible—as you well know."

"So?"

"You saw my face."

"You bastard," Laura said.

That made the American smile.

"You people killed Betsy Watkins," Roger said. "Then bombed the plane."

Antoine checked his watch. "Enough."

But Roger pushed. "You killed Betsy and blew up the plane."

"The box, please."

"Say it. *Say it!*" Roger shouted.

"I fucking heard enough of you," the American said, and rammed his gun to Roger's forehead.

Laura screamed, and Roger waited for his head to explode.

But Antoine stopped him. "Why is that so important I say these things?"

"You're going to kill us anyway."

Antoine made a what-the-hell shrug. "Yes, we are. And, yes that was us."

The silent gunman made a side glance to Antoine for the cue.

"Your name," Roger insisted. "What's your name?"

"Your last wish, my friend. A man about to die

deserves to know his dispatcher. Antoine Ducharme, my friends. Something to take with you."

Then he turned to Laura. "Author Wendy, you know what my favorite line in your book is? No? Then I'll tell you. It's at the end when your Detective Kate Krueger captures the killer in his own bedroom. She says, 'People are like salmon, they go home to die.' "

The cue.

"No-o-o," Laura cried.

As the American raised the gun to her head, Roger grabbed the shovel and swung it like a baseball bat. The blade caught the jar at the midline in Antoine Ducharme's hands, shattering it instantly.

An uncontrollable gasp escaped the man's throat as fluid and glass shards sprayed him. Pathetically he tried to cup the Elixir which seeped through his fingers with his own blood and onto the dirt.

By reflex one of the men took aim at Roger's head, but thought twice and whipped him across the mouth.

"That was very stupid," the Ducharme said, looking at his fingers dripping red. "Very stupid."

He picked some glass out of his palm, still trying to save some mixture.

Roger spit some blood. "Now you have nothing but us."

"You have more," Ducharme said, trying to compose himself. "You have more. It would be insane to store it all in a jar."

Antoine muttered something in French, and the silent gunman dropped to his knees and put the barrel of the pistol to Laura's forehead.

"I am going to count to three, and when I do your wife's brains will be all over these walls. I will not fuck around any longer. Three seconds and she's dead."

Ducharme had no idea about the cabin. For all he knew, the two of them had camped out in the Subaru all night.

"One . . ."

Laura's face was shocked in terror.

"Two . . ."

Roger looked at the gun to Laura's head. "No! Don't. I'll take you."

"Then do so quickly. I'm cold."

The gunman pulled back.

"There's a cottage about a mile from here," Roger began. But he never finished.

Out of the shadows, a figure flew at the gunman.

Brett.

He seized the man in a headlock from behind and pulled him to the ground, all the while with his free hand yanking away the pistol. It had happened so fast, the man was stunned.

In the flurry of movement, Laura butted the American in the genitals with her head. With a pained grunt, he folded in the middle but not before taking aim at Laura. Roger leaped to block her, when an explosion rocked the cave.

The American fell face-forward.

Brett had shot him with one hand, his other still in a chokehold on the first man.

Brett jumped to his feet with the pistol raised. The American was not dead. But his arm landed in the flames, and he rolled away yowling. The bullet had caught him on the elbow.

"Don't friggin' move," Brett screamed.

The American rolled in pain, but nobody else moved. Brett grabbed the machine pistol off the ground so that he had a weapon in each hand fanning Antoine and his men. He looked wild. He looked like he wanted them to make a false move so he could blast them to hamburger.

Laura pulled herself up and helped Roger to his feet. His lip was bleeding.

He got his own gun from the American's belt. "And you wanted basketball," he said to Brett.

But Brett did not laugh, nor did he regard Roger.

"*Up! Up!*" he shouted.

The American with the ruined elbow and smoking sleeve stumbled to his knees. When he hesitated, Brett kicked him in the butt.

"Fucking kid!"

Brett kicked him again.

He looked half-crazed. Days of fear and anger had come to a ballistic head.

Antoine muttered something vicious in French, and Brett sent the toe of his boot into Antoine's shin.

He would have filled him full of lead had Roger not pulled him back.

"Outside!" Brett yelled.

"Brett!" Roger said, holding his hand out for the guns.

But the boy would not respond to him. He was locked into marching the men outside himself.

What cut across Roger's mind like a shark fin was that Brett's mind had snapped. That the sheer horror of seeing his parents about to be executed had momentarily deranged him, and that once outside in the daylight he would line them up and blast them dead.

Laura tried to reason with him, but he stonewalled her too.

Brett stuck the nine-millimeter into his belt. The machine pistol he gripped in both hands like a movie cop. He then rammed the back of one men. "Hands high."

The man raised his hands.

He stabbed the man in the skull with the gun. *"Higher!"*

The man reached as high as he could. With one hand Brett reached around and tore the man's belt off his pants and tossed it to Roger to tie his hands. He then whipped the belts off the others and tossed them to Laura.

When the men were bound, Brett pushed them toward the entrance, still moving under that weird autopilot.

"Wait," Roger shouted. He picked up one of four notebooks. He looked at it for a moment, then opened it and tore out the pages and fed them to the fire.

"What are you doing?" Brett screamed. "We need those."

"No, we don't."

Brett said nothing, remembering the ampules back at the cabin.

Roger tore out another handful of pages and tossed them on the fire. Then another and another.

While the fire flared, he tried not to think of the years of drudgery they represented—the meticulous around-the-clock record of everything he had done since returning from Papua New Guinea—Methuselah's first year, his weight, chemistry; maze test results; the molecular diagrams, equations, diagnostics; the primates, Molly, Fred, Jimbo—seven years' worth. Work that had consumed his waking hours, that had filled him with inestimable dreams. Page after page.

It was like self-amputation in razor slices.

When he was done the fire roared.

Laura took his hand as they watched for a moment. When he was satisfied, he said, "Let's go."

As the others started out, he yanked the golden ampule from his neck and tossed it into the fire.

He then he fell behind Laura, passing Brett who hadn't seemed to notice and who waited to close up the rear as they all moved out of the cave.

Brett did not shoot them. He was more interested in returning to the cottage.

They had parked the Subaru in the woods out of sight from the road. But the men had found it. The seats were slashed, the ceiling vinyl torn out, glove compartment cover pried off, the floor trap opened. They had even gone through the engine compartment looking for containers of the serum.

Luckily, the engine still worked. Brett rode in the rear with the machine pistol trained on the three men. Laura drove, and Roger nursed a bleeding mouth beside her.

As they headed back to the cottage, Roger tried to get Brett to come out of his daze, but to no avail. It crossed his mind that he might have to overpower his own son when the car stopped. It also crossed his mind that the men might try something desperate to escape.

"Brett, that's not a regular gun. Squeeze the trigger and thirty rounds will come out."

Brett didn't respond, but Roger was certain he got the idea. From the way the men sat frozen, they got it too.

They drove the rest of the way without another word. Yet Roger couldn't help but feel irrational pride in his son.

At the head of the logging road was a clutch of police and news vehicles. Uniformed officers waved them to stop.

As Laura braked, Brett shouted, "*No!* Don't stop!"

Laura leaned on the horn and motioned frantically that they were coming through. The police recognized them, but before they could force Laura to pull over, two agents of the FBI glanced inside.

"It's them," one of them shouted.

Roger recognized Number 44 from the Town Day race.

"Pull over." Guns drawn, the two agents tried to open the locked doors. They wanted them to surrender right here and get into the waiting black Hummer.

But that was not the agreement. Nor was Brett going to let them. "Keep going!" he shouted to Laura.

Laura lowered the rear window so the agents could see Brett with a TEC-9 machine pistol trained on the three men.

"They tried to kill us. We're not stopping."

Number 44 wore an FBI photo ID: William Pike. The man with him was Eric Brown. Roger recognized the name. Brown sized up the situation, then shouted for the police to let them through.

Instantly three motorcycles pulled out to escort them to the cabin, several vehicles pulling behind.

At the bottom of the road was an even larger swarm of people and vehicles—unmarked cars, news vans, police cruisers, people with cameras, even some locals with kids. Maybe a hundred or more people.

On the lake floated two pontoon TV helicopters and a seaplane. It was insane, Roger thought. How the hell did they assemble so fast? And up here in the middle of nowhere! The nearest major town was Lake Placid.

Somehow the word had leaked, no doubt from the broadcast people to keep the story breaking from minute-to-minute.

Roger would bet his life they were here not to clap eyes on the FBI's most wanted man but the guy who wouldn't die.

What bothered him was all the people moving in and out of their cabin. Men in uniform and in plainclothes. They had probably torn the place apart for Elixir. He scanned the front yard and whispered a thanks the old fridge had broken down.

As Laura pulled near the broken lawn fountain, one reporter kept up a monologue into his microphone as he trotted alongside:

"The lakefront house was deserted, and wild speculation was that the Glovers had either taken off or were abducted. But as we speak, they are returning in a black Subaru Outback . . ."

The police waved them into the drive, and the crowd made a path. In the distance Roger spotted a frontend loader waiting in the event that he announced the Elixir supply was buried.

People were shouting and pressing around the car with cameras while the police tried to keep them back. But it was impossible. They had not expected the media blitz.

Laura parked as police and FBI jackets made a wall around them. Agent Brown carried his gun low but he wanted Brett to surrender the weapons.

Roger pushed his way to Brown. "Get these people away."

He didn't know what kind of trauma Brett was suffering, but he was not responding to him or Laura. And the charge of the crowd might make him start firing. "Don't touch him, and he won't hurt anybody," Roger shouted. He was smeared with blood. "These are the bad guys." And he pulled Ducharme and the others out of the car.

Brown barked some orders for the police to clear a path.

Reporters shouted questions and cameras were jamming for shots. Brett looked at the breaking point. His eyes were still wild, yet he stuffed himself behind the men and pushed them to the steps of the cottage.

Somebody made the mistake of pushing into Brett. He flashed the pistol at him in reflex, and the guy jumped backward. Nobody else interceded.

The crowd parted like a school of fish for the three bound men and the boy in the weird trance with both hands gripping the large black gun.

Without a word, Brett marched the men single file to a step shy of the porch where he commanded them to turn and face the crowd.

He then climbed onto the porch behind them and held the gun to the back of Ducharme's head.

"Brett, *no!* Don't do it. *Please!*"

But he did not hear Roger. Nor his mother's cries.

Nor did he see the marksmen on the old woodpile, their high-powered rifles trained on him.

"Tell them," Brett said to Ducharme.

The crowd hushed and pressed in, a wall of humming cameras and directional microphones all gawking at the boy and his hostages.

"Tell them!"

"Tell what?" Ducharme asked.

"Tell them how you killed Betsy Watkins and blew up the plane."

Ducharme made a bemused smile. "If I don't, are you going to kill me in front of the whole world?"

Brett pushed the barrel of the gun to the base of his skull. "You bet your friggin' life I am."

Ducharme looked over his shoulder. When he saw Brett's face his smile fell.

"One . . ." counted Brett.

The crowd gasped and police marksmen raised their guns, not certain where to aim, or what to do. They couldn't shoot a boy on global broadcast.

"Two . . ."

"Brett, don't," Laura pleaded. "Not this way."

"Three!" And he rammed Antoine's head with the gun again.

"Okay," he said and swore in French. "What do you want me to say, you crazy kid?"

"The truth. Tell them the truth."

"Christopher Bacon did not kill Betsy Watkins . . ."

"Keep going," Brett warned. "The plane . . ."

"He did not plant a bomb on flight 219. It was associates of Quentin Cross."

"And you."

There was a long pause.

"And you!"

"And me."

"Louder."

"And me."

"Louder."

"And me!"

The crowd exploded, reporters jabbering all at once. Brett looked over to his father and for a second he flashed his father a smile.

"Friggin' cool," Roger said.

Ducharme ignored the questions and looked over to Roger. "So you have a boy do your bidding for you."

"Like his dad, he's older than he looks."

The FBI was humming to get its hands on the compound. But the crowd was restless for Roger to come to the mike.

After Brett surrendered the guns and the police took away Antoine Ducharme and his men, Brown and his agents tried to corral the Glovers into the house to retrieve the last of the Elixir, wherever it was. But that was not the deal.

Roger had promised a news briefing, and they were going to get one. And live cameras guaranteed that.

Roger moved onto the porch with Brett and Laura by his side. Behind them stood several uniformed police, Brown, and his agents. Brown held a hand radio that kept him in moment-to-moment communication with unseen superiors.

That bothered Roger. He sensed conflicting lines of awareness. This was not protocol. It was sloppy. It had gone public. It set forth conditions the Feds were reluctant to address.

Shortly Brown moved to the top step and waved his hands to quiet down the crowd.

"I'm Eric Brown of the FBI, Madison, Wisconsin Field Office. Mr. Glover has agreed to make a few brief statements before we leave. When he's through, we ask that you please return to your vehicles and depart the premises."

"What about questions?"

"This is not a press conference."

There were shouts of disapproval. Roger turned to Brown. "I can take a few questions."

Brown cocked his head to hear whoever was in his earpiece. He muttered something into his phone. "Just a brief statement," he said flatly.

Roger moved to the mike. "I had originally intended to give a statement of our innocence of the charges, but fortunately that's been established.

"I don't know who those men were, but the fact that they intended to kill more people underscores the dangers inherent in the substance, including some misconceptions the media's latched onto.

"In spite of all the claims, I am not immortal. If you cut me I'll bleed. If you shoot me I'll die. There's no way of knowing how long I'll go on, but it's not indefinitely because eventually my internal organs will give out. Whenever is anybody's guess."

People tried to stop him with questions, but he held his hands up and continued.

"Second, for all its appeal, Elixir is fraught with terrible dangers—personally, medically, socially, and morally. I need not go into details, but I cannot stress enough that the substance presents more problems than it solves. And I speak from experience."

"What kinds of medical problems?"

Brown tried to cut in, but Roger took the questions. "You've seen videos of animals fast-forward aging. That's the consequence of withdrawal."

"Is that what would happen to you?" shouted a red-haired woman.

Brown who was back-and-forth on his radio phone cut in. "There will be no more questions. Otherwise we will terminate this briefing."

The crowd did not like that, but quieted down.

Roger continued. "A key term of our agreement is that the entire supply of Elixir be turned over to Public Citizen for research into its cancer-fighting properties exclusively. Second, that research protocol and data be closely monitored to prevent application to human prolongevity.

"For the record, the government understands and agreed to those conditions."

"Finally, contrary to reports, there are no hidden caches of the substance. The world's entire supply is at this site."

Another stir rippled through the crowd.

"Where?" somebody shouted.

Brown and his men closed around the Glovers.

"Where's the rest of it?"

"How much is left?"

Suddenly the crowd was restive and firing questions.

The police started to push back the reporters, until a tumult rose up and people began shoving. A line of uniforms pressed against the crowd.

Things were nearly out of hand. In a moment batons would start swinging and heads would be bloodied.

"I'll take questions," Roger said to Brown.

"No, you won't." Brown's men began corralling them inside.

Roger didn't like that. They were doing all they could to separate them from the media, to get their hands on the compound and haul them to headquarters in Manhattan. Another agenda had taken over.

Roger grabbed the microphone from a uniformed cop. "Hold it. I'll take your questions."

Brown made a move for the mic. But somebody squawked something in his ear. Whoever was calling the shots wanted this over with peacefully.

Brown pulled Roger aside. "Those aren't my orders."

"You've got a hundred million people in those lenses. *They* are your orders."

Brown's resolve cracked as he motioned the police captain to pull his men off the crowd.

When the place settled, Roger spoke: "I'll take your questions, but orderly and with a show of hands, please."

The crowd pressed to the porch again.

When they calmed down, Roger said, "Okay."

The place erupted, hands flapping like cornstalks in a wind. A wall of directional mics and camera lenses poised on him.

"Dr. Glover, you said you may not live indefinitely, but is it true you haven't experienced any effects of aging since you began taking Elixir?"

"True."

"How old are you?" another shouted.

"Fifty-six."

A stir of amazement passed through the crowd.

"What about Mrs. Glover?"

Roger took the question. Laura had wanted no part of this. "We're the same age, but only I've taken the serum."

"Mrs. Glover," another reporter shouted. "Can you tell us why you decided against it?"

Again Roger took the question. "Just that she did."

But the reporter persisted in his attempt to engage Laura. "Do you regret that decision?"

"No," Laura answered.

"Has it caused problems for you as a family?" shouted the woman with the red hair and a TV 4 cameraman.

"Yes," Roger said without explanation.

"Dr. Glover, I'm wondering about the long-range effects of Elixir," shouted another. "If it doubles or triples the lifespan, wouldn't that mean you've invented a higher order of the human species—a kind of superman?"

Before he could answer, two other reporters blurted out questions. When they calmed down to hear his answer, more questions followed. Brown flapped his hands to tell them one at a time.

Roger was beginning to regret this. "You're missing the point. The compound will not be researched for longevity. Even if the side effects can be eliminated, it's dangerous and wrong—like human cloning, which is also banned. . . ."

But nobody was listening.

He looked at Laura. She looked frightened. Brett stood beside her, numbed by the spectacle.

"If someone were to have a transfusion of your blood, would they live forever too?"

"Is it true the Elixir will prevent diseases?"

"Would the substance make anybody younger?"

Roger suddenly understood what Jesus must have felt like after raising Lazarus. Probably everybody in the village came after him with a laundry list of dead relatives.

He tried to answer, but the questions were coming rapid-fire. And the answers weren't registering. It was impossible.

"How much do you have to take for it to work?"

"Does it work on children, too?"

"What about very old people?"

They weren't getting it. They didn't have a bloody clue. And the millions catching it all would hear only *eternal youth*.

And tomorrow Larry King would call, and Barbara and Oprah. And he would be hounded by publicists and agents. And movie and book offers would come flooding in. And pharmaceutical companies would be calling with fabulous contract offers. And telephone calls in the middle of the night: *"Hey, Rog, it's Charlie from Swanson's Steak House. Whaddya say, just a little eternity juice for your favorite waiter?"*

As he stood there before the foaming crowd, the future lay its lurid self out in front of him. Laura was right. They would hound them like jackals. No matter if he didn't have more than two cc's in his possession, they would be after him for samples.

Worse, they would go after Brett because he was

young and vulnerable. Kids cornering him in the school-yard. *Mom's getting really old and depressed, can you help me out? Steal a little of your old man's stash. He'd never know.*

And, if you don't, we'll blow your head off.

They'd be on the run again. New names, new IDs, new escape plans.

He glanced at Laura and Brett looking in fright at the crowd. People were screaming at once.

How much would it cost?

Could it come in tablet form?

Would it work on the family dog?

What about population problems?

Does it bother you that some people view you as the devil?

What if it gets out?

They're not going to live like that, Roger thought. *Not on his life.*

"That's it," Roger said to Brown.

Brown nodded and took the mic and announced the press conference was over.

A roar rose up, but the uniforms poured out from the sidelines to clear the area. Brown and his agents started to move the Glovers inside when Roger shouted, "It's not in there. Out here."

Brown turned to the state police captain. "Clear them out of here. All of them."

The captain was about to pass the order on to his men when Roger grabbed Brown. "Clear the place of the cameras, and rumors will fly that you're holding back on the stuff. Just move them back."

"You're not calling the shots," Brown snapped.

"How badly do you want it?"

Brown stared at him for a moment. "What's your problem, Glover?"

"The people in your ear."

Frustrated, Brown snapped around and told the

captain that the media would stay, just push them back to make a path.

Then with Laura and Brett by his side and three dozen cameras locked on them, Roger moved down the steps and across the open yard to the snow-covered fountain which had stood there unnoticed and undisturbed by the mob.

Beneath the skim of ice and melting snow lay 204 ampules of Elixir, cool and safe.

Brown looked at him to ask if he was joking—the fountain?

"Pun intended," Roger said.

And he poked his hands through and removed a clutch of glass ampules.

A wave of dismay rose from the crowd as they watched Brett and Roger load the ampules into two black plastic containers, then seal and affix the locks.

As they walked away, reporters scribbled notes and jabbered away into their microphones as the cameras zoomed after them and the federal agents on their way to the Hummer. The Hummer would take them to helicopters, which would transport them to FBI headquarters in New York City for processing.

When they got to the vehicle, a man in a dark suit appeared from nowhere. He was surrounded by several others, including FBI jackets.

"Mr. Glover, I'm Ken Parrish, Director of the FBI. And this is Dr. Janet Jamal of Gordon Medical School and Dr. Warren Castleman."

Castleman held out his hand. "It's a pleasure to meet you finally, Dr. Glover."

Parrish had left out Castleman's affiliation because Roger would recognize the name. He was the FDA commissioner. Roger did not release his grip on the carriers.

"We'll unburden you of those," Parrish said.

Zazzaro stepped forward, but Roger pulled back. "That was not the agreement. It's going to Doctor Nathan David of Public Citizen."

Parrish's face hardened. "What agreement?"

Roger felt as if a tremor had passed underfoot. "The agreement I made yesterday with President Markarian."

Parrish's face did not crack. "I can assure you that they will be in safe hands."

"I give you my word," Castleman added. Jamal agreed.

They were trying to pull a fast one, Roger thought. Like most medical research universities, Jamal's lab at Gordon Medical was funded almost entirely by the federal government and overseen by the FDA whose commissioner, Warren Castleman, had been personally appointed by the president. They had no intention of turning Elixir over to the Public Citizen. They didn't give a rat's ass about determining the enzymes that prevented cancer cells from replicating. What they were thinking was social security and demographics and avoiding huge tax increases for younger voters, and who knew what else. Maybe the foreign crazies were right about genetic imperialism.

"I don't give a damn about your word. It stays with me until I see Nathan David in person." Roger could feel Laura nudge him toward the car.

Parrish's face flushed in anger, but he was also aware of the wall of cameras humming at them. He made his best conciliatory smile. "Fine." And he backed away to allow them to get inside the Hummer.

Brett jumped in with Laura.

But Roger did not follow. Instead he walked across the yard by himself to the media people. He found the TV 4 woman with the red hair. While the feds stood waiting by the cars, he pretended to shake her hand while slipping her the audiotape of his conversation with the president.

Discretely she closed her hand around it. She pressed toward his ear. "What's this?"

"Protection for my wife and son."

"Gotcha," she said.

Then Roger went back to the Hummer and got in the back seat between Laura and Brett, the two carriers in hand.

Brown took the front seat beside the driver. Zazzaro, Pike, and another agent took to the rear.

Outside Parrish and his men stood stonefaced as they pulled away. Laura took Roger's hand. "If looks could kill," she whispered.

Roger nodded.

He was sitting directly behind Brown with the other agents behind them. Nobody said anything, but all he could think about was the firepower under the jackets of the men in back, and the naked vulnerability of their own three heads.

The Hummer fell behind police motorcycles and three escort vehicles. Behind them pulled two more FBI vehicles, and tailing the procession were several press vans forming an extensive caravan. Roger wondered how far the authorities would allow the press to dog them.

With the escorts, the trip to the heliport on the Vermont side of the Crown Point Bridge would take less than an hour.

Outside, the blanket of snow had already begun to melt.

As they proceeded to Route 10, Roger considered his gut instincts: What if, when they arrived in New York, the Feds decided to prosecute in spite of the promise? Who would stop them even with the news footage about an agreement? All they had to say was that such matters would be determined in a court of law, which had outstanding warrants for their arrest on a battery of charges beyond murder and sabotage.

What if Janet Jamal and associates apply for a patent of some production process and market Elixir?

Or if some sleazeball creep like the late Quentin Cross

*decides to process a few hundred ccs of his own on the
side?*

Or if the stuff got out like Laura's renegade Russian
nukes scenario? The Antoine Ducharmes of the world
were a dime a dozen.

Where was the control? Where were the watchdogs?
Who would prevent the horrors from becoming global?

Then he began to raise some hard questions regarding
their own future. He knew in some primitive way that
he was a liability. The Feds would have to monitor a
sustaining supply for him indefinitely. That was inele-
gant. And it was risky. It made the three of them vulnerable. And him expendable.

What if the Feds had a .38-caliber slug with his name
on it—one to be put through his brain one evening while
walking to his car? The papers would momentarily la-
ment just-another-senseless-act-of-violence.

Worse—and the question he kept coming back to, the
one that had been snapping at him for days: What if
somebody decided to go after Brett and Laura to get at
his dole?

The brutal conclusion that Roger reached as they
made their way to the FBI choppers was that he was as
much a liability to them as was Elixir. That Laura and
Brett were in danger for their lives as long as he remained alive.

The realization was stunning. And, yet, it had been
squatting there all the time licking its chops.

From a back pocket of his mind he heard a familiar
voice. *The treatment comes with a cyanide pill.*

An even worse punishment for them, because he
wouldn't just die. They'd find him one morning like
Wally and Abigail.

Roger put his arms around his wife and son and tried
to blank his mind of all but thoughts of them.

•   •   •

Because the local police had been alerted, the traffic was stopped at the few intersections for the motorcade to pass without sirens.

While Brett checked out the scenery through the windows, Laura relaxed her head against Roger's shoulder. He kissed the top of her head.

Her hand slid to his shoulder as she kissed him on the mouth. Suddenly her head picked up. She could not feel his emergency ampule. Her eyes widened for an explanation. Before she could say anything, he pressed his finger to his lips and shook his head so Brett wouldn't know.

But she wanted to know why it was missing. He hadn't removed it all these years. Never. Even when he showered.

He shook his head to say he'd explain later.

But what would he say? That he did it for Brett's sake, a gesture of closure? A renouncing of temptation? He could always get more. There were 204 amules between his feet. They would arrange regular maintenance dosages with medics from Public Citizen to keep him alive.

Or was it motivated by some darker impulse he was only beginning to understand?

"I love you," he whispered.

Laura nodded and kissed him.

There were age spots on the back of her hand.

The caravan rolled through small villages to Port Henry. Outside people looked in wonder at the motorcade this far upcountry, and the long line of news vehicles dogging them.

In the distance they could see the high arching steel bridge spanning the southerly end of Lake Champlain from Port Henry to an open field on the Vermont side where several helicopter transports waited. The bridge was a high steel structure of two generous lanes. Two

New York state cruisers waited by the side to keep the lane open.

They were halfway across the bridge when the driver slowed.

"What's the problem?" Zazzaro asked.

"Those trucks. There wasn't supposed to be any oncoming traffic till we got across."

Through the windshield they could see two eighteen-wheelers in the oncoming lane. One continued pass them, but the other slowed and turned a sharp left coming to a stop, blocking both the lanes on the far side of the crest.

"What the hell?" The driver checked his rearview mirror. "Aw shit!"

Behind them the other truck screeched into a jackknife, cutting off the trail of cars about five back.

They were trapped.

Before they knew it, the rear doors of both trucks opened up and out poured dozens of people with automatic weapons firing.

A screech of tires and the motorcycles skidded sideways. Two drivers were thrown to the side, the other ended up with his leg pinned under the machine. As he rolled in agony to pull free, somebody shot him dead. A chatter of guns and the others were killed.

Laura's scream filled Roger's head.

Zazzaro and Brown instantly had their weapons drawn, and behind them the men produced Uzis. But they were far outgunned.

From behind came a volley of automatic weapons as men from the rear truck unloaded their magazines at the escort vehicles and at the first press cars. Windshields shattered and people screamed as the bullets sprayed the convoy.

"They're killing everybody," Brett cried.

Ahead Roger could see a wall of people with guns marching slowly in formation toward the Hummer. They were all wearing white jumpsuits. And red shoes. All holding weapons.

And in the lead wearing a flowing white robe and clutching something to his chest was Lamar Fisk.

Brown was on his radio phone calling for support. But they didn't have a chance to get here in time.

Zazzaro opened the door with his Uzi raised.

"Don't!" Roger shouted. "They'll wipe us all out." From the dashboard he snatched the mouthpiece to the outside loudspeaker flicked it on.

"Fisk, this is Roger Glover. Stop shooting," he shouted. "Hold your people back. I've got what you want. I'll bring it, just stop shooting."

Laura grabbed him. "Roger, they'll kill you."

Through the windshield they could see Fisk raise his hand. The mob stopped. So did the gunfire.

Roger pushed open the door and gripped the two carriers.

"No, Roger," Laura screamed.

"Dad, don't go!" Brett begged.

"It'll be a bloodbath otherwise," he said.

Zazzaro pressed in front of him. "I can't let you do that."

"Then you're going to have to shoot me," he said and pushed his way out.

Laura and Brett were still screaming for him to stop as he moved away from the vehicle.

Brown jumped out after him. He had explicit orders to get the serum into federal protection, no matter what.

Roger knew that now, but it was no time for anybody to play cop. "There's an army of them with more firepower than you've got in fifty miles," Roger said. "Go tend your wounded."

Brown heard the cries of the men behind them. He saw the wall of white uniforms and the weapons. It wasn't worth the sacrifice. "Just give them the shit and haul ass."

"Dad," Brett cried. "Daaaad."

Roger looked back. *I love you, beautiful boy*.

A quick glance at Laura. Her face was twisted in horrid realization.

Then he turned and walked toward Lamar Fisk and his army in white.

From behind him, the dozens from the first truck closed around Roger, leaving in cars the dead and wounded, and those who had been spared. The Witnesses had no more interest in them. Nor in the distant sounds of sirens. Nor the media people cowering with their microphones and cameras running.

Nobody tried to stop Roger as he approached Fisk. But all their weapons were trained on him—automatic weapons stolen from military arsenals.

As he approached, he noticed the looks on their faces. A wild intensity. Perhaps rapture, perhaps drugs. Men and women, young and old, mostly white, but with some blacks and Asians. Some women holding babies.

"It's all here," Roger said. "Please let the others go. There's been enough killing."

Fisk raised his bible as Roger had seen him so many times on the news. The look of bloodless piety in his face. " 'And one by one the Angel of the Lord opened the vials and poured forth the plagues upon the earth . . .' "

Roger stopped a few feet before the man. He raised the twin cases. "It's all yours."

But Fisk disregarded his plea. "*This* is the one true elixir," he shouted, holding up the bible. "This is the only way to eternal life. Not your snake oil."

The creep was going to preach to him first, Roger thought.

In unison the Witnesses cried "Alleluia."

Roger said nothing. The man was not to be reasoned with. He was beyond reason. He was beyond the moment. Beyond this bridge. Beyond the here and now. His eyes were huge glazed orbs. He looked insane with mission.

Roger's eye fell on Fisk's other hand, half-hidden in the folds of his robe.

"Lay them down," Fisk said.

Roger set the two boxes between them.

"Open them."

Roger unlocked the boxes and opened them.

He then stepped back as Fisk inspected the contents. When he was satisfied, he nodded at a woman who overturned the contents making a large pile of glass ampules.

"Vials of abomination," he said.

All around him guns poked angrily in the air. For a moment, Roger saw the Okamolu warriors. "Fisk, please let the others go. You have what you want."

Roger braced himself to be shot dead. That was also what they wanted. Death to the Antichrist. He just wished it didn't have to happen in front of his wife and son.

Fisk shook his bible at him. " 'And I heard the voice of a great multitude, and as the voice of many waters, and as the voice of mighty thunder saying "Alleluia, for the Lord God omnipotent reigneth." ' " And he stomped his foot onto the vials, the contents splattering.

That was the cue. Instantly others began to smash the vials under their shoes.

As Roger stood there, they crushed each of the ampules until all that lay on the tartop were shards of glass and wetness.

When they were through, they dropped their weapons and embraced each other across the shoulders, forming a circled wall around Roger and Fisk.

It was insane: They had just killed a bunch of people, and now their faces were glowing with beatific light as if at any moment Jesus Himself would materialize.

Spontaneously they broke into a chant of "Alleluia" and kicked and stomped the smashed glass.

It was then Roger noticed the red backpacks they were wearing. Fisk, too.

"Alleluia."

"ALLELUIA."

The chant got louder, and the Witnesses began to jerk as if the syllables were being pumped out of them by unseen forces.

"AL-LE-LU-IA."

"AL-LE-LU-IA."

"AL-LE-LU-IA."

Over the chanting, Fisk's voice rose: " 'And I saw the beast and the kings of the earth, and their armies gathered together to make war against Him that sat on the horse and against His army . . .' "

"ALLELUIA."

"ALLELUIA."

While Fisk bellowed on, his people looked to the sky with beaming faces and jabbering mouths, all locked in unison, impervious to the police gathered on the banks of the lake and the media people behind them and the sound of sirens approaching from both sides.

" 'And the waters shall run red with blood . . .' "

"ALLELUIA."

"ALLELUIA."

Fisk's face was huge with intensity, the tendons of his neck swelling, his long red hair flowing like tongues of flame as he recited the doom and gloom and pumped with the rhythm of the chant.

In the movement Roger noticed something small and black in his hand.

" ' . . . and death and hell were cast into the lake of fire. And whosoever was not witness was also cast into the lake of fire . . .' "

"ALLELUIA."

"ALLELUIA."

Some kind of remote control device.

Of course, Roger thought. Of course.

THIS is how it will end.

This is my death.

In a feverish pitch, his tongue slashing out the words with a spray, his eyes bulging in their sockets, his body appearing to swell into its huge white folds—Fisk reached his crescendo:

"I am Alpha and Omega, the beginning and the end, the first and the last."

As Fisk raised his left hand, still howling in verse, Roger considered bursting through the Witnesses to make a flying dive off the bridge. He saw an opening between some women and children—a fast sprint could do it. He might even survive the sixty-foot plunge. In a flash he ran through the moves in his head.

No.

He looked back over the heads to the Hummer.

Laura and Brett were out of the car. Brett started to run toward him, but Brown caught him. He, too, saw what was coming.

Thanks, thought Roger.

"DAAAAAD."

Laura was holding onto him, crying for Roger to get away.

His eyes locked on them. For a brief moment, all time seemed to stop, as if the world had turned to a still-life.

"I love you," Roger said.

Before the final syllable was out, the moment exploded in a brilliant concussion of light.

EPILOGUE

Brett's body burned as he pumped the last two miles of the bike path that took him around the southern shore of Lake Mendota.

It was a splendid April afternoon. The sun was high and the air sultry, and a gentle breeze swept off the lake, churning the tender new leaves of the trees along the path. It was a wonderful day to be alive—the kind of day that should last forever.

He had been in lab since eight that morning, antsy to feel his muscles hum. He completed the last test around two, changed into his helmet and tights, and took to his wheels. He felt so good that he added an eight-mile detour to the usual thirty-five-mile ride.

At twenty-one years of age, Brett Glover was in peak physical condition. He had kept up with wrestling right through Pierson Prep, making UW varsity in his freshman year. His senior season ended with a 24-and-2 record and a defeat of last year's champ from Michigan State at the MWC Conference last month. With the season now over, he kept in shape on the bike and inline skates. He had to because the rest of his days were spent in class or labs.

Occasionally Carolyn would join him on a ride, though he usually did these fast runs by himself. Carolyn, a senior psyche major, was his girlfriend of two years. Next year, they would be staying on for grad school—she in clinical, he in biochem like his dad. They talked about getting a place together, but it was just talk, because Brett wasn't sure he was ready for cohabitation. He liked his privacy.

On the southeastern stretch of the path, the slant of the sun on the water made him think of that other cold-water lake a thousand miles from here.

His father's death had left a void in Brett's life that could not be filled. It was something he had over the years learned to live with, falling back on the memories that at times would relieve the pangs of sadness.

He could still see his father lying beside him in his room, hear him reading about Jack getting the best of the giant. He could still recall them playing catch in the yard, jogging around the Pierson track, running Town Day races, practicing wrestling moves, doing school projects together—images as warm as yesterday's sunshine.

He could still hear Roger explain to the press that he wasn't immortal. That he didn't have X-ray vision. That he couldn't heal the sick or raise the dead.

He could still hear the explosion that left a gaping hole on the bridge and in his soul.

He could still hear his mother sobbing. She had endured so much in that awful week. They all had.

He steered off the path and over to Lake Street, then cut across the library mall to State.

Students milled about, thinking about finals and papers and summer vacation.

For a long time people had asked him about Roger:

If that hadn't happened on the bridge, would he have gone on forever?

Why didn't he make a run for it? He could have made it. The cameras had caught the whole thing. He seemed to have just waited for the end, as if he knew.

Did his dad ever tell him the formula? And was it true that all you needed to make the stuff was a couple drops?

And, of course: Did he have a supply buried some-place?

What Brett could answer he did so vaguely. After seven years, the spell had broken—as in fairy tales. Eventually people stopped wondering, accepting the conclusion that the world's only fountain of youth had been destroyed in a monstrous moment that had claimed his father.

Likewise, nothing more was heard of Antoine Du-charme and his associates, who were convicted of com-plicity in murder and sabotage and sentenced to life without parole.

Brett's mother was back in Eau Claire and writing. Her pen name was Wendy Bacon, but everybody still called her Laura. She had successfully finished the sec-ond of her mystery series to good reviews. The third was nearly done. Luckily, Roger had taken out a large life insurance policy, leaving them enough money so she could write full time. Besides, at sixty-three, she was not a hot commodity in the job market, as she said.

Six years ago, they had received a letter addressed to Roger from a missionary in a village in Papua New Guinea. Sadly, his old friend Iwati had been killed in the eruption of the ancient Omafeki volcano the year before. Destroyed, too, was the small lake island and the only known locale where grew the *tabukari* orchid with the odd scent of apples and rotted flesh. No age had been given for Iwati. But Brett had an idea.

He peddled down Johnson Street to his apartment.

Later Carolyn would drop over, and because it was Saturday they'd probably have some wine and pizza and watch a video. Maybe *Blade Runner* again.

He carried the bike upstairs. He was hot and sweaty and looking forward to a long shower.

But before that, he headed to the kitchen and pulled a quart of grapefruit juice from the fridge and downed half while staring at the photo of Carolyn magneted to the freezer door. She was dressed in a bridesmaid gown at a friend's wedding, looking as fresh and beautiful as the gardenias in her hair. She was the first woman he had ever loved. The first woman he felt comfortable confiding in. The first woman he thought about spending the rest of his life with. Carolyn knew everything about him.

Or almost everything.

He pulled open the freezer door. From behind the stack of veggie burgers and pints of frozen yogurt, he removed the little white plastic box, furry with frost.

The ice seal melted in his hand and snapped open.

It still looked the same after all these years—still chained and encased in gold. He could almost feel the heat of the fire as his hand shot in to pull it free.

He flicked open the end and removed the glass tube.

Some things didn't change. Like the first time, he held it up to the ceiling lamp and felt a tiny thrill shiver through his loins. The light caught it from behind.

A shaft of frozen eternity, waiting to thaw.

About the Author

GARY BRAVER teaches creative writing and popular culture at Northeastern University. He lives with his wife and two sons outside Boston, Massachusetts.

Visit Gary Braver's Web site at:
www.garybraver.com

Coming soon from the author of *Elixir*, an astounding new medical thriller

GREY MATTER

Gary Braver

Rachel Whitman has everything. She's young and affluent, and her husband is the CEO of a booming dot-com company. They have a big new house in a flossy Boston suburb, plus all the brand name "toys" that go along with wealth. Best of all, they have a gorgeous and sweet little six year old boy named Dylan.

But Rachel isn't truly happy because Dylan has learning disabilities.

Tortured by the idea that something she did in her past has caused Dylan's problems, Rachel becomes obsessed with a secret medical procedure that claims to turn slow children into geniuses.

Should Rachel and her husband risk their new fortune on the experimental procedure? Unaware of the consequences of the brain enhancement operation, Rachel can't know that the costs of the procedure go far beyond financial ones.

> **"Among the best of recent contributions to its genre because of its engaging plot and the issues it addresses."**
>
> —*Library Journal* on *Elixir*

Visit us on the web at www.tor.com